THE GODDESS, THE SCIENTIST, AND THE ELIXIR

SHADOWS OVER BYZANTIUM
BOOK ONE

CLAUDIA LINWOOD

CARAVANSERAI
PUBLISHING

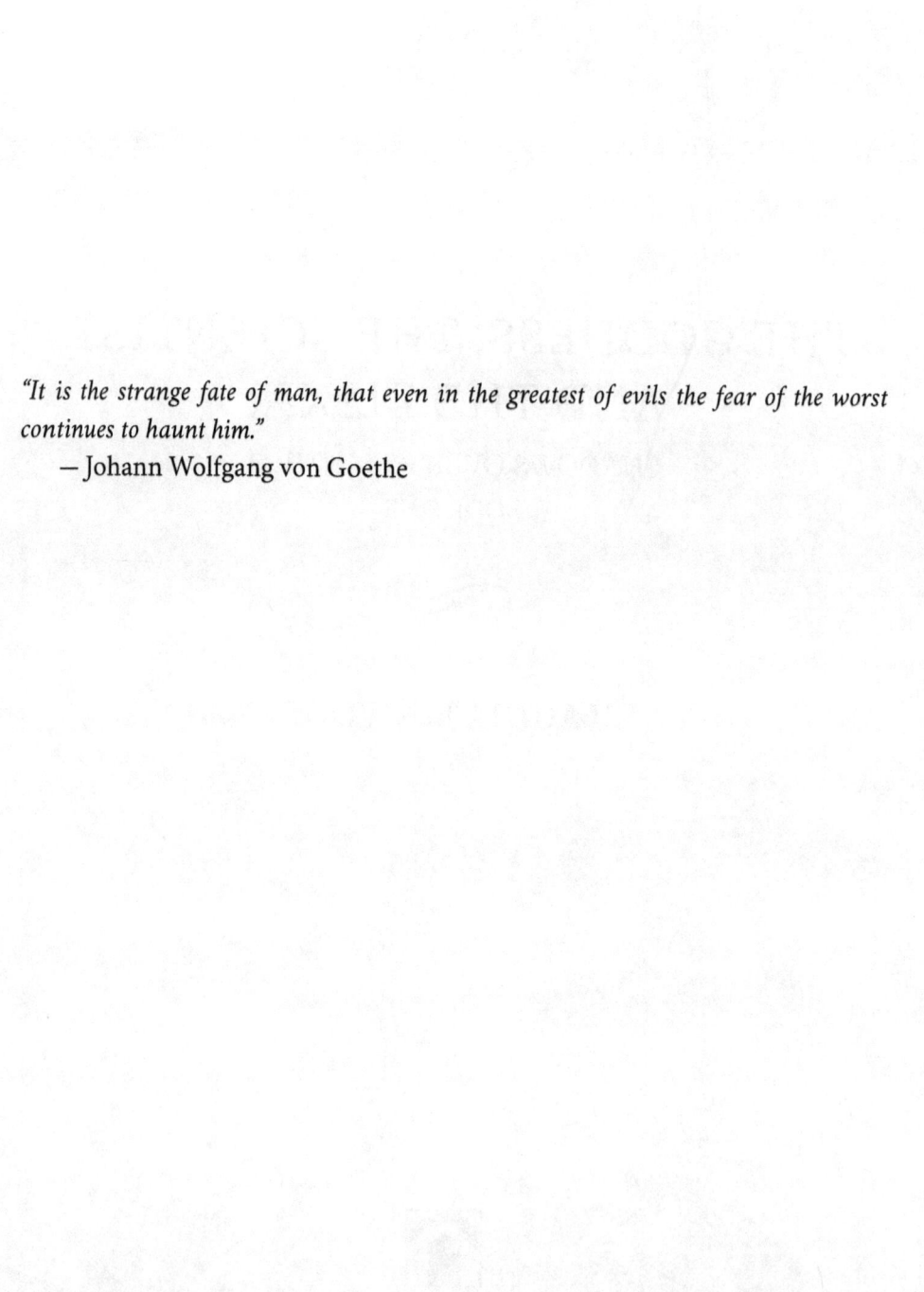

"It is the strange fate of man, that even in the greatest of evils the fear of the worst continues to haunt him."
  — Johann Wolfgang von Goethe

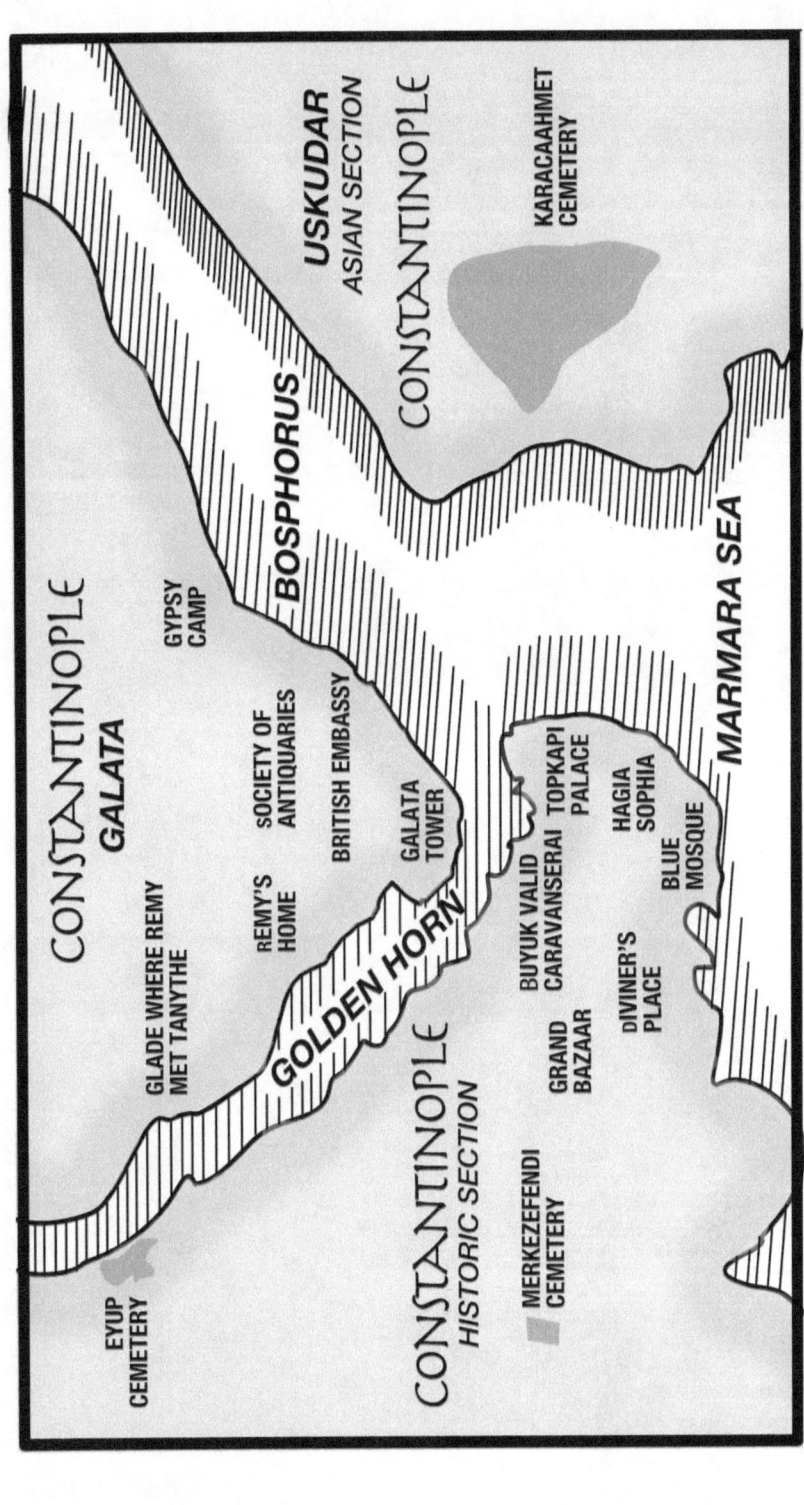

CHAPTER 1

*L*ord Remy Derrien grasped the stone on the necklace concealed beneath his clothing, his only link to the goddess.

He only meant to examine a half-buried trunk cast from the seabed in an earthquake.

By the time he understood what he had found, it was already too late.

-

TWO YEARS EARLIER, CONSTANTINOPLE, 1771

Despite glimpses of gold in the surrounding clumps of dirt, Remy was drawn to the ordinary half-buried trunk, partially covered in barnacles. He had the servants clean the trunk, then watched as they trundled it across rough hills of debris to his laboratory at the Society of Antiquaries. The sea breeze tangled his hair with the spicy-sweet smell of Constantinople's famed roses as he wondered if any of the Society's fellows experienced the same odd tingling from the hundreds of buried objects under his feet. He looked down at the mud caking his boots. Mud composed of those poor souls and their treasures entombed under the sea: blacksmiths, cooks, soldiers, pirates, kings, queens, prophets, scholars, all jumbled together regardless of status, their secrets forever sealed in time.

While the servants cleared away the debris brought in with the trunk, Remy examined it. Despite being buried in the seabed of the Golden Horn Waterway for thousands of years, then heaved up in the 1766 earthquake five years ago, most of the metal showed only a hazing of rust at the edges, and the wooden bands looked sturdy and without rot.

Curious.

Before he attempted to open the trunk, Remy set a large piece of gray carpet beside it to hold what he unpacked. A simple padlock lay flat against the front, fastened to a brass hasp. Rectangular with rounded corners at the bottom, a metal arch for a shank, the lock resembled those used in Ancient Rome. Remy failed to pry off the front in an attempt to access the inner workings. A more forceful blow to the lock could cause the seemingly sturdy trunk to fall apart, damaging the contents.

He slid a length of sturdy brass wire, eight inches straight, then two inches angled at twenty-five degrees, through the keyhole at the lock's bottom left corner. This should access the spring mechanism near the top, which held the shank in place. Pressing the brass wire down where he surmised the spring was located, Remy pulled on the shank, which slid out neatly, as if he had used a key.

"Aha," he said aloud, pleased that he had solved this minor puzzle.

The trunk's domed lid creaked like old bones as he lifted it. He cringed, expecting the stench of rotting decay and a jumble of broken objects to sort through, the same as in many other trunks he had opened. Instead, the earthy smell of fertile soil wafted into the air, and Remy imagined he might discover a treasure trove of priceless objects or ancient scrolls that would contribute to the world's knowledge, making his name in the sphere of science and natural philosophy. So far, in his capacity here, he had found nothing that would garner the fame he needed to rescue him from the dreary fate of the second son of a marquess.

The clothes at the top of the trunk were neatly folded, as if just packed. He lifted a tunic of soft red linen edged with an unfaded yellow geometric border. Beneath it, a pair of matching trousers.

A scent suddenly filled the room, rich and floral, like gardenias in full bloom. He paused, sniffing. As he placed the garments aside, the scent shifted, now spicier, like grated orange peel. He inhaled deeply. Odd. He had uncorked nothing, yet the air shimmered with fragrance. Was the scent real, or conjured by his mind?

Layer by layer, more garments emerged, cotton shirts, linen wraps, underthings. All impossibly preserved. Remy looked at his hands. Unpacking this dead man's luggage felt like desecration.

A chill skated up his spine. The sensation, faint at first, of eyes on the back of his neck, thickened the air. He paused, gripping the brass wire again. It trembled slightly in his fingers. He turned. No one was there. The laboratory lay silent. The sunlight slanting through the top windows lit the dust specks as if they were tiny stars drifting lazily, undisturbed for years. And yet...

The feeling remained. Someone or something had been here. Or still was.

With its four-foot-thick walls and sturdy doors, the old palace housing the Society kept out the cacophony of the city and should have done the same regarding trespassers. A perfect place for his laboratory's supplies, equipment, and the growing artifacts collected by the project. But now...fear tormented him.

Still, he pressed on.

Tucked in the garments' folds, an alabaster flask caught the light. He opened it, and the sharp perfume of patchouli burst out, heady, sensual, overwhelming. A vision flared unbidden: a veiled woman, a blade glinting from beneath her pillow. He jammed the stopper back in, his fingers unsteady. The scent had power. Impossible, inexplicable. It should have faded long ago, but it wrapped around him like ghostly tendrils, cold and inescapable.

A primal instinct screamed at him to look behind. There was nothing, only the suffocating wrongness that clung to every surface of the laboratory. He was a natural philosopher, a scientist. These feelings were the antithesis of his profession.

He turned back to his project and found a compact cooking pot. Then, from a purple silk pouch, he drew out five brass bells linked by a chain. Charms to ward off evil.

"Balderdash," he muttered in disgust. The man had drowned in some catastrophe, his body lost at sea, and no one to give him a proper burial. Perhaps he should have gone for ten bells. Remy laughed aloud at that, though the sound died quickly. The lab, usually comforting in its quiet, now pressed in like a crypt.

He bent over the trunk's remaining contents, his fist pressed to his lips, pondering the owner. What wars had he fought in? How old was he when he met his end?

This trunk contained a singular collection of an ancient soldier's artifacts, and, with permission, he could write it up for a Society meeting. But his father would shake his head and say, as he had many times before, 'That is all well and good, but I'll not have you spend your life digging up unfortunate, deceased people's belongings.' He would rather have Remy saving people's souls. But Remy doubted that he or anyone else could save souls.

He surveyed the items he had unpacked, each of them fresh and clean with no sign of the passing years. What he was seeing was impossible, yet the evidence was sitting there in front of him.

His wife, Pheodora, would claim that the trunk had a spell on it. Even though Phe was educated and from an established, aristocratic British family, she was as superstitious as the natives of Constantinople. Why, he knew she stole off to the gypsy camp to see her soothsayer and purchased magic charms from the Grand Bazaar.

A dense mass of thin, gauzy cloth with a faint tint of azure, shining silver in places like a fish's scales, lay in heaping mounds across the bottom of the trunk. Pulling on one section, he drew it out, but it seemed endless. When he let go, a leather pouch dropped from the folds, spilling out five ivory dice marked with black circles. Clacking in his palm, they sounded as cheerful as children's toys. But Remy did not smile.

With caution, he reached under the gauzy cloth, hoping to avoid any unsheathed weapons. He might find just the treasure he needed. After all, this trunk had proved decidedly unusual.

Something rough brushed his skin. A gasp escaped his lips as an unnamed terror expanded in his chest, uncoiling like a serpent, making it hard to breathe.

He lifted out a straw-colored length of linen, perhaps a shawl, wound around a large object. Steadying his hands, he unwrapped it slowly.

The same coarsely woven material made up the sizable bag inside. It felt heavy, worn and discolored, stained yellow and mottled with large patches of rust-red and black.

Blood?

The drawstring was double-stitched and tied in a tight knot. When he finally loosened it, he drew a breath, his first proper one since touching the bag. Remy laughed quietly, nervously, at this absurdity. He inhaled, ragged and hesitant.

Pulling the bag open, he slanted it forward at a low angle.

A necklace slipped out, its silver chain coiling like a living thing onto the carpet. A large, teardrop-shaped crystal nestled against the fabric, cool and luminescent, its inner depths flickering as if lit from within.

He stared into it longer than he meant to. Then, almost absently, slipped the chain around his neck.

Grasping the bag, surprised by its weight, he cupped it underneath so the cloth would not tear. The objects remaining were large, shifting heavily.

Remy tipped it forward. Three objects tumbled onto the carpet.

He heard his own scream before he understood it.

Dropping the empty bag, he leapt back. His chair crashed to the floor with a loud thwack, like a pistol fired in the laboratory, the sound echoing, boring into his skull.

In the noise's shroud, he gawked in stunned silence.

On the table before him lay three severed human heads, staring back at him with their glinting eyes.

CHAPTER 2

From deep inside the dark, cold place, voices spoke, pulling Tanythe from thick clouds of oblivion. She blinked. The voices grew louder.

This wasn't the first time she had been fooled by her longings. Usually, those voices, her wishes for rescue, faded as she drifted closer to awareness. But these persisted. Could it be? Voices, real ones, for the first time in eons.

She opened her eyes to the darkness inside the bag.

For a long while, the trunk had moved, jostling the items surrounding the bag, her prison. A thud marked it being set down hard. More voices. Then a sudden bang, startling but welcome, a rare intrusion into her silence. After that came a sound like a mouse clawing at metal, then creaks and a squeal, unmistakably metal-on-metal.

A haze of light filtered down to her, dim and distant, like the pale yolk of a dying sun struggling to rise. She widened her eyes, desperate to see. But inside the bag, only shifting shadows met her gaze.

Someone had opened the trunk. Or perhaps it was another cruel vision, conjured to drag her toward despair. But then: a tremor. Not in the world, but within her. An emotion she thought long lost shuddered through her—hope.

Hope that they might be free again. Hope to fulfill the boon granted them by the gods.

She listened to the clink of metal, the rustle of cloth, and the occasional words spoken near her, as if a person leaned close. The silence that had kept her company for eons was breaking.

Tiny beads of light leaked through the warp and woof of the linen bag. In the dimness, she saw the familiar outline of Leukan's head, his severed head. His power shielded her, even now, keeping them both from the malevolent presence of Bahl.

She should have been prepared. Goddesses often sensed glimpses of the future. But the centuries of nothingness had dulled her. Then came a sensation. Heat from below, as if a soft hand rested beneath her. A hand, warm and hesitant. She sensed anticipation from the person and shrank away, wary. If they expected treasure, they would be sorely disappointed. And disappointment could turn to anger.

Tanythe's hope flickered, replaced by terror rivaling that of the moment she was beheaded. She was more helpless now than then.

But no, she still held power. Long dormant, now stirred by fear. Weak, but present. She gathered what courage she could and waited.

Bright light burst into the bag as it opened. She shut her eyes. Cool air rushed over her. The bag was lifted and tilted. Her crystal tumbled out first, the silver chain jangling before falling still. The first time she had seen it since it was thrown into the bag alongside her and the others.

Then, she, Leukan, and Bahl banged against one another, tumbling out onto a surface where they were exposed to light, air, and the gaze of whoever had opened the bag.

They were as vulnerable as newborns.

A voice cried out, "Nooo!"

A loud bang followed, echoing like a rock striking a wall. Wincing, Tanythe kept her eyes closed, yearning for the safety of darkness. She had heard enough screams and clashing steel on the day her throat met the sword. Now came a silence, taut and dangerous, like a beast crouching before the pounce.

She dared to look.

A man stared at her, his face twisted in horror. Pale skin gleamed with sweat. Dark curls tangled around his face. Brown eyes wide, their gaze pierced her.

A soul she knew.

7

Abdosir? She tried to speak, to whisper his name, but her lips, unused for eons, betrayed her. Her voice would not rise.

His scent reached her, a faint musk mingled with sea salt. She longed to press her face into his hair, to hold him against her and revel in his aliveness.

This man, this vessel of Abdosir, had delicate hands, his fingers trembling like a sea creature's eye stalks, searching for meaning. In his eyes, disbelief, but also curiosity. Perhaps, somewhere deep inside, he remembered what they once were.

In the chaos of the bag opening, the man had touched her brow. That simple pressure awakened memories of Mirjhna, of his hands warm on her body when she had been a goddess and he a prince. That touch, his touch, was unmistakable.

Warmth flooded her.

But fear lingered in his eyes. Fear of memories, perhaps. Long ago, when he first beheld her, it was awe and desire that filled him.

She looked up from the carpet where her head now rested.

He ran a hand through his curls. His full lips parted slightly.

She had never felt so exposed, yet power tingled along her face and neck. Rightly so. This man knew her. As Prince Abdosir, he had once worshipped the goddess Tanythe. And would again. Worship would feed her strength.

He still stared, transfixed. He wore a dark jacket, a white shirt, and a kind of turban wound around his neck, blending into the fabric.

She blinked.

He gasped.

The door burst open. A voice shouted in a language both familiar and foreign. A man in a plain robe, a servant, surely, rushed in wielding something like a broom.

Panic flickered across Abdosir's face. He grabbed the crystal, now hanging from his neck, and shoved it beneath his tunic just as the servant reached him.

The servant froze, eyes darting. Then he saw the table, the three heads.

With a strangled cry, he dropped the broom and turned to flee, nearly tripping over its handle as he scrambled away.

Tanythe felt a smile form, one that threatened to burst into laughter. She stifled it, holding her expression steady. What would Abdosir think, seeing her grin at the poor servant's terror?

But he didn't notice. His focus remained fixed on her, his gaze sharp with concern. Had she unbalanced him so?

She wished for a mirror. Was her face decayed? Eyes bloodshot? Cheeks peeling? Hair falling out in gray clumps?

He stared into her eyes, reached out, then withdrew, his pupils wide as coins once dropped into her shrine's pool. She refused to blink and searched his eyes.

Fear. Desire.

Familiar.

Then his pupils shrank, his eyes bulging.

Fear reclaimed him.

He turned and fled, swift as the servant, though with far more grace.

CHAPTER 3

*L*ong ago, Abdosir had come to pray at their shrine. As Tanythe bathed in the clear pool, she saw him hesitating at the entrance, a silk pouch of deepest purple in his hand. She lay back in the sacred spring's cool water, floating, her hair undulating around her in soft caresses.

He knelt at the shrine, placed gold coins in the brass vessel, and set a wick in an oil lamp. The flame took hold as he held the wick to the fire of the lamp beside it. His lips moved as he watched the flame, his eloquent prayer a poem of desire. She called silently. He broke his reverie and looked toward the pool.

Abdosir stood above her as she floated on her back, his desire all too evident. Taking pity on him, she vanished, leaving him wondering if he had imagined her naked in the clear pool, her pearl skin reflecting the golden sun rays, her red hair flaming around her.

He had offered a silver chalice set with pearls and sapphires, mindful that she was the Goddess of Water. A fitting offering. Her power was growing exponentially.

She knew the worries of the small folk scattered through the countryside, their excitement as well as their fear at the enormous tent of zebra and tiger skins that had been erected on the land where Abdosir was building a palace dedicated to her. The people were uncertain whether Prince Abdosir merely desired a new palace amongst the fragrant cedars or was readying to seize their lands.

Inside his magnificent tent, Abdosir sipped wine from a crystal cup as he studied a scroll at his silver and brass table. Just as the sun set on the horizon, Tanythe appeared in a part of the tent that escaped the light of his oil lamps.

"Abdosir," she murmured, her voice as gentle as sea waves brushing the shore.

He leapt from his divan, pulling his djanbiya from his jeweled scabbard, the curved blade sparkling in the golden light of the hanging lamps.

"Who dares trespass?" He took a fighting stance and looked in all directions. [Enter your work phone number here]

She appeared under one of the lamps, a mirage in a pool of light. Silver threads glimmering through the diaphanous layers of her gown, woven so spiderweb thin that the cloth was hailed as the breath of heaven. The pale flesh of her body shone through like a pearl, her nipples the blush of a just-bloomed rose.

Abdosir dropped to his knees, still clutching his djanbiya. A warrior doesn't give up his weapon, even in the throes of desire.

"Goddess Tanythe," he said, his voice thin and strained.

"Fear not, Prince Abdosir." She tired of having to say that phrase to her worshippers. Leukan had commented how he had never seen her ferocious aspect. Of course, he wouldn't; he was a god.

Tanythe put her hands on either side of the prince's face and raised him to standing. She smiled as his djinn dropped to the silken carpet.

He pulled her close, his breath heavy with restrained desire as befitted royalty. He caressed her face, then slowly trailed his hand to her breast. His left arm swept behind her back, his right under her thighs, and in a swift and graceful motion, he carried her to his bed, silks and gauzes hanging from the surrounding gold and emerald frame. He removed his necklaces of pearls, diamonds, and emeralds, his gold cuffs, and tossed aside his cloth-of-gold robe until he stood as naked as she was under her diaphanous gown.

He studied her for a moment. She could feel his hesitation, feel him unsure of what to do with a goddess radiating light and power in his bed. She reached for him.

He kissed her long and slow, the breath of heaven the only thing between them.

* * *

1771 Constantinople

THE LIGHT FILTERING through the high window above Tanythe dimmed, and a boom of thunder heralded the rain drumming almost as loudly on the roof. The room darkened.

In her mind, she saw the man who had opened the bag, his expressions flickering from one emotion to another like light on water. A ripple of joy cut through the sadness she had borne since she had seen Leukan die, since she had failed him.

This man, who had just left the room, did not know it yet, but he was her prince, come to worship once again.

CHAPTER 4

*L*ord Remy Derrien, on his rather early morning walk to the Society, looked up to see that fog had rolled in, almost as thick as London's, obscuring the grand old buildings of Constantinople that he passed. Remy had threatened his servant, Kahlil, with a beating if he said a word or gave even a hint about what he had seen before he fled from the laboratory that day. In the event that Kahlil told a friend or relative, the incident would spread like the plague throughout the Grand Bazaar. And that tale would make Remy either a laughingstock or a demigod. Which it would be was a mystery to him, the same as this amazing and confounding city.

As he navigated the slippery cobblestones, Remy considered whether, if it came down to it, he could actually beat Khalil. He pictured himself holding a— what would he use to beat the poor man? His father, the Marquess of Wearsely, complained of Lord Dalton, who would beat whichever servant caught him in a temper with whatever was at hand: a whip, a cane, a birch, and, on one occasion, a salted eel.

Remy laughed to himself at the kerfuffle that had caused. A salted eel. It made for some good gossip. Lord Dalton was a scoundrel at best. Khalil was a good man. Besides, if Khalil had mentioned the incident to someone, the tale would most likely vanish into the stew of tittle-tattle that comprised the whole of Constantinople. Then again, perhaps Remy's threat would most likely do the trick.

That day in the laboratory, Khalil had been unnerved, but not more so than Remy. When the contents of the bag spilled out, Remy had cried out and leapt up, his chair crashing to the ground in a resounding bang, as loud as a gun's report. When Khalil bounded in to save him from an imagined disaster, they had locked eyes. Though their worlds were as different as possible, they came together in the raw horror of what they had seen. And that should have been enough to shut anyone up.

As Remy continued through the morning mist on the way to his laboratory, he tried not to picture the contents of the stained linen bag, but his mind wouldn't let it alone, much as one would worry a sore tooth or gawk at a gory accident. Distant thunder rumbled over the Bosporus, a chorus to the muezzin's haunting prayers, which echoed eerily off the majestic stone edifices, and he looked up at a tall minaret rising into the mist. Ancient buildings loomed above him, the tops of dozens more minarets vanishing in the fog, the city remaking itself at every turn. His mind meandered through its own kind of fog, and he directed it to a clear path. Yet invariably, his thoughts twisted back to what had spilled from the bag.

A camel shambled from the mist, overshadowing a man on a donkey leading the camel by a fat rope. Remy stepped into the street, only to retreat as another camel followed, then another, trailing the odor of stale urine and vomit like a prized fragrance—a seemingly endless line of dromedaries, mesmerizing him with their gait's odd rhythm of both legs on the same side moving together. With part of his mind occupied in this fascination, a deeper part finally grasped that he was actually here, in this fabled city, rewarded with a prestigious position that just might enable a marquess' second son to succeed in something other than the clergy. The last camel sauntered past, made his contribution to the accumulated droppings on the cobblestones, then Remy stepped carefully across the street and continued to the Society.

Ominous claps of thunder boomed through the streets and resounded even louder through the stone and marble buildings as if giants were playing ninepins. Remy opened his umbrella in anticipation and picked up his pace, but he couldn't outstride the storm. The hammering rain drew a curtain over the city and distorted the muezzin's prayers into disquieting static, which again put Remy in mind of the macabre conundrum awaiting him in the laboratory.

* * *

SITTING at his imposing mahogany desk in the Society of Antiquaries' distinguished old palace, Remy felt naked, his body bare under the loose mohair kaftan, feet practically unshod in sandals. Vulnerable in a way he hadn't experienced since his first weeks at Trinity College, Cambridge, before he arm-wrestled his way to respectability. Rainwater dripped from his wet hair down the back of his neck, giving him a chill. He wrapped a damp shawl, turban-like, around his head and scowled. Anyone would think he was a servant seated at his master's desk.

Albie, his patronizing Trinity roomie, who inherited a dukedom a year after graduating, would have a laugh now if he happened through the door. Remy could hear Albie's imperious voice, one eyebrow raised, 'Well, well, if it is not Lord Remy Edric Derrien, gone native in Byzantium.' Of course, Albie would use the ancient name for Constantinople, ever disdaining what he called the barbarian days we unfortunately inhabit.

Remy glanced through the window. The gloom of the rainy spring morning made it look like nightfall. Beside the window, his wet Superfine coat and breeches hung on hooks, limp and wrinkled like a shriveled corpse. His linen shirt, cravat, and stockings dripped puddles on the marble tiles, their soggy white shapes blurring into ghosts, giving him a bit of a start each time he looked outside the ring of light from the oil lamp on his desk. He absently placed his hand on the crystal at his chest, set in a delicate silver mount hanging from a silver chain with unique elliptical links. Touching the stone, which at times looked clear, at times faint blue as if it were the purest water, calmed him. He kept telling himself he was not a thief, even though the crystal belonged to the project, as did everything in the trunk where he had found the bag.

Earlier that morning, before he had stripped off his sopping clothes, he placed another log on the hearth fire Kahlil had laid, but the fire was slow to catch. Remy kept glancing at the pale flames, waiting for them to flare up and fill the room with a burst of warmth, but was met with only an occasional snap of the dry wood, which broke the silence of the old palace.

He stopped writing, straining to hear. Tentative footsteps tapped on the hard marble floor in the hall. Most probably Simmonds-Snow, Lord Arthur Simmonds-Snow, if you will, fellow of the Society of Antiquaries, London, same as Remy. Would Simmery dare try to sneak into Remy's laboratory without permission? He curled his lips in amusement at his nickname for Lord Simmonds-Snow, whom he found pompous and affected. Somehow, the word simper had come to mind when Lord Simmonds-Snow's smile would subtly transform into the suggestion of a smirk, making Remy feel like a second-class citizen. Simmery might be the elect head of the project, the Governor, but his position was merely an administrative office. Not a merit award like Remy's, giving Remy dominion over the laboratory and project artifacts. The Gov knew Remy's importance, but Simmery's family was older and wealthier than his, so Simmery saw himself as cock of the walk.

Remy had locked the building's front door after he entered this morning and left his umbrella next to the forgotten black one, folded like a crumpled bat in the oversized ceramic holder. No one would know he had arrived early. People forgot umbrellas in the holder all the time, making it impossible to gauge the current population by umbrella check. He glanced at the clock ticking on his mantle: 7:04. Too early for Simmery. Must be one of the other Society members—they were the only ones besides the Governor who had keys.

But if Simmery had heard about the contents of the bag. . .

Even if circumstances were normal, Remy did not have the laboratory ready for an inspection. Eyeing his office door, closed but unlocked, he slid open his desk's top drawer, wincing at the squeal, and fumbled for the key. Perhaps he could lock the door before whoever approached could try the handle. The footsteps continued, coming closer.

"Blast." Remy's muted outcry came at him from in front, then bounced off the plaster wall behind as if in reply. He pulled the shawl off his head, damp hair falling to his shoulders, taking the chill from the air and transferring it to his flesh. If it were Simmery, at least Remy wouldn't look as if he had gone totally native, turban and all.

Light from the window darkened, and the patter of more rain clashed with the ticking of the mantel clock. The footsteps stopped. Remy's office door creaked open. A flash of lightning illuminated a tall figure shrouded in a dark robe with a peaked hood. It stepped into the room just as a tremendous boom of thunder made Remy jump upright beside his desk.

He eyed his double-barreled pistol hanging on a hook near the door, secure in a leather holster beside his drying clothes. But he remained still, his body reacting to the odd smell before his brain fully registered it—pungent incense covering a scent of—decay?

The figure stopped in front of the door, ignoring Remy, who tried to find the glimmer of eyes inside the hood but was met with impenetrable darkness.

"State your business," Remy said, surprised that his voice didn't wobble in trepidation.

But the intruder turned abruptly and left.

The singular creak of the laboratory door opening—Remy was sure he had locked it—had him pulling the loaded pistol from his holster.

The laboratory contents were his project, under his protection: the choice debris from the monumental earthquake of 1766, five years ago, which heaved these ancient curiosities out of the Golden Horn Waterway near the Grand Shipyard. Curiosities that the London Society of Antiquaries sent him here to examine and catalogue with the best available scientific equipment of 1771.

Confidential Curiosities.

Remy stood at the laboratory's threshold, pistol at the ready. The trespasser had stopped before one of the tables arranged with artifacts. Remy squinted. A faint light around the trespasser grew brighter. Was it his imagination? He glanced at the long, thin window near the ceiling, where a few stray beams of early morning sunlight fuzzed through the haze of a cloud-dark day—a stab at forgiveness for the dawn's vicious storm.

Remy entered the laboratory. "See here, you do not have permission. Leave. Now."

The intruder gave no sign that he had heard. By heaven, the man would need to be forced out.

The trespasser strolled by the gold, silver, and copper coins, with images of Nero, Caligula, Darius, and Xerxes. He merely glanced at the table holding a few pieces of exquisite jewelry glittering on black velvet. Any thief would be stuffing his pockets by now.

Remy shook his head, trying to displace the fog that filled his brain. He pointed his pistol at the man. "State your business or leave."

Remy stepped directly into his path.

CHAPTER 5

*A*s if Remy were not in the laboratory, the intruder glided around him and stopped in front of a table along the rear wall stacked with equipment and odds and ends. From underneath, he pulled out the metal and wood chest, now locked with a massive padlock.

Remy cocked his pistol. Aimed it at the intruder.

"Put that down. Then step away, or I shoot."

The trespasser set the chest down in a bare space on a table that, just a moment ago, had been covered in a jumble of parts and broken items. Then the man opened the chest.

Simply opened the chest.

A peculiar dizziness invaded Remy's head, and the pistol sagged in his hand. The padlock had been custom made. The locksmith had assured him it was more than secure.

Remy took a breath. Aimed his pistol again at the intruder. The man couldn't ignore him and get away with it.

He pulled the trigger.

Nothing but a resounding click, which rang off the laboratory's stone walls.

Misfire. This damp weather be damned.

"Stop." Remy lunged for the intruder, but he swiveled, leaving Remy grasping at air. As if nothing at all had happened, the man reached inside the chest and lifted out the bag.

"Give me that. You have no right." Remy snatched the bag and almost lost his balance as the trespasser gave no resistance. He straightened to his full height, shorter than the man. How he wished for his English clothes, the authority they gave him. He stood there, holding the bag, and almost laughed aloud at the common phrase implicating himself as victim. Sobering at this thought, Remy heard the rain start again, rattling like bones on the clay roof tiles.

A flash of lightning, as bright as a burning desert sun, illumined the room. Remy gaped at the green moss and dirt clotted on the trespasser's hooded robe. This close, the cloying odor of decay carried from him, overlaid by pungent incense, a perfume of dark tombs with looted sarcophagi—from Remy's studies: *sarkophagos, Greek:* eating flesh, carnivorous.

Remy looked directly into the dark interior of the intruder's hood. A cold claw squeezed his brain, oozing out scenes of marble temples, tomb paintings lacerated with age, and chanting worshippers, all veiled by swirling smoke. A priest's shining blade slitting a girl's throat, blood spurting. Burnt offerings twisted on a charred stone altar, shapes Remy recoiled from discerning. Under tall marble columns, shade partially hid a beautiful man and woman, his elaborate black braids and gold circlet rivaling her jeweled red tresses.

So like those in the bag.

Remy stifled the scream that built in his throat and hiccuped a huge inhale. He still stared into the dark of the intruder's hood.

There was nothing there. Remy blinked and reason stepped in. Rain beat on the roof as if it were locked out, and the day, the day was surely darker, and the lamps in the laboratory—he hadn't yet lit them.

The man reached out and grasped the bag that Remy held.

His flesh touched Remy's. Warm flesh, but somehow more revolting than if it were damp with rot. Something tingled through Remy's hand, snaked into his body, a jolt so strong he almost lost his grip.

The trespasser tugged at the bag Remy held.

For reasons he couldn't fathom, Remy let go.

With great care, as if it were a delicate laboratory instrument, the trespasser placed the bag on the table. A spherical shape rolled to the opening.

One of the heads, which still looked as if it had just been separated from its body, as if it had been alive only seconds ago. Each time Remy viewed these aberrations, his brain juddered as if he had been a recipient of Jean-Baptiste LeRoy's electroconvulsive therapy.

The intruder took the head and gently set it upright on the table. The head of a clean-shaven man, skin like polished ebony, a noble profile, and strong jawline. His thick hair, deepest black, was intricately braided with what looked like amber beads woven into the strands. His ears, like curved shells, bore gold earrings. The glowing golden lines of a spiraling tattoo covered what was left of his neck.

Hard earned, they were.

Remy could have sworn the intruder spoke, but he hadn't heard a sound. Yet the words in his mind were not his. Did the intruder refer to the heads —that obtaining them had taken its toll on their murderer? Remy put his hand to his forehead. Had he just believed the intruder said these words, put them into his mind? By God, he was a philosopher of the natural, a scientist, a man of letters who studied the material world, not like the inhabitants here in Constantinople, so superstitious they saved para, their silver coins, in order to consult an astrologer regarding important decisions in their lives.

The trespasser, intent as if he were searching for something specific, reached into the bag. He pulled out another head, almost an opposite of the first: swarthy skin, scraggly black beard and hair, thick neck like a Minotaur, eyes dark with evil.

For a moment, Remy glanced away, fearing that those eyes could direct their malevolence into him. The trespasser set the dark-haired man's head some distance from the first one. With no hesitation, he reached into the bag and pulled out the last head.

The woman. Devastatingly beautiful.

A sense of odd displacement flooded over Remy—a disorienting déjà vu— the same as after the shock had passed when Remy had first seen her. Her glittering blue eyes, her bountiful red hair, wispy scarlet curls framing her face, longer locks curling around her poor severed neck in a nest of flames, entranced him. Her pink lips, partly opened, looked as if they might speak.

Tanythe.

Again, Remy had heard no sound, but the name sat in his mind, as though someone had just begun reciting a poem.

Remy drew back. He hadn't thoroughly examined or catalogued these three heads. Dreading a repeat of the dreams he endured the night after first opening the bag and emptying its grisly contents on the table, he had saved them for last.

In the dream, there had been fog. He couldn't see where he was, couldn't remember. Incessant mist worried him like gnats. Then he was running through walls of icy rain. The fog swirled around him in his laboratory. Someone was there, stalking him. The fog grew thicker, the stalker more menacing, even though Remy couldn't see him. Remy stepped backwards, trying to see his pursuer, put his hand on a table, felt something round and warm. Jerked his hand away as he whirled around to see the heads staring at him with their eyes. Alive! The stalker wrapped his arms around him from behind, cold and stiff as if he were a corpse. Remy had screamed himself awake.

This same dream occurred more times than he could recall. Each time it started, he recognized it and tried to wake, but couldn't. The dream unfolded as if he were reading the same chapters in the same book and was unable to put it down. It was torture, magnified because he knew what was awaiting him and could do nothing. Nothing.

Remy bent his head, put his hand to his forehead, and pressed hard. If he broke down here, in front of the intruder... Why, the man could do unimaginable things. With a deep inhale, Remy straightened. He patted his pocket. Empty. His pistol. Where was it? He stopped himself just before he looked wildly around. Mustn't let on how panicked he was. Forced himself to look directly at the stranger.

The intruder held the woman's head level with his own, looking into her eyes, her scarlet locks tumbling around them, as if in an embrace. His hands looked strong, elegant, and were dark as ebony, contrasting with the creamy alabaster complexion of the woman. A faint glow surrounded them both.

Remy reached for something solid to steady himself, but he wasn't near anything substantial and his hand met only empty air. Had he seen the woman's lips move with the blink of her eyes? A surfeit of heat rose inside him

—*how dare the interloper besmirch his woman with such intimacy?* Remy rocked on his heels. *His woman?* Had he really thought that?

The image of his double-barreled pistol sitting near the microscope bloomed in his mind. How could he have been so careless?

He rushed to retrieve it.

Shaking with a rage he hadn't felt since he shot and wounded Lord Devon that November in the duel the damn fool had insisted upon, Remy cocked the hammer. His mind raced back to that time: how a conversation on alchemy versus natural philosophy, or science, could induce one to demand life-threatening combat was beyond Remy. But in contrast, he was here now and had a solid reason for rage.

He curled his finger on the trigger and aimed his pistol at the trespasser.

"Put the heads in the bag and set it back on the table," Remy said, his voice surprisingly firm.

The trespasser slipped the heads back, one by one, lingering on the woman's.

Had the man heard and obeyed? Remy had the impression the intruder was merely going about his business, that his actions were coincidentally what Remy had requested. Well, he would soon see if he was correct.

"*All* the heads." Remy waved his pistol and the intruder obeyed.

Perhaps the man was coming to his senses.

"Set the bag on the table and step away." Holding the pistol with both hands, Remy kept it pointed straight at the trespasser.

They are mine in more ways than you can imagine.

The words resounded in Remy's mind, as if someone had spoken them. This was the third time messages like this had appeared from nowhere. These words evoked feelings inside him: the overabundance of joy, the escape from mortality in the act of love, the insatiable hole of grief from the death of a loved one. Feelings opposite enough to tear a human apart.

As Remy struggled to keep focus, his world began to disintegrate, as if the trespasser had fired upon him with a different kind of weapon, one not of the physical realm.

He foundered, struggling with his overpowering emotions. He tasted salt and gulped a sob. By god, tears streamed down his face. Through his blurry vision, Remy saw the intruder tuck the sack into his robe and turn toward the door.

Remy gripped his pistol. His hands shook. The crack of the pistol almost deafened him, as if he were firing inside a mausoleum. In the instant of the bullet's leaving the barrel, he saw the trespasser jerk forward, his hood blown behind him.

The image froze in Remy's brain.

Nothing was there.

The darkness inside the hood was just that. A void. A vacuum. Nothing.

Remy clutched the pistol, his only anchor in this world. It seemed he stood there for a long time, breathing the rotten-egg smell of sulfur, the warm gun in his hand, sparks like fireflies in the gray smoke swirling around him.

Coughing, he tried to wave the smoke away, but there was so much. The burning in his arm made him grimace as he approached the dark shape on the floor. The intruder's robe lay there empty, as if a laundress had dropped it on her way from the drying line. Remy probed the black cloth with his sandal.

There was no body.

He ran out of the laboratory, past his office, through the hall, and into the wet morning. A few vendors were setting up. He inquired, but they had not seen anyone. At any rate, he couldn't very well go into a description—a headless, naked—what? All he had seen was a figure in a robe walking around his laboratory, then the empty robe lying on the floor. He searched through the streets. The intruder had only a few minutes on him, but the man was nowhere to be seen.

In a cold, misty drizzle, Remy walked back to the Society's building, the spring morning growing even darker with more clouds gathering. Shadows massed under the Society's massive arches. The vivid colors of the calligraphic tiles covering the facade looked almost monochromatic in the dimming light.

Back inside, Remy stood over the robe, then knelt beside it, picking up parts of it, smelling the odd scent of the cloth. He was certain that when the thief's hood had blown back, nothing was there. By the same token, he had felt the man's touch, seen him hold the heads. Remy clasped his hands tight in front of his chest, feeling his flesh, warm, real. This could not happen in his laboratory. He did not believe in magic, in the nonsense of alchemy. He was a natural philosopher, a scientist, a modern one who studies theoretical knowledge, yet one who does not balk at getting his hands dirty with necessary experimental activity. What many call a man of science.

He slammed his fist onto the robe—empty on the floor like the husk of a cicada—and reeled from the pain in his right biceps. Confound it. He put his left hand to his upper arm and brought it away, wet and sticky. Blood soaked the upper sleeve of his kaftan. He rolled up the wide sleeve. His skin was discolored, still bleeding from a circular wound. The bullet must have penetrated the intruder if there was a body under the robe, and ricocheted off the wall into Remy's own arm, his wrestling arm.

Lord Simmonds-Snow would have apoplexy.

But Remy could easily concoct a simple cover—he was robbed at gunpoint and shot while defending the laboratory. But in truth, he was no hero. What manner of being had he allowed to steal his prize specimens, his future, and his reputation?

He had kept the heads his secret. After all, they were immortal. If he could find out how and why, he could change the world.

He would choose a few of the Society's more valuable items and hide them. Say the stranger took him by surprise, shot him, and absconded with the treasures.

Unaccountably weak, Remy slumped against the wall, his arm numb, images flitting through his mind: the trespasser looking into the woman's eyes, her lips moving; the trespasser's hood blown back to show nothing there; the sentences planted and spoken inside his brain. An ache from deep in his body blotted out the tingling in his arm, the dizziness clouding his thoughts. Remy clutched the crystal around his neck.

"Tanythe, Tanythe, Tanythe," he whispered over and over.

CHAPTER 6

The man who had opened the bag, the man Tanythe knew as Abdosir, had, in the end, put each of their heads back into the bag and carried them away. He had stopped; the bag clenched tightly in his hand as if he thought they might escape. All was quiet for a moment. From inside the bag, Tanythe listened. Creaking sounds, which must have been a lid opening. The man moved the bag, then set it down, and she, Leukan, and Bahl settled onto the various objects that she felt through the linen. The lid closed with a groan, muting all outside sounds. Again, they had been put away. For how long?

Tanythe had recognized this man from another life, and he recognized her from then. But he did not know that—not in a way he would understand to act upon it with awareness. He had placed her crystal around his neck, a sure sign he would, in time, come to his senses in the most literal interpretation. And then, as Abdosir, he might rescue them.

Had it been a few days or weeks since he stowed them away once more? It seemed a short time, but long. She had seen light, breathed fresh air, and encountered another human who didn't threaten her with a sword or an axe. Tanythe had become impatient for more.

From inside the trunk, she barely heard the door to the room open. Then the man, Abdosir, spoke loudly. She recognized his strange language with its precise enunciation. His voice deep, threatening. Outraged. He was angry. Very much so. Footsteps, more than just the man's, advanced toward the trunk.

They came near enough for her to sense things about them. She could feel the heat of their bodies. She recognized Abdosir's scent, quintessences of cooling mint and pine sap mixed with charred wood. The other emitted an ever-changing smell of dark earth just plowed, sweet with grass, then sour with the stink of decay.

The physical atmosphere outside the trunk came through as intense, a standoff. Two beings scrutinizing one another to see who would make the first move or turn away. Did this situation involve the contents of the trunk, or was it happenstance that they merely stopped here at this stage of their altercation?

The creak of the hinges from the trunk's lid filled Tanythe with anticipation of seeing Abdosir again. She felt a vibration through the bag and was sure that one of them had gripped the bag, then raised it. Light shone through the mesh of the linen as it held their weight, bunching Bahl, Leukan, and herself together as if they were apples from the market. They bumped against one another, helpless against whoever carried the bag.

A frisson of despair flooded through her. They had come so far, for so long, would they be destroyed before they could fulfill their destiny? Tanythe sought Leukan to see his expression, to confer through their eyes, but could only see Bahl smashed in between them, his brows squeezed into a scowl. It must be the other person, not Abdosir, who carried the bag, for she caught the odor of earth, grass, and decay. In a dizzying motion, the bag swerved. She clutched with her phantom hands for anything to steady herself.

"Give me that. . ." The rest of his words were garbled. It was Abdosir's voice.

Then the bag swung in an agitated manner, as if the two were tugging at it. During all this, a feeling of familiarity flooded Tanythe, one that she struggled to place. Then the motion stopped. Something solid supported them. She shut her eyes at the brightness of what must be someone opening the bag, then two hands pulled out Leukan's head, leaving Bahl and her behind.

Leukan. No. Do not go. This could be the last time she saw him.

She held her breath, listening for sounds of swords, the grunt of hand-to-hand fighting, but all was silent. A little later, through the uncollapsed end of the open bag, she saw Leukan's head placed on the surface outside. Hands reached inside and took Bahl. She tried to move, but of course, she couldn't. Besides, where would she go?

Then the hands were on her face, strong, colder than warm. She felt as if she were lifted high, but kept her eyes lowered. Her courage had abandoned her. She stole a quick glance. A robed figure held her up.

Faced with the black void inside the hood, Tanythe jerked back. But of course, that movement was only in her mind. The robed stranger held her near his face, eye to eye, except that the inside of his hood was as black as a deep well. If she were able, she would have screamed. Yet the hands held her with a tenderness so familiar she forgot her fear in trying to recall the memory that would solve this puzzle. She could have sworn the being was trying to send a message, but it couldn't penetrate.

Then she knew.

The robed figure, a man lacking a head. The attempt at mind talk. That touch she remembered and cherished from long ago.

Leukan.

So Leukan's pleas to the gods had kept his body as alive as his head for all these centuries. Oh Leukan, what I would give to make you whole, to make me whole, to run my hands over your body, kiss your lips, hear your powerful voice. She tried to mind talk with him. She attempted again and again, but Bahl's curse still held in that regard.

"Put the heads in the bag, and set it back on the table," said Abdosir. He pointed a small object made of metal at Leukan. Tanythe heard a slight click. The man, Abdosir, was even angrier now. She could see his eyes glaring at Leukan.

Leukan set her down as if she nested in soft leaves and feathers. He slipped Bahl's head into the bag, then his own. He gazed at her. She could feel him staring from the black void inside his hood. The confusing circumstance that Leukan's head was behind her in the bag, and his body stood in front of her, and all that encompassed, she would consider later.

"*All* the heads," said Abdosir. He brandished the metal object at Leukan. Abdosir acted as if it were a weapon of some kind, but it was so very small and had no sharp blade.

Leukan placed her head inside, clutched the bag in his hand, and tucked it inside his robe. She near fainted with relief and relished the odd cold heat from his body. Then he moved fast. Oh, Leukan, we have waited for this—

An ear-splitting explosion surrounded them, greater than a blow of the storm God, Enlil's mattock, a fearsome combination of axe and adze. Inside the bag, Tanythe cringed, fearing debris from the explosion would crush Leukan and the bag he held. The thundering sound boomed from the walls and ceiling as an unimaginable force pressed into the bag, pushing her against Leukan's head, forcing them both into Bahl. Leukan's body was blown backwards as if a bull had charged into him. They were lifted. For a long moment, she knew they were airborne. Had Leukan lost hold of the bag? No, it was closed at the top, so he still clutched it.

When they began spinning faster and faster, she sent Leukan's body what power she had. Then, as if they were suddenly let go, they were thrown out and away, going faster and faster. Pricks of light through the linen weave became a smear, a comet streaking through the sky, the fading path a memory following behind. The sensation of speeding remained. They had been in a trunk, then out in a room. Surely they should have smashed into a wall by now, and that would be the end of them.

But Tanythe saw only darkness, heard only silence.

CHAPTER 7

MEANWHILE, IN THE SYRIAN STEPPES, LAND OF THE PHOENICIANS. PRESENT DAY

The rocky incline leveled out, making Darius uneasy. Although he could see the faraway hills, he had lost sight of the grassy meadow where his sheep grazed. He dug his oaken staff into the soil of the next rise, anchoring himself before pulling upward. At last, the cave. Was that a white shape inside, or was he imagining what he hoped he would find?

He started at the unearthly sound that bellowed from the craggy mouth of the Cave of the Spectres. Darius started. A slippery chill spilled down his spine, and he gripped his staff so hard his fingers turned white. He had stayed away from this place. Best not to tread where there were spirits.

Then he almost laughed. It was only the hollow cave exaggerating a sound he heard countless times each day—the bleat of a sheep. He stepped inside only because Frona wouldn't come when he called. Stubborn and ready to birth, she had wandered in. In the dim light, he saw a tiny lamb at Frona's teat. His flock's keen sense of smell would have warned them of predators, so the cave was safe. But he didn't think sheep could smell spectres. He held his staff at the ready, unsure how one fought a spirit.

Frona licked his hand as he knelt. She had taken to her newborn, and the lamb's hold on her teat proved strong. A good sign.

Strange how easy it was to see inside the cave. He looked up. Light filtered down from somewhere in the rock ceiling, though he couldn't find any clear openings. The light suddenly brightened, glinting off something near the floor.

Darius patted Frona as he stood, not wanting to alarm her, and moved toward the far end of the cave. There he found brass incense holders and blue crystals arranged on a stone altar.

To his left, he noticed a sunken area. As he stepped closer, he saw cracked earth at the bottom dotted with puddles. A spring must have once flowed from the rock wall above—its surface smooth and stained white from long-past water. These puddles must have formed where the light broke through the ceiling.

He returned to Frona. The lamb stood firm, and to his grateful surprise, Frona followed him out of the cave. Darius kept close to the ewe and her new lamb, watching its progress, happy that Frona took to her new one. Still, his thoughts kept wandering back to the cave.

The next week, after his brother came to relieve him, he visited his aging *Yiayia*. When Darius mentioned the cave, and the stories of old gods she shared with him when he was a child, she looked up from her weaving and her eyes grew moist. Fierce with determination, she insisted she was up for the trip.

Early the next morning, Darius arrived at her house. His Yiayia handed him an old clay fire pot, coals glowing inside, the outside bound in a thick wicker casing. He slung the wicker loop-over his shoulder, wondering why the coals were necessary. They wouldn't be brewing tea or heating bread, scallions, and cheese—the lunch she had packed in a woolen bag.

At the cave's mouth, she sat on a boulder to rest while Darius placed a steadying hand on her shoulder. She smiled up at him, radiant, as her gaze swept across the rocky hills speckled with red, yellow, and orange spring blooms. Bleats from grazing sheep mixed with birdsong and the lilting cadence of his grandmother's prayer, the same one she had recited before his childhood stories.

When she stood, she waved off his help and reached into her bag, pulling out a bouquet of blooddrops bound with string.

"The eight red petals are sacred to the gods of this cave," she said, handing him the bouquet.

Straightening her shoulders, Yiayia walked directly to the altar, as though she had always known its location. Darius laid the blooddrops beside the crystals. At her instruction, he placed the fire pot on the far side to keep it from wilting the flowers.

From the center of her woolen bag, she removed a vial of oil, lengths of cotton string, a brass oil lamp, and tear-shaped incense.

"Before you came to me," she said, her voice reverent in the old language, "I dreamt of this cave. It is time."

She poured oil into the lamp and soaked the string. Guiding the string's end into the fire pot, she lit it from the coals. The flame rose straight and unwavering. She lit the incense. Smoke curled to the ceiling, its myrrh scent conjuring sacred silence, broken only by a steady dripping sound.

Darius turned. His grandmother's hand trembled as she pointed.

At that moment, golden sunrays broke through the dark ceiling, striking the altar and the dry basin. A trickle of water streamed from the rock, becoming a rivulet as it flowed into the sacred pool.

His grandmother began to chant.

Darius joined her. The ancient words forming in his mouth, filling the cave, summoning the gods.

CHAPTER 8

LATER, CAVE OF SPECTRES, SYRIAN STEPPES, LAND OF THE PHOENICIANS. PRESENT DAY

*L*eukan became aware that his body lay straight and stiff in a place unknown. He could not open his eyes or move his arms and legs. Gathering strength, he searched his mind, trying to recall where he was and why. He felt his muscles gradually tensing. With a great heave, he bolted upright and opened his eyes, blinking as debris fell onto his skin.

He had been buried. What little of his body that he could see was covered in white—a winding sheet. Dead. He had been dead.

Calling on his element, terra firma, he waited for his strength to replenish, then tore through the winding sheet's material on his right side, the ripping noise made him want to cover his ears.

He saw his hand and forearm rise from the earth as if he were in a nightmare. Communing with terra firma, asking for her favor, he bent his fingers. When he could feel them, he began to work his elbow back and forth until his entire arm was free. Scrambling his fingers at the top of his torso, he loosened a strip of the cloth and unwound it as much as possible. With his free arm, he dug out the other. The struggle took longer than he would have believed, but his torso was free. In a short time, he had dug out his legs and freed them from the burial shroud.

Leukan lay back for a moment, gaining more strength while he gave thanks to terra firma. As he attempted to stand, he found his legs as shaky as a newborn fawn's, so he clawed his body upwards, slipping and sliding while the soft soil crumbled under him. And finally, he pulled himself from his own grave.

Sitting on the earth, Leukan brushed off what dirt he could see clinging to him, which was difficult since the soil's color proved as black as his skin. He reached to clear his eyes, but his hands cut through the air where his eyes and head should be.

Waving about, his fingers grasped nothing. Again, he attempted to stand, but his legs, still gaining strength, proved weak, so he crawled over the stone-strewn ground, scraping his bare skin. One more attempt, and he lurched to his knees, his power growing.

He was in a cave. Fresh red flowers lay on an altar beside flickering oil lamps. One lamp's flame fluttered fitfully as it devoured the last of the oil through the wick.

With his renewing power, his legs worked enough to bring him upright. He staggered through the cave, halting abruptly at the edge of a spring-fed pool, and just missed tumbling in. His reflection rippled on the pool's surface, revealing brief glimpses of his bare body. Leukan dropped onto his stomach and scooted forward toward the water, his compressed reflection abstracted into black slashes.

He cupped the water, his hands tingling from the chill, and brought the blessed liquid from the sacred pool to his lips, tipping his palms toward his mouth for a drink. The water splashed onto his shoulders, wetting his body at the same time he became aware of his close-up reflection in the water, which had become as still and clear as a looking glass.

His gasp at the icy water's shock filling the cave like the hiss of a serpent as he stared at his stub of a neck, his gold tattoo defaced by the weapon that had taken his head.

How was he seeing without eyes, hearing without ears, thirsting without a mouth, thinking without a brain? All the sensations using the organs originating in his head were operating as if they had noticed nothing missing.

A beam of sunlight appeared on the pool's surface, so bright Leukan turned away at the blinding reflection. He squinted, trying to stop the memory of the long blade exploding in a harsh burst of sunlight as the glinting edge cut into his neck.

Hatred, fear, and horror tore at his insides. His remembrance had turned back years, centuries, millennia. He knew this cave as his first temple. He knew the Shaman Bahl, who wielded his death sword. Knew his worshippers, dust now, who had used the last of their strength to scrape a shallow grave for him. But he—he was alive?

He had asked a boon, no two boons—from the gods above him. From a god to a god. *Tanythe?* He had felt her beside him. He still felt she was with him. A physical presence.

He closed his eyes, only the sensation of closing his eyes, and saw a dark, clammy place, so cramped as to be claustrophobic. The bag where Bahl had stowed their heads.

He called to Tanythe, but saw only darkness as a smothering shroud of silence enveloped him. Bahl's sword had decapitated them both, and a shaman's sword, even the shaman's soldiers' swords, would be spelled. The blades used on him, on Tanythe, had parted them in more ways than the physical. No matter how much of his still-limited power he used, Leukan could not bring up their mind talk. How cruel that they were murdered, crueler still the curse which silenced their secret communication.

Tanythe. When she was whole, he would hear her voice inside his mind, and she his in the same way. They were linked in that manner over any distance.

He walked back to his grave, a rectangular hole with messy heaps of soil and stones mounded around the edge, smooth places with smudged streaks where he had pulled himself out. A chill shuddered through him, but he hadn't the power to create a robe for himself to cover his nakedness. His feet sank a little into the cold earth. It felt so like home.

Digging his toes into the dirt, he felt something smooth, different from the soil. He knelt, scooped out more soil, and pulled out a black hooded robe. The length and breadth suited him and he shook it, but not too much, for he craved that the earth be close. Then he slipped it on. The cloth felt warm and cool, like his element.

There was a crude grave beside his. With some vigor, he removed the heavy stones. When he dug his hands into the earth there, the force of terra firma magic nearly knocked him backwards. It pleased him to be in his element.

Now that he had returned to life, he accepted her blessing as he scooped out handfuls of dirt and rock from the grave, bloodying his fingers.

Tanythe.

She lay in her grave. Her lovely body, pale as white rose petals, her nipples shell-pink, her delicate wrists bare—her jewelry stolen by Bahl's soldiers, stolen the same as her beautiful head.

Leukan beat the ground with his bloody fists. *Oh, Divinities.* She had come to the grave stripped of everything. Searching for her necklace, he dug frantically into the dirt around her body.

Then he remembered.

All these centuries, all these millennia, he had felt the magic of her crystal with them in that accursed bag.

As his power grew, he sat back, stunned by the new dichotomy of being here with his body, and knowing he was simultaneously with his head, which lay somewhere far, far away. This was new. He had 'found' his body just now, but his life, his awareness, had been with his head since the moment he was decapitated.

Leukan shook the soil from his hands. This was the call. A summons. It was time.

He stared at Tanythe's body, seeing, oh so long ago, the crystal necklace shining on her silken gown. The stone colorless, yet filled with color: like the sky, palest blue, or sunset's vivid gold and turquoise, or opaque as a wintry fog. Borne of sea foam from waves pounding the shore, rainbows in the thick mist of cascading waterfalls, reflections in pools, glassy still. All were symbols of Tanythe, Goddess of Abundance, source of life-giving water.

The musical sound of the spring trickling into the full pool gave Leukan a vision of their cave when the Ivory Temple was at its zenith. The hundreds of oil lamps glowing, reflected like twinkling stars in the clear pool, the holy fragrance of incense amidst the haunting chants. This cave was the inner sanctum, the original place of worship, centuries and centuries before the temple's construction.

Oh, the power Tanythe had then. And would possess once more.

Leukan prepared for his quest as he scraped the dirt back into her grave, covering her soft skin. He placed the stones gently on the smooth, mounded earth. Tanythe would stay in their sacred cave and absorb power from their new worshippers and the sacred pool with water the azure of her eyes. Leukan glimpsed the altar, the flame still burning in one oil lamp.

A devotee would soon arrive and refill the oil, light all the lamps, offer more flowers, and see his grave open and empty.

All would soon hear that Leukan, the God of Earth, one of the Gods of the Ivory Temple, had returned.

CHAPTER 9

VPHOENICIA, 2500 BC, LEVANT REGION, EASTERN MEDITERRANEAN

Tanythe struggled to keep her expression blank, not a blink or a grimace, while Bahl's acolyte held her severed head by the hair, dangling it in front of the shaman. Both men grinned at their prize. They must not discover she was still alive, for they-knew gods and goddesses could die.

She held her eyes open and kept the same vacant expression as Bahl came near. Stopping, he peered at the ground, bent his stout body, and snatched something from the dirt. He shook it and held it up.

Tanythe used all her power to keep from exclaiming, to keep her face dead. She watched, not daring to move her eyes, while that son of a cur, Bahl, raised her lovely crystal to the sun, the stone shining its pure light.

"This is what the goddess used to kill our brothers-in-arms," said Bahl as he stepped closer. She could smell the pungent incense on his robe and sour sweat under his costly perfume. He held the crystal above her head so his acolyte could see.

Tanythe longed to extend her arm and snatch the gem from the impertinent shaman. She began to reach out, bade her elbow straighten, and her fingers grasp for the crystal, but no arm moved, no fingers stretched. Even as she sent a burst of power through her fingers, she could not touch her jewel. She was aware that she had been beheaded, therefore separated from her physical body. Yet she still felt as if her body were attached, that she could walk away from this scene and retrieve the gown and jewels the soldiers had stripped from her. She pondered this phenomenon, but broke off to stop her eyes from following her precious necklace as Bahl held it before him, his beady eyes covetous.

The acolyte's hand, gripping her hair, trembled ever so slightly.

Bahl slipped her crystal around his thick neck.

The acolyte gasped.

"Ah, do not fret, Onaster. My wearing this will reduce tenfold any power left in that beautiful head, and render the stone harmless to us." Bahl clapped his acolyte on the back, making the man's hand wobble, which swung Tanythe's head back and forth.

"Two gods." Bahl held up Leukan's head to show Onaster. They guffawed, raucous and crude.

Tanythe called on her power to punish them, but stopped. She had used most of the power she had left, keeping her eyes still, keeping from spitting at Bahl. Keeping from weeping at the sight of Leukan's severed head hanging by his braids in the Shaman's meaty fist.

Dirt smeared Leukan's cheek. Blood dripped from his neck and reddened his black braids, staining the woven-in amber beads. His dark eyes, shadowed now, stared at her. She saw life in them still, the same life she felt rushing through her.

She thought back to what must have happened: Leukan had seen their defeat, seen that it would ill use his power in attempting to destroy Bahl. So he deflected his magic into keeping them alive.

Bahl's acolyte held her head at arm's length and studied her. "Pity you didn't take this woman for the harem."

"There is no trusting a goddess alive and unhappy," Bahl said. He conjured a linen sack, loosened the drawstring, and set Leukan's head inside.

The acolyte placed his soiled fingers on Tanythe's lips. Revolted, she flinched.

"Did you see that? She moved," said Onaster. He brought her head close, squinting his tiny almond-shaped eyes at her. She inwardly cringed at the stink of his unwashed body, the reek of his breath.

"Have you never seen a fowl with no head running around in the dirt? Same thing." Bahl shook the bag, settling Leukan's head deeper.

"What does a grand shaman do with a god's heads? Pikes at the gate?" Onaster eyed her mouth, watching for another movement.

"Nothing so crude. I asked the King for these, and he granted them to me. I shall tease out the essence of gods with my magic. They will suffer in the place where gods dwell." Bahl held out the sack, the opening wide.

"Put the goddess's head in."

Tanythe saw Bahl smirk. Then the weave of the linen bag took up her line of sight as she settled next to Leukan's warm flesh.

Bahl tightened the drawstring.

She was alone with Leukan, who had given her life in death. When they dropped her into the bag, she had attempted to look into his eyes, hoping to affirm that they still sparked with life, but she was facing away from him. Now, in the dark, she could only feel his head next to hers, still warm, not cold and dead.

No matter how she tried to communicate, she could not access his thoughts. Surely he had thoughts as she did, or had he given her all his power? Was he now merely dormant, like trees in winter?

The bag swayed slightly with Bahl's steps, dim light filtering through the weft of the flax strands. She heard men greeting him with respect as Master Shaman. Then the bag moved differently, and the light vanished. Odors of stale bread, dried meat, and fruit permeated the bag. From all sides, objects pressed into them. The bag lurched upward amid creaks of leather, then the earthy smell of a horse infused the interior. Soon, the thuds of its hooves drummed on a solid road, the bag moving to the rhythm.

Tanythe opened her eyes. Pricks of dim light shone through the square gaps in the linen's weave, and the same rhythm rocked the bag. Her drowsy eyelids closed halfway. She must have slept, for this is how she felt when she awoke in her human body. So very strange. Her body, physically severed and far away, still sent messages from her limbs and torso.

The reassuring warmth of Leukan was beside her. How long could she contemplate their fate? To what end? What of Prince Abdosir? Had the soldiers destroyed his beautiful marble palace? Would her poor prince's head be the next to join them in this bloodstained bag?

Abdosir had not called her with the shell she had given him. When she placed it in his hands, he had cradled the silver-fitted conch shell, his eyes shining with tears. A prince with caskets of jewels, glittering necklaces of pearls and emeralds, who recognized that all his riches were a poor second to a goddess's gift embedded with a goddess's magic.

Abdosir had lifted the shell to the light, the inside spirals a shiny, deep rose, hidden inside the shell's aperture. The outside was partially overlaid in finest silver embossed in vines, leaves, and mythical creatures, and set with sparkling moonstones, sapphires, pearls, and blue topaz. The colors of water, Tanythe's element.

"Speak into the shell when you need me. I will hear and come to you," she had said.

He had looked up, holding her gaze, and kissed the shell's glistening rose-colored inside. "Come to me now," he said into it, his deep voice spiraling through the shell's inner sanctum.

And she had heard as if he were whispering into her ear, his breath hot with desire. She was drawn to him by the power in the shell, and wondered if her feet had touched the ground as she glided into his arms, the many translucent layers of her cloth-of-heaven gown slipping off until she was naked when he held her to his chest.

But earlier, as the armies poured into their temple, she had heard no whispers in her ear, no hoarse cries for help. Reluctantly, she left her reverie, the image of the shell glistening in her mind as she paid heed to the sound of horses thundering toward them. Was it their conqueror, King Gydrl's army, arriving to protect the Shaman? Shouts, swords clashing against metal, against wicker and leather shields, dull thuds amidst agonizing screams, the sharp scent of coppery blood. She reeled at the sensation of Bahl's power surrounding her. Then another magic, strange and strong.

"Ah, so this pathetic street magic is yours?" Bahl's voice bellowed with rage, but she could hear fear at the core. The two magics intertwined. Bahl groaned. Sounds of fists, flesh to flesh, the clang of swords, always swords.

Dim firelight flickered through the opened bag, and something heavy with the tang of rancid sweat and blood came to rest between her and Leukan. Demon's eyes reflected the flickering firelight and stared straight into her.

By the gods. Bahl's head.

CHAPTER 10

PHOENICIA, 2500 BC, LEVANT
REGION, EASTERN MEDITERRANEAN

So Bahl had lost the battle. A frisson of triumph rose in Tanythe, then dampened as she tried to feel Leukan's presence through the chaos of Bahl's ongoing death throes beside her. Give it time. The Shaman soon would pass from life and become a lump of festering flesh. Better that than his ebbing malevolent magic scattering her thoughts.

Light flared as someone opened the bag and dropped an object inside. As the object hit the bottom of the bag, Tanythe raised her arm to block the stark brightness, but met with only a phantom arm. Squinting in the glare, she peered through her lashes, glimpsing swarthy skin stained dark with blood and, next to Bahl, a portion of Leukan's black braid, his dark iris ringed in a thin circle of gold. Below in the shadows, a glint of silver and the clear curve of a shining substance.

The bag closed. Plunged back into darkness after the shock of light, she considered the object carelessly tossed in after the Shaman's head. At that moment, Tanythe had felt the faint presence of her power. A soft glow rose from behind Bahl and Leukan, eerie as a lost star inside this merciless prison. It could only be her beloved crystal.

Someone lifted the bag. Her head knocked against Bahl's, and she felt heat radiating through the linen, bringing the pungent smell of horse. As the horse's hooves hammered out the speed of their travel, she felt only a faint jostling. Bahl's conqueror must have stashed their bag inside a saddlebag tucked close to the horse's warm flank.

Tanythe prayed for sleep's blessed oblivion.

After days of riding with the man, she became used to his scent and harsh guttural language—most probably a Thueycur from the Thunder Steppes. But she never adjusted to the presence of Bahl, her murderer, pressed against her. She hoped the horse's uneven strides would jostle the shaman's head so Leukan would come to rest beside her.

Her thoughts stopped as she focused all her attention on the Shaman. His flesh was still firm, not decaying into a mushy, revolting mass, and the only smell she could detect was the clove oil in his hair. Bahl had not decayed. The force of his gaze had not lessened.

By the gods, he was as alive as she and Leukan. How? Was this his perverse magic, or had he stolen theirs?

When Tanythe next awoke, she wasn't sure what had disturbed her blessed slumber. The Thueycur was still riding, but his pace had slowed. As she roused from her sleep haze, the cool air's briny scent brought her to attention. The ocean, her element, greeted her with a welcoming handshake of power. Salt air surrounded them, accompanied by the chaotic clamor of a port city: mixtures of languages, creaking ship's masts, dull thuds which must be cargo loading and unloading, drunken singing, horses' whinnies, cart wheels clattering on cobbles, screams of seabirds, street seller's cries. Aromas of baking bread and roasting meat made her salivate. How she yearned for the pleasure of eating. Strange that, for she hadn't allowed herself to think often of things she missed.

In the jumble of tongues, she heard the Thueycur's familiar voice and a language she knew, with the word *Byzantium* repeated in a long conversation. The bag jounced with the sound of the man's footsteps. The city noises and the ocean, her element, roused her worldly desires. She tasted them eagerly. By those hints and clues from outside, she could perhaps decipher their fate.

Death was still a possibility.

The smell of salt air faded, overtaken by dust, rancid sweat, and the burning oil of a lamp. Hinges creaked, the rustle of objects being moved, and the feel of a hard surface under the bag. Objects pressed against her, pushing

Bahl closer. She smelled the musty odor of dye used on silks. Then the cloying scent of fresh gardenias almost choked her. This was foreign to the Thueycurs —they were raiders whose women usually rode with them, carrying the same weapons. Scent would give them away to their enemies. So the Thueycur had stashed the bag with his loot.

Evidently, he was rearranging his spoils as she felt the bag lifted, then set down, several times over. Each time, a distinct scent wafted into the bag: the costly perfume of coriander and myrtle, spicy and tart with citrus; sometime later, woodsy patchouli, then sweet sandalwood. The odors faded. Fresh smells drifted through the bag: the bitter spice of olives, the sweet tang of dried fruit, and the smokiness of cured leather. She heard tinkling bells, then the clank of iron on iron accompanied by a burned smell, the jingle of coins, and the rustle of cloth like soft grasses in a breeze. The bag shifted and, as it settled, she felt pressure from all directions.

Then, a subtle sensation that all sounds had less presence. The Thueycur must have placed them near the bottom of the trunk among his prize possessions.

She winced from the squeak of hinges, then a numbing quiet settled over them, and the bright noise of life became muffled. Panicked, she tried to move her legs and arms, attempting to claw her way out of the cursed bag. Of course, her limbs would not move. They did not exist.

Buried.

A hard jolt set her attention straight. They were moving. The surrounding objects resettled against the bag. Once again, the disconcerting feeling of life being sucked away surrounded her. She tried to find something to latch onto, anything other than Bahl's very real presence inserting itself on her.

Over and over, she would awake to the same darkness, the same airless, tomb-like atmosphere, and succumb once more to the endless rocking motion. This repeated time after time after time in what could have been days or months. She couldn't guess when she lost all sense of time, which had blended into her dreams...her dreams of Leukan, the White Temple, their worshippers, the celebrations, the feasts, a blur of her life.

She opened her eyes to the darkness, alive now with—what? This awakening among countless awakenings felt different.

There. A surge, a quickening in the endless rocking rhythm.

Her mind worked swiftly. The Thueycur had booked passage on a ship and had stowed the bag in a chest with his other valuables. The immense power of the ocean, the near-infinite quantity of water, had given her the peaceful sleep and dreams that she had begged for.

Now, after her hiatus, her senses had become sharpened.

A violent see-saw of the ship rocked them, then a change in the slant as if the vessel were climbing. Her stomach lurched—how could she feel that? A sudden drop followed, as if the vessel were plummeting down a mountainside. Objects smashed into the bag where she was imprisoned, mashing her into Bahl as if they were soft fruit.

Gripped by fear, Tanythe blinked, eyes wide, straining to see in the blackness. They could be crushed. She cringed at the shouts and the ship's motion battering her every which way, different from the muffled garrulous carousing of the crew before she had left her senses behind to the blessings of sleep and dreaming. Waves pounded the ship, crashing into the vessel like enormous trees slamming into the forest ground, the ship's timbers groaning as if a fiendish giant was wrenching them apart. The Thueycur's thick guttural exclamations shrilled like an old woman.

Objects banged into the bag with the ever-more violent pitching of the ship. Tanythe tried to see Leukan, hungering for what his eyes might say to her, but the darkness in the bag was as impenetrable as ever. Finally, his magic touched her like a warm hand, and she knew their power still endured. So far. A soothing peace washed over her.

The Thuecyur's harrowing scream jagged through the din, prickling her scalp with a terror akin to when the soldiers had held her, when she glimpsed the sword swinging toward her neck. Then the Thuecyur's scream stopped as suddenly as if someone had muzzled him.

Creaks and moans of splintering timbers sent a torrent of dread into her marrow. She, Leukan, and Bahl slid back and forth as the ship rolled to one side, then another. A rush of heaving movement propelled them in a different direction, then an earsplitting explosion, and the sensation of catapulting through the air. Tanythe reached to steady herself with her vanished arms as she succumbed to the sinking vessel's dizzy spiraling.

A feeling of coldness, unlike anything she had ever known, engulfed her as the trunk sank further and further into a stillness resembling a silence of the deceased. Then the abrupt stop, the feel of something impossibly solid underneath them, as if they had reached the bottom of the earth.

From above, a vast amount of water, beyond imagination, pressed down on their trunk. The earth below held them like a nest cradles fledglings. Sand, rocks, granite, they were Leukan's source of power.

Now the God of Earth was safe in his realm on the Earth's floor. And Tanythe, Goddess of Water, lay in the bosom of her mother, the Immense Ocean.

* * *

SUFFOCATING SILENCE.

Tanythe dreamed. A sunset, but no birds sailing silhouetted in the yellow-orange brilliance, no breeze teasing her silks and tangling her scarlet locks. All was still while darkness stole over the earth. She pictured the moon, unreachable, glowing white-cold. Heavenly bodies staring their indifference through the years, centuries, eons.

Then, among the many layers of sleep, piled upon her through time like hundreds of woolen blankets, something roused her. A dulled sound. A slight motion. Tanythe opened her eyes to the same blinding darkness as she labored to make sense of the movements and unidentifiable sounds.

Echoing booms roared through the water, as if entire mountains toppled onto the ocean's floor in a monumental cataclysm. A grinding sound, like huge mill stones raking over one another, vibrated her teeth, and soon after, the dizzying sensation of being tossed end over end.

Then everything settled. Tanythe waited, then cursed the hope that blossomed and welcomed the drowsy drift to oblivion. Her dreams kept her company.

After days, centuries, or eons, a different dream roused her. She had flown up and up, spiraling like a leaf caught in a turbulent updraft. And here was sound once again, muted but becoming clearer.

She opened her eyes, but saw only darkness. An abrupt movement sharpened her senses. Scraping, metallic noises made her long for her hands so she could clamp them over her ears to drown out the terrifying dissonance. She gritted her teeth, fear squeezing tears from her eyes. A long-forgotten prayer circled inside her mind as she envisioned the spheres of the planets coming undone.

She listened. Sounds, muffled as if she were in a house of many rooms, and down three flights of stairs there might be someone knocking at the door. She kept listening, and now and then there came a snippet of noise, sometimes closer, always a little closer.

CHAPTER 11

1771 CONSTANTINOPLE

*S*taggering from the impact of the man's weapon, Leukan stumbled out of the palatial building, the foul smell of smoke trailing him. He held tight to his treasure. By all divinities, the weapon's voice rivaled that of the mightiest crack of thunder. Deceivingly small for so much power, the weapon had pierced him with such force that he found himself in the ethereal realm, still clutching his treasure.

When he insisted on keeping the bag, the Divine Ones had ejected him from their realm and deposited him here, on a rain-slicked street.

Transitioning at such a pace from the spirit realm to the corporeal had been dizzying, and he lurched like a drunkard. The few people he encountered gaped. Some pointed. A woman screamed and dropped the basket she carried, scattering red and green produce.

He took cover in a shadowy alley just as a boom of thunder echoed between the narrow stone walls. When the man's weapon had struck him, his robe had peeled off like a useless husk, reducing Leukan to a naked, headless body. He looked down, his bare legs still encrusted with dirt from his grave. A trickle of blood leaked from a small hole in his chest.

In the alley's shadows, he crouched on the ground, scooping handfuls of dirt over his bare feet. He set one hand on the cool, dark earth, the other on his burning wound. The scent of rain, earth, and fertile loam mixed with the coppery odor of his blood as his hand grew warmer on his flesh. When his palm burned hotter than his wound, he removed his hand.

A smudge of gray over firm flesh marked where the hole had been. A blood-black line trailed from it. Brushing off the smudge as he rose, he leaned against the cool stone wall and assessed the amount of strength he had lost from the wound and subsequent healing. Leukan closed his eyes. Of course, the view of the plaza from the alley vanished, even as he had no eyes, no lids to slide down into velvet blackness, and no head —at least none attached. All of this invaded his thoughts as his body siphoned power from the earth, just as a tree received nourishment from its roots.

Could the people of this time see him as a naked human body without a head, or was he still so lacking in power that only he could detect his earthly form? But even a lone bag floating through the air would frighten a human.

Leukan clutched the bag against his chest. Upon emptying its contents, he had thanked the gods when he saw his and Tanythe's heads alive. But his praise had dried on his tongue when he beheld the shaman's swarthy face. With horror and shock, he had viewed Bahl's scraggly dark beard, his bull neck severed like theirs, his eyes glowing dark with evil *and life*.

Life!

The Shaman Bahl, the most majestic sorcerer since King Solomon, so the rumors said, had achieved the greatest feat of all: immortality. And Bahl was not a god, as were Tanythe and Leukan. Yet Bahl had escaped death.

What a turn of fate, to be a king's greatest sorcerer and meet the same end that he had dealt the gods his king called false. Bahl had decapitated Tanythe and Leukan, then by some celestial reckoning, Bahl himself had been beheaded. Leukan stifled the impulse to toss Bahl's head into a rubbish heap. Best to keep his enemy at his bosom, where Bahl would have no room to thrust his shaman's blade.

Outside the alley, as the sun broke through the early morning clouds, more people walked the streets, and merchants began opening their shops. Leukan positioned himself so he could remain hidden, yet still see if anyone came searching for him. Seeing without his eyes. Perhaps his body held onto long-ago habits, enabling his senses to still function.

At a sudden clang, his body jerked. He flattened himself against the wall, the chill of the stone sinking into his bare skin. Hearing without ears. Odd, how he kept a running catalogue of his sense functions.

Across the paved plaza, a portly man picked up a huge tray, the brass still vibrating from its impact on his shop's stone porch. Next door, an old man hung herbs outside under an awning as his assistant brought out linen bags of spices, opening them so that mounds of bright yellow, red, and orange were shown to entice customers.

On the adjacent shop's porch, a woman and three young girls hung scarves, robes, and hats on wooden ladders, making a hall of clothing which led into the shop. Leukan fancied the saffron-yellow robe on the top rung of the ladder. That would be his first article of clothing since the robe he had found buried beside his grave in the cave. The woman brought out a lustrous blue silk robe embroidered in gold, but thieves would pursue him for the value of that one. A dark brown hooded robe that one daughter held up for inspection by her mother looked humble enough and would blend in with the city's crowds.

Hands on their hips in unison, the woman and her daughters scrutinized the goods arranged on the porch before entering the shop. Leukan tried to will his body into the hall of garments where he could hide, but after the man's potent weapon had penetrated him, his power remained deficient.

If he waited, perhaps there would be a ceremony in the far-away cave temple, giving him enough power to conjure a proper robe, or to transport his human body into the garment shop. In his grave, he had rested in the arms of terra firma, who had lovingly preserved him according to his plea.

When he first rose from the grave, life flickering inside him like an ember waiting for the breath of air to ignite, his power had been weak. Eventually, it had grown from the new devotees' worship in the cave temple. Each flicker of each flame, each spiral of incense smoke circling to the cave's roof, each release of the incense fragrance was a prayer, strengthening him.

After Leukan awoke from his grave, his long-lost head had cried out to him. He had directed his body onto the path presented, immediately flowing through time and space as if he were in a coracle shooting through a river's foaming rapids. Before he could assess how long it would take to reunite his head and body, he stood on a fine marble floor in a hall of statues, mosaics, and paintings, the beckoning so strong he could feel forces pulling him toward his head.

Were it not for the man who interrupted his quest in the room of treasures, Leukan's reunion with his own head would have been seamless. He would be whole now. As it was, he had communicated with the man but failed to mesmerize him. The unexpected summons and the mystical travel had sapped him of power more than he realized. Still, some time had gone by. He would try to mesmerize one of the shopkeepers.

Peering from the alley, he saw more people milling through the street. Perhaps he could navigate to the garment shop in the same way he came to this city. He closed his eyes, found a similar sensation from before, and began threading a path to the shop when a boost of magic from inside the bag pushed him from the alley.

Tanythe's powers.

And now, that sensation of free falling.

A man exclaimed, pointing at Leukan as he stood naked and disoriented midway between the alley and the shop. The magic had stopped. He couldn't bring it back. Leukan held the bag over his privates, ducked into a crowd waiting by a food stall, and made his way from one clump of people to another until he was in the shop's garment display.

He had been a dignified god, but was now reduced to status below a beggar. All because of Bahl. Leukan set the bag on the floor, pulled the brown robe from the ladder, and slipped it over his shoulders.

A shrill little voice called from inside the hanging garments, the language different from the man who possessed the heads, "That will be one hundred akce."

The smallest of the three girls emerged from the garments, scarves draped across her arm. Leukan quickly pulled the robe down, but her face was on the same level as his still-bare lower half. Unconcerned about his nakedness, she looked up at him just as he pulled the hood over the space where his head should be, a space filled only with his invisible ethereal body.

Her scream rivaled the boom of the brass tray that the merchant had dropped earlier. Leukan sped from the shop, brown robe flapping.

By all the gods, he had forgotten his bag.

As Leukan ran back, he used his power, boosted by the increasing magic from Tanythe, to float the bag higher than the shop woman could reach. All three now surrounded the young girl who was babbling. They turned, stunned at his reappearance. Before they could react, he snatched the bag and fled, leaving behind a chorus of shrieks.

In the alley behind the shops, Leukan found an unlocked door. He tumbled into a dusty storeroom piled with familiar items from his long-ago time of existence in the world: wooden trunks, straw baskets, clay jars. He sat cross-legged on the earthen floor, absorbing terra firma's power.

After he and Tanythe had been thrown from the ocean floor by the grace of their elements, Leukan had sensed his strength growing. A seed tentatively sending its roots into his element, earth—absorbing nutrients, responding to the sun's warmth in the soil, and sprouting from water's nourishment, Tanythe's element. Their new devotees had compounded this abundance in the cave.

He could feel Tanythe's power exponentially exceeding his, and rightly so. Leukan had searched the man's mind whose weapon had almost prevented his escape, and had found this: the man loved Tanythe. A man of this time, whose affinity for Tanythe gave her increasing power.

Leukan settled the bag in his lap and leaned against the wall. He had glimpsed Tanythe briefly in the room of treasures while the man threatened him with a small metal weapon, seemingly harmless. Now he could look upon her uninterrupted for the first time in millennia. His hands trembled as he opened the bag and cradled Tanythe's head in his lap. He held her facing him. Her beauty overwhelmed him, much more so because he hadn't beheld her for so long. Tears filled his eyes, his phantom eyes, as tears filled her beautiful azure eyes.

She blinked, and he read the expression in her eyes, her face, the full knowing of what he meant to do. He set her in his lap, pulled out the head with dark braids beaded in amber, and lifted it onto his neck. He struggled to still his shaking hands as he felt the warm weight of his own head settling onto his long-lost body.

In his mind, his words rang out as if he were proclaiming them from a stage at a great king's court:

Tanythe, Goddess of Abundance, source of life-giving water, that of placid ponds to raging seas, I beg this boon. Bind my head to my body, giving it the vibrant life we had together—

Leukan's breath caught. He would not assume that he and Tanythe, god and goddess, would be the same, not in such a strange time as this, not after so long.

He continued:

Give me the vibrant life I had before. All my thoughts, feelings, and knowings, from the tiniest flickers of awakening to the overwhelming floods of realization. Make it complete. My offering is my life from this moment on. All that I have.

In his expectant joy, there loomed sadness, for Tanythe could not *hear* his mind talk, but like all prayers and supplications, the goddess would know and grant this. He could see it, the glow in her eyes, her sudden warm smile. Joy.

Was the head he held to his neck becoming warmer? He could have sworn he felt the stirrings of his tissues and blood vessels striving to join, the subtle vibration of thickened blood liquifying.

"There. It's the bag I saw floating. See—" A woman in a garment almost as poor as Leukan's stolen robe stood at the threshold of the alley door. An armed man in a strange uniform accompanied her.

Leukan sent a curse. He had been lost in his plea to Tanythe. Nothing had registered outside his reunion with the goddess.

"What is he doing? Is that—?" The soldier strode into the room. "You! Stand. Hands where I can see them."

Leukan slipped his head into the bag, scooped up Tanythe's head, securing it in the crook of his arm, and walked through the solid door at the rear of the room. The woman's screech of surprise cut off as he exited into a shop, thankfully not yet open. He pulled his hood over the space where his head should be and placed Tanythe's head inside the bag with Bahl's. When only a few people passed by, he exited onto a cramped street closed in by the many buildings' overhanging second floors.

He had used most of his power when he appealed for Tanythe's help. The walk through the solid door took the remainder. But it could have been worse. The man, obviously some kind of soldier, could have used a powerful weapon like the man in the room with treasures and the heads. Leukan touched the place on his chest where the projectile had pierced him. Nevertheless, a boon interrupted, not a good omen.

Would Tanythe take this as a sign they should not return, that their time had expired when they were decapitated those long years ago? But surely she would have the same hope as he had clung to.

CHAPTER 12

PHOENICIA, 2500 BC, LEVANT REGION, EASTERN MEDITERRANEAN

Dark. Dark as old blood.

Bahl opened his eyes wide, seeking any vestige of light, but it was as if his lids remained shut. This caravanserai extinguished all lamps after the drinking ceased and the whores were bedded. He moved to throw off his covers, but couldn't rid the sensation of being smothered. Flailing, he tried to rise, to place his feet on the hard stone floor, but he remained immobile, a block of wood in the dark.

Inside his mind, scenes illuminated, then faded, like a bard unfolding his tales. He saw himself clutching a linen bag that held his glorious future—the severed heads of the gods of the Ivory Temple. King Gydrl had granted him this bounty: Bahl, shaman to the Magnificent King himself. With the gods' powerful essence, he would become greater than the king himself.

The visions of his glory faded, replaced by one of a battle. A fierce magic met his own, planting a stone of fear heavy inside him, pressing out his pride in his new possessions. With a taunt from a pursuing enemy, an entwine of magic bound his sword hand as if it were immersed in deep water. Bahl failed to parry his opponent's thrust and watched the scene unfold so slowly that it must have been a dream. The glinting edge of the blade descended in halting steps toward his neck.

Then the blow. He gripped his mount with his thighs, tried to raise his sword, but only in his mind. His arm was dead weight. Disbelief filled him as his world erupted in blood and blackness, his sword lost, his horse screaming in terror.

Then the shock of soul-rending agony reached so deep inside that Bahl failed to feel. Fear prickled his skin when rough fingers brushed his scalp and seized his hair. He saw his enemy's blood-spattered face twist in satisfaction. Then the coarse weave of a linen bag closed around him, scratching his face. He glimpsed blood staining the gray weave, the red of the goddess's hair, the blue of her eyes, the god's dark braids interwoven with amber beads. Red. Blood red.

Pinpoints of light pierced through the bag's mesh weave. He could neither move nor turn, so he let his eyes rove in every direction and stopped in shock. The male god's eyes stared back at him, the irises ringed in gold.

Alive. By the conjurer's blade, alive, just as he was.

Bahl had heard whispers of the gods' immortality, but these gods he had killed with his own sword. They had bled red, just like him.

He looked into the darkness, fearing to see more. But beside him, the warmth of the goddess's flesh pulled his thoughts back. How long since he had stuffed their heads into this bag? Days. Their decaying flesh should be as cold as a crypt in winter.

But it wasn't.

The bag's interior became lighter, and he caught the glimmer of the goddess's eyes.

Alive, like the god's.

With his own sword, he had cut off their heads. He saw their astonishment, watched their helpless death throes, like the hundreds of enemies he had slain. He never would have believed these were immortals, but the proof lay on either side of him.

The life he had sought, he never found. The Great Gods of Light gave death to mankind. Life, they kept for themselves. And despite all his power, he was still human.

But now? Now he was as alive as the goddess facing him inside this miserable bag.

He had been galloping from the enemy when they surrounded him. He had lost. The bag, stolen. His eyes widened as he grasped the unthinkable.

He was in the hands of his enemy, inside the very bag he had once gloated over.

His body had toppled from his mount. He had seen it then, saw it now in his mind. Blood spurting from his neck as bright as rubies in the sunlight, his hand grasping the bag even in death. The enemy chopped it off to get the bag. His body? Trampled by the army following the man who took his life. Eaten by wolves. Picked apart by vultures. Consumed by worms.

He shut his eyes, welcoming the darkness, but it offered no solace. The visions kept coming, now that he had let them in.

With his natural gift of magic, Bahl had sought a life of power, but only found servitude to a more renowned master who garnered all the praise. Praise that should have been his, Bahl, the Great Shaman. Now he had gained another chance.

He could not tell if this life after death would last. Yet he knew he lay between two gods, whose immortality must be giving him life.

He would find a new body. But how would he manage affixing his head, which held his immortality, onto a new body?

He must find a way.

He would use the gods.

And he would seize the secret of life for himself.

CHAPTER 13

1771 CONSTANTINOPLE

"Good Lord, Derrien."

A voice filtered through the dark reveries of Remy's brain like a nightmare coming to life. Remy opened his eyes. Was that a silhouette of a man standing over him?

"Have you gone native and decided to—" The man knelt beside him. "Your arm is all bloody." The man looked around, nose wrinkling. Remy blinked, trying to focus. Confound it. Looked like the Gov.

"Smells like gunpowder," the Gov muttered, rolling up the wide sleeve of Remy's kaftan. "By God. You've been shot. Might be a bullet still in there. Let's get that wound dressed. Can you stand?"

Remy raised his head. He was sprawled on the floor of his laboratory, barefoot in native sandals, his limbs wrapped in the folds of a kaftan. His arm burned. His skull throbbed. And he'd been robbed—by that... that headless creature.

Later, in the Society's guest suite, Remy sat stiffly on a featherbed in one of the more luxurious rooms while the physician worked on his arm. The sharp tang of vinegar engulfed him, and he grimaced at the sting as the physician cleaned the wound. A third glass of brandy sat on the bedside table, half of it inside him along with the first and second glassfuls, swirling his thoughts like the samiel winds.

Remy once again envisioned the headless thief holding Tanythe's beautiful head, her eyes blinking at him, her mouth moving. Since the incident, Remy couldn't stop the glimpses of her flitting through his mind, images he had never actually seen: Tanythe, her head now on a lovely body floating naked in a pool of clearest blue water, her pale skin tinted aqua, her red hair snaking around her as if she were embraced by a sinuous water creature. She must have sparked his usually dormant imagination.

"All set," the doctor said, motioning to a servant who whisked away the bloodied cloths. "I've left some packets of powders on the table." He indicated a stack of small triangles, folded brown paper tied with string, the numbers one, two, and three inked upon them. "Take one of the packets following the numerical order, about every two hours. Let the powder dissolve in water. Mind, only six per day. If the pain gets worse, call me. You should be feeling better now that the bullet's out. Would you like it? Souvenir?"

Dazed, Remy nodded yes. At least he'd have something that had touched the thief, that went through his body. He grasped his arm, horror rising. By Jove, the bullet went through the thief's body. Then the bullet ricocheted off the wall and lodged in Remy's arm.

A revulsion unlike any he'd known convulsed through him. It felt obscene. As if he'd committed some unnamable taboo, something akin to devouring human flesh. He gagged. Bile surged up his throat. He seized the brandy and drained it as if it were water.

He was defiled.

And lo and behold, just as the thought passed through his mind, he saw Tanythe, whole again. That lovely head on a wondrous body, clothed in a semi-transparent blue gown glittering with sparks of silver like distant stars. He saw himself there with her. In the vision, he held a shell, cool in his hands.

Remy looked at his own hands. Empty. Even though he felt the curves of the smooth shell that he held in his vision, felt it in his grip. Here, in the Society's guest room.

Drawn back into his vision, he lifted the shell to his lips, spoke into it as if in conversation with Tanythe. A conch shell—*Turbulent pyrum*, the giant conch, a species of marine gastropod mollusk native to the Indian Ocean. This very shell's marvelous whorls and apex had been fitted in silver, swirling with flowers and winged creatures, studded with moonstones, pearls, sapphires, and blue topaz. A blue silk tassel hung from a silver bead at the tip. Hidden on the shell's underside, the aperture, the satiny opening into the interior, resembled a lady's privates in shades of delicate pinks blending to red.

Remy lay back on the soft feather bed. He closed his eyes, seeking sleep, but Tanythe and the shell, a phantom in his hand, refused to vanish. He willed his body to relax, but it disobeyed, tense with questions. Who was this Tanythe? And the shell. What was the significance? He flexed his right hand, still feeling the shell's curves and the texture of the silver emboss.

These images came out of nowhere when he was awake, perhaps from the shock of the escapade with the thief. A prick of pain made him clutch his arm and simultaneously cleared his mind. Had he actually been robbed by a headless man who fancied ancient living heads that seemed to talk to him?

Lately, Remy had been under pressure. His appointment from the Society had caught him by surprise, a pleasant one, yes, but pressure all the same. He was honored. This was his step up.

He'd left his valet behind in London, per the Society's suggestion. As for his wife, Pheodora, he had insisted on her coming later, once he had settled in and found a house. Frankly, he wanted solitary time to think, and what better place to ponder his future than while contemplating the endless ocean as the ship cut through the magnificent, huge swells?

Arriving in Constantinople had been like getting punched in the face. Camels lumbering past multi-colored tiled minarets. *Bedu* in indigo robes with curved *janbias* tucked into vivid sashes. Women veiled and shrouded in robes of black, green, blue, maroon, and purple, their hands hennaed in swirling blood-red designs. The Grand Bazaar stocked with fruits and vegetables he'd never before seen. Spices piled in mountains of red, ochre, yellow, and green. Fantastic jewels, brass plates, pitchers, lamps, and odd implements. Bolts of exotic silks radiant as fire.

Then Pheodora had arrived, and with surprising enthusiasm, embraced the city.

Settling in and setting up his laboratory had forced him to place his feet firmly on the ground, and he had tried to keep them there. But now...

Remy stared at the arched ceiling in the guest room at the Society of Antiquaries as he lay in bed. He had never been delicate, but this wound had set him back physically and mentally. This was his chance to succeed as a man of letters, a natural philosopher, and a modern scientist with a discovery that would put his name on the map, so to speak. But now, doubt clouded his mind.

When he first opened the stained linen bag, had he seen living heads, or were they merely ancient but skulls exquisitely preserved? Perhaps the shock of the grisly contents sparked some dormant madness in Remy, something inherited but latent for all of his twenty-five years.

If he didn't make every effort to hoist himself from this dark hole, he would sink deeper and deeper.

Simmery must have noticed that the robbery had changed Remy. Yet the Gov would associate Remy's disorientation with the fact that he had been robbed and shot in his own laboratory. That bought him some recovery time. Once again, his mind flicked through the event, and Remy put his hand to his forehead as if that would stop the images from repeating. It was over, done with. The heads were gone, probably for good, and good riddance. He raised his arms and stretched, pressing his legs into the thick mattress, and nearly yelped as a searing pain ripped through his right biceps.

Blast, how could he forget about the bullet wound?

He sat up straight, drawing his knees up, his feet rumpling the bedcovers. The room began to spin. As if a curtain had been raised on a stage, a scene appeared in his mind: his laboratory, a few weeks before the theft.

That Wednesday, Remy had left the heads scattered on the table in his lab, his chair overturned, as he fled the same as Khalil. Despite his shock, Remy had the presence of mind to lock the laboratory door, then shelter in his office until time to leave, when he made for home. Early the next morning, he arrived at the laboratory ready to face the monstrosities and perhaps his insanity.

Taking one look at the heads scattered on the table had stopped him cold. He couldn't bear to face them, yet he stayed rooted to the spot and stared at the abominations, hoping he would eventually see ancient yellowed skulls sans flesh—see them as they should be after thousands of years.

But no, they had still looked as fresh as life itself. What on earth was that smell? He walked to the other end of the lab. The odor had vanished. Perhaps it was merely his imagination, which had been remarkable of late. Back near the heads, the odor proved strongest. He sniffed a strong, slightly sweet scent with a dark, musky aroma. By Jove, it was the Gov's cologne, *Attar Al Paculi*. The man reeked of it.

Remy went to the door and exhaled, a kind of cleansing of the palate to see where the smell first originated. He caught a whiff of the fragrance by the doorframe, then on the table by the heads. Next, at the microscope, especially when he put his eye to the lens, where the odor proved especially strong. He sat heavily on the chair in front of the microscope. A red hair lay on the specimen pad.

He stared at it as if beholding an apparition.

The scene unfolded before him—Simmery snooping in Remy's very own lab. Simmery discovering the heads, peering through the microscope at a hair, possibly looking at skin samples. Remy could only imagine.

Did the Gov KNOW about the heads?

Of course, in any of his meetings with the Gov, Remy could easily have acquired the aromatic scent on his clothes or even on a report or note given him. Then, sitting in his lab, the smell would permeate whatever was nearby. As for the red hair, in Remy's shocked state after discovering the heads, a hair could have attached to his hand or sleeve, and he might have unknowingly transferred it anywhere in the laboratory.

If Simmery had indeed been snooping and found the heads, he would be furious that Remy had not informed him of the discovery. Would he suspect Remy had stolen the heads himself and faked the robbery so that he could study the heads in secret? Or would he think Remy had hired a brigand to steal them, shooting Remy in the process so Remy would seem innocent?

All the happenstances of the last weeks swirled in Remy's head. From his bed, he gazed at the Society's impeccable guest room. The costly carpets from Persia, the tables polished to a russet sheen, the cut crystal water pitcher, and matching drinking glass sparkling in the light from the back garden. Then he thanked the Lord that the guest rooms were as far away as possible from his laboratory.

His wound throbbing, Remy ripped open the packet from the doctor marked number one and dropped the powder into the glass of water on the tabletop beside his bed. The small grains sank as they dissolved, clouding the liquid, the murky water much like his mind since the theft. He envisioned the Gov in a fury, sacking him, revoking his Fellowship in the Society.

Remy put his hand around the glass and glimpsed Tanythe in the water, holding the shell out to him, the blue and purple jewels sparkling, her red hair swirling, almost filling the glass.

He picked up the clouded water, shut his eyes, and drank. Then he lay back on the soft pillow.

He let out a long sigh. Hoping against hope that the medicine could help him sleep and obliterate his painful imaginings and corrupted visions.

CHAPTER 14

*R*emy awoke to the fragrance of honey. Orange tulips fanned out in a cut-crystal vase. He squinted into cornflower blue eyes, blinking through the gaps of bright green leaves.

"Dear husband. Shot?" Pheodora set the vase on the bedside table in the guest room of the Society of Antiquaries and took his hand. Her graceful fingers entwined with his.

"Never in all my imaginings of you laboring in your laboratory did I think that you might be shot." She shook her head, the gold silk tassel hanging to the side of her elaborately crimped cerise Turkish headdress bobbed in emphasis.

"An explosion, fire, chemical intoxication, perhaps… but shot? Why, when the footman brought me the note, I chased down a nipperkin of our best brandy on the way out the door." Pheodora let go of his hand, crossed to a seating arrangement fringing the window, and dragged a chair to his bedside. She wore native dress again: pink silk trousers, *salwar* that resembled blousy fat balloons extending to her slim ankles, a long sheer *gomlek*, like a chemise, and an ankle-length purple *entari*, an outer robe with the ends tucked up. But for her flaxen tresses peeking from under her headdress and those startling blue eyes, she might fool someone into thinking she *was* a native.

"It's just a scratch," said Remy.

But it wasn't. The doctor had dug out the bullet, and it had hurt like hellfire. Still hurt. Throbbed like the devil, as if that creature, that thief, had infected him with an exotic disease from the grave. He shuddered. Closed his eyes. Pheodora had noticed. Who would not notice this pathetic display?

"Why, dear." Pheodora moved closer, her eyes brimming with tears. "Let me see it." She lifted the woolen coverlet and pulled it down to his waist. The cool air felt good. Did he still have a fever?

She pushed up the loose sleeve of his nightshirt, her eyes widening. "Dear, your bandages need changing."

He blinked, and she was suddenly back with a leather case. She tucked up her billowing white under-sleeves and, as if she were a djinni, appeared on the far side of his bed. He must have dozed off for a minute.

"Let us have you sit now." She slipped her arms under his back and helped him up. Stronger than she looked. He had never realized it. He shook his head, confused at his weakness. Fever would do it. And the shock, probably.

"Raise your arms. Wherever did they obtain this odd nightshirt?" Pheodora pulled up the kaftan's sleeves. "Here, roll to the side. The nightshirt is under you." He felt her warm hand on his skin as the shirt slipped up his back.

"There. Now, on the other side." He rolled onto his left hip. With all this rocking, he could still be shipboard.

"Finally." She dropped the garment on the floor, leaving him in his linen drawers. "I'll see that the Society has a proper nightshirt for the next guest," she said, with crisp disdain.

He blinked. Pheodora seemed a vision. There. Then not. As though appearing in and out of focus like specimens beneath his microscope.

"Did you know the last time I was in your laboratory, I looked at a peacock's feather through your marvelous microscope?" she said brightly. I had purchased some tail feathers at the Grand Bazaar. . ."

She prattled on as he focused on his thoughts.

Incredible. How on earth had Phe picked up the analogy in his thought about the microscope? But his thoughts were scattered, and he could have said something about the instrument out loud and not remembered it the next second.

"...the feather seen through the lens was like a brilliant silken carpet..." Pheodora droned on. Her words, light and sunny, like birds chirping, faded into another's that resounded in his head: *Hard earned, they were.* The thief's words.

Something soft and cool at his back. Pheodora was stacking pillows behind him. He leaned into them. Ahh—

"...the feathers looked as if they were woven in uniform rows, the barbs of the most vivid greens and.."

Tanythe. A name that seemed to emanate from the crystal he had placed around his neck.

"..blues, oranges, and purples flowed into one another. And the feather's eye, like..."

They are mine in more ways than thee can imagine. The thief's words wound around his brain. What did they mean? He must have imagined those words. Insanity creeps slowly, insidiously, until it overtakes—

"...Remy, when I took my eye from the microscope, the laboratory seemed drained of all color, and I had to stay in the chair until I regained..."

Phe's words spun in his head. With his open eyes, he could actually *see* the letters of the words she spoke coming apart, spinning in an alphabetic swirl. Remy closed his eyes, but the letters, their serifs' sharp points, showed white on the blackness. He leaned hard against the pillows, his hands clutching at the covers, trying to stop the increasing spinning.

The same vertigo that had twirled him into unconsciousness after he slumped against the laboratory's damp wall now stole his sight and balance. His hearing blunted, but for a loud buzzing racket, and those words, always the thief's, like evil spirits in his head. *Sokor Körmös,* what they called demon spirits here in Constantinople, according to Khalil and Pheodora.

Thoughts jumped at him from the darkness, standing out in the confusion before he absorbed them. He now resided in this fabled ancient city, the city of Byzantium, where the Crusaders had fought with Sultans and their elite corps of Janissaries, where harems existed in bejeweled inner sanctums of marble palaces.

Pheodora. She had been in his laboratory again using his microscope. Had she somehow seen the heads?

The thief. Was he merely an ordinary thief? Perhaps the pressure of being thrust into this exotic, foreign environment, hoping to succeed at his wildest dreams, had made Remy believe that a headless, mystical thief had stolen the heads.

Could he have hallucinated the heads? There were other treasures in the trunk, albeit treasures only because they were so ancient. Were the heads merely skulls? Bone and teeth and empty eye sockets that, by weird turns of his fears and insecurities, had been transformed into an outlandish hope to fulfill his dreams of success?

The buzzing in his head gradually ceased. His eyes cleared.

Pheodora sat by his bedside near the table and flowers. Another small table had appeared to her right, on which sat a leather case and a brass bowl of water. Folded white cloths were stacked beside it. How long had he been out, unseeing, questioning? He didn't know what to call his strange exit from the here and now.

"Remy, do you need to lie down again?" She reached out, resting a hand on his chest.

He shook his head ever so slightly. Mistake. The slight motion almost caused him to toss the contents of his stomach.

"This is beautiful." Pheodora reached for his chest and held out the crystal, the chain pulling on the back of his neck. The necklace he had found in the trunk where the heads had lain for centuries. The necklace that he now believed was Tanythe's.

"Why, the stone is as clear as pure water, yet I sense a blue light coming from it. Oh!" Pheodora dropped the crystal. The stone struck his chest with a dull thud.

"It shocked me!" She examined her hand, then rubbed it briskly. "Where did you get it?" Her question sounded like an accusation.

Remy couldn't speak. All he could think of—the word tingling at the tip of his tongue—was *Tanythe*. He coughed for lack of anything else, which made his arm hurt. His mind was too muddy to make up anything clever and plausible.

"The Grand Bazaar, the week I first arrived," he blurted. Well, at least that was believable.

Pheodora eyed him. "I should never wonder at what you come up with, Lord Remy Edric Derrien. Why, I never thought I'd see the day when Sir Natural Philosopher—" Remy frowned at her. "Err, Sir Scientist, would need a talisman." She gave him another peculiar look, those eyes probing like the lens of his microscope.

"Well, a change of countries brings out new things in one. Why, look at me." Pheodora held out her arms and exhibited her Turkish costume. With a wry smile, she flicked the gold tassel hanging from her cerise headdress, then pulled a gold chain from her blouse with a shiny glass medallion the size of a guinea coin hanging from it. The outside circle was lapis blue, the next white, the next gold, then a solid black dot in the middle.

"A charm to protect me from the evil eye. See, we are not as different as you think," Pheodora said, her voice like the froth on a pint. She let the medallion fall back inside her blouse.

"Take it out again so I can see it." Remy studied the crude eye composed of uneven circles. Rather hypnotic if you looked for long. He could have sworn the circles rotated in opposite directions to one another.

At the snap of a sharp click, he raised his head. Pheodora had opened the leather case next to her and pulled out a gilded box. "You know, when I first came in and set the flowers on the night table, you were mumbling in your sleep." She gave him a look. "It sounded like your mother's name, Janice."

Tanythe. Remy started to correct her. What was he thinking?

"Why do you look so, so...wary? It is perfectly permissible to call one's mother's name after a shock. After all, I don't recall you ever being shot before."

She pulled the lid off the gilded box, removed a glass bottle of clear liquid and several lengths of cotton cloth, then set them on the inside of the box's lid. From the case, she removed a pottery jar, pulled out the cork, and poured a gold viscous liquid into a brass bowl beside the box.

"The bandage may be stuck due to the blood and fluids that have dried on it." With liquid from the bottle, which turned out to be water, Pheodora wet his old bandage, then began unwrapping it.

He wasn't ready for the hurt. Unsticking the bandage must have reopened the wound. It felt as if she had punched his arm. "By Jove, Pheodora, do you want to finish me off?"

"Silly. Remember, it's just a scratch," she teased, washing around the wound with a wet cloth. The sharp odor of vinegar made him draw away.

"Keep still. You will make me put something in the wrong place, and it might sting horribly." She dipped a clean cloth into the golden liquid and slathered it onto the wound.

"Ah, the bees make an incredible substance," said Remy as he soothed his nostrils with the sweet, balmy scent as honey calmed his wounds.

"How did you know honey draws out infection?" Remy asked as he watched her sort through several lengths of cloth.

"Quinton, Rymon, and Trinian. You'll know them better as Quin, Ry, and Trin, my three rowdy brothers." Pheodora chose a bandage and held it out, gauging the length. "Our nannies were hopeless when it came to the boy's cuts and scratches. And Mummy was always away at parties, or riding, or in the midst of a card game, or sleeping, so the boys came to me. They had seen me help the veterinary surgeons who doctored the horses, cows, sheep, and the hunting hounds. The surgeons would let me look through their kits and assist them. Things like holding the medicine jar, dumping out a pot of pus drained from a wound—"

She eyed him.

He must have made a face.

"Rather nasty, don't you think? But I felt so very important. Even if they sent me to fetch a drink from the kitchen, a servant's job. You know, a little girl all beribboned with ruffles and lace. They hadn't the faintest idea I was learning anything. Oh, and the surgeons would always use honey on the infections and wounds, and the boys wouldn't screech and threaten me when I put it on their wounds."

"There." Pheodora sat back, viewing her work. "If the doctor scoffs at it, wait until next time when I apply one of my other secret formulas." She packed the rest of the bandages in the box, stoppered the honey jar, emptied the water into the flowers, and slipped all of them into her fine leather compartmented case. A case he had never before seen.

"Let me arrange for you to come home to convalesce. I never see enough of you." She kissed him on the cheek. He pulled her close, wincing a bit from his awakened wound when he set his feet on the floor as he contrived to place her in his lap.

"Not in the Society's guest room, Remy. Even though it does have a scandalous appeal. I don't fancy Lord Simmonds-Snow, dear Snowy, popping in and catching us." She kissed him on the mouth, long and slow, then wriggled from his embrace and dragged the chair back into position.

"I'll arrange it with Snowy and return with a carriage in a few hours. It will be more healing for you to be away from work." She adjusted the window curtains. "Is this too bright?"

"The light is perfect. You rode?" Remy raised his knees on the bed and leaned forward, stretching his back.

"Derya needed the exercise, and so did I." She gazed at him. "Why didn't they send you home after you were shot? Don't they know you have a wife? They see me here. Surely, they don't think I'm your assistant?" She flashed a big grin, the tease.

He wanted her in his bed. His arm be damned.

Pheodora sat beside him, the mattress pushing her next to his body. He caught a whiff of some exotic scent. The warmth of her next to him made him feel almost healed. She looked into his eyes.

"Remy, take care here. There are things… Constantinople harbors ancient mysteries so complex that neither you, with all your sophisticated natural philosophy or science, nor I can fathom their depths. Some of these things are the epitome of evil."

He wrapped his arms around her and held his wife close, glad to be going home.

Pheodora did not know the half of it.

CHAPTER 15

hrough the window, the garden looked inviting, but Remy had become exhausted yesterday from sitting out too long. Still, recovering from the bullet wound at home, away from the laboratory, had brought relief.

Each time he began reflecting on the incident, Remy attempted to blot out the images, the voice he heard in his mind, and the smells. Yet he would awaken in the night, the sour, sulfurous stench from the black gunpowder combustion filling the bedroom. He would sit bolt upright in bed, the thief's words fresh in his brain, his image so vivid that Remy searched the room, fear prickling his skin. The black-robed figure seemed to hover near the door. No. By the window. Now, beside the bed. Reaching for him. The thief by the door. No, near the window. Now, next to the bed, reaching for him.

Then Phe would stir in her sleep, rustling the covers, and he would put his hand on her back, her warmth driving the phantoms away.

This was no ordinary wound. It should be healing faster, and the dreams. These all-consuming thoughts and creeping fears should have faded by now. Yes, the bullet had torn through the thief before striking his biceps, but it had missed arteries and vital organs. He stared at the ceiling, sleep impossible, his mind shocked into endless queries of whys and hows regarding the incident.

Unbidden, his memory pulled him back. Two days ago, Wednesday, he had discovered the heads. Thursday, he had found the Gov's cologne permeating his laboratory. That Friday, he had hoped for an ordinary day with no unearthly phantoms, no disconcerting discoveries. That morning, Remy had unlocked the front door of the Society's building, pausing to regard the newly mounted brass plaque beside it, the letters light gold in relief on a dark background:

The Society of Antiquaries, London & Constantinople

London: Est. 1707

Constantinople: Est. 1771

His branch here, in this historical city, had been recognized.

He had traced his fingers over the etched date, 1771. *This* year. He was a part of history. A hundred years from now, someone would lightly brush their hand over this date and wonder about those Society members who, so long ago, came here and lived in this alien land. A surge of pride flowed through him, almost eclipsing the disquieting incident on Wednesday.

Fortified, he had stepped over the Society's threshold into the marble-floored hall of the former palace. The cupola's high arched windows flooded soft light across faded mosaics, scenes of mythical hunts, pastoral serenity, and domestic rites. Life-sized Roman statues stood in niches: Phoebus, Diana, Bacchus, and others he couldn't identify. A whole pantheon cast in stone.

That Friday, Remy had grasped the crystal that now hung inside his shirt, unlocked the laboratory door with shaking hands and forced himself into the laboratory. Cutting off his thoughts, he entered. A vivid vision of the heads, their liquid eyes glaring, made him turn back, but he forced himself to an about-face and sat at the table where the heads lay in disarray.

He stifled a scream.

Remy blinked. He was in bed at home in Constantinople, awake in the dead of night. His vision of the heads faded but the scream withheld in the laboratory vision blared inside his mind.

Beside him, Phe moaned, turning in her sleep, dragging the covers with her, then lay still. He could hear her deep-sleep breathing start again.

As if it were laid out before him, he viewed the laboratory just as it was that auspicious Friday as he sat at the table where the heads had spilled from the stained linen bag. The man with the ebony complexion facing away from him, the woman lying on her cheek, and the bearded man face down. The bag that held them lay crumpled into a heap behind them, just as Remy had left the trio on Wednesday. On Thursday, he couldn't bear to be near the heads long enough to set their positions right.

He looked up from contemplating the bedcovers. The black rectangle of his bedroom window had become the pale blue-gray of first light. Remy lay back on his pillow, now chilled from the night air, desperate to sleep. But no matter what distraction he threw at it, his mind would not be deterred.

That Friday in the laboratory, he had donned thin leather gloves. Gently, he lifted the swarthy man's head with the sparse black beard and piggish-devil eyes and set him inside the bag. Breathing hard, he put both hands on either side of the ebony-complected man's head and lifted him. Catching those coal-black eyes ringed in gold, bright and staring, Remy nearly dropped the head. He strengthened his hold. Simultaneously, a great swell of sorrow tore through him, tears flooding his eyes as he envisioned the woman, whole, her beautiful head on her naked body, soldiers marching her out of a cave. Was this a vision from the ebony-complected man, whose head was warm in his hands?

The emotion was so overpowering that even now, at home in his bed in the dark, Remy wiped his eyes with his nightshirt sleeve. When he had placed his hands on the woman's head, her warmth penetrated his gloves. He held her gently and found himself staring into her eyes, just as the thief had done. He had come to his senses, still holding her head, the wall clock informing him he had held her for a quarter of an hour.

These people. Who were they?

Devils? Gods? Prophets?

After stowing the bag in a trunk and securing it with a new padlock, Remy had plodded back to the table where the heads had been. He absently sat, the task accomplished. Then stood up, panicked. Would they have enough air in the trunk? Hurrying to the back of the room, he paused, his hand on a table to steady himself. By all heaven, they had been thrown from the depths of the Bosphorus in a great earth upheaval. They had been locked in a trunk under-water, then silted over for centuries, buried in the depths of the sea. Remy put his head in his hands, then recoiled.

He still wore his gloves, which had touched each head. Remy tore them off and threw them on the floor for Kahlil to toss into the rubbish bin. But when he looked at the table, he still saw them there. Alive.

Just as alive as he was.

The right side of his body had a chill, and he pulled at the bedcovers, rolling Phe closer to him. It was better to be at home. He had endured worse dreams in the Society's guest room. During the day there, he had insisted on the door being locked, fearing that any moment the thief would glide into his room with a macabre weapon and finish him off.

But the thief was no ordinary ruffian. He had lovingly lifted the woman's head and stared into her eyes.

"Blast." Remy struck the mattress with his fist.

"The thief had come into the laboratory to retrieve *his own* head." Remy blinked as his voice broke the night's silence. He looked over at Pheodora, on her back now, her breathing still slow and even. Blessed sleep. He shook his head.

Why on earth hadn't he realized the thief's mission before? He was losing his deductive skills, as well as most of his senses, so carefully honed in his studies at Trinity. The practical, detached observation of the new methodological natural philosophy or science had become second nature to him. He had relished applying rational thought and reason to the enquiry of the material, finding it a logical way to demystify the physical world.

This was the philosophy of the future.

A philosophy he was supposed to be putting in place. His thoughts niggled back to his conundrum. Now that the thief was in possession of his own head, how would the man put himself together? Was this a question that espoused natural philosophy/science, or had he veered into an area of madness? A headless man stealing into a laboratory to retrieve his severed head?

As if in answer, his brain called up a verse in a singsong rhythm:

"Humpty Dumpty sat on a wall,
Humpty Dumpty had a great fall;
Threescore men and threescore more,
Cannot place Humpty Dumpty as he was before."

The rhyme from Remy's childhood slipped from his lips and sounded entirely too loud in the bedroom in the middle of the night. Still, he hadn't disturbed Phe. Hmm, the rhyme could be prophetic. He must find the thief, if only to discover how he would reconstitute himself. Remy pressed his fingers to his brow. When he had encountered the thief, the thief had *spoken* to him three times:

Hard-earned, they were.

Tanythe.

They are mine in more ways than thee can imagine.

Why hadn't Remy tried to communicate with the thief then, rather than threaten him? The man had obviously attempted to engage him on a personal level, not adversarial. When the thief had behaved like a gentleman, albeit a desperate gentleman on an impossible mission, Remy had conducted himself like a lout.

As a gentleman, a natural philosopher, and a man of science, Remy was obligated to find the thief. To communicate with him, especially if the man was what he believed he was a being of another realm. Remy placed his hand on Phe's arm, her warmth reassuring in the dark night.

A being from another realm?

Was he becoming completely unhinged?

CHAPTER 16

*R*emy kept his hand on Phe's arm, her warmth soothing as she slumbered beside him. The night seemed to go on forever. Nestling into the coolness of his pillow, he attempted to quiet his mind, but it would not be tamed. Instead, it began to sift through plausible explanations for the living severed heads and the headless thief who had stolen them.

Perhaps his desperation for a great discovery had driven him to believe that three mummified heads in an ancient trunk were alive.

Preposterous. He wasn't that far gone. Yet.

Then again, the thief might have been a common ruffian, a bit touched, who had stumbled upon the strange heads in the bag and become sidetracked. And what had Remy seen when the thief's hood slipped off just as the bullet struck? Likely a visual delirium brought on by the sheer anxiety of having to shoot someone in his laboratory.

But more had happened on that Friday. He would sort through it now, slowly, properly. The last time he had tried, fear had overtaken reason, and he'd screamed himself awake, startling Phe clear out of bed. He wouldn't let that happen tonight, only because he was wide awake.

In the laboratory that Friday, after securing the heads safely inside the trunk, Remy had sunk into his chair and placed his hands on the table where the heads had lain. His palms and fingers rested in something wet, viscous, and rather sticky. Repulsed, Remy had jerked his hands away.

A clear substance tinged pink in some places and gold in others coated his palms and fingers. Smelled, hmm, like rosewater and black pepper. No, like puddles in the old market where they sold camels once a month. Wrong, it had no scent at all.

He had held his hands up, noting that the gel-like stuff coated the table's metal surface in a thick layer. Secretions from the heads?

Disgusted, yet intrigued, Remy sniffed his hands. The delightful fragrance of rosewater, then the foul odor of drains. He whipped his fingers away and spat on the floor, wrinkling his nose at the offensive smell.

After scrubbing his hands clean, he rummaged through the nearest cabinet and found the perfect vessel: six and three-quarters inches high with straight sides, the top narrowing to a two-inch neck sealed by a glass stopper.

As he collected the substance with a metal scoop and deposited it in the jar, he found it gave off no odor at all. The substance was more gel-like than he had originally observed, so it was fast work to gather it. He had only a smidgeon of the gel left at the table's far corner when, at a blur of movement to his right, he whipped his head in that direction, his body rigid with dread.

What if the thief stood just behind him?

From his chair, Remy turned sharply, searching the room for some grisly apparition, only to glimpse a fat black fly buzzing the table. He swatted it but missed. His laboratory was not a fetid stable where flies fouled the surfaces.

Remy managed to swat the insect midair. It dropped to the table, twitching. He should have been more careful. As he attempted to brush it off the surface, the fly shifted toward him, and he inadvertently crushed it right into the last bit of gel on the table.

Spindly legs and a veined wing floated in the clear, viscous substance.

Ruined. Contaminated.

Remy sealed the main jar with the pristine gel and set it on a nearby shelf. Then he turned back to the mess, fly parts suspended in the last remaining droplets. Keeping an eye out for more flies, he set the spatula in the gel and began to fish out what looked like part of the fly's wing when it fluttered.

He jerked back, heat pounding.

Before his eyes, the dismembered body parts drifted together, as if compelled by unseen threads. They floated together, fitted in place, and reformed on the table like a finished jigsaw puzzle.

A whole fly.

Unable to move, Remy stared at the reassembled insect.

Had he truly witnessed what he thought he had—the crushed and dismembered insect coming together?

The fly sat motionless on the table surface. Those spindly legs Remy had just seen floating in the substance were aligned in perfect symmetry at the sides of the fly's body, its long hairy feet resting in the gel. The fly raised its wings up and down slowly, as if testing them.

Thin black veins snaked through the transparent wings, resembling lead strips in stained-glass windows. Plodding out of the substance, the fly turned. Remy could not take his eyes off of this... this miracle.

In an effortless motion, the fly buzzed high into the air near the open casement window. Remy's eyes stayed locked on the insect as it sailed through the window into the vast outside.

The fly had been crushed. Parts of it floating in the substance.

Remy bent down, his nose almost touching the table. The sparse liquid that had held the dismembered fly looked clear, pristine. He brought a magnifying glass over and studied the substance. Not one black speck.

Another fly had not landed on the table. The fly that appeared had been crushed and then reconstructed from its original body parts. Remy was absolutely positive about this. The unnatural occurrence was no mistake. After being reassembled, the fly looked normal. And had flown off as if nothing had happened to it.

Remy sat, stunned. Had he concocted this from his imagination? He forced himself to rise from the chair. Determined to preserve what he could, Remy retrieved a smaller jar from the supply cabinet, one with the same glass stopper as the larger vessel. He returned to the table and tried to scrape the contaminated residue inside, but there was too little. Just a thin, sticky film. He wiped it up with a clean cloth and sealed the cloth in the small jar.

Remy slumped in the chair and once more stared at the table. If Pheodora asked him what he had done that day in the laboratory, he could truthfully say, *stared at the table*.

This was the miracle he had viewed that Friday. Another conundrum related to the three heads. Remy sat up in bed now, pulled his knees close to his chest, and wrapped his arms around them, his feet pressing into the mattress. He stared at the crumpled bedcovers, the ridges and folds silvered by faint light from the window.

These unearthly phenomena were becoming a pattern. He had been left with only what he had seen, what he had experienced.

No proof of any of it.

Fat lot of good that did him.

He could tell no one, not even Pheodora. Anyone he told would conclude he was afflicted with a mental derangement. As if many of those who knew him had not already come to that conclusion.

That Friday in the silence of his laboratory, he had stared at the table's clean surface once more, bemoaning his fate. He had just witnessed a miracle. But his observation was all he had. A mere fly. Remy could already hear the jokes, see the smirks spreading on the faces as he turned away.

With the substance and the small amount on the cloth safely sealed in jars, could he prove he had found The Elixir of Immortality?

CHAPTER 17

PRE-HISTORY, SOMETIME
AFTER EARTH WAS CREATED

*L*ight and pain.

Leukan thrashed through what he remembered of his creation. He gave names to sensations and vague impressions, names that he now knew, from where he could not tell. Rumblings and terrifying ear-splitting sounds shook his very being as immense shapes above him exploded into fountains of fire. The earth beneath him split. Giant crevices opened into voids.

Threaded through the chaos, piercing the silences, came complex, repeating sounds, resolute and unyielding. A call. A name. What he now knew as his name.

Blurry slabs of shape and form shifted endlessly, joining and separating. Searing fire flowed into him. Agony. He emitted a sound long and loud, startling him when it broke one of the sudden silences. He gasped for breath as the five daughters of the Divine Ones graced him with the five senses: sight, hearing, smell, taste, and touch.

Overwhelmed, he fainted when they removed the veil that limits all mortals. When he revived, he beheld That Which Had Been Hidden.

And he knew he was a god.

Leukan. He was the God Leukan, his body formed of cold earth and scorching fire.

Above him, the Divine Ones' chariots ascended into the clouds, the sky vivid orange and violet, their voices as clear as the stars, celebrated by the ceaseless sky-wheel's haunting song: *He must find his way. They had done all that was needed.*

Leukan, desperate, begged them to stay, to help. He searched his brain for the Divine Forms, their true voices, but found only fleeting impressions, for even gods could not clearly discern the precise shapes of the great Divine Ones.

His newly formed body, created from earth and fire, soon shriveled from thirst. Crawling across the cracked earth, desiccated and incomplete, he despaired. How could they abandon him, those who had labored to bring him into being? He collapsed, life given, now fading. Was he to die so soon after being birthed by the Divine Ones?

He looked at his hands, the sparse flesh dry and shrinking around thin bones. With little time left, he could barely keep his hands steady. Leaning against a rock. He forced breath into words.

"Divine Ones, I beseech thee. Show me how to live."

The earth trembled beneath him.

Soil and stones rained onto his body, dust rising into yellow clouds. Little strength remained, and he scraped away the earth covering him, but removed only a pittance until he lay exhausted. Half-buried, his throat too dry to swallow, he prepared to take his last breath.

The roiling dust cloud poured more dirt upon him. Surrendering to the earth, Leukan felt free, something he had never felt in this brief life, even though he knew fear again, knew that the immense power given him would wither. That he would die.

As he waited, as life gradually departed from his body, he became aware of a heightened energy from the earth flowing into him. Giving to him.

With great effort, Leukan thrust the soil from his body. He plunged his hands into the earth, his strength faltering and rising in uneven waves while he continued to scoop out soil and rocks. Why he did this, he knew not, but kept digging as his nails split and his fingers bled. He scraped rock and soil from around enormous boulders and heaved them aside. His muscles weakened the deeper he dug, and the soil grew heavier, turning to mud from the moisture of the depths. Still, he scooped the earth out, his limbs and torso coated in slippery muck.

Then, from one side of the deep pit, a trickle. Clear liquid, carrying a scent of freshness.

Leukan plunged his bleeding hands into it and brought them to his lips. Coolness kissed his tongue, and he knew it was good.

He drank.

"Water."

The name formed on his tongue and passed from his lips.

The liquid filled the hole, lifting him upward. It overflowed the edges, gushing onto the parched land. Transparent, save for the gold glints of sunlight and the flickers of turquoise shade, the water burbled its pleasure as the ravenous earth consumed it. Bubbles appeared, gathering in masses on the fast-flowing water's surface, bursting as the turbulence riffled, forming a layer on top of the water.

Leukan had never seen such. He reached into the substance and found it so light he could scarcely feel it.

"Foam," he whispered, and it vanished in his palm.

The frothing white foam formed pale flesh, and the reflected blue of the sky became piercing eyes. A rose petal, blood-red, caught in the current, lent its pigment to flowing tresses and its fragrance to the flesh. Lit golden by the warm sunlight, a woman rose from the stream like a glowing pearl.

Leukan had followed the Divine guidance. It was done, his strength used up. He collapsed into a muddy heap.

She stood above him, her red hair dripping water onto his parched skin. She held out her hand. With a last effort, he grasped it. Leukan could not remember how, but he somehow stood and embraced the woman.

She kissed him.

Strength flowed into him the same as when the first thin trickle of liquid quenched the withered earth. Water roared into drying oceans, gushed into barren river beds, and soothed the cracked earth as it created magnificent waterfalls, ponds, and lakes. Terra firma burst into bud and bloom as the God of Earth and the Goddess of Water created abundance.

* * *

TANYTHE. Goddess of Water.

Leukan. God of Earth.

One could not exist without the other. Earth to hold the water and nourish the seeds, flora, and fauna. Water to sustain all things to plentifulness.

At the very first, the Divine Ones had shown Leukan how miserably he would fare without Tanythe.

He would never forget.

* * *

UNDER A MOUNTAIN in a jumble of rocks, Leukan formed a cave, its walls a jumble of rocks. Tanythe placed a gently flowing spring inside. But the cave dismayed Tanythe with its darkness and foreboding atmosphere, and the spring became weak, the water flow erratic. Leukan called upon the sun to bore its way through the craggy ceiling. When the bright beams illumined the cave, Tanythe cried out in delight, and the spring flowed fast, the pure water pooling in the gathering golden glow.

"Ah, Tanythe whispered, "now the Goddess of Water and the God of Earth have a shrine." She plucked a crocus from the wreath crowning her fiery hair and offered the lavender and white striated bloom, the pistil bright gold, to the streaming sun rays.

"A symbol of hope," she said, her voice sweet and clear as the spring itself. "This flower shall bloom through snow and fallen leaves, at the last of winter."

In the shadows, a jasper altar appeared, its rare green and blue veins glowing in the flicker of flames from golden oil lamps. Tanythe turned to Leukan, her sapphire eyes bright with the promise of life yet to be born.

* * *

Much later. Phoenicia, 2500 BC, Levant region, Eastern Mediterranean

AS KING GYDRL'S SOLDIERS, intent on destroying them, poured down the hills into their valley, Leukan glimpsed his and Tanythe's cave shrine as it was those many thousands of years ago. Oil lamps flickering behind the sun rays that slanted through the cave's ceiling, the cool spring paying homage to his beloved Tanythe.

When the distant noise of the soldiers' war cries and thuds of their horses' hooves reached them, Leukan took the goddess's hand and turned their temple, the thick marble columns tinting gold in the first rays of the sun. He had asked the Divine Ones' protection and smiled at the evidence, for the soldiers would attack when the sun's full brilliance, reflecting off the white marble, would blind them.

He drew his sword, basking in the strength surrounding them, surrounding the temple. What did a god and his goddess have to fear? They had their powers to protect the temple, to shelter the small folk cowering inside, whose fervent devotion afforded their gods even more power.

In the brightening sunlight, Leukan's long sword gleamed. Forged by the god of thunder in the volcanic fires deep under the earth, honed from secret metals, whetted on diamonds, blooded on the flesh of evil, purified in Tanythe's waters.

Beside him, Tanythe clutched the glittering crystal pendant on the silver chain around her neck. He felt power surging within it, ready to flatten the hordes with the force of water's mass and weight.

Leukan smiled.

They were invincible.

CHAPTER 18

PHOENICIA 2500 BC, LEVANT REGION, EASTERN MEDITERRANEAN

*L*eukan swung his sword, its Divine Force hacking through the soldiers heading for their temple. The troops flattened like sea grass in a tempest. More soldiers crowned the distant hill, spearpoints catching the rising sun's brilliance, their war cries a cataclysm of locusts.

Beside him, Tanythe wielded her crystal, and the soldiers fell to the ground, weapons torn from their hands as they howled in fear and outrage. The few survivors scrambled to their feet, faces twisted in panic, and limped away, leaving blood trails in their wake.

As Leukan squinted at the black-robed figure who appeared on the distant ridge, he touched Tanythe's shoulder. The figure raised his arms.

Leukan staggered backward at the magic released. Soldiers swarmed from behind the figure, down the hill, chanting in unison. Even as Leukan's sword grew cold in his grip, he raised it, calling its power, but the blade's power felled only the first dozen men. The rest clambered over their fellow soldiers as if they were part of the terrain. When Tanythe raised her crystal, half of the soldiers slowed, their cries shrilled with pain, but they bore forward, as if against a stiff wind.

"Twas no idle boast, King Gydrl, about his shaman, Bahl," Leukan muttered as he wielded his sword once more. The soldiers did not falter. Their taunts had become decipherable amid their fierce war cries.

"Our followers," Leukan said, his brow furrowed as he glanced at the temple, the men fighting around it, the women holding the steps and portico. How much time did they have?

"I will bring them to the cave." He looked into Tanythe's eyes. "Go. Build our power there." She met his gaze, and clutching her crystal, fled to the cave.

As Leukan dealt blows to Gydrl's troops with his sword, he scuffed up the ground, feeding his power. Dirt flew into the air and separated into minute particles, billowing as thick as a dust storm around the temple and cave, shielding Leukan's followers while they easily picked off Gydrl's soldiers.

They fought their way to the cave, Leukan, all the while calling on strength from his element, earth. With each bludgeon, each bloody wound to one of his followers, Leukan's strength ebbed. He sucked in his breath at the pull in his gut, while his magic spilled like his worshippers' blood.

Finally. The cave's entrance. Just ahead. Their spirits lifted. His men fought harder. They would make it. Leukan wiped his arm across his eyes, but the opening of the cave blurred. His men had faltered, their confusion dizzying him.

The shaman, Bahl, loomed before them. His broad body, clad in an inauspicious black robe, blocked the cave's opening, his magic making it difficult to breathe. "At last, I meet the God of Earth," he said, a sneer in his voice.

Leukan planted his feet firmly into the soil, desperately trying to replenish his exhausted power. He met the shaman's eyes.

"Thy soldiers are like flies, easily swatted, but obnoxious," Leukan said, his voice still strong, thank the Divine. He stepped forward and swung his sword, leaning into his pivot to garner more strength. This dark shaman's head would adorn the steps of the Temple of the Goddess of Water and the God of Earth.

One with the motion of his weapon, Leukan anticipated the feel of his honed blade ripping through Bahl's muscle and sinew, crunching through the vertebrae of his thick neck. But his sword hit something solid, the metal ringing as if he had struck an anvil. The shock of it vibrated into Leukan's hand, then his arm, and up to his shoulder. The recoil knocked the sword from his grip. Without hesitation, he swept it from the ground as he faced the shaman once more.

Bahl's grin at Leukan's astonishment made Leukan's gut churn.

"Your power is depleting." Bahl indicated Leukan's followers falling all around him. The shaman readied his sword. Leukan swept his sword into position to block, but the shaman proved lightning fast. The blade slammed into Leukan, slicing a long gash in his ribs where a strange and strong magic penetrated him.

He pulled more strength from the earth and managed to keep his balance. By Terra firma's fire, this Bahl was more than the rumors Leukan had disbelieved. Much more. In his mind, he called for Tanythe to burst forth from the cave. Her power renewed, her followers ready to fight.

Through the haze of pain and the deprivation of his departing power, Leukan raised his sword. He brought it down, intending to slice the shaman in two, but Bahl stepped aside easily, and Leukan's sword cut through the air.

In a blur, Bahl slammed the flat of his sword blade into Leukan's wound.

Leukan grunted in surprise as he lost his balance, landing hard, eliciting laughs from the shaman's soldiers. A little more than an arm's length away, his sword lay on the ground. He gritted his teeth through the pain and reached for it, using more of his magic, but a soldier suddenly stood between Leukan and his blade, pointing the arrow nocked in his bow at Leukan's heart.

Bahl eyed his soldier, who edged closer to the God of the Earth's sword. The shaman nodded at the weapon, and, with a sinister smile, said, "Pick it up."

The soldier set his eyes on Bahl for a moment, stashed the arrow in his quiver as he slung his bow over his shoulder, and lifted Leukan's sword by the grip. As he held the sword out to his liege, the pommel, a spherical black stone, reflected a narrow band of light across the soldier's hand. The man turned to Leukan, his eyes lit with the strange light, and dropped the sword, falling on top of it.

Bahl kicked the man off the sword, careful not to touch it. "Fool. But he gave his life at my command."

Leukan barely registered the words as he glanced away from the cave's entrance, where a portion of Gydrl's soldiers were engaging with his soldiers. He met Bahl's gaze. If Tanythe could lead their soldiers out soon, he still had a chance.

"You could have killed me. Why didn't you?" Leukan asked Bahl. He sat up and rested his hand on his side. Blood flowed freely through his fingers, his strength fading. An unfamiliar coldness filled his body. Bahl's magic, eating his power as soon as Leukan's proximity to earth restored it. He kept glancing at the cave's entrance, but not often enough for Bahl to notice.

At last, a band of soldiers streamed from the cave's darkness.

Not his soldiers.

Bahl's soldiers.

The cold grew in Leukan's body as they parted, holding Tanythe for him to see, naked but for her crystal, her red hair undone and falling to her knees.

He tried to rise, but was too weak. As he watched Tanythe, he remembered his birth, his weakness from learning Terra firma's ways. The moment the earth gave way to a trickle of water. The miracle of her. Now, again, he pressed his hand to the ground.

Nothing

Tanythe gazed at Leukan, her blue eyes calm. Her hand moved to her crystal. A wave of power shattered the soldiers around him, staunched his wound. He took up his sword. He would turn them into a bloody pile of flesh.

Just then, a soldier ripped the crystal from her neck.

Leukan fell to his knees, bleeding once more.

"Tanythe!" He cried as the soldiers massed around her. She possessed inherent magic other than through her crystal. By earth's fire, had Bahl driven that from her as well?

Power roared into Leukan. Tanythe's power. But it dove deep inside him where he could not reach it. He was still weak, still bleeding.

Tanythe, let me use it, he called to her in his mind, but her magic plunged deeper inside him. *If I cannot use it, take it back. Save thyself.* Leukan plunged his sword into the ground, reached up, stifled a groan, and took hold of the grip, pulling himself upright.

She gazed at him, unflinching, her eyes penetrating his very soul.

In his mind, her voice: *Hundreds surround us. Save the magic I sent. Use it when you have an advantage.* Then she directed a small force that knocked him to the ground, for it took little.

As he struggled to his feet, a tall soldier, his leather armor red with blood, marched her to where Bahl stood. The shaman nodded. The soldier seized Tanythe by the hair, lifting her so that her toes barely touched the ground.

Bahl looked Leukan in the eye. He swung his blade, slicing through Tanythe's neck. Red fountained into the sky.

"No!" Leukan jumped to his feet, his furious roar absorbed the clamor of the soldiers. With every bit of his strength, he reached deep inside and drained the earth surrounding him. A low rumble rolled through the ground. The earth shook. Trees crashed. Buildings crumbled. Great cracks opened, swallowing soldiers and common folk alike. But he saw only Tanythe's stare. Heard only what her eyes had told him:

That she would die. Die for him.

With residual power from the earth's upheaval, Leukan took up his sword. The shaman Bahl appeared before him and pointed at the temple, the steps red with blood. The white columns and marble walls glowed a faint red, then burst into flames. An impossible conflagration.

"A potent magic that burns even stone." The shaman's voice crackled like the fire.

Leukan charged. Sword raised, his blood streaming down his arm. He would slay this man. Defeat his ruinous magic. With the shaman gone, their temple would be restored.

The shaman flicked his little finger.

Leukan held his sword raised to the sky, but could not move. His legs and arms were like a statue's.

What magic was this?

"You wonder at my power? Magic such that even a goddess can die." The shaman motioned to the tall soldier, skin bronzed with sun. His hard leather armor shone through bloodstains as he came near. Leering, he held up Tanythe's head.

Tanythe, so beautiful, even in death.

Leukan struggled to overcome Bahl's spell, but it held. Desperate, he made a silent request:

O Divine Ones' Earth, keeper of life's secrets and strength, I call on Thee.

Tanythe, Goddess of Water and Abundance, has served thee well. Grant this Goddess life in death, growth over decay, renewal over demise, so she may rule once more with me, her counterpart, God of Earth.

Could his waning magic help grant her life in death, growth instead of decay?

"I see your pitiful magic trying to defeat me. You cannot," Bahl said. The flames from the temple fire tinted the shaman's face red, a demon's countenance.

"I burned your temple in Arwad, killed your worshippers, and razed the city. But I grant you, a failed god, this knowledge. Much of your magic is from those who believed in you. Now they are gone. To be a true god, you must gain many more worshippers." Bahl stood by while his soldiers began binding Leukan with chains.

To the soldiers, he said, "There's little need. When I release my spell, he will stagger as he attempts to stay upright." The soldiers dropped the chains at Leukan's feet as he watched the white temple blacken and crumble into the scarlet flames. Would this be the end of him?

Leukan could not conceive of it. He called on the Divine Ones' Earth and begged for himself what they had granted Tanythe. As his request left him, Tanythe's gift of magic buried deep inside his body showed itself in all its glory. At last, he could defeat Bahl.

"Your goddess saved you for nothing." Bahl glanced at the smoldering ruins of the temple and signaled his men. They forced Leukan to his knees. The tingle of power from the earth funneled into him and joined with Tanythe's.

This would not be his end. He was a god. Leukan put one foot on the ground, then the other, and rose to his feet, the magic vibrating through him. From the corner of his eye, he glimpsed Bahl raise his sword, the blade shining silver through Tanythe's blood.

As if called somewhere else, the combined power inside Leukan vanished, leaving only a vast hollow space. He turned his head.

A blur of white and silver caught his eye just as a dull thud reverberated through his body, exaggerated in the hollow created by his vanished magic. Searing heat tore through him.

Leukan flinched at the nauseating dizziness and puzzling loss of control. A warm liquid flowed down his chest.

His knees hit the ground.

A fountain as red as Tanythe's hair spurted over him, splashing onto his face and in his eyes. His hand lifted in answer to his command, but he lost sight of it when the rocky ground came into view, slowly, so slowly. The scene around him changed as if he were revolving. He could only watch, wide-eyed, his mind trying to gauge what had happened.

Bahl came into view, laughing raucously.

Leukan's own body was inexplicably far away, something horribly wrong with it.

Soft clouds in the blue sky rained long strands of red. Was it Tanythe's scarlet hair? Far away, his arm flopped limp, as his body tried to tell him something. But he could not understand.

His face hit a hard surface. Sand stung his eyes. Grit papered his tongue. His hands would not obey his command, or his legs. He blinked as he settled into the dust.

Disbelieving what he saw.

His body, a few arm lengths away. His neck, a stub of red with muscles, veins, and bulging tissues. The golden tattoo on the side of his neck, ruined. Blood pooling around his body Still, so still.

For a moment, he could not breathe.

He had seen his head tumble from his own body.

Something seized him by the hair and lifted his head. The gray linen of a sack brushed his face. Inside, he saw Tanythe's blue eyes recognize him, her mouth open slightly.

He knew that expression. It said, *Not you, Leukan. I saved you.*

Then her face changed, a spark of recognition in her eyes, and her mouth closed, her lips almost curving upwards.

It was then that he understood. His request to the Divine One's Earth had summoned the magic she sent him. That magic now granted him what it granted Tanythe.

And now she realized what he had done.

CHAPTER 19

1771 CONSTANTINOPLE

*P*heodora carried Remy's breakfast tray without a clink or clank from the china as she navigated the uneven flagstone path through the garden. How she managed that with her hips swaying enticingly, not missing a step, was beyond Remy. But that movement, for him, indefinable, had bewitched him since courtship and still kept him sleepless some nights.

His thoughts strayed to last night's smoldering session in bed and his surprise at the fascinating positions she had initiated. He was sure those were in compensation for his first night home after being shot when, in her love-making throes, she had reopened his bullet wound. Luckily, he'd managed only a deep grunt, manly and stoic, though within, his nerves had screamed as if stretched on the rack.

Aside from that painful pleasure, and several other wholly painless ones, Remy had been plagued by restless nights, rehashing the Society's incident over and over until the early hours. Sleep eluded him most days, and when it came, it arrived in unsatisfying fragments. He had dozed off more times than he could count during the days.

He did not dream, or so he believed, even though Pheodora insisted everyone dreamed. Some just suppressed them, she said, and had given him *that look*. Since the incident, though, several times he had awakened in the night, sweating, the wisp of an image in his mind as fleeting as the thief's departure from his laboratory. Possibly evidence of a dream. Hmm...Or a symptom of something stranger.

But here in the garden, under the shade of the magnolia's huge leaves, with songbirds flitting through the Judas tree's explosion of deep pink blooms, his nighttime ruminations seemed illusory. The robbery, the heads, even the Elixir —some bizarre fantasy. After the incident, Simmery, reveling in his importance as Governor of the Society's Special Project, had insisted Remy take five days' absence.

Meanwhile, the Gov worked his connections at the British Embassy. Today was day three of Remy's leave. Simmery had sent the note he was now rereading, the language prideful, informing Remy that Ambassador Sir James Porter had assigned five British soldiers to search for the thief and his loot.

Remy, aware of Phe's eyes on him, looked up and passed her the note. She scanned it, leaned forward, and placed her hand on his arm. "Remy, did you know you dozed off while reading this?" She gave him a teasing smile. "And Snowy's writing is not *that* tedious." She tapped her fingers on the note.

"Snowy is plodding onward through the mystery. He will find the thief. Don't worry." Pheodora pushed back her chair and stood, brushing off her baggy trousers. Her jeweled belt sparkled in the sun.

He had meant to ask whether the gems were real.

"Do you want to come inside and continue your mid-morning nap?" She put her hand on the back of the chair as though readying to launch herself toward the house. "Dr. Havenard said sleeping would be good for you."

The sun shone on Remy's face and shoulders, filling him with warmth. "I'll stay here. Feels refreshing to be outdoors. Amazing, this climate. In London, we would be shrouded in cold, clammy fog, the fog drip making us unbearably damp." He pushed deeper into the chair's cushions.

"I'll send a maid to fetch the dishes. She'll drop off tidbits and a pot of tea." Pheodora tilted her head, questioning.

"Wonderful, perfect. You go on." Remy waved her away as he attempted to recall his last thought before she'd read the Gov's note. Something about the Gov. He watched Pheodora walk through the garden to the house until the path took her behind the rose bushes. A brief thought of their bedroom interlude last night seamlessly transitioned into the Gov's persistent interference, this instance sending British soldiers out searching for the thief. Not the first time Simmery had intruded in their bedroom.

Remy had pleaded ignorance of what the thief had stolen, saying the thief had ambushed and shot him, that he barely noticed the thief carried a bag as he fled. Of course, the Gov had been champing at the bit for a list of missing items, even though he well knew that Remy would have to return to the laboratory to make an assessment.

Remy envisioned sorting through the many items that had been delivered from the excavation site to the Society's huge basement, trunks, boxes, clay pots, and other findings too large for containers. He let out a sigh of frustration, for he wasn't yet in shape to rush over and search out treasures that had been hidden for centuries.

Since they had not yet thoroughly explored the excavation, he could compose a fictitious list of what the thief had stolen, and no one would be the wiser. Finding the heads—that shock had put him off his duties—but the discovery of the Elixir had set him back on track. Now he had the means to focus.

A week or so before the robbery, Remy had planned experiments using the Elixir but had to postpone to prepare his monthly report on the excavation's progress and the items he had examined. Of course, he would not include the heads or the Elixir.

He considered those his grand discoveries but had failed to reconcile them with his new philosophy of the material world, of science.

He savored the words Elixir of Life and leaned back in the chair, splaying his arms on the straw arm supports. Remy rested his mind as he viewed the garden teeming with all manner of life: jasmine, rosemary, roses, bees— perhaps each touched by the same mysterious principle. With the Elixir, he could heal those who suffered, maybe even more.

His mind swirled with the knowledge he had crammed into his head at Trinity College about the ancient philosophies, including alchemy, bleeding into the new theories of the 1700s. Remy and his Trinity colleagues were proud to be on the cusp of the new philosophy of science, which promoted reason, with the view that all that exists is ultimately physical. A discipline more precise, reliable, and open than the alchemists, who obfuscated their findings with arcane symbols and abstruse language to keep their secrets.

But now…Now Remy associated the discovery of the heads and the Elixir with the very philosophy he and his colleagues had disdained—that of the ancient pursuit of alchemy. He reviewed the three major goals of alchemy. The first was the transmutation of metals. Everyone was familiar with alchemists attempting to transform common materials into gold. The second goal was the transmutation of human life from mortal to immortal. The third was the creation of an elixir that would prolong life indefinitely. Remy and his associates, modern men of letters, regarded these goals as superstitious and backward.

He set his elbow on the arm of the chair, leaned his forehead into his palm as he closed his eyes, listening to the breeze swirling the leaves. He caught a whiff of the rose's sweet fragrance and rosemary's tart smell. Then the heads' faces loomed before him. He sat up straight. How on earth had he arrived at a point where he had to face these disturbing objects, this strange matter?

He rearranged his body in the chair, opening his eyes to the garden. A balmy breeze ruffled the tree leaves and flowers, bringing the scent of jasmine from the vine covering the wall by the gazebo, the white flowers alive with bees' orange and black stripes. A rogue bee hovered for a moment near his ear, its loud hum droning into the chorus of the many bees as the insects zoomed from flower to flower.

The bees' buzzing reminded him of how the inside of his wounded arm felt from time to time. After the doctor removed the bullet, Remy kept the projectile, not as a souvenir, but intending to hide it. He didn't want the Gov or one of the nosier members of the Society to discover that it came from his pistol. Everyone believed Remy's story. That the thief had shot him, then fled.

Remy had placed the bullet in a brass box purchased during his first visit to Constantinople's world-famous Grand Bazaar. The lid, inset with a panel of opaque glass, featured a peculiarly entrancing design of crude asymmetrical circles: the outer of cobalt blue, then black, white, azure, and, in the middle, a smaller solid black circle. He had seen this design on Phe's necklace and remembered that she called it a charm to protect her from the evil eye.

Later, he learned the symbol was a *nazar boncugu*, the name deriving from Arabic. *Nazar,* meaning *sight, attention, or surveillance. Boncugu,* meaning *bead. Bead of sight.* The amulet protected one from the evil eye, just as Phe had said. By Jove, at times she could be unnerving.

At any rate, the brass box was a fitting place to house the bullet. After he became aware of the symbol, Remy saw it everywhere, in all manner of jewelry, fabrics, pottery, brass, and ceramic objects, and painted over doorways and on walls.

He had not mentioned to Pheodora that he had kept the bullet. If she knew, she would insist on glorifying it in some kind of arrangement, box framed or under a glass dome with feathers and moss or some other artistic materials, and would not understand, given his deliberately incomplete explanations, why he wanted to keep it hidden.

At the first opportunity, he would view the bullet under the laboratory's microscope. He was overjoyed when the Society purchased the very microscope he suggested, the one he coveted: a Cuff's, which incorporated the most innovative design, well-constructed with a superior mechanical operation compared to other microscopes. Why, it even had a concave mirror that concentrated light rays onto a sample—

That odd sensation in his wound again, resembling the bees' buzzing. Remy brushed a small cloud of gnats away as he placed his hand near his wound, but refrained from touching it. A superstitious act at best, but the blasted thing was unpredictable. At the moment, his arm felt as if a snake slithered through the muscle and tissue, spiraling around the humerus, the upper arm bone, like in a caduceus. Remy looked down at his biceps, half expecting a viper's triangular head to break through his skin where the bullet had penetrated.

Despite the warm breeze wafting through the garden, a dreadful shiver vibrated his body, invoking the image that had been seared into his brain after he shot the thief. The thief's hood blowing backward from the bullet's impact. The bang of the pistol echoed in Remy's ears, while the stench of sulfur filled his nostrils, and he squinted from the sting of the billowing gray smoke. Wavering in front of him like a phantom was the image of the thief, his hood thrown back, revealing nothing but a cross-section of bloodied tissues, veins, and bone where his head had been severed from his neck.

Remy saw again the thief's robe, encrusted with soil and mold, lying flat on the floor of the laboratory, as empty as a corn husk. He had failed in his frantic scramble to catch the man, to retrieve the heads. In frustration, he had banged his fist on the laboratory floor. At the memory of the pain, he gripped his arm hard.

"Damnation." He inhaled, an abrupt intake, as fresh pain radiated through his body from his firm grip. He had done the same back in his laboratory. A fringe of blackness clouded the edge of his vision, here in his garden, as if a thick swarm of gnats were about to shroud him. The blackness, the droning in his ears, the sharp pain zigzagging in his arm—that was all he remembered after he failed to retrieve the heads, after he had knelt on the floor to examine the robe.

As the images faded from his mind, Remy found he was leaning forward, fingers tight on the edge of the wrought-iron table in front of him. He scanned the garden, assuring himself that he sat firmly in the rattan chair with the flowered print cushions, that his feet were flat on the flagstones.

But his mind ranged far and wide, retracing his steps, desperately seeking the one bit of evidence left him. And no matter how he had wanted his body, prone on the floor of the laboratory, to rise and hide the intruder's robe, he had lain there, growing unconscious, waiting for the Gov to find him.

Now, days after the whole thing was over, he suddenly remembered what he should have done, but couldn't. Hide the robe. And the question he should ask, but hadn't—

Where was the blasted thing?

CHAPTER 20

*R*emy decided to carry on with his plans, even though Pheodora had said the servants were all in a pother about the possibility of encroaching foul weather. But the afternoon turned out mild. A cool breeze drove the small waves lapping against the caique, a rounded-hull vessel painted white at the bottom, and gold above, adorned with vivid designs. He had been impressed when the captain explained that the caiques were constructed to be rowed in either direction. How very clever.

Leaning over the caique's side, Remy let his hand trail in the cool water, small bubbles from the turbulence tickling his fingers. He wiggled his fingers and breathed in the bracing salt air of the Bosphorus Strait. The Society of Antiquaries, the British Embassy, and his home were just across the Bosphorus in a section called Para or Galata, names used interchangeably for the same place. This practice of multiple names for one locality was wildly confusing to a newcomer, but annoyingly common in these ancient Eastern lands. Para, Galata, their origins as tangled as the city's streets.

Remy let go of his thoughts as the seabirds screeched like miniature banshees, a high note to the splashing and gurgling of the caique's oars slicing through the water, and the synchronous whoosh-chunk sound of oars feathering and unfeathering. The caique traveled faster than he had expected. With each pull of the oars, he looked to the south toward historic Constantinople, where the ancient buildings clung to the skyline, dominated by Hagia Sofia's immense dome, bright white in midafternoon, but shining golden, almost blinding in its brilliance, at sunset.

Flanked by four minarets like needles striving to pierce the clouds, their metal points glowing as if they were on fire even in this light. Once a Byzantine church, now an Ottoman Mosque, its name, Holy Wisdom, outliving the empires that claimed it. Behind him, he glimpsed the afternoon sun shining on the waves of the Golden Horn Estuary, teasing at the magic of sunset, when its waters would glow as if molten gold had spilled from a goldsmith's forge into the channel.

Since the robbery, Remy had nurtured a hankering to be on the water, to be alone, away from the familiar, from anyone he knew. He had tired of sitting around the house waiting to heal, reading, sleeping, worrying, and watching Phe come and go on her visits: her language lessons, her shopping, her plays, and who knows what else.

When the caique pulled onto land, Remy became disoriented by the unfamiliar crowded streets set amongst the tall stone buildings and, feeling claustrophobic, he hired the first Turkish coach to pass by the landing. They called the coaches arabas—yet another Turkish word Lord Snow thought he ought to memorize. Usually relishing the new and unusual, he had never experienced this type of panic before, and blamed it on the incident, the heads, and the thief. He placed his hand on his wound, then removed it. What was done was done.

"Karacaahmet Mezarlığı," he said to the araba diver, the Arabic twisting his tongue. Remy now had French, German, Italian, and was near to perfecting his Arabic, which was necessary as his household resembled the Tower of Babel. His servants were English, French, German, Russian, Greek, and Turkish. He lived in a medley of sounds, vibrant and full of the variety of life.

"First trip, good sir?" the driver's waxed mustache twitched as he spoke.

"Third," said Remy. Three visits, yet he was still unaccountably drawn to Karacaahmet Mezarlığı, the oldest and largest cemetery in Constantinople established in the mid-fourteenth century. Its thousands of sepulchers and graves held sultans, grand viziers, imams, courtiers, statesmen, and poets.

The driver gave him a knowing smile, assuming an assignation of some kind. Remy raised his eyebrows, leaving him to his risqué fantasies. Better than the shrug Remy had started to give him.

He leaned back on the araba's cushions, viewing the crowds in the street who seemed to represent the world's nationalities: Greeks in white petticoats and gold-embroidered jackets, Albanians clothed in primitive sheepskins, Arabs in brown burnooses and white turbans, Persians in flowing gowns and black caps, and Armenians in Turkish costume and red fez. Circassians, their chests crisscrossed with cartridges, swords at their sides, and daggers in their girdles, dervishes in tall brown hats. Interspersed among them, veiled women passed silently, only their dark eyes peering from the folds of transparent veils, their voluminous dresses of white, green, red, blue, and purple hiding their shapes.

The street noises came in waves, the loudest rising and falling like sea swells, a relief after the laboratory's deathly quiet. Yet he was heading to a cemetery. Remy shook his head. The irony.

Constantinople rivaled London in size, though not so populous, but the burying fields seemed to stretch farther than the city itself. Odd that such a great deal of land was lost this way. At the arched entrance to Karacaahmet Mezarlığı, Remy bid the driver to return in three and one-half hours, handing over five extra paras.

As he stood on one of the lower paths, the slender pillars of the grave stones towered over him, the different shapes on top resembling heads. He shivered at those silent stone crowds and gave a start when he noticed the slanted, blinking eyes at their base. Then he let down his guard, for he had been fooled twice before by the cats, the only living inhabitants, who slunk through the shadows amongst the graves, their eerie yowls piercing the wind.

He strolled amongst the dead, the fresh air tainted for a brief second with the rank sharpness of feline urine. He stepped over jagged cracks threading through the graves and pathways. Then he stopped next to a section of neatly kept graves, trees, and shrubs, where an area of broken earth and tumbled gravestones exhibited the chaos of the great earthquake five years ago, which had brought him to Constantinople. Remy breathed the sweet, then fetid odor of the brown dirt not yet covered by weedy growth. The footprints of cats' paws had sunk into the dirt and smoothed the rough clods.

He reached over a wrought-iron fence and touched a gravestone's beautifully carved flower, then recoiled as his sleeve caught on the arrow-shaped tip of the fence rail, scratching his arm. As he walked past the gravestone pillars, he noticed the differences: carved turbans topped men's stones, tiaras topped princesses', and other women's bore scalloped circles carved with open flowers for living children, closed for those who died. Seeing this dismayed Remy, for Phe longed for a child.

He pulled his jacket close, the chill unusually penetrating, yet invigorating. The path led him from the intermittent shadows into full sun, warming him to the point of drowsiness such that he desired to lie in the dirt mound on a fresh grave. But he pressed on, up a series of steps meandering up the hill, passing large cypress trees, the gravestones in their shadows staring, crowds and crowds of the dead.

A bright spot of sun marked the front of a sepulcher, fading into the shade of a green bower. Arched windows, set in the marble walls, contained the most elaborate *jaali* that Remy had seen. The skills of the craftsmen who carved those latticed stone screens, the elaborate swirls mimicking Arabic calligraphy, astonished him.

Through one of the jaalis, Remy glimpsed a flicker. Eyes wide, he froze, unsure whether it was something or someone. Again, movement. A flickering lamp perpetually lit for the sultan buried there. Nothing more.

On edge as never before, Remy tried to regain any sense of calm, but it seemed impossible. This was becoming a natural condition for him now after the incident. Feeling the need for a bit of contemplation, he found a bench sheltered under a tree-like rose hedge and sat under the blood-red roses, inhaling their peppery fragrance while he viewed the marble pillar that stood before the sepulcher. The dappled sunshine brightened gold-filled letters carved on the pillar. He recited the verse aloud, feeling the Arabic shaping his tongue:

We come into this world;
We lodge, and we depart;
He never goes, that's lodged within my heart.

Remy pulled his jacket close, attempting to protect himself from the sadness that filled him. "I have felt this way time and again." Remy looked around, shocked he had said that aloud.

"In my dreams, I feel the earth shake under my boots, see my house crumble, crack, and fall, trees crashing onto the roof, great crevices yawning in my garden, swallowing the fountain and flowers. All turning the black and brown of the earth. I see the fire of the volcano, the slow burn of lava burying all in its path." Remy swallowed and let go of his jacket while the breeze ruffled his hair. He had said that aloud to the cats, who merely stared at him, the same as the tombstones.

"The cold comes and goes. The cold of the earth in the early morning summons me. I walk barefoot in the garden, Pheodora calling that I forgot my shoes. The scorpions! I - I—" Remy whirled around. Someone's eyes were on him. He clutched his necklace, the crystal warm from his body. The necklace from one who should be dead, but lived. One he had never spoken of.

"I have seen what should never be," he said, eyeing the flickering golden flame within the sepulcher. "In my laboratory, three heads thrown from deepest earth. Yet still living. I hear their voices in my mind. One of them answered questions that I had only thought. I have visions of the severed heads. The woman, her beauty. She sends visions of things that I later find. Things that are real." Remy rose from the bench. His left leg tingled with numbness. He flexed it.

"And all this longing for the earth, the cold, and the visions of fire deep underground. They do not come from the woman Tanythe. They have come only after the bullet pierced me." Remy clutched at his wound, the pain reassuring him of what he had stated.

"The bullet passed through the thief's body, then pierced me. It left a residue, something inside me from the thief. Something insidious?" He looked up. The shadows had grown long, slanting over the sepulcher. He watched the perpetual flame flickering occasionally.

"I fear I am catching a grievous disease in my body and mind. There is no one I can speak to.

I am alone like you. Only I have no flame flickering for me."

CHAPTER 21

*P*heodora hid behind the sepulcher adjacent to the one where Remy sat on a marble bench. She was confident he wouldn't recognize her, as she had dressed the same as any Turkish woman going into the streets to shop, visit friends, or visit a cemetery to pay respects.

She looked down at her *serigee,* a lovely deep-green silk garment that covered her entirely, concealing her shape like a voluminous tent. A *murlin,* a solid silk veil of matching green concealed her face save for a slit for her eyes. Another veil covered her head.

Why, she could probably walk past him, and he wouldn't bat an eye in recognition. Remy had convalesced now for four days, including the one spent in the Society's guest room—the other three at home, which had gone by too fast. She enjoyed having him home, though not under these circumstances. Tomorrow marked his final day of leave. He seemed improved, physically at least, yet still he hadn't spoken of the incident. He was hiding something. Of that, she was sure.

By some quirk of the sepulcher's acoustics, Pheodora had heard every word Remy uttered. His visions, his fears, his ramblings about the bullet, and the oddities he called "heads." She had hoped following him would bring clarity, but she was more in the dark than before

Her husband had spoken a woman's name, Tanythe. From what he said, this woman existed only as a disembodied head.

Was Remy going mad?

He was so very learned, not a man of superstition. Had she not heard his voice with her own ears, she might never have believed what he said.

The deepening shadows on the white marble sepulcher dulled the gold inscriptions to murky brown, and she had long tired of reading Arabic, her fluency as good or better than her husband's. She waited. If he lingered much longer, she would have to sneak out before him. No matter how famous the Karacaahmet Cemetery, it exuded all the creepiness of any graveyard, and she could not fathom staying after sunset.

Just then, Remy rose from the bench, swiveled around abruptly, and looked straight at her.

She dared not move.

He turned and hurried down the paved marble walkway, stepping around the part that buckled in what must have been the last earthquake. The sun falling toward the horizon made it hard to see Remy once he had traveled a few yards past the sepulcher's iron fence. H seemed to vanish into the tall cypress trees haunting the graveyard, leaving behind only the fading rhythm of his boots on stone. Soon even that sound became indistinguishable from the rustling of the leaves.

Darkness seeped from the shadows, bringing what seemed like hundreds of cats weaving around the tombstones, their slanted green, blue, and gold eyes peering at her from all directions. She cuddled the blue-eyed calico kitten she had found, its pink paw pads gently batting her fingers, claws mercifully sheathed.

Tucking the kitten into a wide pocket in her silk serigee, Pheodora followed the path Remy had taken, careful to keep her gait slow. It was the only exit, and though she was sure of her disguise, she didn't want him to glimpse her. She had planned to surprise him on the eve of his last day at home, perhaps even tease him, hidden behind a Turkish woman's veils. But the afternoon had taken a perilous turn.

Would Remy return to their home or roam to some other unimaginable place in this mysterious city? If he chose home, which she doubted, her cook had instructions to tell him that Mistress was visiting the Sultana and to give him his favorite supper: *lahmacun,* a large thin circle of dough with minced lamb and vegetables, topped with onions, tomatoes, and parsley, and seasoned with cayenne pepper, paprika, cumin, and cinnamon, then baked to a crisp. Remy would eat at least two.

And she would join him soon after she followed him home. Perhaps she would pay the driver more and arrive before Remy.

Pheodora slipped behind a cypress tree as wide as three stout men while Remy stepped into a coach that had been waiting. He clutched at his jacket. A new, rather odd habit, given his fussiness about his clothes, as was usual for a gentleman of his rank.

Minutes later, she joined up with her two maids and footman, who had waited discreetly in a nearby park kiosk. People were picnicking that evening, enjoying coffee and sherbet. That had been her original plan, a quiet surprise outing for her husband.

Her footman hailed an araba. Grateful to be out of the cemetery and undiscovered, Pheodora tried to set aside her unease. Inside the coach, she idly studied its poetical mottos intermixed with paintings of nosegays and baskets of flowers, but Remy's more serious words kept encroaching on the silly verses.

Should she confront her husband about his odd revelations, or try to discover what Lord Simmonds-Snow knew about the incident when Remy was shot? Snowy had advised against revealing that she was his goddaughter. "Too soon," he had said. "Remy must first come to trust me." They needed to form a bond, and Snowy was eager to do so, if only Remy would stop treating him as a rival. Which was understandable, she supposed, in one so brilliant.

They left the araba and boarded a caique to cross the Bosphorus.

"Give him time," Snowy had once reminded her. "He needs time to trust." She was sure the fact had been mentioned at their wedding, when Snowy had been introduced. But what groom remembers such trivia on his wedding day, even one with a mind like Remy's? At least that might shield her from blame, should it ever come to light.

Trust.

Pheodora inhaled deeply. Why was her husband so guarded? She had assumed it was the pressures of his new role, one he had coveted for years, and the strangeness of Constantinople. Remy had mentioned little about the robbery, the shooting, or the thief. Just a brief description with few details. Apparently, there was much, much more.

What he had revealed at the cemetery certainly explained his reticence. The aura of the peculiar about the robbery and Remy's words today had her crossing her arms tightly against her chest in vexation, causing the kitten to meow loudly. Her maid and footman looked at her in alarm as she drew the little darling out from beneath her *serigee*.

"I shall call her Sultana," Pheodora said.

CHAPTER 22

*R*emy congratulated himself. Since yesterday, his last day home recovering, he had experienced no further episodes of odd sensations in his wound, or dread of the thief taking revenge for Remy's shooting him. Perhaps his monologue at the Karacaahmet Cemetery had exorcised his demons, so to speak.

Anxious to leave for the Society, he had foregone breakfast at home, but his stomach differed in its opinion. He tapped his foot, eagerly watching while the street vendor scooped up dough shaped like a wagon wheel minus the spokes, sprinkled it with sugar, and slid it into an open iron oven. Waiting for the pastry to cook, Remy breathed in the early morning aromas of Constantinople: smoky wood and charcoal fires just-kindled, the savory sizzle of marinated meat and frying onions, and the heavenly fresh-bread whiff of his wheel cake. The vendor removed the flat shovel holding the pastry, slid it onto a palm leaf, and drizzled a golden line of honey around its crisp circumference. Remy couldn't help salivating while the vendor set the hot wheel cake, cradled in a palm leaf, in his open hands.

He let it cool a moment before taking a cautious bite. Glorious. He devoured the warm, sweet concoction in no time, an auspicious start to his first day back.

But as he neared the Society's old palace, his bandaged arm began to throb, as though it dreaded the place where it had been wounded. A figure emerged from the shadows of the portico. Before Remy could cry out, the morning sun revealed the scarlet coat of a British soldier.

"Good day, sir," the soldier said, withdrawing a folded paper from inside his coat. "Name and position, if you please."

Remy looked him up and down, black tricorn with white trim, immaculate uniform. By Jove, the Gov had followed through, even stationing a guard at the Society's entrance. If they had found the thief, surely the Gov would have sent word. Or had he left Remy in peace during convalescence?

With his most proper tone, Remy answered. "Lord Remy Edric Derrien, Fellow of the Society of Antiquaries of London and Constantinople, Natural Philosopher, Scientist, and Director of the Constantinople Project." He couldn't suppress his smile. How official the string of words sounded. Words that described him and his esteemed position.

"Noted," the soldier said, scanning the list. "But, sir, you are not on the accepted list." He looked up, a frown beginning where his tricorn hat met his forehead.

"What?" Remy's voice bounced back at him from the enclosed portico. What was Simmery playing at? Had he sacked him?

The soldier ran his broad finger down the paper once more. "Sorry, sir. I will need to escort you inside. Clear it with Lord Simonds-Snow." He opened the door, gestured for Remy to go first, and followed him, hounding at his heels.

Inside the hall, Simmery turned from a conversation with Lord Jonas and pounced.

"Welcome back, Derrien. How are you, old chap?" The Gov checked himself from clapping Remy on the shoulder. "Your arm?"

"Hardly know it's there. Thank you, sir," said Remy, hoping to avoid conversation about the bullet or anything else concerning the robbery.

Lord Jonas offered a hearty handshake. "Bravo, Derrien."

"Thank you, Jonas." Remy nodded, warmed by the man's genuine enthusiasm. Jonas, a fellow long stationed in Constantinople, seemed one of the few who truly embraced the city's strangeness. Folder in hand, Jonas tapped it against his trouser leg. "Must get back to my desk. Welcome back." His hard leather soles echoed down the hall, bringing an unwelcome tingling in Remy's body as he recalled the sound of the thief's footsteps outside his office that early morning, the day of the robbery. A disconcerting sensation gripped him, and he felt himself sinking into a hole where he had no control over what happened next.

"Lord Simmonds-Snow, please clear this gentleman. He is not on the list," the soldier stated as he shifted closer. Probably itching to arrest him.

Remy took a defensive stance.

"At ease, David. This one's cleared. The clerk will send you an updated list." Simmery waited until the guard had gone before turning back to Remy, his brows furrowing.

"No one and nothing," The Gov shook his head, his Roman nose looming over his turned-down mouth.

"Beg pardon?" Remy hated it when the Gov became cryptic. It meant he was thinking too much.

"The thief. Nothing. No sign of him or the stolen valuables. Did the thief say anything?"

"No." Remy was careful to keep his tone light and innocent.

"I see you've met David, our guard. He'll be posted at the front all day into the evening, daily. We've put a new lock on your office and laboratory door. Best if you lock them both when you're inside, also when you leave." The Gov reached into the pocket of his brown and white striped waistcoat and handed Remy a brass key. "Here, guard it well. I kept an eye on the servant who lit your hearth this morning. Must not take any chances, you know. Welcome back." Simmery ducked into his office, only to emerge again.

"Priority, Derrien. As we previously discussed, do your best to determine exactly what the thief stole. I need that list. And your monthly report, if you can manage it, despite your interruption. That would be jolly good." Simmery leaned close, the strong, slightly sweet scent of his Attar Al Paçuli cologne making Remy almost gag.

"And anything not included in your last report." Simmery's whisper sent his warm breath along the edge of Remy's ear, causing a shudder to skim down his spine. And bang. Just like the adder under the rosebush in Remy's garden, the Gov had struck. The Gov had tried to hide it, but Remy could see the ambition in those crafty light brown eyes. And something else…A piercing look, a kind of knowing in the slight dilation of the pupil, the peculiar shine in the iris, as one would get from a lover who suspected, or knew, you had cheated on them.

"Yes, Lord Simonds-Snow." Placid respect placated the Gov. After all, the man was his senior by at least ten years. As Remy made his way to his office, he waited until he heard Simmery's door close to wipe the sweat from his forehead.

Weeks ago, Remy had avoided attending a noon meal at the British Residency, pleading a deadline. He had intended to use the time viewing recovered items he hadn't yet seen and avoid unwelcome interruptions. That was when he had encountered the heads. His piercing cry of "No," more a scream, the crash of his overturned chair, and a wide-eyed Khalil fleeing the building would have had the entire Society rushing from their offices like moles popping from their tunnels. But as luck would have it, they were all feasting at the Residency.

After his discovery, Remy resolved to keep the three heads a secret until he could study them thoroughly, until he found precedent for such things. But with Kahlil, despite Remy's threats to keep him silent, most likely whispering about his Usta's or Master's taboo treasure to who knows whom, Remy had to brace himself for a future confrontation with someone in the Society. As far as he knew, Kahlil, himself, and the thief were the only ones who had seen the heads. He frowned, at least in the last thousand years or so.

Remy paused before his office door. The key in his hand slick with sweat as he imagined tackling the robber, only to wrap his arms around a stinking corpse, the robber's body fluids squishing onto him. He grimaced and shook it off, managing to fit the key and turn the lock. The door opened with a loud click.

Morning light filtered through the window, but his office remained dim. He trimmed a fresh cotton wick and lit his oil lamp from the flickering hearth fire. The same old office, everything in place, but somehow different after the theft, as if any otherworldly creature might appear at any moment and, instead of stealing, would bring an unearthly object or inflict harm in a bizarre manner.

Remy had delayed examining the heads, rationalizing his hesitation as scientific caution. He didn't want to think why, but now that they were gone, he forced himself to own up. Squeezing his eyes shut, he admitted it:

He was afraid of the heads.

Afraid of those bright eyes full of life. Afraid they might speak. Afraid to touch them. If he took a skin sample, would they scream? Sitting at his desk, he covered his ears as he imagined the man with the ebony skin opening his mouth in an agonizing screech.

Having a guard at the building's entrance was both comfort and curse. If the thief returned for something else, then Remy wouldn't have a chance to— to what? What could he do that he hadn't already done? Seize the man? Strip him of his robe? Well, perhaps talk to the man. After all, the thief had tried to communicate with him.

"Blast," Remy slammed his fist onto the desk. A missed opportunity that might have set things on a different course.

He rose from his chair. Sat back down. Put his hands on his desk and pushed himself up. *He would have to face the laboratory.* If he failed to do so now, he might never be up to the task. He took the oil lamp from his desk, the warm glow soothing. Each succeeding footstep to the laboratory door became more difficult. The lamp's light wavered in his trembling hand.

At the laboratory door, he set the lamp on the floor and unlocked the new lock as shadows from the lamp leapt up the walls, ghostly and menacing. He retrieved the lamp, holding it tight as if it were the only solid thing in the world.

Inside, weak morning light from the high windows barely illuminated the tables, the glass beakers, the microscope, and the discoveries set out here and there. Remy forced his feet to hold to the floor, or he would have bolted. The stink of sulfur from the pistol he fired made him wrinkle his nose. For a moment, he swayed, almost dropping the oil lamp as the weeks-ago blast from his pistol rang in his ears, the thief's hood blown back from his…his headless—

The cold, hard wall met Remy's back, and he braced himself against the plaster, clutching the lamp. His breath came in sharp bursts until he thought he would faint. Would Simmery find him sprawled on the floor, lamp oil ablaze around him?

The chill from the wall reached inside him as his breath mercifully slowed, bringing him round. The light from outside grew brighter. He looked up. A cloud passed over, dimming the light once more.

He would have to open those high windows, rid the room of that sulfur odor still in the air. He pushed from the wall and walked through his laboratory, lighting the lamps with his oil lamp's flame. With each new flame, items on the tables glittered, but their brilliance only reminded him of the heads' bright, living eyes.

How could he have simply let go of the bag? If he hadn't done that, he might have frightened the intruder away. But deep down, he doubted it. The thief was not an ordinary man.

One of the things that the Governor, Simmery, did *not* know.

CHAPTER 23

*R*emy paced the laboratory, stopping at the empty table where the thief had last set the bag holding the three heads. Moving from table to table, he double-checked the lists on each of the preliminary reports he had completed. The comprehensive report would take more time. He had made no written record of the Elixir or the heads, keeping his most significant discoveries secret. Regrettably, he had postponed experiments with the Elixir to focus on the reports. Again, he turned and checked the table where he had last seen the heads, hoping against hope that their bright eyes would stare back at him.

But the heads…gone. Stolen in a macabre fashion beyond belief. He cursed himself for failing to record more notes on their appearance, the smallest observations of their movements.

As if it were now a do-or-die mission, he was seized with a compulsion to know anything and everything about them. Finally, when he had no specimens (he cringed inwardly using the word *specimens* for them), he felt ready for the task. Perhaps he could glean some information from the trunk where he had found them. He started work on his reports, but thoughts of the heads, what little he knew about them, kept nagging him. He could take an hour…

They kept two lanterns in the laboratory, but Remy could find only one, his favorite: copper, square-shaped, four openings with arched tops, and a hinged loop for carrying. He trimmed the wick, refilled the holder with olive oil, struck a match, and set the wick alight.

Once certain the wick had caught, he locked both the laboratory and office doors and slipped the key into his pocket. The basement door creaked open. Stale, damp air rushed up to meet him, redolent with dust and decay. The basement, carved centuries ago into bedrock for some unknown purpose, now served as the palace's foundation, a common reconstitution in ancient architecture.

He made his way down the long, winding stairway, keeping one hand on the rough stone wall as he stepped carefully on the treads, which were about three inches higher than normal and sunken in the middle from centuries of use. The stairs must descend three or four stories and seemed never-ending as they curved around the wall.

Finally, he stepped onto a solid stone floor that opened into a vast space and raised the lantern to cast light over a larger area. Directly ahead, nestled into the wall, was a large niche raised like a stage beneath a high, arched ceiling. At its center, exactly in line with the stairs, stood a block of deep purple-red porphyry, three feet high, six wide, and nine long. Such rare stone was known for its imperial symbolism.

A dark purple rectangle, like a stain, marred the center of the stone's top surface, surrounded by a border of the original porphyry. For Remy, this rectangle, different in texture, hinted that this had once been the resting place of a sarcophagus.

When he had time, he would examine the wall behind the stone block. Its uneven surface suggested a concealed door.

Beyond the niche, he watched for the broad white line he'd instructed Khalil to paint, marking the six-inch drop into the rest of the basement, and rubbed his head at the memory of his fall the day he missed the step. He began the search for the trunk where he had found the heads, detecting the faint stench of mud and rot from the site where the earthquake had disgorged the objects from the Bosphorus. The Society had not finished excavating, and there were still treasures under the mounds of earth beside the sea.

The Society here would not have existed if not for a man in a tunic and baggy trousers who arrived after the earthquake at the British Embassy with a bronze bull's head the size of a man's fist, possibly a Minotaur. He claimed he dug it from the side of a great mound beside the Bosphorus that had covered his boat. The resident paid him fifty kurus, a month's salary for an average worker, and sent soldiers to stake the claim. A letter stating that valuable objects had been discovered went straight from the British Embassy to the Society of Antiquaries, London, which, after a unanimous vote, chartered the Constantinople version.

Except for the British guards who secured the site, Remy's finds would likely be in the Sultan's vaults, never to see the light of day.

He almost passed by the trunk, forgetting he had laid a piece of heavy linen over it, pinned with a note stating he had reviewed the contents. Marveling again at the sea chest's almost pristine condition, he removed the cloth. The wood and metal had resisted decay, perhaps treated with some preservative. Remy made a mental note to look into that.

A week after he had disembarked in Constantinople, shaky on his new sea legs, Simmery had arrived and assumed the head office of governor. He had handed *all things from the quake*, as Simmery called them, over to Remy, instructing him to be thorough. That vote of no confidence, instructing him to be thorough, rankled Remy to no end. And that rankling had turned into an irritating itch that Remy couldn't scratch, which had, in turn, plagued him no matter how he tried to counter it. The phrase was a blatant insult to Remy, a graduate of natural philosophy/science from Trinity College, University of Cambridge, United Kingdom, where Sir Francis Bacon, Sir Isaac Newton, and John Dryden had studied.

Eager to delve into his project and impress the Gov, Remy had cataloged many of the items at record speed. But after discovering the heads, he scarcely remembered in what shape he had left the trunk's contents. *Haste makes waste.* His father's voice, clear as day in his head. But Remy had ample excuses with which to reply.

Positioning the lantern, he set a piece of gray carpet on the floor to hold his discoveries, took a breath to fortify himself and opened the lid. It creaked like the last step of the third-floor staircase in Murray House, his family's summer home in Marel, Scotland. The trunk's lid stuck halfway, then with a firm pull, opened fully.

He peered inside, met with a whiff of exotic scent that smelled strongly of gardenias, bringing to mind paintings of sirens in luxurious harems, which he vividly remembered from first opening the lid. Remy breathed in deeply, but to his disappointment, the fragrance faded as quickly as a wisp of smoke.

The thin, gauzy cloth that had hidden the bag of heads filled more of the trunk than he recalled. After all that had transpired since he first opened it, he couldn't trust what he believed he had seen before. Remy tried to find the end of the cloth, but that proved impossible, so he lifted a handful of fabric near the corner. A beautifully embroidered silk purse lurked there. Inside: three gold bangles, pristine. Then another purse, gleaming with pearls, lapis-studded earrings, and fine goldwork.

Had he missed these before? Very likely. He had been shaken by the heads. There could still be more treasures hidden. As he pulled out the fabric—dear heaven, had it grown?—his fingers struck something solid. A sizable object, bundled like a mummy in a separate piece of the same cloth he had been grappling with. Remy carried the bundle to one of the basement's examining tables and pulled up a chair.

He lifted a flap of the delicate fabric. Why, it was so finely woven, so thin, that the room seen through it became filmed in a faint azure haze that winked of silver. As he studied the fabric, he discovered the thinnest silver threads in the weave. He'd never seen or felt cloth like that.

Separating the layers resembled unwinding a mummy. Someone had taken great care with this. When the object lay revealed, Remy stared, disbelieving, the wondrous fabric forgotten. He kept his eyes open as long as he could, sure that the object would vanish if he blinked.

The shell.

Exactly as he had seen it in his mind while recuperating after the robbery.

Tanythe.

The woman's name sat weightless on his tongue as if he had been properly introduced. Perfectly normal to have ancient severed heads tossed from the Bosphorus in an earthquake end up in your laboratory. Perfectly normal that the disembodied heads, after perhaps thousands of years, were living. Perfectly normal to know one of their names. To converse with her in a vivid vision through a shell…then to find that same shell inside a trunk in the basement. He glanced around, half expecting colleagues to burst from behind crates and urns, roaring with laughter at the ruse. But of course, that was ridiculous. No one knew about the heads, and the shell had been revealed to him in a vision. No one could have known about it.

He lifted the shell, still half expecting it to vanish, leaving him certain that his mind was disintegrating. But it lay in his hand, heavy with silver. A fine specimen of a conch shell. The species known as the divine conch, *Turbinella pyrum,* just as he had identified it from his vision. The whorls, apex, and body whorl to the basil tip of the shell were marvelously fitted with silver, untarnished, embossed with mythical creatures amongst swirling vines and leaves, inlaid with quality sapphires, blue topaz, pearls, and moonstones. He turned the shell over. Smooth, glistening pink whorls tucked inside the coarse exterior that wasn't silvered.

Remy's muscles jerked as if he had abruptly awakened from a deep sleep. Had he just kissed the inside of the shell? He stared at it, then set it back on the cloth, which formed around it in sparkling azure folds.

Immediately, his thoughts cleared. He had not realized how lost he'd become in its beauty. How swiftly it had clouded his sense of self, of memory, of purpose.

After bundling the shell in the fabric, Remy tucked it inside his coat, took hold of the lantern, and hurried up the stairs. In his office, he stashed it in a file drawer behind his desk. As he closed the drawer, some of the fabric stuck out as if attempting to escape.

He reopened the drawer. The fabric fell away, revealing the shell in a cool underwater blue setting, the silver fitting and gemstones shining as if lit by moonlight.

A pressure weighed on him.

He dropped to his knees, clutching his chest. The walls closed in. He was underwater, wedged in the trunk beside the heads and the shell, beneath the glacial blue Bosphorus. Outside, an araba clattered by, bringing a pop to his eardrums. With a deep heave of breath, the pressure vanished, and Remy inhaled like a drowning man breaching the surface.

By Jove, he was on his knees in front of the file drawer, the key neatly turned in the keyhole, the locked position, nothing protruding from the drawer. He must take hold of himself. If anyone had seen him...

He rose to his feet. The desk lamp pooled in a ring of yellow light on his efforts to complete his report, calling him to work. In his chair, Remy faced the stack of papers. Took his quill pen from the bronze pen holder. The white paper sheets glared, taunting him.

The end of the week might be the end of his position at the Society if he did not write something brilliant in his report.

And the only brilliant information he had was the truth.

The damning truth.

CHAPTER 24

*A*fter the struggle for the bag in what was called a laboratory, after the terrible explosion, Tanythe saw tiny flecks of light shining through the weave of the bag. She, Leukan, and Bahl were being carried at the pace of a walking man. Then the flecks gathered into a smudge of light, like the trail of a comet. The bag must be moving at an impossible speed. Who possessed it now? Leukan, or the man in this life that she called Abdosir?

Her mind filled with visions of Leukan whole. She and Leukan together, when the White Temple and the sacred cave still served their worshippers. But even those visions began to fade as a more pressing question arose.

Where was her body?

After she had relived the horror of her capture, of her beheading, memories of her body were as dreamlike and indistinct as mist. What remained was pain: Bahl's soldier yanking her hair, the sharp pinch of scalp, the spurt of the reddest blood she had ever seen. And the strange sensations: her body falling endlessly, her limbs helpless against the ground, reaching for Leukan, for strength, for life. Tears slipped down her cheeks.

She opened her eyes wide when she felt Leukan's touch through the bag. She was certain of it. He lifted her out, the rough linen sliding across her face. They were in a dusty, windowless room, cluttered with objects stacked on the floor and shelves along the walls. Leukan placed her on a crate, just far enough away that she could see the whole of him when he sat, and then he removed his own head from the bag, leaving only Bahl inside.

Tanythe felt her power stir. She flowed it into Leukan's head as he placed it upon the stump of his neck. The severing had mangled a part of his golden tattoo, their once intertwined symbols of earth and water. A flash of a silver blade slashed through her mind, muddying her senses. She squelched the image. It would not do to relive her beheading.

How best to reconnect the tattoo's lovely lines? But that was a trifle compared to what must come: blood, veins, nerves, muscle, bone. And the vast gathering of thoughts, dreams, and knowledge, scattered through the ether.

"You!"

A man stood in the doorway, dressed like a soldier. His gloved finger pointed at Leukan. Leukan held his head to his neck with both hands, his whole being absorbed by pulling Tanythe's power deep into his inner workings.

Tanythe sent a warning. The last she could manage as she abruptly ceased threading and weaving his flesh, blood, and bone. Even so, she tried waking him from his trance with mind talk, but the avenue remained dead now that she had disconnected from his body.

Divine Mother, help him escape.

She held her breath. Her power had receded from Leukan and had not yet returned to her. Helpless, she watched as Leukan blinked, danger dawning in his eyes. In a flurry of movement, he thrust his head back into the bag with Bahl, grabbed hers, clutched it to his chest, and ran for the door, which was chained and secured by two iron padlocks.

She felt his heart pounding against her cheek. When he resurrected his body, he had exhausted most of his power. She closed her eyes and gave him what remained of hers.

At last, Leukan stopped running. The bag sat on a hard surface. Again, the touch of his hands on her skin made her sigh in relief. The coolness of fresh air was invigorating, but fear made her squeeze her eyes tight, imagining a new horror ready to fill her vision.

But warmth, the sun upon her face, made her nearly swoon. Eons had passed since she felt the soothing energy of that star. A soft breeze stirred her hair.

She would look. What else could she do?

She gathered her courage, letting her eyelashes shade her eyes, fluttering like antennae, testing the light, tasting the brightness, prepared to recoil. The resinous scent of pine and the sharp tang of cedar filled the air. Tanythe opened her eyes, the brightness a shock and a gift. The sound of birds trilling, a flutter of wings, their shadows making trails through the sunlight. And a musical tinkle, changing with the swirl of the wind. A stream burbling nearby.

Leukan set her head on his lap and stroked her hair. The tenderness of his touch, so unlike his earlier, perfunctory handling, made her long to feel his firm body beside her again. He tilted her head so she could see the stream just beyond the stone where he sat. The water frothed and burbled as it rippled over smooth gray stones, deepening to clear azure in pools, then becoming shallow, moving faster and mirroring the sky and the trees, marked by shadows as it coursed away, until it lay hidden in the forest. She felt his exhaustion. He had fled with nearly nothing left. And now he called to her, reaching for her power.

They were alone at last. No one to shriek in alarm. No one to interrupt the sacred work of making themselves whole again.

Leukan lifted her head, his powerful hands cradling her, and waded into the stream's shallows. She breathed the droplets from her element's frothing current and reveled in the music of the clear water, her power renewing, growing every moment.

Midstream, he set her head on the flat surface of a rock. As he sprinkled her with water, each droplet shimmered, her magic responding to her element. She kept her eyes open as he submerged her head; the water swirling cerulean and turquoise around her, shining as her presence polished the currents. When he lifted her, she felt her power radiate into him.

Back on shore, Leukan placed her on a large rock slightly away from him. Alarmed at the distance, she soon understood. It gave her full view of his body, perfect for the work that lay ahead. He pulled his head from the bag. Holding it in his hands, he stayed utterly still. A strong sensation bore into her, and she knew he was invoking her power as a goddess. Then another, as if what he was doing had been amplified. She struggled with how to grasp and understand it when—

Tanythe

His voice inside her. Their mind talk. Her eyes teared as she heard him for the first time in eons.

Our cave temple. We have worshippers. The spring is flowing. The altar's lamps flicker with flames emitting the fragrance of scented oils. Flowers freshen the dankness of millennia of neglect. Thy lovely body lies in its grave, safe. And alive, Tanythe, alive like mine.

She could hear his joy in the mind talk.

He stroked her cheek.

She dared answer.

Leukan, beloved. I–I must not waste power on words now. I am readying to make you whole.

As he settled his head on his neck, carefully ensuring it faced the proper direction, her power grew. She finally understood: the man called Lord Remy Derrien, formerly Prince Abdosir, maintained his focus on her, continuously bolstering her magical essence.

Tanythe, I can feel no connection with my body, even with my head properly set upon my neck. I had thought—

Tanythe reached for his hand. After all this time, she still manipulated her phantom limbs. Touch can soothe and calm, and Leukan sorely needed that in this moment.

This is new for both of us. Concentrate on holding your head steady as I work.

Her power responded as she directed it deep inside his head. She connected the tiniest blood vessels and muscle fibers, the lymph system, arteries, delicate bones of the spine, and the numerous visible and invisible fountains that gave life. From the ether, she gathered Leukan's thoughts and feelings, that which made him flesh, and the ghosts of his spirit dispersed by the violence to his physical body. She left the spaces to be filled by that which was high and infinite, that with no name, that which was inconceivable even to gods and goddesses.

Working outward, Tanythe seamed together Leukan's flesh, the delicate tissues, fat, and blood vessels, finally melding the designs of his tattoo and smoothing the join of the skin back to front, side to side, leaving no scar.

She invoked that same highest source, which flowed even as the stream burbled in its bed, but which brought oh so much more.

Leukan, do you feel the connection in your body?

Leukan sat still, so still. Too still, even as all that was around them continued in ceaseless motion. Doubt flitted at the periphery of her thoughts like the blue dragonflies hovering over the stream nearby. If she had made one mistake, Leukan would sit on the stone forever, heedless of her.

I—I do not feel any different.

Thank the gods, Leukan's voice. He would again inhabit the human realm. She waited for his heart to meld the two bloods, the blood from his head with his body.

This transformation had taken its toll. Even with his head separated from his body, Leukan's divine self had been intact, as was hers now. But until Leukan came fully into consciousness in his body, his divine self would be mostly in the shadow world.

She reached with her powers to make sure his flesh was warming, to regulate the pulse of blood through his veins, but only a phantom touch of her magic met his flesh and then passed through it. To rectify anything gone wrong would take more power than they both had so early into their renewing.

They would be fodder for whatever beast happened upon them: a leopard, a pack of dogs, otters, even a colony of ants. That might be their end. Unless she could somehow absorb more power and speed his flesh's rejuvenation to completion, then call Leukan's divine presence back into his body.

She sent a plea to Lord Remy Derrien, the only one who could hear her mind talk, for she had subtly placed her name in his head. He must come to help them—

Tanythe

A whisper from Leukan. Still, mind talk. Or had he truly voiced her name? She watched his lips.

Tanythe

His lips did not move, and there was an odd twist in the sound of her name. That was not Leukan's voice. When he told her he felt no different, had that been their last mind talk?

Show me where you are. I will rescue you.

The man, Remy, called her name and answered her plea for help. Her power strengthened from his contact, and she gave that magic to Leukan, whose head had drooped slightly forward. With what strength she had left, she called again to Remy. Her voice would grow clearer and louder for him as he came closer to her.

Tanythe envisioned herself, whole, in their sacred cave, pouring oil into three gold lamps on the altar. Lighting the wicks, offering prayers that Remy, her Abdosir, would find them before nightfall and that Leukan be restored to the powerful god that he truly was.

In her vision, she raised her arms, silver bracelets glowing with moonstones and watery blue sapphires, the clear crystal in her necklace radiating like the full moon.

A goddess beseeching the presence that imbues the starry heavens, that fuels the fiery sun, that turns the great sphere E-Rath.

CHAPTER 25

"*A*h, there you are." Simmery stood in the Society's main hall, clutching the blue folder containing Remy's report to his chest, conspicuously, deliberately, so Remy couldn't help but notice. The Gov might as well have waved it about. A sinking feeling stole Remy's words.

Simmery opened the folder, holding the papers at an angle, squinting at Remy's neat script as if trying to coax out hidden truths. "Thorough," he muttered. "Thorough on the discoveries I have seen. But something is missing."

Remy stood rooted to the floor, his scalp tightening around his skull. What had given the Gov that idea?

Simmery leaned close. "I was certain we had something special in those artifacts. Something more unusual." His slippery words had the tone of a fellow conspirator. He motioned Remy into his office.

A tickle zigzagged down Remy's throat at the overpowering fragrance trailing from the Gov. Remy cleared his throat. *Attar Al Paculi*, the same obnoxious fragrance he had detected in the lab by the heads. The Gov might as well have left a calling card. People grew desensitized to their fragrances, unaware of how they lingered, exposing secrets.

Remy's skin twitched, the same as Atabey's did when flies bit him. By heaven, Simmery *KNOWS*.

Inside the office, the scent thickened. Remy sat in the upholstered chair in front of the Gov's desk, struggling not to cough.

"Beg pardon, Lord Simmonds-Snow. Bit of a frog in my throat."

Simmery poured water from the pitcher on the side table into a glass and brought it over. "Here, old chap. Hope you're not coming down with a head cold. We need your head clear."

"Thank you." Remy coughed, nearly spilling water on the carpet. The repeated mention of head in the Gov's last sentences was not accidental. Remy struggled to give an expression of nonchalance at Simmery's insinuations, which were dead on.

Yes, something was missing. Three extraordinary items, living beings. Remy had been hiding something magnificent in the laboratory. Something that could turn natural philosophy/science on its ear.

He pictured Tanythe's head, her bright scarlet hair, her azure eyes alive and intelligent. Her voice in his head like the irresistible sirens luring Odysseus. Remy raised his hand to his forehead, then moved it above his head, intending to delete her image. What was he doing? Tanythe's beautiful likeness was not floating above him for Simmery to see. He lowered his hand, keeping his face expressionless.

"Perhaps," Simmery said, "you're currently working on an addendum?" Suspicion clouding his eyes, Simmery tilted his head at Remy, his beaky nose inching closer as if the Gov were a bird who might suddenly snatch a morsel of Remy's flesh in his sharp bill.

Remy put his shoulders back and sat military straight, the floor firm under his feet. He would not be the Gov's morsel.

"I am, sir. Quite right. We've yet to unpack every trunk or crate. Some were damaged and require delicate disassembly. And we've been focusing on what's already here in the building. I'd meant to propose reopening the original site for excavation. If it pleases you, perhaps we could meet to discuss that?"

Simmery rested a hand atop Remy's report, a smirk playing at his mouth.

"Well, Derrien," he said, voice smirking too. "We do not need a meeting. I would like all the items here reviewed before we collect more." The Gov skewered him with a glare. "Especially the items most valuable and special."

The Gov was playing him like a cat with a mouse. If Kahlil had spoken of the heads, Simmery would assume Remy had bypassed him—shared discoveries with a lowly servant. And Kahlil, like all the servants, was constantly angling for advancement.

Remy recalled how Kahlil flinched upon entering the laboratory, always clutching the talisman at his neck, murmuring prayers in that hypnotic cadence. The boy stepped over the threshold as if it might bite and jumped whenever Remy brushed past.

Remy mentally reviewed his report. It began with his scientific observations, followed by a thorough catalog of recovered artifacts. In a detachable section, he'd included a fictitious list of stolen items.

Fictitious because the only thing the thief stole was the heads and Remy's sanity.

Simmery opened his mouth, but Remy beat him to it.

"We may have something that we looked square in the face, thinking it was ordinary, only now to discover its great value. What the thief stole may give us clues," Remy said with as much authority as he could muster without getting the Gov's dander up. He kept his statement as vague as possible.

Simmery looked down at his desk, his lips pursed. "Of course, with you unconscious after being shot, we are at a disadvantage. Still, the soldiers gathered odd reports from the day of the robbery. Some citizens claimed to see a cloth bag floating through the city, moving at the pace of a man walking fast."

Remy fought to maintain composure.

"And," Simmery went on, "a police officer and a fishmonger claimed they saw a man in a brown robe remove his head and flee with a woman's head. Red hair, mind you. Clutched to his chest." He clucked like a maiden aunt.

But the whole thing was mere show. When the Gov emphasized the woman's red hair, Remy had raised his eyebrows in surprise, but his stomach had clenched as if the Gov had brandished his finger at him in blame. Had Simmery noticed the fear that flitted across his face? Yet the Gov continued, not missing a beat.

"Surely an overactive imagination colored that report. But if the thief stashed our artifacts in a bag and kept to the shadows on a dark rainy day, many here who are superstitious would have thought the bag was floating. And a black robe disappears easily in the gloom."

Simmery stared at him, eyes like magnifying glass lenses.

Remy struggled to breathe. It came in tight little sips, as though through a drinking straw. That look. That certainty.

Simmery must have found the robe the thief left in the laboratory.

Remy had given the Gov a description of the robber. Around Remy's height, black hooded robe that shadowed his face in the dim light of the stormy morning. Remy had not included: when he shot the man, the hood blew back, revealing he was headless.

"As for the report about the fishmonger," Simmery added, "a soldier swore the man led him into a storeroom, removed his own head, and fled through a solid door."

A pause. A soul-searching stare.

Remy's insides shifted, jelly-like. If he had to rise now, he might need a cane.

The burden of secrets he kept threatened to undo him. Even if the Gov had seen and examined the heads, Simmery didn't know that the thief had no head. That Remy had shot the thief and was wounded by the bullet's ricochet. That only the thief's robe fell to the ground when he was shot, his headless body nowhere to be found.

"These dark days," Remy said hoarsely, "this ancient city. Superstition and fantasy abound."

Simmery didn't know that Tanythe called to Remy with a voice inside his mind. Or that the thief had spoken to him the same way. Remy nearly reeled at the insane list he had recited in his mind.

The Gov reached out and clapped Remy on his shoulder.

Remy barely suppressed a groan at the pain that shot through his wound.

"Beg pardon, forgot which side was shot," Simmery said lightly. "Derrien, you are quite pale. Are you all right?"

Remy nodded, careful not to clutch his throbbing wound. He did not want to draw attention to the wound, for he had essentially shot himself. Another of his many secrets.

"Well, aside from reports of a floating bag and that flight of fancy about a man removing his head, the soldiers had a dry run." Simmery leaned towards Remy, his expression serious. "I would like you to search for the thief. Are you up to it?"

Remy nodded. "Feeling fine, sir." His voice came out hoarse, frog-thick.

Simmery turned to go, then stopped. "Best arm yourself." The Gov laughed. "I mean, take your pistol."

CHAPTER 26

*R*emy sat in his office, staring out the window, the long black hand of the mantle clock marking the minutes. Tick-Tock, Tick-Tock, Tick-Tock. Enough to drive one crazy.

He had requested the Society's carriage but canceled it, sending a message to Tarek, his stable boy, to ready his horse. He could be more independent without a coachman nosing in his business.

Reconsidering, Remy had thought it best to start the search on foot, for witnesses had seen the bag floating as if someone were carrying it, so the thief must have fled on foot.

Simmery had sent a note listing names and whereabouts of witnesses the soldiers interviewed. He expected Remy to interview them himself, writing that perhaps Remy would gather a clue that the soldiers had missed.

Remy scoffed aloud. Most certainly, he would, since the soldiers thought the man was merely a common thief. He leaned back in his chair, his arm intermittently pulsating in pain from Simmery's careless touch. Just this morning, Pheodora had hurriedly covered her initial expression of alarm as she dressed his wound. She mentioned, with exaggerated casualness, that the wound might need to be reopened as it showed signs of swelling.

Remy put his hand near the wound, then withdrew.

The thief had jerked forward at the crack of Remy's pistol shot. His hood had blown back. Try as he might, Remy could not fill in the blank space between that and the thief's black robe resting on the floor as flat as a playing card. Everyone assumed the robber was a brazen peasant, but the being was more mysterious than anyone could imagine.

And Remy was the only one who knew.

It was a moment before he realized he had become lost in thoughts of Tanythe, seeing her clear blue eyes light up as she stared at him. He fumbled with the crystal necklace under his shirt. Outside the window, the light had assumed a peculiar brightness, and inky shadows puddled equally distributed around objects.

The mantle clock ticked like a metal hammer against stone, yet all was hushed. Time seemed to have stopped. Noon, when the sacred stillness of the otherworld seeped primordial chaos to the surface. So his professor of Classical Greek had drummed into him. Remy had scoffed at those ideas. Until he encountered the heads.

Lord Remy Derrien, Tanythe has need of you.

Remy sat as straight as an arrow. Confound it, words in his brain. The same way he had 'heard' them when he encountered the thief. He would respond this time. This would be his chance to find the thief. But how? How would he respond?

He heaved himself out of his chair. Made sure his double-barreled pistol was loaded, then tucked it into his coat's outside pocket and slipped his cartridge box into the inside bottom pocket. No holster today. He wanted the pistol hidden.

As he took his hat from the hook by the window, he became aware that words had passed his lips. He had whispered, "Tanythe, show me where you are. I will rescue you."

It was as if someone had guided his speech, having him respond without a thought.

An array of brilliant stained-glass colors invaded his mind, vivid reds, blues, and greens played by light like a piano. Colors grew dark, faded, then assembled into an image of Tanythe, a picture as sharp and clear as if her head were sitting on his desk, lit by the light from his window. Surrounding her, the colors assembled into a leafy glade amongst tall pines and cedars next to a fast-flowing stream sparkling in sunlight. This scene faded and renewed, as ephemeral as a cloud.

How would he ever find a simple rural setting with no distinct landmarks? It could be anywhere around Constantinople beyond the city walls.

Think of me. I will lead you to us.

Remy set his hat on his head, locked his office door, walked down the hall, and out of the building. Tarek, his stable boy, holding Remy's saddled horse, met him. He handed the reins to Remy.

"Sahib, I am here," the boy said breathlessly, "I do not know how. We traveled as fast as a wish." He glanced around, clearly disoriented. "It must be—

I think a djinni brought us here."

CHAPTER 27

*B*efore Remy could thank Tarek, the stable boy darted off, spooked by the djinni he imagined had brought them here.

Remy winced. After all that had happened, who was he to question the existence of a djinni, or any spirits and strange beings, or even Tarek's beliefs? He stroked Atabey's forehead and ran his hand down the stallion's silky blaze, extending to his nostrils. The horse blew on his fingers, calm in contrast to Tarek.

"Will you lead me, Atabey? Help me follow Tanythe's guidance?" Remy murmured as he caressed the stallion's deep chestnut mane. Atabey's neck shivered as if he were shaking off flies, and he stamped his front hoof as if answering yes. These Turkish horses differed from the breeds of the colder countries. They were not as strong, but they made up for that with their swiftness and gentle nature.

Remy had planned to follow the Gov's list of witnesses who knew anything about the thief and proceed with interviews, but there would be a change of plan. Simmery had specified that he search for the robber, and finding Tanythe was, without doubt, part of that.

The thief had been after his own head. Remy recalled the robber's hands being as dark as ebony as he held Tanythe, so his head must be the noble one with the matching complexion and black braids beaded with amber. If correct in his earlier observation, he was thankful the thief's head wasn't the one with sinister, beady eyes.

Could the robber have discarded Tanythe's head? Yet he had looked upon her lovingly, as much as one without a head could look. And Tanythe had said, *Think of me. I will lead you to us.*

Hmm. Remy had been so befuddled at hearing her voice that the import of the last sentence had not sunk in until now.

'Us.' So, the three were together, or, at least, Tanythe and the thief's head.

Atabey had been properly warmed up from his swift trip to the Society and started at a brisk trot. Full of surprises, these Turkish horses. For a moment, Remy thought the horse was leading him straight home, but the stallion took an abrupt left between two towering stone buildings, one with a keyhole arch over a wondrous hammered copper door, and down a dusty alleyway where Remy had never ridden. Gripping the reins, he began to turn Atabey around, but stopped. Atabey might as well lead, for Remy had no other directions.

They entered a small bazaar on a crowded street. Shafts of sunlight poured through narrow beams above, striping the crowd and beasts with bright orange. Atabey kept his head, spooked neither by the yellow pi dogs that crossed his path nor the shrieking children. When the stallion halted beside a stall of sweets and snorted, refusing to leave until the dark-eyed beauty gave him a pink candy and a smile, Remy put it together.

Blast. Young Tarek, with his insatiable fondness for sweets and ladies, must have detoured here countless times before he brought Atabey to the Society. The horse was merely retracing his habitual route.

Remy's insides hollowed as his suppositions crumbled. Despite the odd things that had transpired, this conversing with Tanythe was surely the result of fever dreams concocted by the physical and mental shock of finding things living that shouldn't be. Oh, and being shot by his bullet, which had pierced an unearthly creature, infecting Remy's flesh with God knows what.

Just then, the vision of Tanythe filled his mind. Her eyes lit with an expectant, yet quizzical gaze. Remy leaned forward in the saddle, the pull undeniable, as if Tanythe had *him* by the reins. He rode out of the bazaar and halted Atabey under the dense shade of a large ginkgo tree that must have been hundreds of years old, the bright green leaves like lady's fans with vaguely scalloped edges. After fumbling in his pocket, he pulled out the Gov's directions to the witnesses the soldiers had interrogated. From here on, Remy would not let his foolish infatuation with a bewitched dead woman drive his quest.

When Remy presented the paper plastered with seals of the Society, the British Embassy, and the Captain of the Janissaries of Constantinople, the janissary sent his servant for tea and ushered Remy inside. The janissary told Remy that he had been especially spooked when he saw a man holding a severed head to his headless neck. Fingering a talisman of the ubiquitous evil eye, he relayed how the man had walked through a solid door as if it were not there. When the janissary had made it to the street where the door led, it proved impossible to find the strange man.

Remy attempted to look shocked at the outlandish tale, as most people would have done, which only led to the janissary launching into a recitation of his credentials to show his reliability. During this onslaught, Remy showed the appropriate empathy, all the time fighting to quash Tanythe's renewed call and the impulse to rush out the door, leaving his reputation in ruins.

When Remy mounted Atabey, the horse whinnied and fought the reins.

"Blasted, Atabey," Remy muttered. "We're going home. Pheodora will be thrilled to see us early and give you a carrot and me a kiss." But Atabey whirled around and trotted toward neither the Society nor home. He wouldn't stop or turn.

"What's gotten into you?" Perhaps the horse had been stung by a wasp just as Remy mounted. Again, Remy tried to turn him, but the stallion proceeded into a smooth trot, heading northwest, which eventually led out of the city.

"I'll sack that bloody Tarek. Where in heaven's name did he take you out here that you like it so much?" Remy sat in his saddle even as his wound began to throb and let Atabey take the reins.

CHAPTER 28

*W*ithout hesitation, Atabey continued his pace through the city. They trotted past a garden, the fruit trees' plentiful blossoms as white as a fresh snowfall. Remy let his horse turn onto a paved street fronted by a magnificent open-air exchange, with arched roofs on massive pillars above crowds perusing the many goods in the shops.

On towards a domed mosque, the twin minarets like swords pointing to heaven, as if to warn that one would soon become like those in the graveyard beyond its flowering gardens. Remy pulled his coat close as they passed the mosque's cemetery. The tombstones' blank faces, under turbans and tiaras, stared solemnly from beneath the dark cypresses.

Had his handling of the heads and the taint from the bullet that passed through the thief affected his destiny? He pondered the perplexing puzzle of whether the heads were an abomination or a heavenly gift. Would the answer condemn him to hellfire or praise him?

Think of me. I will lead you to us.

The same unbidden voice. One that spoke inside his mind, at his laboratory, at his desk, and now as he rode Atabey past a seemingly never-ending cemetery. Remy gazed at a white marble sepulcher, opalescent in the sunlight, pale rose, mint green, and azure. The azure taking shape, becoming Tanythe's eyes, then fading into the shadows of the tomb's ornate curves. Her image filled his mind and eased his anxiety.

To his left, small waves on the waters of the Golden Horn threw the sunlight in his eyes. Across the estuary, Remy caught glimpses of the seven hills of Constantinople and one of the ten gates in the grand city's walls. Opulent palaces lined the banks, fruit trees blooming in pink, white, and crimson, and bright gardens with rainbows of tulips. Remy became transfixed as one multi-storied grand palace eclipsed another in majesty, with soaring domes, tiered fountains, and regal gazebos.

When he next noted where Atabey had taken him, they were passing meadows with vivid flowers waving in the breeze, the fragrance of spring perfuming the air. As they traveled further from the city, the straight trunks of cypress trees rose to the sky on either side, darkening the now-narrow road. The trees' scaly foliage jittered in the wind, brushing away bird song and permeating the air with the smoky odor of their pungent oil. Oil used by the Egyptians as an embalming unguent. Had the heads been through a similar treatment as the Egyptians' mummifying process? They could have been immortalized in a sacred ceremony, with substances now lost, by the famed priests of their enormous temples.

There were fewer and fewer people on the road, and Remy looked behind him, the towering cypresses hiding all beneath in deep shade, reminding him of the cypresses in the cemetery they had passed—how long ago? From the elongating shadows, it looked to be about two hours after noon. He had experienced nightmares like this: letting his horse take the lead in a strange land and becoming disastrously lost with grievous consequences. How could he have been so blindingly stupid?

Think of me. I will lead you to us.

The voice resounded through his mind and ignited his resolve as the image of Tanythe bloomed there: her azure eyes, her scarlet tresses, her ivory complexion. Yet his fear of being lost so far from the city dampened his enthusiasm for her mind talk and her message.

He would finish this task and be done with it. Find the thief, please the Gov, and discover the secret of the Elixir. He pressed his boots firmly into Atabey's flanks. The stallion's rhythmic walk became a trot again, and he showed no protest at taking Remy's instruction.

The cypresses on the wide path thinned, now interspersed with cedars and pines. They passed under a tree covered in delicate ferny leaves and the most marvelous blooms, like airy spheres of downy yellow feathers.

Atabey snorted as he walked further into the forest. Here, the foliage and trees grew in thick groves, not at all like the landscape in Remy's vision. Atabey pricked his ears, and Remy gripped the reins, searching the thickets and foliage for any threat. He saw nothing obvious but heard a slight murmur under the birds' calls, the rustling leaves, and the padding of Atabey's hooves on the sandy path. The sound gradually increased, and they broke into a clearing of sorts.

Sunlight reflected off a stream flowing over stones and noisily cascading into waterfalls, which siphoned into quiet pools or joined with several rivulets placidly proceeding along the sandy banks. One of the sweetest sounds Remy had heard in a while.

He stared hard at the landscape in front of him. It proved the exact image from his vision when he had first heard Tanythe's message: a leafy glade amongst tall pines and cedars next to a fast-flowing stream sparkling in the sunlight.

Think of me. I will lead you to us.

He focused on her phrase and again saw Tanythe in his mind, her pink lips mouthing the words. Oh, how he wished she would 'say' his name.

The words, louder now, if words in one's head could have a volume attributed to them. Remy vanquished his nagging reasoning, which insisted that he must find the way back before dark and give up this insanity. He had come this far. He would finish it.

In the blue-black shade shrouding the stream bank, a vague shape formed. Remy reached for his pistol.

A man.

Pointing the weapon, Remy walked Atabey slowly forward, but the stallion balked, then reared slightly and spun around, dancing in panic as Remy fought for control. He clutched the reins, threw his arms around Atabey's neck, his pistol tight in his fist, his legs gripping the stallion's body. What the hell had gotten into Atabey? He'd never been such a skittish bastard.

Sunlight beamed into the shadows, highlighting the man who sat perfectly still on a flat-topped boulder, his head slightly bowed. He wore a robe.

Tanythe's head was about two feet from him on the boulder. Remy stared at the man. He looked familiar somehow. Blast. Why had it taken him so long to put it together? It was the head with the ebony complexion from the laboratory, attached to a body. Lord in heaven. How—

With an unearthly squeal, Atabey reared, catching Remy by surprise. Grasping at the reins, the saddle, anything, Remy clutched his pistol as he slipped off the saddle and slid down the horse's rump. He hit the ground and sank into the stream bank's soft sand, his leg hitting something hard. The pain had him gritting his teeth. Behind him, a loud splash obscured for a moment the sound of the running water in the stream.

Blast. He felt around him in the sand. Had his pistol landed in the water?

He sat up and turned. A pain ran through the back of his head. His leg began throbbing at the same time as his old bullet wound. No sign of the pistol. It must have sunk.

Atabey? The sound of the horse's hooves thudding on the dirt alerted him when he was thrown, but in the confusion—his pistol flying from his hand, the jarring impact as he hit the ground—he failed to identify which way his horse had gone. He spotted clumps of dirt and gravel to the left of where Atabey had spun round, and more dirt clods surrounding the deep hoof prints leading toward the woods where the poor creature had fled from the terror in the shadows.

Remy struggled to his feet, wincing at the pain in his leg, his head, and his wound. Confound it. In a heartbeat, he had been reduced to a cripple with no transport and no weapon.

He hobbled over to the boulder that the presumed thief occupied. His robe was different, brown like the Gov had mentioned in the soldier's report, the hood hanging behind him. Remy pictured the black robe, mildewed, clotted with dirt and debris, on the floor of his laboratory. The thought stood out in his head as if someone had shouted it: *Simmery had the robe*. The dreaded feeling of his foundation dropping from under him had Remy clutching at the nearest boulder.

He was sure Simmery knew about the heads, so it stood to reason he had taken the robe from the laboratory after he found Remy unconscious. For a moment, Remy smelled the Gov's *Attar Al Paçuli* cologne.

On the boulder beside the thief, Tanythe looked up at him, her eyes full of concern.

You are hurt. Please sit beside me.

He couldn't do much more, anyway. Remy hobbled over and sat next to her on the cold boulder. He had been closer to her, even held her, but now she was actively acknowledging him and his state. He fingered the crystal inside his shirt.

Keep the necklace on. Place the crystal on my cheek.

The shadows were dappled now, light and shade rustling in the breeze, the stream burbling as if nothing had happened or ever would. And the thief sat still. Remy eyed him. Was he breathing?

Yes, Leukan is breathing, but that is not your concern. Yet.

Remy pulled the crystal from inside his shirt and leaned over, placing the smooth surface on her cheek.

Tanythe closed her eyes.

Which part, if healed, would help you recover your mount?

"My leg, for I must walk to find my horse, then ride him." As the words left his mouth, the pain left his leg. He stood and, little by little, put his weight on his foot, then on his leg. Healed. Like the Elixir healed the fly. Tanythe narrowed her eyes at him, and he had the distinct impression that she knew he had gleaned the Elixir from them.

Take my head and submerge it in the stream for eleven counts. Then bring me back here.

It was one thing to pick her up when she hadn't spoken to him or looked comprehendingly at him. But now, it seemed almost indecent, for they had not been properly introduced. Remy nearly laughed aloud. He had not always been so strait-laced, not until he had come of age, gained entrance into society, and was expected to impress the ladies. His mother and sister had nagged him into this narrow area of manners.

You have my permission. Tanythe smiled.

He had never seen her smile with her eyes, laughing as if she enjoyed his thoughts of being strait-laced, and it made his stomach a bit giddy. But he was not a schoolboy. He placed both hands on either side of her head, lifted her, and carried her to the stream. His arm ached. His head throbbed. At the slight sensation of vertigo, he wobbled, worried he might drop her.

Remy knelt beside the stream.

Tanythe blinked, and he thought he saw her nod. He placed her head under the cold, clear water. One, *two, three.* Her red hair streamed behind her with the current. *Seven, eight, nine.* She opened her eyes underwater. *Ten, eleven.*

He lifted her out, her hair trailing into the water as if it didn't want to leave. He rose to his feet. Difficult with his hands full.

Her hair, dark as rubies when wet, dragged on the ground. As Remy placed her on an adjacent boulder to Leukan's so Leukan wouldn't get wet, they both looked with alarm in the direction of something very large crashing through the underbrush.

A whiffle, a nicker, and Atabey stood at the edge of the clearing. He pawed the ground, snorting to call Remy from danger. Remy had stayed still, feeling for a nearby threat, but he observed only the strangeness of Tanythe's head on the rock and Leukan nearby, sitting motionless with his head bowed.

Walk to the stream. Wash your hands of me. Then stroll to your mount. When you are beside him, place the crystal on his neck where he cannot see it.

Remy felt Atabey's eyes on him while he rinsed his hands in the cold water. Careful to shake his hands slowly so as not to startle the horse, he held them casually at his side as he walked over.

"Atabey, it's all right now," Remy cooed as he crept closer, wishing he had some carrots, Atabey's favorite treat. Almost imperceptibly, he moved his hand up from his side, then closed his fingers around the loose reins.

"Old boy, you returned." He exhaled as he drew close beside Atabey, who nudged him with his nose, almost sending him stumbling.

"Atabey, don't be angry," Remy said softly, rubbing him behind the ears as he laid the crystal on his neck. He held the stone, which sparkled on Atabey's deep chestnut coat. The stallion huffed, his ears pricking.

Be calm, we will be kind to you.

As soon as Tanythe's words were in his brain, Remy spoke them without a thought, without processing that she had put words there, without thinking what they were, what they meant. His hand trembled, but he kept the crystal against Atabey's neck.

As Remy waited for Tanythe to speak into his mind and let him know when to remove the crystal, he studied Leukan and Tanythe. A slight breeze rippled the leaves' shadows over them, making them seem to move, emphasizing their strangeness, which was as tangible as the crystal he held in his hand. Hairs on his neck bristled just like Atabey's, and his fingers twitched on the crystal, itching to tuck it back into his shirt. The urge to leap onto Atabey and flee was unbearable.

Truly, he understood his stallion. From somewhere came the thought that the crystal was transferring Atabey's fear into him. He seized upon it and mused over the possibility until Atabey nuzzled his hand. As if a sand timer had run out, Remy knew it was the moment to remove the crystal.

Calmer now, Atabey followed him to Tanythe, then pulled in the stream's direction. Thinking he needed to drink, Remy walked him there and found a mound of green grass and grain covering the surface of a large boulder next to the water. He turned and caught Tanythe smiling while Atabey grazed on his feast.

These were miracles: healing Remy's leg, calming Atabey, then giving him food. But they were selfish miracles. Tanythe needed the horse to take her and the thief back to the laboratory. And she needed Remy to be able to ride.

But what would Tanythe do? What could she do when she became angry?

CHAPTER 29

*A*tabey finished the mixture of grass and grain, then drank deeply from the stream. He seemed content now, thanks to Tanythe's intervention, and Remy tied the stallion to a tree, leaving about two feet of rope so he could move and not hurt himself if he became unnerved by the heads again. But the crystal seemed to have taken care of that.

With Atabey safe, Remy leaned against the tree trunk and studied the thief that Tanythe called Leukan. He still sat on the boulder, his body slouched in the same position as when Remy first saw him, his dark braids hanging past his shoulders, the interwoven amber beads winking in the dappled light. Leukan's gold tattoo, now neatly aligned to the rest of his neck, was complete, and no scar showed where his neck had been severed. The glittering design, could it be genuine gold tattooed into his skin? looked to be two separate symbols combined.

How had the thief reassembled himself so completely? If Remy could discover this technique, he could become a wizard of a physician and be of help to many. He possessed the qualifications. A few of his Trinity College colleagues had studied natural philosophy/science alongside him and were now practicing physicians and chemists. His disagreements with them on such cures as phlebotomy, bloodletting using leeches, and prescribing the poison mercury for purging had led him to believe that the state of doctoring needed much improvement.

Leukan hadn't moved since Remy first saw him, not a twitch or blink or any of the normal minuscule motions of a person at rest. Remy folded his arms over his chest and studied Leukan to the point of rudeness, waiting for the thief to clear his throat, scratch his neck, or sneeze.

Remy envisioned him, naked and headless, fleeing through the streets with the bag clutched in his hand, somehow finding a shop and procuring the brown robe he now wore. He must try to trace his path. But what was he thinking? He had found the thief, and his name was Leukan.

The stained bag lay nearby, a large bulge keeping it from lying flat, most probably the third head, the one with the beady eyes. Who were these beings? Why had they been beheaded?

Remy stopped his musing, for if Tanythe and Leukan could speak inside his mind, perhaps they could also glean his thoughts. An insect whirred nearby and bumped against his ear. He pushed away from the trunk and swatted it, only to send the bug into his hair, where it became tangled. It buzzed and clacked, its prickly legs sticking into his scalp as it frantically tried to take wing. Panicking, Remy worked to untangle the insect, hoping it wasn't poisonous, when out of the corner of his eye, he glimpsed a sparkle of silver in a sunbeam illuminating the stream.

He shook his head, the insect buzzing off, thank God.

"Confound it," Remy muttered under his breath as he walked down the slope to the stream bank. He chastised himself for not bringing a spare pistol or even a knife in his saddlebag. As he stood on the sandy bank, he stared into the stream.

The afternoon sun slanted through the trees, illuminating the sandy bottom littered with smooth rocks in shades of gray, blue, green, and maroon. Silver minnows scurried through the clear water, avoiding the occasional gray-blue fish three times their size as it meandered by, but there was not a flicker from anything metallic. It must have been a small wave from the waterfalls reflecting the bright sunlight. Still, he walked the bank, checking the water every few feet as he followed the curving stream bed. The dappled sunlight shone for a moment into the dark shadows of a submerged log.

Remy leaned forward but couldn't find the shape he thought he had seen.

He pulled off his boots and woolen stockings and rolled up his trousers as he debated whether what he glimpsed was his pistol. The water was colder than he had felt on his hands when he submerged Tanythe's head, and the rocks and pebbles off-balanced him as he waded to the log. Minnows nibbled at his feet but fled when he reached into the water to dig around where the sand had built up near the log. Halfway to the center of the stream, where the water deepened, he stepped into a hole up to his knees just as he felt something smooth and long under his fingers. He gripped the object and pulled out his pistol. Holding it in front of him, Remy waded to a rock in the sunlight and perched on the smooth surface to dry out.

As he held out his pistol, water and sand dripped off it. The barrels were plugged with sand, and the powder was soaked. He would have to unload it, then let it dry completely before he could even think about shooting it. Rotating the frisson forward, Remy exposed the flash pan and discarded the powder. Then he moved the hammer to a capped half-cocked position to arrest the trigger so it wouldn't fire. But he had no cleaning rod or bolt puller jack, making it impossible to unload the pistol by pulling the bullets out through the muzzle. The metal would probably start rusting by the time he returned to the city.

With the barrels plugged, the insides couldn't possibly dry in the time it took to get back. But if the pistol dried, and if by some crazy chance, he panicked and forgot the barrels were plugged, firing the gun could be fatal, for there could still be enough powder residue left. The gun would explode in his hands. It would be a rare event if that happened, but he had heard stranger things relating to pistols.

As he approached Tanythe, she blinked, which always made him start. She smiled at that. *I give thanks for your traveling here. When you think of me, it grows my power, so I ask that of you. As you see, the thief, as you call him, is whole now. I beseech you, take us to a safe place.*

Remy opened his mouth to ask one of his many questions, but couldn't find his words.

It grows late. You must help Leukan onto your mount.

Leukan was still in the same position on the boulder as when Remy had first arrived in the glade, so different from when he had roamed restless around the laboratory, gliding like a djinni. Some type of mental derangement had occurred between when Leukan had been in the laboratory and now.

Tanythe's eyes clouded, and a slight furrow appeared between her dove-wing brows.

Leukan will not hurt you.

Yet something about the thief kept him away. If he began to lift him and Leukan regained consciousness, would the man become violent? He was larger than Remy, and those with mental disturbances could strike out with great strength.

Watching for even a twitch of motion, Remy walked toward the thief when Remy's muscles bunched, and his senses came alive to something horribly wrong. Leukan had not moved, Atabey had not whinnied, yet Remy practically vibrated.

He stopped focusing on Leukan and whirled around, seeking the threat.

On Tanythe's boulder, which was positioned about four feet from Leukan, an enormous rat sniffed Tanythe's head, its long pink tail like a worm on the rock's surface.

"Get away!" Remy jumped at the rat, who shied off for a moment, then continued sniffing, its whiskers brushing Tanythe's cheek. Her eyes were closed.

Remy drew the pistol from his pocket. Held it high like a club, knocked the rat in the head, and swept it off the boulder, leaving a trail of blood.

Tanythe opened her eyes. Blood spattered her face.

Keep me safe.

She looked up at him, and a surge of strength filled Remy's weary, bruised body. He fumbled in his pocket for his handkerchief and blotted her face gently. Then lifted Tanythe and placed her head inside the bag with the beady-eyed man's head, wondering what role that one played in this complex trio.

He placed the stained bag inside the roomy saddlebag on Atabey and closed his eyes for a moment in relief. Then untied Atabey and led him to Leukan. Sensing a change, Remy looked up. The glade and forest had become shadier, and the breeze cooler. The sun was leaving them as it made its way to the western horizon.

"Can you stand?" Remy asked the thief, worrying how he would place a large, limp man into the saddle and then mount next to him without the man falling. Leukan's dark black eyes stared straight into Remy's.

A surge of quiet horror vibrated through Remy. This man had put words into his mind when he was headless, but now that he was complete, he was not communicating. His dark eyes had a dull gloss and no gold ring around the iris, different from when Remy had studied his head on the table in the laboratory before Leukan had stolen it. Different in an eerie way.

Then Leukan nodded.

Remy stepped back, his scalp tingling as if it had been pricked with pins.

Leukan will not hurt you. Please keep him safe. From inside the saddlebag, Tanythe had accessed his thoughts.

Envisioning himself on Atabey, holding Leukan straight in the saddle, Remy placed his hands under the thief's armpits. He took a breath and pulled him upright, then quickly moved to his side, placing his arms around Leukan's torso. As Remy walked them forward, Leukan almost fell on his face, but Remy stopped and braced him, wondering how the man's legs held his weight. Something was working in the thief's body. They stayed still for a moment. Then Remy started toward Atabey, Leukan's arms swinging limply, his legs stiff but still holding him and stepping as Remy pushed him forward. He was like a life-sized puppet, a nightmare in the calm glade.

Step by step, they made their way. Remy noticed a flow of strength inside his own body, and he lifted Leukan into the saddle as easily as if he were a child.

"Steady, Atabey. This one needs some help." Remy kept up the same gentle conversational tone that he used with his horse when he groomed him. Even with a stable boy and a groom, he liked to work with his stallion.

Remy stood on the ground beside Atabey and held Leukan in the saddle, bracing him upright as he swung up behind him. To keep the thief steady, Remy would have to hold him against his chest with one arm, managing the reins with his other hand.

Atabey snorted.

"I know it's more weight than you're used to, old boy, but you can do it. We've done—"

Atabey neighed. A greeting.

"Well, I see you've found the thief. It is the thief, isn't it? Did you shoot him?" Simmery stopped his gray stallion at the edge of the clearing.

CHAPTER 30

Shocked by the Gov's sudden appearance, Remy couldn't find his words. He held Leukan against his chest to keep him upright, his other hand holding the reins, attempting to keep Atabey under control against this surprise intrusion.

Remy's hand went numb. He gripped Leukan tightly, flexing his hand to keep the blood flowing. He had better answer the Gov before he started accusing him of anything and everything. After all, he had caught Remy red-handed.

"Yes, it is the thief. No, I didn't shoot him this time. Can you help me transport him to the Society?" How the hell did the Gov find him?

"Of course I will help, Derrien. I saw you leave the janissary's house, but you were a hill away and I could never catch up. Until now, of course." The Gov rode toward Remy, but halfway there, his horse balked, whirled around, and stamped back to the edge of the clearing.

When the Gov gained control of his mount, he sat in the saddle further away than before and gave Remy a knowing look. "Granted, Atlas is disturbed by the rather catatonic thief in your saddle, but he has not reacted to other similarly odd people so strongly." Simmery eyed the saddlebag attached to Remy's saddle. "What's in your saddlebag?"

Remy sat silently, holding the thief, holding the reins. By God, he knows. Am I imagining this? Imagining that he knows?

He visited us several times. We could not get him to hear us.

Tanythe. Of course. She was out of sight, but could still hear. And for all he knew, she could probably see what was going on outside the saddlebag and read everyone's mind as well.

Remy's body wanted to drop the reins, let the thief fall. Wanted to lie down on a soft bed, give in to what was happening. But he had to control Atabey, had to keep the thief in the saddle. And now, he had to admit to the Gov that he had kept an important discovery from him.

Would he sack him here and now?

"Derrien, horses do not lie. Something besides your catatonic rider is disturbing Atlas. I believe that something is in the contents of your saddlebag." Simmery eyed the bag as if it were the incarnation of evil.

And perhaps it might be. God knows Remy didn't.

Atlas whinnied. Atabey whinnied back, with a little snort at the end.

"Strange that Atabey is calm with whatever is in the saddlebag. It is almost as if he has been bewitched," said the Gov.

You must tell him. He knows. Tanythe, again. Could she control the Gov's reaction?

Atabey whinnied another greeting, and Atlas chimed in with a nicker. At the sound of hooves on the path, Remy turned in the direction the horses were looking. He reached for his pistol but had to hold Leukan and the reins. His pistol was no good anyway, and he should have stashed it in his saddlebag. He was making mistakes. He'd better take more care.

Pheodora trotted from the forest on her white mare, her large straw sun hat tied over her headscarf. "My, you two look as if you had just seen a djinni." She gave them a broad smile, then frowned. As she rode to Remy, her horse reared. With difficulty, Pheodora guided her mount back to the tree line where they had broken into the clearing.

She called back to them. "Derya is afraid of that man with you, Remy." Pheodora dismounted and spent some time crooning to Derya. After the horse calmed, she tied the reins to a sturdy tree branch and walked over.

"Hello, dear. Fancy meeting you here," Remy said in a cheery voice. Saved from the Gov for the time being. "What the hell, Pheodora? Riding all that way alone. You've heard the stories. The British are not the most popular people here in Turkey. And your fancy Turkish clothes are too rich. They are bait for thieves." He sounded angry, and he was angry. And frustrated, and worried about his position. What would the Gov do in front of his wife?

"I had Lord Simmons-Snow in my sight the whole way, and I have my pistol." She looked up, those blue eyes unconcerned. Still, they were another dead giveaway that she was not a native.

"Who is that man riding in front of you?" She leaned forward, eyeing Leukan.

"A colleague hurt on a mission," the Gov answered. "We need to get him back to the Society before nightfall."

Hmm. Simmery had come to his rescue when a moment ago, the Gov had been about to confront him about the heads, anger building in his voice.

"Lord Simmons-Snow, can you ride guard? My weapon is out of commission." Remy glanced at Simmery's pistol in a polished leather holster.

"I can follow," Pheodora said. "What else do you need, Remy? Lord Simmonds-Snow?"

"A strap, or something to tie, uh, John to me." Remy straightened Leukan, but the man, almost a dead weight after the long walk to Atabey, still slanted sideways in the saddle.

The Gov studied them for a moment, then dismounted. He pulled his pistol from his holster and stuck it in his coat pocket, then unbuckled his holster belt. As he walked over to Remy, he slid the belt from the loop holding the holster. He stopped and held out the belt. "This won't go around the both of you, but I can buckle it around John's waist or chest, and you can grip the back of the belt. I think that's the best we can do."

"Good idea. I'll hold John while you work with the belt." Remy straightened Leukan again as Simmery approached. Atabey huffed and stepped backward, ears pricked.

Hiding the belt behind him, the Gov slowly backed up. "I should probably slip you the belt without Atabey seeing it. It's either the belt, me, or both that makes him skittish."

"I can put the belt on him. Atabey likes me," Pheodora piped up. She retrieved the belt from the Gov and climbed onto the boulder where Tanythe's head had been. She looked at her hand, shook it, and wiped it on the boulder.

"There's blood on this rock," she said, then squinted at Remy. "It's also on your forehead, Remy, and your hand." She gave him one of those motherly glances as she motioned him over.

Atabey had moved as close to the boulder as Remy could direct him. "Steady old boy," he said.

Pheodora held out the belt and looked directly at the thief. "Hello, John. I am Pheodora, Remy's wife. I will put this belt around you so Remy can hold you securely," she said sweetly, her eyes growing wider by the minute as she secured the belt around Leukan.

"There." She let go of the belt and steadied her footing. "Remy, grip John like this." Pheodora held her hand palm up with her fingers curled. "That way, he should stay steady in the saddle." She pressed her lips together and stared at the thief.

"John, we'll soon have you safe and sound." She patted Atabey on the forehead. "And Atabey, you are such a good boy, yes, you are."

Remy positioned Atabey parallel to the boulder where Pheodora stood, blocking the Gov's line of sight. He leaned sideways, as close as he could to her. "Follow my lead. The belt is fine, just pretend. Don't let the Gov know," he whispered.

"The belt is too loose. Can you tighten it, Phe?" Remy said aloud as he pretended to fiddle with it on the opposite side, where Simmery couldn't see. He slipped off his necklace and palmed it into Pheodora's hand as she feigned to tighten the belt.

"The problem is here," Pheodora said, her voice carrying over the burbling stream.

Remy kept his voice low, so the wind wouldn't whisk it to the Gov, but forceful enough that Phe could hear it. "Place the crystal on Derya's neck, and count to eleven, then remove it. Do the same for Atlas."

She gave him a puzzled look.

"The Gov's horse, his name is Atlas. The horses won't be skittish about John afterward," Remy said.

"There, does that work for you?" Pheodora slipped the crystal into the pocket inside her sleeve.

"Much better, thank you. You have a way with horses," said Remy, setting the stage for the Gov and Pheodora.

Pheodora sat down on the boulder, slid off, and frowned at her horse, making sure the Gov noticed. "Derya needs calming before we leave. I have something I can share with Atlas, if it pleases you, Lord Simmonds-Snow."

She rummaged through her saddlebag, pulled out three carrots, stuck two in her belt, and gave the third to an eager Derya. While Derya crunched her treat, Pheodora held the crystal to the mare's neck as she counted to eleven silently. She walked to Simmery and held up the carrot. Atlas nickered.

"May I give him this carrot?"

"Atlas speaks for himself," said the Gov, laughing.

As the Gov's horse munched his treat, Pheodora dangled the necklace from her hand. "Please indulge me, Lord Simmonds-Snow. Hold this crystal to Atlas's neck for a few moments. I will let you know when to remove it."

Smart of Pheodora. She didn't know Atlas well enough to place something on his neck with the Gov mounted on him. Didn't want to have another injury.

"Some Turkish voodoo?" asked Simmery in a jocular manner. To Remy's surprise, the Gov seemed amenable.

"My groom swears by it. And Remy stole it from me. That's why Atabey is so calm around John. I just used it on Derya." Pheodora moved closer.

Atlas lunged for the crystal.

"Do hurry and take it, before this ravenous animal eats it." She moved to the side, giving Atlas the extra carrot while holding the crystal out to the Gov. He placed it on Atlas's neck.

"Like this?" Simmery asked.

Pheodora nodded, obviously counting. After eleven seconds, she said, "There now, that should do it." Pheodora held out her hand.

The Gov studied the crystal, turning it this way and that. At one moment, the light shone a bright rainbow on his face. "Looks ancient, and the metalwork on the chain is fascinating. Where did you find this?"

"My groom got it for me. And I have him looking for another for Remy. Would you like one as well?"

Remy felt a beam of pride in his wife. Pheodora gained such rapport with everyone that they welcomed and accepted her eccentricities.

"Let us see how this works first. Wouldn't want to put you to the trouble yet." The Gov glanced around. A cool breeze blew off the stream. The shadows had grown longer in the glade, and the woods' bright green had turned darker.

"We have approximately two hours before sunset. I think we can make it most of the way. By deep twilight, we should be almost to the Society." He turned Atlas in the direction they had come from. "As discussed, I shall take the lead. Remy, you ride in the middle since you have John. Pheodora, as you said, you will take up the rear."

With a sobering look, the Gov said, "We shouldn't be out of the city at night, vulnerable as we are. And we don't know when John might recover from his peculiar state and give us trouble."

CHAPTER 31

*R*emy checked the shine on his shoes, which looked to be markedly uneven. He would have to speak to his valet. The door to his dressing room creaked open. He looked up, surprised to see bright colors, for his valet wore befitting somber tones.

"Phe, what on earth are you doing awake? After our hurried journey home last night, I thought you might stay in bed today." The vivid colors of her native costume had thrown him off.

"I couldn't sleep in. The strange occurrences of yesterday kept running through my mind." She yawned, then sat on the edge of the chair by the window and leaned forward, her elbow on her knee, her hand supporting her jaw, and watched him.

He set one shoe back on the stand, holding the other in his hand as he recalled that his father, the Marquess of Wearsely, swore that one could tell how a man managed his life by the sheen of his footwear. Remy had never found that maxim to be a good indicator, but perhaps the Gov went by the same compass as his father. And he wanted to impress the Gov in any way he could, so it couldn't hurt to throw shined shoes in with everything else.

Pheodora strolled to him. The drape of her Turkish clothes and tightly cinched jeweled belt revealed his wife's figure in a way that dramatically surpassed the infernal hoop skirts and hard bone stays she had worn in London, insisting they were the newest styles from France.

Her perfume, the sweet floral scent of lavender and spicy bergamot, had him taking a deep breath while she straightened his cravat as if she even had a clue how to tie one. She patted his cravat and looked up at him. "Why on earth are you getting dressed so early? Surely Snowy won't show his face until late afternoon, if at all."

"Must needs. I shall go in today, so I might as well dress now. The Gov will arrive at some point. He's like an old maid with the project. Hands-on. Too hands-on." If she only knew what had transpired. But this little talk should serve as a fair warning, so she wouldn't be shocked if Simmery sacked him. Remy set the shoe on top of the dresser so his valet would polish it again.

"At this very moment, Cook is supervising a marvelous Turkish breakfast. I hope you can find time for it." Pheodora sighed as she lounged on the divan, her gold-embroidered and jeweled slippers winking from under the damask of her lavender pantaloons. He imagined her among the amazing ladies she described from her visits to the sultan's harems.

"It seems as if our adventure occurred only a few hours ago. Or a week. Time is the strangest thing." Pheodora stretched her arms and rested them behind her head on the embroidered pillows. She gave a little laugh. "Your man needs to redo your cravat. My straightening it mussed it even more." She looked around. "Where is he? Shouldn't he be assisting you now?"

"The necessary. Couldn't wait." Remy peered into the looking glass and fiddled with the blasted neckwear. "He seems to be most regular."

Pheodora raised her eyebrows, a sign of disapproval. "Drinking?"

"I subtly check his breath and his balance. No drinking that I can detect over the powerful odor of his peppermint candies, which could be a sign in itself. He may be one of those who can function inebriated." Remy peered into the mirror and smoothed his hair. He would rather stay home today, face Simmery tomorrow.

"Your curls are lovely." Pheodora sat up, extending her feet on the carpet next to the divan as she studied her jeweled slippers, moving them so they caught the light just so. She looked at him. "Lovely curls like a choirboy. You are a bit like a choirboy, Remy. That's part of your charm."

He scowled into the mirror. "Wonderful, now I feel even more manly."

"That's what I'm here for. To enhance your manliness." She rose and kissed him. Her lips pressed tender and warm on his, and he pulled her close as he fumbled with his trouser buttons. Remy removed his cravat, then his shirt, and embraced her as he gently maneuvered them onto the divan. The soft layers of her Turkish trousers and coat, and vest, and all the underthings that women put in the way of men seemed interminable. He peeled off silk and then velvet and then damask and then linen…

"Finally." He had reached actual flesh. "Dear, do you add extra layers to arouse my passions?" He kissed her mouth, her neck, her breasts.

"You've found me out," she whispered in his ear. Her breath, like soft feathers, ran down his neck, and he kissed her. Returning his kisses, she ruffled his hair.

He ran his tongue down her smooth stomach and found the rose between her thighs. There he floated in a place with no worries, the pleasant sensations slowly expanding into a pressing urge.

Pheodora moaned, her fingers playing on his back.

"I need you inside me now," she whispered and placed her arms around his shoulders. He slid his body onto hers, kissing her mouth as he plunged deep inside her.

Tanythe.

My God, had he said the name aloud?

He gasped at the burning on his back as Pheodora raked her fingernails across his flesh. All the sensations, the urgency, merged with the pain blazing across his skin. Remy lost all concentration in a release that collapsed him onto Pheodora, a sweating, panting creature in its most basic state.

* * *

"YOU SHOT THE MAN!" said Remy as he set his cup of coffee on the table harder than he meant, eliciting a glance of disapproval from Pheodora at the clink of china on the wrought iron. Featuring coffee rather than tea, the bountiful Turkish breakfast on a cool spring morning in the garden was much too pleasant to have this conversation. But Phe must not go around shooting someone merely because she imagined a threat. Things like that could cause the Sultan to turn even more against the British, who didn't have the same standing here in Turkey as the Italians and French.

"*You* could have gotten shot." Remy kept his voice steady, stopping it from rising higher. "What if the man had fired back?" Remy's stomach churned with queasiness as he imagined Pheodora being wounded or killed. There's no telling how incidents like that could go. He pushed his empty plate away.

Phe stiffened in her chair and seemed to rise like a cobra flaring its hood. "I had no choice. Under the folds of his burnoose, the man was slanting a pistol at you when I fired. I saw the unmistakable glint of metal."

Glaring at him, she took a *simit* from her plate and bit into it, a few sesame seeds from its doughy ring sticking to her lips. She dipped a silverware knife into the bowl of hummus and set a dollop on her plate beside the black olives.

"You *think* you saw a pistol slanting up?" Remy tightened his shoulders at the condescension in his voice and checked to see if Phe noticed.

"What? How could you believe I might have imagined that? That I would have shot someone based on a careless observation?" She faced him, the knife upright in her hand.

"I was there. It was twilight, and it was difficult to see," said Remy.

She huffed. "The man rode his donkey out of the shadows, where I clearly saw the barrel of his pistol. He meant to rob you. Us." Phe laid the knife flat on the table with a loud thwack as if daring him to contradict her.

"You never mentioned that the peasant had a pistol, that he aimed it at me," said Remy. "The sun was setting. I couldn't see behind me and had my hands full, keeping John straight in the saddle and guiding Atabey."

Pheodora picked up a green olive from the tray at the center of the table, brought it to her mouth, then set it on her plate. "I tried to explain, but we were too far away from one another. And the drama worsened back at the Society when you and Snowy almost dropped poor John as you slid him from the saddle, then hauled him inside as if he were a puppet." She plopped the olive into her mouth.

"And you deserting us, leaving Snowy and me to deal with John in the guest room. What did you run off for?" She tipped her coffee cup and swirled the liquid. Nearby, a cuckoo started its repetitive *goo-ku, goo-ku, goo-ku*, dominating the birdsong in the garden.

Last night, Remy had left her and Simmery in order to hide his leather saddlebag, which contained Tanythe's and the beady-eyed man's heads, before the Gov got his hands on it. Today, he must find the courage and calmness to confess to Simmery about the heads, all the while pretending that the Gov didn't know about them.

"I had to check on the horses and secure the front door. You cannot tell me you've forgotten about the robbery." Last night, the three of them had been exhausted. Even Pheodora had lost her usual spunkiness. When he and Phe were finally home, they turned the horses over to Tarek and fell into bed.

"After you shot the man, I glanced back and thought I saw him grab his leg. I doubt he was fatally wounded," said Remy. He placed his hand over hers and stopped her from toying with her cup.

"I hope not. But he deserved it, meaning to kill one of us." She squeezed his fingers and looked at the trees above them, the shadows of the leaves playing with the sunlight on her face. "Where is John from? That odd tattoo on his neck. I've never seen a gold one. And the way it glitters. Those braids. And the hooded robe, like a monk. Whatever does he do at the Society?" Pheodora asked.

"John had been there for a while when I arrived. He is a historian, rather eccentric, with a specialty in the Byzantine era." How long could he keep up this lying? "How did you follow the Gov?"

These past weeks, Remy had caught Pheodora staring at him as if she were working a puzzle. He suspected she had been spying on him, but her suddenly turning up at the stream was the first proof he had. What if she had arrived when he was submerging Tanythe's head in the water? His skin prickled with gooseflesh at that image. What on earth would he have said?

She slipped her hand out from under his to flick a lock of hair from her eyes, then dipped a piece of simit into the hummus on her plate.

"I saw Tarek hurry off with Atabey and thought I'd catch you at the Society for an afternoon ride. Then I glimpsed you disappearing around a building and Snowy, his horse at a trot, after you." She tilted her head, eyeing him suspiciously, and bit into the simit. "When I finally caught up with you two, Snowy was going on about his horse reacting to something in your saddlebag."

Remy sipped his coffee, avoiding her piercing gaze as he stalled for time to think about what to reply. "The Gov is so proud of Atlas that he cannot admit the stallion is overly skittish about nothing in particular, hence blaming my saddlebag. Has he cornered you yet with Atlas's pedigree? He's a Bedouin-bred Arabian stallion."

"Snowy's been interrupted at our gatherings a few times, so I have not had the privilege of the whole lineage. But what I have heard is very impressive." Pheodora toyed with the olives left on her plate. "But what *was* in the saddlebag—Oh!"

A small calico kitten landed in the middle of her plate, skidding in the hummus.

Pheodora laughed. "Oh well, I was finished anyway." Her eyes gleamed at the kitten as it gulped down the remains of her breakfast.

"Don't you feed the little thing?" Remy set his napkin on the table and moved his chair back.

"Of course, but she's growing and is hungry all the time. I don't think she got enough to eat in the ce—"

Pheodora stopped abruptly. Remy tilted his head. She had started a word, one that began with an "s" sound. A word she didn't want him to know.

Phe rose and kissed him. "Are you going now? Snowy may not even show up today."

Remy hoped so. "I need to check on John."

And Tanythe. And try to figure out Simmery's game.

CHAPTER 32

*P*heodora was correct. They had experienced quite enough last night, riding from the middle of nowhere back to Constantinople. She didn't know that the Gov and he were returning the heads, rather two heads and one completed person, to the laboratory.

There was no light under the Gov's door, and it was 11:40 in the morning. Before checking on John, Remy stopped by the laboratory to remove Tanythe and the other head from his saddlebag. In his fatigued stupor last night, he had decided it was safer to leave them in the saddlebag, out of sight.

Suddenly weary, he sank into a chair. Perhaps he should have slept in. Remy had received a jolt from his breakfast coffee and a second burst of energy from deciding how he would confess to the Gov. The energy drained away when he envisioned how Simmery might react. After he took care of details in the laboratory, he would have Khalil brew him a strong cup.

He forced himself out of the chair and placed the saddlebag on the table where the heads had always rested after he had removed them from the trunk. Located near the laboratory's rear, the table was boxed in, out of sight of any casual observer admitted to the laboratory. He unlatched the saddlebag's flap.

Leukan is just as he was.

Tanythe's voice at last. Remy pressed his fingers against his forehead, the pressure and warmth a comfort. He had wanted desperately to hear her voice once more and kept trying to reach the sound of her deep inside his brain. Well, it had come to that, hadn't it?

He reached into the saddlebag and placed his hands on either side of Tanythe's head. Listening for her voice, he closed his eyes, alert to the sensation in his hands and body. A dreamy feeling, two bodies joined, breathing into one another, each existing for the other—

His breath came heavy. His heart pounded. Remy opened his eyes. For God's sake, he was in the laboratory trying to put things right. If the Gov caught him like this...

His mind focused solely on his task, he placed Tanythe's head on the table in the same position as when he thought the Gov had last seen her. Her eyes were red, and she wore a weary look, the same as Pheodora had after their hurried ride back from the glade. Remy set the other man's head near hers, the man with the dark, beady eyes. Then he gazed at Tanythe.

Yesterday in the glade, when he wondered if Leukan was breathing, Tanythe, her head sitting on the rock beside Leukan, had answered with mind talk.

But Remy had never asked her a question out loud. What if Simmery barged in and heard him speaking? The door was locked. Still, the Gov had a key. But Remy needed to know.

"What is wrong with Leukan? He was energetic, and I could hear his voice inside my brain when he stole your head, all the heads." There, he had said it. The echo of his voice still hung in the air.

Tanythe's eyes sparkled, the redness gone. She looked up at him, making his breath come tight and hard. *You can see that Leukan found his head.*

Tanythe's voice, inside his mind, was as musical as a sweet harp. Remy stayed his hand from caressing her cheek, her hair.

She smiled. *I bonded Leukan's head to his body, but my weakening power failed to complete the task. This unfinished task is what you must do.*

Her voice stayed inside Remy's head. He sat in the chair in front of her, his elbows on the table, his head in his hands. How could he possibly do what she asked? Make a man whole. Put life into him. Did she know about the Elixir? He looked up.

A burst of air came from her mouth.

Startled, he scooted the chair back, making a loud scrape. Had she sighed? How was it possible?

Yes, I know you have a substance that provides what you call a miracle. Later, we will discuss how to make Leukan whole.

"I may not return," he said, and stood, ready to leave for Simmery's office. Could she save him from the Gov's ire at him for concealing her, Leukan, and their companion? Remy silently pleaded, 'Please, give me anything,' and stayed beside her, waiting. He began to ask for help, but he could not admit his weakness. She had confidence that he could make Leukan whole.

Her eyes moved.

His body tingled with hope. She was more than what he saw. He had seen only a fraction of what she could do.

But she turned her eyes away, and Remy knew. Somehow, he knew she was picturing Leukan, her azure eyes with the same expression he had dreamed of seeing when she looked at him.

CHAPTER 33

*A*fter breakfast, Pheodora had leaned close to Remy as he kissed her goodbye, then he ran his finger down her cheek in a small caress. She watched her husband walk slowly down the steps. Remy slumped his shoulders, and he held his head down more than he needed to for navigating. Things he did when he was troubled. The driver held the door open. Remy got in. Seeing her in the doorway, his glum expression brightened, and he gave her a broad smile as the driver closed the door.

His goodbye kiss, the warmth of his lips on hers, took her back to their intimacy earlier that morning, and to his valet, who returned at the most inopportune time. At least Remy's cravat would be proper now. Nothing else was. Her smile grew, and even if she had wanted, she couldn't have stopped the broad curve of it as she strolled to the stables. Atabey and Derya greeted her. A dull whiffle from Atabey, who was deep in his oats, and a sharp nicker from Derya, who received a carrot.

She took Derya out for a ride, then had a brief conversation with Tarek and made sure the other stable hands saw her there—this would be her cover if Remy became curious—then she slipped to the corner where the *araba* she had hired waited. The driver pulled away the fringed scarlet cloth covering the coach, and she felt the lurch of the horses, the tiny bells on the harness tinkling like a carriage in a wonderland. They made their way leisurely to the Society

164

while she peered through the abaya's gilded wooden lattices at the marvelous gardens, flowering trees, and people in all sorts of colorful dress, going hither and yon. Constantinople was a real-life wonderland, but like all fairy tales, the ancient city possessed a sinister side, hidden by marble palaces, harems enclosing jeweled ladies, mosques adorned in vibrant calligraphic designs, ivory-tower minarets, and age-old walls.

Remy had mentioned that he would meet with Snowy today. By his tone of voice and his fidgeting, she could tell he was worried. By his failure to look her in the eye at breakfast, she guessed he might have a secret related to the meeting. At the Society, she would inquire if the Gov was in. If so, that meant Remy was likely with him, which would probably last a while since Remy would struggle to broach the major subject that troubled him.

Then she could begin her sleuthing.

When she arrived at the Society's portico, the guard, introduced to her by Snowy, let her in with a scowl of disapproval after informing her that the Gov was indeed in a meeting. Explaining that her errands had brought her close by, making it convenient to give the Gov important documents from London, she patted her leather manuscript case. Since he was preoccupied, she would see her husband first. She gave the guard a wan smile of thanks as he reluctantly let her in. Creeping down the hall, she saw light under Snowy's closed door and heard muffled voices. She hoped one of them was Remy.

Her key refused to slip properly into the laboratory lock. Fortunately, she had three copies made. The second went in smoothly but wouldn't turn until she jiggled it, lifting the key slightly. The door opened. With a furtive glance behind and seeing no one, she slipped into the laboratory, where the sharp tang of alcohol, a lingering whiff of sulfur, and the faint odor of rancid decay met her. Always different, these laboratory smells.

She locked the door.

Before she heard another key in the lock, she hoped to be on her way home. The laboratory wall clock read 1:30. Pheodora removed the agate, quartz, and opal stones from her bag and set the opal under the microscope, just as Remy had shown her. She peered closely, taking her time in case she needed to provide a reason for her presence. Then she lifted her eye from the microscope, surveying the laboratory. She would start at the back and make her way forward.

In the Karacaahmet cemetery, she had overheard Remy say something about 'three heads thrown from the earth,' and that he heard their voices in his head. He had mentioned a name, a strange name. Tanythe. At home, he had acted normally, except for restlessness in his sleep punctuated by mostly indecipherable murmurings. From what little she could glean from Remy's expressions and subtle reactions to their conversations, his bullet wound had something to do with all of this.

Had the thief shot him with a poisoned bullet? Perhaps she would find something in the laboratory that would explain everything.

The front tables displayed various treasures that Remy had mentioned. Farther back, tables were neatly stacked with labeled and numbered crates and boxes. One crate, when opened, released the smell of mold and musty old houses. Inside were two mud-encrusted urns and pottery shards. Another held fine wooden chests with brass fittings—one locked, another containing laboratory equipment. These were likely spares or new pieces.

She looked up. Had she heard a voice? Everything was so quiet. It was as if she were in a tomb. The laboratory, the corners still in shadow, had become eerie, even with afternoon light shining through the high casement windows. She had better hurry.

More tables held open boxes, works in progress. They contained metal bowls, jewelry, coins, scrolls, glassware, tiles, cloth, and strange instruments. Some were mundane tools, others exquisite art, which reminded her of her father's antiquities at Tynewold Manor.

Remy had not exaggerated about his workload.

Again, a voice. She looked behind her. Could the voice have been inside her head? The atmosphere in here was unnerving. And it would be most frightful for her if she were caught snooping. Perhaps the voice was her imagination after all the odd things that had occurred.

Pheodora leaned against a table and peered into the room's dark corners. Her stomach growled, startling her for a moment, then reminding her that perhaps she had indulged a bit too much at breakfast.

As she moved through the laboratory for a final look around, something else Remy had said at the cemetery struck her: the bullet had passed through the thief's body, then pierced Remy, and Remy feared he had caught a disease. How could that be possible?

She hurried, searching for anything that looked suspicious. Finding herself boxed in, she turned down a narrow aisle formed by crates and a tall chest. There she encountered a table isolated inside a U-shaped alcove.

Curious.

The table was empty except for two life-sized heads. A man and a woman. Incredibly realistic.

For a moment, she could swear an icy hand gripped the back of her neck. Her scalp prickled.

Pheodora glanced around anxiously. She had been here too long and was becoming haunted by this place and these objects, compounded by the old palace in this ancient Byzantine city. All of which were plying curses on her. Like on Remy.

She focused on the table again. These must be the ones she overheard Remy mention at the cemetery. She crept closer. An odd sensation blossomed inside her skull, as if a wick had been lit, the tiny flame bursting into a flare of intensity. A flash of red and orange obscured the heads with their shining eyes, then roared into a torrent that poured inside her, filling her with a power so fresh and forceful that Pheodora saw the heads on bodies.

In this, this vision, the woman approached her, adorned with moonstones, pearls, and sapphires, her red hair curling around her ivory body. Her diaphanous gown blended into the blue and opalescence of an ocean, soft white peaks of sea foam swirling at her feet, forked lightning feeding the silver-white glow of her jeweled diadem.

The man stood stocky beside her, rough to the lady's smoothness, his dark eyes pools of bubbling lava. His left hand gripped a gleaming double battle ax, and on the same side, half a pointed bronze helmet outfitted his head. His right hand held fanned-out Tarot cards, the figures moving. On that side of his head sat half a pointed conical cap, the material shining with winking stars.

This power can be yours, resounded man's gruff voice in her mind. She pressed her fingers to her forehead. Her vision of the woman and man blurred, and she stared at them, now reduced to their heads only, situated on the table.

This laboratory was surely haunted. Heart hammering, she pulled her necklace from inside her blouse, the medallion with the eye staring out from her chest to protect her as she moved away and found her way to the door.

Just a quick look again, she told herself as she fought her better judgment.

Pheodora glanced at the table once more. The woman's eyes shone blue in the light, the man's black as a midnight pool.

She stepped forward. The base of the man's neck sat crooked on the table. Why, it was uneven, not finished as a sculpture would be. It-it looked as if it had been severed—

She backed away.

These were real.

Real human heads.

A nightmare. She was in a nightmare. The man blinked as his mouth moved. "This power can be yours," he said aloud in the same gravelly voice she had heard inside her head.

The scream that tore from her throat filled the laboratory. It bounced off the plaster walls, growing louder and louder. She clawed her way through the air backward, far away from the table where the heads' eyes glinted at her. Her fingers clasped something smooth.

The door, a hundred steps ahead of her, opened. Something shadowy came at her. She threw what was in her hand. A loud crash. She gripped the next thing behind her.

The shadow kept coming for her.

She flung whatever she held and desperately clutched behind her for another. A man caught her wrists and pushed her against a wall.

The gruff voice in her head told her to be still. Undeterred now, the shadow lurched for her. She struggled with the man who held her.

"No! Let me go!" she screamed, but the man who held her didn't understand that she wanted him to let her loose so she could flee from the shadow.

The shadow hurled itself at her, colliding with her. She winced but felt no impact, just a coldness as if she were naked in a blizzard, the snow forced horizontal by the howling wind going straight through her skin, deep inside her.

She fainted for a moment.

Do not be afraid. I will give you great power.

That same gravely voice that came from the disembodied head. The vibration of the words resonated inside her from organ to organ. It was as if she were the shadow man's tight-fitting suit, and he was buttoning himself inside her, making himself comfortable.

"Enough," said a voice outside. A familiar voice. She blinked and focused on what was in front of her. Remy, her husband, his face distorted in anger, his hands hard on her wrists. She ceased struggling. It was over.

Whatever had frightened her had done worse than she feared. The man on the table had somehow become a part of her. She glanced at his head, his eyes dull and half closed.

A waterfall of new thoughts and sensations cascaded into her, filling her over and over. Power flowed inside her. Something she had always wanted, but this…This was something she could never have imagined. She felt as if she had wings and could fly. Magic sparked inside her, full of light and promise and intrigue. Just as the sun set on the earth and sunlight paled into darkness, this magic fell into another realm of shadows and shades, steaming cauldrons, scales and claws, battles, and horrific wounds that had her groaning in agony, but silent in that groaning.

A strange exultation flooded her, born of light and dark.

But it felt like her. And Pheodora knew she would grow to like it.

* * *

"Enough," said Remy. He still held her wrists.

He was hurting her, but not hurting all of her. Pheodora now had two selves. They fought for her favor. At this moment, she chose her familiar self and looked at Remy through her old eyes. Remy, her husband, she told the man, her other self, so he would understand.

She knew she had to please this man inside her, no matter what. But he wanted her to please her husband now.

The next thing Pheodora knew, she was holding up her laboratory key. Remy seemed happy with that and snatched it away from her. At his touch, she felt the man inside, warrior and magician both, settle deeper.

The man's amazing magic filled her, as at home as if he were a welcome guest taking up space inside her house.

CHAPTER 34

REMY'S MEETING WITH THE GOV, WHILE PHEODORA ENTERS THE SOCIETY

"*D*errien, you're noticeably worse for wear." The governor's voice sounded hearty but forced. He looked weak, his eyes dull, his skin sallow. Simmery pushed away from his desk and walked to the door. "Let us adjourn to the laboratory."

"Sir, please, I have something...Remy could not say the words. He would put everything he wished for at risk.

Simmery sat on the couch across from his enormous mahogany desk. "Well, spit it out, old man."

Remy looked at the floor. "I—you know about the bag, the bag with the—"

"Heads. Yes." Simmery leaned into the cushion, his arm resting on the back of the couch. "By God, old man, it took you long enough to tell me. What were you thinking, hiding such a discovery from me?" Simmery's eyes sparked, not dull anymore.

"When I caught up with you the other day, far out of the city in the glade, I recognized one head from the laboratory on John," the Gov said. He looked thoughtful. "So, the thief came to fetch his head. How the devil did he manage to attach it?" Simmery devolved into muttering as if he were alone and talking to himself.

Remy waited, trying to understand what he said, but the words were jumbled beyond deciphering.

"John doesn't work as he should. We will have long conversations about that," said Remy. Simmery glared at him—the hate in those eyes. Remy struggled to keep from turning away.

"I want the truth this time." The Gov said each word as if he were spitting it out. "I should sanction you in front of the Society. There are rules, you know. I am the head of this project, not you. Yes, you received a merit award from the Society in your placement here, but I am afraid you've let it go to your head."

Simmery banged his fist on the upholstered arm of the couch.

"Derrien, you are working in *my* laboratory like a servant in one of my manors, and you must report everything to me. Otherwise, you are working against me. And you do *not* want to do that." The Gov spread his fingers, white now, and curled them into a fist again.

Remy's gut squeezed hard as if that fist were inside him. "The heads gave me such a shock, I-I didn't know what to do. I admit I questioned my sanity and—and..." He hung his head and could not believe he had done such a thing. "I realize I made a mistake, sir."

"A grievous mistake," said Simmery.

Remy tried to think of some excuse that would not make him look so weak in front of Lord Simmons-Snow, a powerful man, a member of the House of Lords, and a prestigious fellow in the London Society of Antiquaries. Of course, Simmonds-Snow would want the prestige of an important discovery. Men like him got all the credit. More money, more prestige, while second sons like Remy suffered insults and ended up as vicars in some run-down rectory in a decrepit northern English burg.

"A mistake you'll regret the rest of your life." Lord Simmonds-Snow rose from the couch, his posture straight, looking fully like the lord of the realm. His eyes bored into Remy.

This was it, the final blow. Would the Gov sack him here and now, send him packing?

A shrill scream tunneled down the hall.

Simmery jerked toward the door and led the way toward the keening sound. A scream and another and another rhythmically punctuated the pounding of their shoes on the marble floor.

Lord Grimond and three of the other fellows of the Society joined them at the laboratory door, followed by wide-eyed servants. A sense of dread permeated Remy. This was how rumors started—how the British could very well be banished by the Sultan. At least, now that Simmery was in charge of the laboratory, Remy's name would not be so prominent in any of the official reports, assuming he was still a member of the Society.

"We'll handle it," bellowed Simmery. With an affronted expression, Lord Grimond turned back, his hands out as if he were scattering fowl, and shooed the murmuring crowd down the hall.

Good job, Remy silently praised the Gov.

The laboratory door was shut. The Gov tried the handle. It opened. He gave Remy a nasty scowl.

"I'm positive I locked it." Remy followed him inside.

A glass beaker sailed past the Gov's head, heading straight for Remy.

Remy ducked, and it exploded into pieces on the wall behind him. He could have sworn that he felt the beaker slightly brush his cheek. They both side-stepped as another almost hit the Gov on the forehead, then shattered on the floor.

Remy ran to Pheodora. Caught her by the wrists before she could throw the beaker she had just grasped in her hand.

"Enough! What are you doing here?" He squeezed her wrist until she dropped the beaker. Remy winced at the sound of more shattering glass, but Phe took advantage and struggled. Her headpiece slanted to the side, eyes glazed like an opium eater's. Surprised at her sudden strength, he wrestled her against the wall, where she slumped and tried to slide down, but he prevented that. She shrank to the side, her complexion drained of color. She looked at the floor, then directly at him. Her eyes! By God, it was as if someone else stared menace at him. He almost dropped her.

She grimaced. Like water draining from a sieve, the threat radiating from her eyes gradually faded as he watched her, then his own familiar Pheodora stared at him, eyes wide in terror.

"Remy, you're hurting me." She shrank back, eyeing him as if *he* were the threat.

He realized he had squeezed her arms even tighter, but her earlier unexplained strength had slipped away, exactly like the menace in her eyes. He loosened his hold on her but kept a gentle grasp. No telling what she might do next.

Pheodora stared at him now as if she had never seen him before, then her head tilted, and her arms went limp.

"Quick, a chair. I think she might faint." Remy directed the Gov, who slid a chair under Pheodora. She collapsed into it, leaned forward, and would have fallen onto the floor but for Remy taking hold of her shoulders.

Simmery stood beside them, pointedly looking at Tanythe's head on the nearby table. The beady-eyed man's head sat next to her, just as Remy had set them out to show the Gov that he was cooperating now, not hiding anything.

"Pheodora, why are you here?" Remy spoke softly as he bent over her.

She looked up, her eyes the Phe he knew, but still huge with fear.

"How did you get in? The door was locked." Remy glanced at the Gov. Pheodora fumbled in her outer robe's pocket and held up a key. Her hand shook.

"You gave your wife a key to the laboratory? After the robbery? After all we've gone through here?" The Gov controlled his voice, but it held a subtle fury that Remy had never heard.

"No, no." Pheodora's words came out hoarse and strained. He could barely hear her. Looking puzzled, she put her hand to her throat and swallowed several times. Remy placed his hand over hers, guiding it down to her lap. Then he pocketed the key.

"I-I h-had one made." Her voice shook, same as her hand, as she looked at the Gov. "Remy didn't know. I-I never told him." Her words shook more than her hand. "Remy has let me into the laboratory when he is here, where he watched me view things through the microscope." Red patches blotched her face.

"Here, Lady Derrien." The Gov had somehow fetched a glass of water. "Please take a small sip."

Pheodora reached for the glass, but she sloshed the water onto her vest and pantaloons. Remy took the glass and held it to her lips. She managed a few sips, then pushed it away.

"I-I came in and s-saw," she gestured toward Tanythe's head. "And if it wasn't horrific enough that you have beheaded heads in here, ones that are hours old..." She caught her breath and gave Remy a searing look.

"One of them blinked." She stared at the floor, then looked at them both, avoiding the heads. "And I...I am not crazy. I clearly saw it. She looked straight at me and—"

The Gov held up his palm and shook his head. She looked up from under her brows as if she might bite him.

"We know. It is a shock, a terrible shock, for the few who have first seen the heads." Simmery looked around. "Derrien, fetch us more chairs."

Remy bolted from the room. He considered calmly walking down the hall, then running to the nearest caique that crossed the estuary to Constantinople, taking an araba to the Hotel Pera, and booking a ship home. But he pulled two chairs from his office into the laboratory, dragging them through the broken glass. He waited while the Governor sat first.

"Sit, Remy. We do not need you looming over us with that gloomy countenance." Simmery waved his hand toward the vacant chair, then leaned close to Pheodora.

"This conundrum has bothered your husband and me since we discovered the heads in the objects we found in the earthquake. Remy leaned toward her as if he could prevent whatever bizarre thing might happen next.

Remy kept his face expressionless. The Gov glanced at Remy. "This is to be kept a secret. A tit for tat. Although I think *you* owe me one." This time, his eyes skewered Remy's, but Remy was determined not to look away.

Pheodora took a glance at Tanythe on the table and whirled back around, facing the Gov and Remy.

"John is one of them, isn't he?" Pheodora narrowed her eyes at them both. "That's why his body doesn't work. My heavens, are you somehow making new people here?"

"No, no. Nothing so macabre." The Gov looked truly disturbed at that accusation and followed Pheodora's glance as she looked to Remy, who sat rigid in his chair, broken glass crunching beneath the soles of his shoes. His muscles nearly spasmed, but no one could tell as he took the accusing stares.

"Who are they? Why were they beheaded?" Pheodora asked.

CHAPTER 35

hat same morning, after checking once more on Pheodora, making sure her maid would send word if she 'took ill,' Remy accepted the umbrella his footman thrust at him on the way out the door and headed on foot toward the Society. This would be his second trip today to his place of occupation, the first this morning in a Turkish coach where he thought of Pheodora and her soft kisses as the coach rocked him almost to sleep.

On this second trip, walking, he tried *not* to think of Pheodora. The strangeness of what he had seen in her after she discovered the heads befuddled and concerned him most deeply. He had left the house as soon as he was convinced she had settled and would stay that way.

Remy noted the vibrant blossoms of ruby red, brilliant white, and flamingo pink adorning the street's fruit trees and thriving in the ubiquitous gardens. However, the day's events, both expected and unexpected, overshadowed the surrounding beauty.

When Remy intercepted Pheodora in the laboratory, she became hysterical and fought him. Before his eyes, she turned into a stranger. Then, as if a switch had been flicked, she became, for all outward purposes, her normal self. Phe's encountering the heads excused her hysteria. He and Khalil had experienced much the same reaction. But afterward, she had seemed changed in a way Remy couldn't rationalize.

At the street corner, he swerved to avoid the energetic pack of street dogs gathering near a rose hedge covered in white blossoms. Recognizing him from his walks, they wagged their tails, then turned to their business.

Unbidden and unwelcome, his thoughts returned to Pheodora. After he and the Gov discovered her in the laboratory and Remy stopped her from throwing beakers at them, he had bundled her out the Society's back door, packed her into an abaya, and taken her home, all the while fearing she would suffer another incident.

She had become complacent, but a foreboding energy at the cusp of emerging seethed inside her. At times, when Phe looked at him, her eyes were not her eyes. She admitted she was drained, had the wits to apologize to him, then fell into a deep sleep, never once mentioning the heads.

Back at the Society, the guard greeted him and opened the doors. Remy nodded, then gave the perfunctory greeting, his voice weak from worry. Would Phe be herself when she awoke, or would he receive an urgent message from her maid?

As he crossed the threshold, another dread dampened his spirit: he would have to face Simmery this afternoon and complete his dressing down, which had been interrupted by Phe's screams tunneling through the Society's halls. Confound it, Pheodora again.

"Well, if it isn't the mysterious man from the laboratory." Lord Grimond breezed into the Society's entry hall and placed his black umbrella in the accommodating ceramic holder near the door. "Are things becoming dull now that they've settled down?"

"Not a bit, Lord Grimond. Did you have a pleasant midday meal?" Remy set his umbrella next to Grimond's. No caste system in the umbrella holder.

"Wonderful feast at the Residency. Seriously, what on earth happened in there this morning?" Grimond adjusted his monocle as he leaned close. Remy must give him something. After all, the man had probably heard every possible rumor.

"A mix-up in schedule and a shock from something unexpected. Nothing Lord Simmonds-Snow and I couldn't handle." Remy attempted to sound offhand. Grimond gave him an *Is that all you'll tell me* expression.

"Perhaps a little later, then. Cheerio." Grimond seemed unfazed. Since his post in Bombay, he had certainly become overfamiliar with bureaucratic obfuscation.

Remy trudged down the hall past the ancient statues, whose eyes he could have sworn followed him to the Gov's office. Earlier in the day, Remy had been in this very office in conference with Simmery, but that had been interrupted when Pheodora discovered the heads. What abysmal timing. Yet he felt a grin cut his face. Seems everyone was finding out about the heads.

Remy knocked at the door as he set his expression suitably sober.

"Enter." Simmery's voice had an edge. Not a good sign. When he saw Remy, he dropped the papers he was holding.

"Close the door," he said, in such a curt and severe manner that Remy almost ducked out, wishing he could close the door from the other side and escape.

"I know what you did and did not do." Simmery put his hands on the desk and stood.

Remy straightened, calm on the outside. Inside, he barely controlled his rage that the Gov's ancestry gave him a higher standing in the Society than Remy's merit status. He met Simmery's intense gaze.

"You failed to inform me until you knew I knew." Simmery balled his fists at his side.

Even while reprimanding him, the Gov couldn't say the word, *heads*, a decidedly puerile name. Remy himself couldn't call them *heads* aloud either.

Go to Leukan. Tanythe's call filled Remy's brain.

After all that had happened this morning, he hadn't given a thought to Leukan. Had the Gov checked on him in the Society's guest room?

"Ahem." The Gov cleared his throat. "Derrien, what has gotten into you?" The Gov pushed back a loose strand of brown hair that escaped from the black ribbon holding his queue. "Beg pardon. How is Pheodora?"

"Sir, she was sleeping when I left, thank God. When I took her home, she was in shock, not her cheery, strong self at all. Her lady's maid is with her." Remy looked at the floor. Simmery didn't know that Tanythe mind-talked with him. How could he impart that there may be an emergency?

"Odd how everything came into the light at once. For me, for Pheodora," said the Gov, suddenly looking weary. He sat down heavily behind his desk and looked up at Remy. "You look knackered. Please excuse my thoughtless-ness. Sit."

Remy sagged into the chair in front of the Gov's desk. The soft upholstery sank with him. Just like he felt—as if he were sinking. Quite possibly, he was. Would he ever be able to return to his laboratory?

Simmery sat up and leveled his gaze at Remy. "This is how it has to be for the time being. I will not have you thrown out of the Society. You and I will study the—"

Remy stifled a smile. Still, neither he nor the Gov would say the name *heads.*

The Gov shook his head. "We must find a more suitable name for them and find their secret. I believe it will be a better project with both of us working together."

"Yes, sir." Remy attempted to rise from the chair, but he had sunk so far into it that he was held prisoner. Pushing hard on the arms, he struggled out of it and stood straight, trying not to look foolish after that pitiful show of becoming vertical.

"I look forward to our collaboration," said Remy with all the sincerity he could muster. He hoped it was enough. He could use the laboratory, but he knew that Simmery, Lord Simmonds-Snow, would take credit for any discov-ery. Remy would still be the second son, the second natural philosopher/scien-tist, and Lord Simmonds-Snow would be the gentlemanly villain who would steal his career. The Gov might as well relegate him to a rectory far from the world of natural philosophy and science.

Go to Leukan. Tanythe's call filled Remy's brain again.

"Sir, with all that has happened this morning, I haven't been able to check on John. By any chance, have you?" Remy took care with his tone. He would have hell to pay if Simmery thought he was accusing him of shirking his duties.

"Before you arrived, I checked on him. He is just the same." The Gov left Remy standing as he bent behind his massive mahogany desk.

"I have something to show you," he said, still hidden behind his desk.

Remy stretched his neck but could only see the Gov's back as he bent over something. What the hell was he doing?

Simmery rose, holding a canvas bundle, which he laid on the table in the corner. He motioned Remy over as he unfolded the canvas. In front of the table, Remy shifted from one foot to the other. Tanythe was unusually persistent. He must invent an excuse to leave.

The Gov lifted a thin, dark bundle from the unfolded canvas. He spread the clumsily folded black cloth out on the table. A dank odor suffused the room, curdling Remy's stomach. His wound throbbed as it had not done for a week. Before he could stop, he clutched where the bullet had entered his biceps as if he had just been shot. He could barely take a breath as he stared at what Simmery had laid out on the table.

Lord in heaven, the thief's robe.

"Derrien," Simmery's voice cut through the thick fog in Remy's head. Something clutched his other arm, and he was being led. Soft cushions under him and behind him. Then the sound of clinking glass. A whiff of an outdoor autumn wood fire and a bit of butterscotch.

"Drink this." The Gov's voice.

This was old Scotch, a fine vintage. And it brought Remy back to focus.

"Derrien, we need to talk." Simmery sat on the couch beside him.

Leukan needs you. Tanythe's mind talk. The third time.

"Yes, Lord Simmonds-Snow, I-I promise we can talk, but it must be later." Remy couldn't keep his hand from shaking.

Simmery took the glass.

Remy struggled to stand. "W-we will talk later about your, *our* project, concerning the... the. . . heads. I must check on John."

Remy ran out the door.

CHAPTER 36

The window threw late morning light on John, or Leukan as Tanythe called him, or the thief as Remy had known him. Three stripes of sunlight slanted across John's chest from the peculiar angle of the beam, the source of which Remy couldn't find. John hadn't soiled himself, and he lay on the bed in the same position as the past two nights. There was no sign of decay.

Why had Tanythe sent such a frantic message? Remy had envisioned Leukan lurching around the room, destroying the place, perhaps injuring himself.

Unsure to do next, he hovered over John. Remy had ridden for hours with the man seated on his saddle in front of him, yet had barely touched his flesh.

Taking a breath, he placed three fingers on the inside of Leukan's wrist. The flesh was cool and slightly damp. He increased the pressure, then repositioned his fingers, feeling for a pulse. Remy's heart beat faster as he searched for the slightest quiver. Then, as if from a great distance, came a hint of a pulse, a slow, slow beat. Remy counted seconds: ten, twenty, thirty. After forty seconds, another quiver, then forty more seconds, and another. Thankfully, they kept coming, fairly consistently.

Tanythe remained quiet.

Remy let go of John's wrist and collapsed in the guest room's overstuffed chair, never letting his eyes stray from Leukan, who lay as still as a corpse. Would the thief die here at the Society? Remy waited and watched until the shadows across Leukan had grown blue and long, like those at the stream when they had left.

Leukan hadn't moved. He lay still and peaceful. Time to check the laboratory. Find a suitable place for the two heads to rest and be safe from servants, other fellows in the society, and nosy wives.

As his hand closed on the cool brass door handle, a sound like a gust of wind ripping through a window sash made him turn. Leukan sat straight up in bed, his eyes wide, breathing rapidly. Remy rushed over and braced him upright, afraid he might tip onto the floor.

Leukan's breath came faster. He leaned over and vomited bright red blood on the Turkish carpet and Remy's shoes.

"No, no." Remy started to call for help, but no one but the Gov knew about John.

John began retching once more.

To hell with it. Remy took a deep breath to allow for his loudest voice, but before he could yell, the door opened.

"By God!" Simmery rushed inside, avoiding the bright red blood pooling on the carpet. "What happened?"

Remy braced John as he retched blood again. "In the blink of an eye, he came out of his stupor and vomited," Remy said as he kept Leukan upright on the bed. But the man's almost slack weight was putting a strain on the awkward position Remy had adopted to hold him. Leukan opened his mouth. This time, nothing came out.

"Put the pillows behind his back. I need to readjust the way he's sitting. He might choke if he vomits again," said Remy.

Simmery stuffed pillows in place. "Fill me in."

Remy repositioned John on the bed, keeping a hand on him so he wouldn't topple. "He lay in the same position as when we first brought him in. Barely had a pulse, a faint beat every forty seconds. Then, without a word, he sat up and vomited blood." Remy held John with his right hand and placed his left fingers in position on John's wrist. "Pulse is stronger and closer together than before."

Simmery placed his hand on John's forehead. "No fever. We need to examine him. Help me remove his robe." Remy gently rolled Leukan to one side, away from the stack of pillows. "Quick, pull his robe up over his hips." He rolled Leukan to the opposite side. "Now, the rest of the robe."

"Take his right sleeve." Remy kept Leukan steady and slid the left sleeve off Leukan's arm. Then they pulled the robe over his head.

"Thank God he wasn't wearing a cravat," Simmery muttered as he helped Remy re-situate John on the bed. "What the devil is wrong with him?"

"Do you know a discreet physician we can call?" Remy wiped the blood from his hands on the soiled covers as they both examined John.

"I think we can do as well as any. We both took the material world studies—

"By God, he's been shot." The Gov looked at Remy.

That sinking feeling again. Would all his secrets be revealed today?

"The wound is old, healed. About as old as yours, Derrien." A peculiar look came into the Gov's eyes. Crafty, scheming—the true Lord Simmonds-Snow at last?

Remy exhaled slowly, forcing himself to inhale again. He had noticed the bullet hole in the thief's robe that the Gov had ceremoniously shown him. But the Gov hadn't noticed it. He wasn't expecting a bullet hole. The robe had many tears, dirt, lichen, and stains; it had been easy to miss.

Remy had never mentioned that he had shot the thief. Everyone thought the thief had shot Remy, and he wanted it to stay that way. He couldn't bear it if the actual story got out—that Remy shot the thief and was wounded when the bullet, his bullet, ricocheted off the wall. That he was shot with his own bullet. He would never live that down. He would be the joke of the century.

Remy's face burned.

"Did you shoot the thief before or after he shot you?" Simmery looked concerned.

Of course, that would be what everyone would believe. No one would ever think of what had really happened. Absolute lunacy.

Remy's head spun in relief. He could have been even more of a hero. Shooting the thief first. Of course, Remy shot the thief before the thief shot him, in a manner of speaking. That was the absolute truth, which says something about truth.

"I-I am not sure. I seem to remember that I had my pistol with me." Remy made a show of concentrating. "Me firing my pistol. Yes. I-I believe so."

Oh, he remembered everything exactly, but was so ashamed of what happened that he had told no one he had shot the thief. He hadn't thought it through.

"Good for you, old man. That should have kept him from escaping. Can't imagine why it would not have brought him down." Simmery clapped him on the back.

Without a sound, Leukan opened his mouth. A small stream of blood poured out.

"Quick. To the laboratory." Remy gripped Leukan's shoulders. "We have things that can help him. Sir, take his feet. Hurry."

They rushed awkwardly down the hall, meeting no one. Hard to explain hand-carrying a naked stranger covered in blood through the building. Just inside the laboratory door, Leukan vomited blood again. Remy held him upright, blood trickling down the man's bare chest, while the Gov draped a blanket over the nearest chair. Remy deposited Leukan on the seat and held him upright, but Leukan's head flopped onto his chest.

"We'll need to lift him onto that table. Can you clear it, sir, while I hold John?" Remy tried to get a better grip while Leukan slid lower, his head halfway down the chair back. "Hurry, he's slippery with blood."

The Gov hastily cleared the table, then bent and picked up Leukan's feet. "Ready?"

Remy nodded as he got a grip on Leukan's upper arms. "Now," Remy said.

They struggled to the table and lifted him onto it. Remy covered Leukan with another blanket and stood there, exhausted, staring at the Gov, who stared back.

Remy placed his hands on the side of Leukan's neck, silently counting. "Every thirty seconds there's a pulse, faster than in the guest room." He looked up at the Gov.

"What on earth are we going to do?" Remy asked.

I know what happened. Tanythe's mind talk. God in heaven, he'd completely forgotten about her.

"Lord Snow, watch John." Remy ran to the back of the laboratory and fetched Tanythe's head. He indicated another nearby table. "Please clear it and pull it over here as close as you can to John. I need to set her down."

"What in the name of heaven are you up to, Derrien?"

Remy set Tanythe's head gently on the table. "I am not sure, myself, Lord Snow, but I beg you. Humor me."

Take my crystal from your neck and wrap the chain around my head to secure it there.

Remy stood next to Tanythe, his eyes on her as he removed the chain from his neck, which seemed to take forever as his fingers, wet with blood, kept slipping off the chain.

"Blast," Remy turned his head as he struggled with the links, now caught in his hair.

"By God, Derrien, why in the name of heaven are you fiddling with your jewelry? The patient is over here."

"And the physician is here." Remy hurried to Tanythe, one hand holding the crystal while he wiped the other on his trousers. With his shirt, he cleaned the blood from the crystal, then wound the chain around Tanythe's head, securing it there.

She looked up at him. *Now, pour fresh water over me and let it settle around me.*

Remy rushed to a table with laboratory equipment and hurried back with a shallow metal tub and a pitcher of water, the Gov eyeing him all the while. He gently placed Tanythe's head inside the tub and poured the water over her head slowly.

"What is this, Derrien?" The Gov hovered near Remy, a grave expression on his face as if he were observing funeral rites.

Remove me from the water and position me to face Leukan.

Ignoring Simmery, Remy removed Tanythe's head from the tub and set her on the table so she could see Leukan, who remained laid out as still as a corpse.

Now, put my necklace around his neck.

Remy struggled with unwinding the chain from around Tanythe's head and breathed with relief that the links hadn't tangled in her hair. He finally had it resting in as proper a manner as he could on Leukan's chest. The crystal, sitting in Leukan's drying blood, looked pristine as if it were just polished.

"That's the same crystal that Pheodora used on my horse." The Gov moved close to the crystal. "By God, look at it, Derrien. It's shining like a beacon."

"I've never seen it do that," Remy said. He kept his voice low, as if this were a sacred service.

Why hide anything from the Gov now? Except for the Elixir. Dare he keep that a secret? The excuse that he wanted to confirm its powers before he disclosed his discovery might work. But the Gov would insist that he'd made it clear he headed the project and that everyone must report to him. Later, Remy would decide. Later. There was much to tell Simmery before that.

Remy pulled a chair over and sat next to Tanythe and Leukan.

"The way you acted, Derrien, I would swear you were taking orders from someone," Simmery said as he brought a chair over and set it beside Remy.

Remy avoided looking at the Gov and focused on the crystal, which still glowed. He sank into his chair, nerves frayed from fear of what might happen to Leukan, of what might happen to him when the Gov learned about the mind talk Remy shared with Tanythe. He wouldn't mention Leukan's trying to communicate with him while he stole the heads.

Just as the Gov took his seat, the room vibrated. They both ducked and put their hands over their heads, eyes full of fear when they met each other's gaze.

"Earthquake?" They spoke simultaneously.

Remy thought sure it was Tanythe's doing, but when he saw her horrified expression, he knew it wasn't. The room trembled.

"Earthquake!" He and the Gov cried again as if in chorus, this time in loud panic. The Gov hurried to Leukan but shook his head and covered him with a blanket while Remy lifted Tanythe's head to carry her with him.

Take only my crystal, but leave us.

Simmery ran to the door. "Derrien, we must go. Now." He held out his hand, gesturing for him to hurry.

As if in a dream, Remy lifted the crystal from Leukan and slipped it around his own neck. He looked up in horror as a piece of plaster exploded on the Gov's head. The Gov's extended hand grew limp. He fell to the ground.

With a grunt, Remy lifted him. Dodging crumbling statues, crashing objects, and the ever-present plaster raining from the ceiling, he carried the Gov into the street.

CHAPTER 37

*R*emy and Lord Simmonds-Snow had not felt it. Neither had Tanythe. But Leukan had.

Remy had set Tanythe's head on the table in the laboratory. Her eyes shining, she focused on Leukan with no sign of alarm. Terra firma, restless in pursuit of Leukan's pleas, had at last deigned to answer one of its own. Her replies could be as gentle as earth shaping into a shallow pond, cradling the water like one cups a kitten in one's palm, or as violent as an explosion of poisonous gases, boulders as large as buildings bursting from a fiery crater. But now, the loamy scent of earth surrounded Leukan, and he breathed it in as the life-giving gift that it was.

On this day, much time would pass before the Society's inhabitants noticed the first tremor, but the earth spoke to Leukan through his very bones. Nourished him with the sensation of magma's circulation, the molten rock flowing inside the earth like veins in Leukan's human body. The heat of that sensation broke him into a welcome sweat.

The sweat of healing. His fingers twitched ever so slightly, a leaf barely trembling in a stingy bit of breeze, then stilled. His blood warmed and took on the coppery smell of one of Earth's elements.

Deep inside terra firma, solids and liquids stirred, and old bones shifted. Rocks, soil, and carbon bore down from the surface, squeezing diamonds from clumps of nondescript matter into the white brilliance coveted by kings. And Leukan drank it in, absorbing every drop of terra firma's gift.

When the earth shivered, too subtle for humans to even prick up their ears, Leukan sat still, absorbing a tribute owed him from one he had ruled thousands of years ago. He reveled in the vigor he received.

"Earthquake!" The laboratory rang with Remy and Lord Simmonds-Snow's simultaneous exclamation as the earth's first major spasm worked to the surface long after Leukan had regained much of his vitality.

Heedless of their panic, Leukan remained silent and still, knowing Remy and the Governor must escape, knowing that terra firma would shield him and Tanythe. As the rumbling intensified, he rose in a perfect symphony of balance and strength. He stood—body and head united—muscles obedient to his command: stand, balance, move.

He blinked. Surveyed his surroundings. The laboratory. Tanythe's head sat near him. His hands reached for his neck, tracing the smooth skin, the raised tattoo. He turned, movements fluid as water, his body refined, strong, as if honed in Olympia.

Remy and Lord Simmonds-Snow had fled. Chunks of plaster crashed down around them, exploding in sprays of white powder. Tanythe sat, helpless, on the table, eyes fearful until they rested on him. She blinked as if to clear her vision, to verify that he was whole at last, her eyes reflecting each emotion, disbelief, astonishment, then relaxing in relief and joy.

Remy's leather satchel lay across from Tanythe. In a moment, Leukan was by her side, opening the satchel.

"Tanythe, the earth will not harm me or those I protect," he said. Silent as a stalking cat, a tremor shook the building. Plumes of white plaster rained down. Bahl's head sat on the table, eyes wide. Good riddance to him.

Leukan placed Tanythe's head inside the satchel, slung it over his shoulder, snatched Lord Simmonds-Snow's cape from the hook by the door, and fled the laboratory.

* * *

THE STREETS BOILED WITH CHAOS. People crying, injured, terrified.

No one noticed a naked man covered in a black cape hurrying toward where the earth spoke to him.

The cemetery beneath tall cypresses swaying with the tremors proved quiet, save for the cats, desperate for shelter, dashing from tombstone to tombstone or scrambling up tall tree trunks. Screams from the streets reached the stone-paved paths, echoing between marble sepulchers. As if in a tantrum, the earth became more violent, tossing gravestones like chess pieces. Coffins spilled from unearthed graves and broke open on impact, disgorging bones, rich silks, gold, and colored gemstones.

Terra firma showered Leukan with blessings as he walked the cemetery paths, taking fealty from the displaced earth and stones. A veritable feast of power. As if it were an escort, a mighty movement heaved the ground up under him, then forced it down, propelling Leukan onto a pristine marble path toward a white marble sepulcher crowned with three domes. The ornate brass and iron gate creaked open as if in welcome. He walked on smooth pavings into the tomb, the cold black soil the quake had scattered inside as fragrant as exotic perfume. A statue of a woman lay broken on the floor, her delicately chiseled hand rising from the mounds of dirt scattered about.

Leukan held the satchel close. Deep inside the ornate sepulcher, the earth gently rocked, welcoming him. A gold wall split, earth pouring in as a greeting. He lay upon the tumbled soil, absorbing the strength and power from centuries of pent-up forces.

* * *

A DUSTING on his nose and cheeks, like light kisses. Leukan opened his eyes and brushed the earth from his face, surprised to feel his warm fingers touch his nose and cheeks, whisking the particles away. For an eternity, he had moved phantom limbs and assumed the soil would stay on his face, his extremities existing only in the aura of light that surrounded him. But now, his arms, his body, were real.

The earth pressed close, covering his legs and torso, filling him with strength, renewing his powers, welcoming him home. A tremor from deep down shivered through the tomb, a tremor only he could sense. The last vestiges of terra firma's acknowledgment that one of her own had at long last returned.

Fine particles of soil fell from him as he rose from his partial immersion, affirming the earth's blessings with his right hand to his heart. Lord Derrien's leather satchel lay inside a niche in the mausoleum's glittering gold wall. Leukan unlatched it. Inside, Tanythe blinked, her eyes opening wide, welcoming him as she peered up through the darkness.

"When we reunite you and your body, we will both have the strength for speech. Perhaps then we can break Bahl's curse on our mind talk." At the rich sound of his voice, Tanythe's eyes lit with a glow that rivaled the reflection of the gold walls. Leukan drew the leather flap over Tanythe's head and latched the satchel.

They would need her crystal. He would have to find Lord Derrien.

CHAPTER 38

*R*emy kicked away debris littering the street in front of him, the motion shifting Simmery's weight on his shoulders. He stumbled and almost lost his balance. With a spot cleared as best he could, he lay Simmery on the hard cobblestones just as another tremor rumbled through the city, inducing screams, shouts, and the gut-wrenching noises of the earth moving.

Falling onto all fours, Remy clutched at the cobblestones, trying to find something solid, some support that could give him solace from the earth tearing under him. But there was no escape.

Lord in heaven, he had no idea how terrifying an earthquake could be. Catching his breath, he knelt beside the Gov, trying to control his panic as he fumbled in his pocket for his handkerchief. Blood from Simmery's head wound soaked into the linen, dripping thick red drops. Tossing the sodden cloth aside, Remy unbound his cravat. Finally, a practical use for the cursed thing. And tied it around the deep cut on the Gov's head.

"Nasty wound. Let's move further into the middle of the street, away from that building," said Lord Grimond from behind him. Remy turned in the direction Grimond pointed, then looked up at the building directly across from them and gasped, inhaling a mouthful of dust. He spat. The four-story structure's facade, cracked and crumbling, was surely about to collapse. As he lifted the Gov by the shoulders and Grimond bent to take the Gov's feet, Remy glanced a few buildings down at the Society's old palace. It seemed untouched, and the remaining fellows and servants were streaming out the front door.

"Lift now," Grimond said, just as the street heaved upwards, then sideways, tossing Grimond to the left, Remy opposite, and the Gov God knows where. With an eerie, prolonged groan and a deafening bang, the earth cracked open down the middle of the street, sliding the Gov into its dark maws.

"Simmery!" Remy couldn't hear his desperate cry over the other screams, over the lumbering cacophony of the earth's readjusting. He ran to where he last saw the Gov and peered down the dark crevice. The white of Simmery's shirt caught a glimmer of light.

"Lord Grimond, over here." Remy beckoned to Grimond, who staggered toward him. The crevice was wider here. It slanted downward at an angle that looked navigable if the rocks and soil held.

Praying the earth would be still, Remy started down, his hand gripping the solid edge at the top. Without a sound, another tremor threw him out of the crevice onto the street. He landed hard on his side, his breath knocked out of him. Gasping like a landed fish, he lay helpless as Lord Grimond squatted beside him.

"Hold on there. Give it a minute or two, and you'll be right as rain. I'll see to Simmonds-Snow." Grimond disappeared from Remy's view as he bent to look into the crevice. Underneath Remy, the ground moved like a living thing. In a sickening wave, the cobblestones buckled. He struggled to rise but found only air under his flailing hands. He fell. Nothing to grasp to break his fall. Perhaps he was joining the Gov inside a crevice.

Remy stared up from the surrounding darkness into concerned faces far above. Dirt and detritus crumbled onto him from the steep sides of the hole where he lay. Spitting out the bitter soil, he turned his head. He had landed on a rough bed of cold, hard earth and stones. My God, he was caught in the jaws of the earth. What would happen to him when they snapped shut?

Yet the earth cradled around him. An odd warmth emanated from the cold dirt, each tiny piece a fragment of a long-dead plant, animal, or human, jumbled together as in a recipe to create something new, something greater than its parts. He turned from the distant voices calling from above as the continuum of life flowed into his body. Heat built inside him, and he could have sworn that, for a few minutes, his body lifted a few inches from the bed of earth.

"We're sending for a rope," someone yelled down. Was it Khalil or Grimond?

Remy's body touched the ground again, settling into his earth bed. He willed the amazing sensation back, but everything stayed inert. He lay still, listening. Strange, throughout these occurrences, Leukan came to mind, as if he were conversing with him. When Remy attempted to change the vision to Tanythe, his mind went blank, then again filled with the image of Leukan.

"We're trying to help the Governor," Kahlil called, his face appearing for a moment at the top of the crevice. The crowd of faces bobbed, vanishing and reappearing, as they murmured one to the other. The earth seemed to sway, probably his distorted senses and the result of his fall. Remy clutched at the ground, now strangely grown cold.

A pebble hit his forehead and bounced off. He turned his head, but shadows obscured where he lay so far from the light. A clod of soft dirt crushed against his cheek, sending grit into his eye. Another landed on his chest. He grunted at the impact. Then the earth dropped out from under him. The faces above receded, bearing expressions of horror as they vanished into an avalanche of pebbles and sheets of soil.

* * *

REMY OPENED his eyes to darkness. Something warm pressed hard on both sides of his body. He tried to reposition himself, but whenever he moved, the space his movement created became immediately occupied by soil and rocks, squeezing him. On one side, tiny pinpoints of light poured through a thick screen.

His body tensed. His scalp seemed to stiffen and shrink. The same feeling he got when the hairs on his head raised like a dog's hackles.

Where the hell was he?

Nearby, Remy glimpsed a flickering movement. Muscles tight with fear, he stared and made out shapes. He breathed the sharp, coppery odor of blood and the rank stench of sweat. Through the dark, a speck of light revealed a pair of eyes. They blinked. They stared, then blinked again, and he knew they recognized him at the same time he recognized them: The swarthy man with the beady eyes.

Remy opened his mouth to scream, but no sound came.

He was inside the bag with the heads squarely between the beady-eyed man and Leukan.

He struggled to stand, open the bag, and crawl out, but he couldn't find his arms. His legs would not obey him.

The beady-eyed man's pupils became pinpoints of light streaming into him like bullet trails fired from a distance, penetrating his body. A bat's wings brushed his skin from the inside. His body filled with spiders, their thin, hairy legs pricking his organs, muscles, and bones like needles. Snakes slithered through his arteries and veins, their scales hard and brittle. Rats' snouts brushed their whiskers on his insides, and their sharp teeth gnawed at his muscles.

Remy's blood ran like a river as he screamed and screamed until blackness covered his mouth in a billowing cloud. He could not breathe. His desperate gasps for air hissed in his ears.

* * *

"REMY!" The slap stung his face. A burst of cold spread over his head, then down his chest. He coughed as he inhaled liquid. Choking. He couldn't get his breath. Hands under his back lifted him at a slant, then pounded between his shoulder blades.

He breathed in deep and long. At last. Air.

No gleaming evil eyes. The rank smell had vanished, replaced with lavender?

"Remy." Pheodora's soft voice. Her smooth hands cradled his face. "I thought you'd never stop gasping." She held a glass to his mouth.

"Here." The water made his dry throat sting. Still, he drank, relieved it wasn't scotch, which would sting worse. With that thought, he opened his eyes and took in their room at the house in Turkey.

CHAPTER 39

"*L*ady Pheodora. Quick, quick. Earth shakes. We go." Even as Remy's wife slept, Bahl could hear what must be her maid's panicked voice. He felt a hand on Pheodora's arm, shaking her body, the body that he now inhabited. Perhaps the maid could wake this woman when he, the great Shaman Bahl, could not.

He repositioned the essence of himself, his phantom body and head, inside Pheodora. Accustomed to being cramped in a bag with the two gods, the space he occupied now was roomy. He should be able to walk about with ease, but this woman, Remy's wife, proved willful and made it difficult for him to have his way.

There it was again. He didn't have to wake Pheodora for him to hear the awful groaning of the earth as it adjusted its foundation.

Still, she slept. He must make her move. If something heavy fell on her, she might die. Then he would be forced to inhabit the maid, and how could he gain proper access to Lord Remy Derrien through his wife's lady's maid?

He kicked and pushed against Pheodora's insides. At last, she opened her eyes.

He could see now. The room was a shambles, objects shattered, the floor littered with debris. As he watched, the earth heaved, toppling a massive wardrobe to the floor with a deafening crash. Pheodora screeched as she bolted upright, bedcovers sliding down her body.

"Lady, earth moves. We go." Bahl felt the hard grip of the maid's hands as she helped Pheodora from the bed.

"The footmen are clearing the way." A woman's voice, another maid, tossed aside the smaller newly fallen debris after the footmen had cleared a path through the larger pieces.

If Pheodora would let Bahl, he could guide her, but her fear and the servants' attempts to aid her as she wobbled down the stairs only hindered him. As things were, Pheodora's body proved clumsy. He guided his mind into Pheodora's, trying once more for control. She was terrified, even more than yesterday at the laboratory when she discovered his and Tanythe's heads, but now that she was more awake, he found a route where she was receptive.

He guided her body as they hurried into the street. When she was safe, Bahl withdrew his influence, keeping his presence more subtle as he left her in the care of the servants. If he retained this much control and sustained it, he could bend this woman to his will and, through her, reach Lord Remy Derrien, who would be his path to Tanythe.

Then Bahl could obtain the boon that would make him a god. Since he had no flesh and bone body, it was a delicate matter working his plan.

* * *

THE EARTH GROANED, a deep rumbling with shrill, prolonged shrieks like enormous millstones straining against an impossible task. Pheodora felt the vibrations in her chest and longed to run and escape the ground trembling under her.

Let go. I will lead you. Just listen.

That voice from her dream, husky and deep. Where had she heard it? So familiar, yet how could something so familiar make her feel violated and helpless?

She squeezed her eyes shut from the brightness of being in the open, from the exertion of trying to push that voice from her mind. When she opened them, she saw her neighbors and their servants spill into the street, some pulling on their vests and scarves. From this far away, Pheodora tried to see if there was any damage to her home, so different from hers and Remy's stately brick townhome in London. Like the other Turkish houses, theirs was wooden, with two balconies on either side of the portico. All seemingly intact, thank the Lord, which was more than she could say about the inside.

Remy's laboratory occupied an ancient stone palace, stone being less flexible than wood. She pictured the Society's high, vaulted ceilings, the dome above the hall, the quake shaking the palace as violently as the surrounding houses. Was her husband safe?

Let me guide you, so you will be safe.

Pheodora looked around, but she knew the voice was the man from Remy's laboratory still inside her, assuring her he would help. Despite her skin growing clammy, her scalp prickling, a warmth radiated from her core.

Her servants gathered close as the last of them streamed from her house. One of the young girls was crying, which sparked Pheodora to worry once more. The Society's building had held up during the last quake. Thinking of Remy, Pheodora clutched her charm against the evil eye, the gold chain taut against her neck.

Remy had relayed Kahlil's frightening description of the 1766 earthquake five years ago. She had seen evidence of that quake in the still-broken pavings of some of the city's streets and many of the beautiful old buildings' crumbled facades. Even parts of the ancient wall surrounding Constantinople, which had stood for millennia, had been reduced to rubble. The same earthquake had brought up the monstrosities she encountered yesterday in the laboratory. That scene grew vivid inside her mind: the head with the beady eyes speaking. *This power can be yours*, in the same gravelly voice she now heard in her mind. Remy, holding her wrists, his voice frighteningly furious, saying the word *Enough*. The shadow, she knew somehow it was the beady-eyed man's shadow, rushing at her, suddenly inside her body, buttoning himself up as if she were a greatcoat.

A new tremor rippled through the solid stones of the street.

Her maid, Anisya, wrapped her arm around Pheodora's waist. "L-lady," Anisya's voice wavered in fear. The footman behind braced them both by the shoulders.

It was only yesterday that the beady-eyed man had inhabited her, and now a disastrous earthquake. What manner of evil had this severed head brought?

Why hadn't Nene Rose sent word that there would be an earthquake? Although Remy had scoffed at what Phe told him of her soothsayer's fortune-telling, Pheodora knew the woman had the gift of foresight. *Gypsy imposter*, Remy called Nene Rose.

"Lady." Anisya tugged her by the arm. "We sit now. More steady this way." On the street cobblestones, her maid snuggled up close, her warmth making Phe aware of how cold she was.

"Less afraid now, no?" Anisya whispered. They had been reduced to this silence of dread, with the earth demonstrating how small and vulnerable they were.

Another tremor shook the ground. Pheodora leaned into her maid. A few screams from the crowd faded into the great quiet, as if a sound might rouse the beast once more.

Pheodora had many things to be afraid of. If she mentioned to Remy or anyone that she believed this man inhabited her, they would put her in an asylum. But she could confide in Nene Rose about the voice in her head trying to take over. In Pheodora's visions, the man had been a great man, someone with power. Otherwise, how was it possible for him to be living without a body? Nene Rose could tell her about this man.

Despite her fear, Pheodora had been polite to him and careful of what she thought and said, just as she would with a guest in her home.

"Lady Derrien?" Her maid clutched her hand. "You must not sleep now. If we need to flee—"

"Even the birds have lost their song," whispered the footman behind them. "Brace for a bigger tremor."

I will aid you with my power.

Pheodora squeezed her eyes closed, trying to shut out the man's voice, when a booming sound louder than a cannon shot made her eyes fly open. They all jumped to their feet, staggering from the violent tremor. The balconies on the house next to Pheodora's splintered to the ground in a cloud of dust and smoke.

The crowd screamed as one, a piercing caterwaul, and craned their necks, trying to see where to go for safety. More cracking, more crashing as parts of other houses broke off and fell to screams and cries for help. The air became foul with dust and smoke. Pheodora spotted red-orange flames in the ruins of a building down the street. Debris scattered in the air and fell to the ground with thuds. Dogs barked. Pheodora covered her head with her shawl and sat down again as one with her maids and footmen on the hard, cold street. They huddled together for warmth, for safety, for reassurance.

The horses' whinnying in the stables broke the silence.

"They feel another one coming," someone called out. The people crowded closer.

Before this, Tarek and the stable hands must have kept the horses under control. Pheodora tried to see the stables, but the house and trees hid them. Still, they must be mostly intact, or the poor animals would be running the streets, fleeing from something impossible to outrun.

You must find your husband.

Was that the man's voice in her head? It sounded different. Perhaps this time, it was her voice, worrying about Remy. Pheodora shook the dust from her shawl. With Anisya and her servants by her side, with the crowds in the street surrounding her, she surveyed the wreckage.

Thousands of years ago, I was a king's magus—

Pheodora shut her eyes, willing the voice to be silent.

—and gained him much gold and many battles. You have seen with your own eyes how I still live after all this time. I can show you the way of power.

She could not stop him. Pheodora put her hand to her brow as if she could touch the voice and know immediately whether it was good or evil. But, of course, her fingers brushed smooth skin, and nothing happened.

Who was this man? What did he want from her?

CHAPTER 40

*R*emy had endured Pheodora's repeated pleas to stay home.

"Surely the laboratory could wait another day," she said after he woke that morning. Then she availed him of all the reasons he should postpone going in. She went at him again while his valet assisted him with dressing for his return after the earthquake.

"See there, merely putting on your shirt and pants has weakened you from your ordeal in the quake, even with the help of your man. It's been three days, Remy. No one would mind your resting one more day." Pheodora pushed a stray curl behind his left ear.

"When I visited Snowy yesterday," she continued, "the doctor had assured him his face would be as good as new despite its frightful bruising. But something deeper has happened to you and is less easily cured." Her eyes clouded with worry.

She attempted to dissuade him one last time as he checked his pockets and waited for the araba to pull adjacent to the porch. He still hadn't convinced his wife he was fine to go to the Society, and gave it one more try. "Phe, I am not weak, merely overcome with the thought of the laboratory destroyed.

"Phe, I'm not weak. Merely overcome with concern for the laboratory. I can't rest until I know what survived. Especially the microscope and other instruments. And with Lord Simmonds-Snow unable to go, it falls to me." With her fondness for the microscope, how could she counter that?

He placed his hands on Phe's shoulders and held her at arm's length. Pheodora, resplendent in her Turkish costume. By Jove, he was becoming fond of his foreign princess adorned with jewels and turbans and those wonderful pantaloons or whatever the ladies called them.

"But, Remy—"

Just then, the araba pulled up, and he kissed her goodbye, putting a stop to her last-minute attempts to dissuade him. She held out a small bouquet of red roses. "Take these. For luck." She kissed him again, a peck on his cheek, and grinned. "Yes, I knew you'd go no matter what, so I cut these earlier. Let's hope the laboratory is intact and you can spare a suitable jar for these lovelies."

Red roses for love. Holding them, their spicy-sweet fragrance filling the coach, he waved to Phe, who waved back, a wan smile below her concerned eyes. But he barely saw her for worrying about Tanythe and Leukan. Had the quake killed them? The araba swayed while turning into another street, and he gripped the wall strap, trying to vanquish the images of the battered and broken bodies he had seen carried from the quake's rubble.

Since the earthquake three days ago, Remy had not heard from Tanythe. At her request, he had left her and Leukan in the laboratory. She had been staring at Leukan, who lay unresponsive on the table, plaster falling around them as the earth shook.

Remy envisioned a chunk of the ceiling crushing them both. Overcome with an emotion he had no name for, he stared out the araba's latticed window at the quake's damage to Constantinople. Perhaps he should have accommodated Pheodora's plea to stay at home a few more days. Falling apart in the laboratory would do no one any good. Already, one member of his family had done so. Phe knew what she was talking about.

* * *

THE ARABA FOLLOWED the normal route to the Society, the horse's bells tinkling gaily, a contrast to the piles of rubble and destroyed buildings along the way. Several times, the driver had to detour because debris filled the street. Attempting another route, he turned down a narrow lane whose overhanging balconies served as a kind of roof, reducing the morning sun to orange-gold stripes breaking up the blue shadows.

They passed under a building's crumbling facade, the rickety wooden balcony tilted at sixty degrees toward the street, clothes draped on the crooked railing, looking as if the bodies had slipped out. Remy counted the seconds until they were out from under the sagging construction. If there was an aftershock, the structure would fall, and, light as the balcony looked in its ruinous state, it could easily crush the araba. He viewed the building out the back window as they left and shivered. By Jove, even a hearty sneeze could send it plummeting to the street. When they encountered a collapsed minaret blocking the way like a long, fat finger in a cone hat laid across the street, the driver was once more forced to detour.

At last, they turned onto the street in front of the Society. During the quake, when Remy had fled outside carrying the Gov, this area had been covered in rubble. The crevices and cracks were still there, but most of the debris, stone, bricks, and metal had been cleared, and the Society building looked the same as when Remy had first seen it months ago. In his haste to check the laboratory, he jumped from the araba and almost turned his ankle.

"Phe's roses," he muttered. Turning back, he picked up the bouquet that he had left on the seat, then paid the driver. He used his key to enter, as the guard wasn't hovering by the front door. Was anyone at the Society today?

In the long hallway, the servants bustled about, cleaning. Several ancient statues from the niches still lay broken on the floor. One looked as if someone had cut it into pieces and laid it out.

"Good to see you, sir. How is Governor?" asked Kahlil as he swished his mop on the floor, making a dark streak through the fine coating of white plaster that dulled the marble's shine.

"He is much better today, thank you." Remy hurried past other servants hauling debris, stuffing small items in their pockets, scrubbing walls, and sloshing water in buckets gone milky with plaster.

Pheodora had restocked the laboratory's first aid kit and made another for his office, so he could help if anyone sustained injuries from cleaning up.

The laboratory door looked unchanged, the doorframe still in plumb. When Remy unlocked it, the door swung open with barely a creak. Heart beating as if he were being chased, he rushed inside. The light from the windows illuminated the room enough that he needn't bother lighting the lamps. He stopped just inside the door, fearful of what he might see.

A ghostly white dusting of plaster covered everything. He paused at the microscope, which seemed to have escaped damage, and set Phe's roses beside it. A red petal brushed the dust, looking powdered with frost.

The two tables Leukan and Tanythe had occupied were coated with the same fine film of plaster dust as if nothing had been there. Which meant they had left soon after he and the Gov, at the earthquake's beginning, unless they had taken shelter inside the laboratory.

"Tanythe. Leukan," he called out, his voice amplified by the plaster walls. He halted, listening, but heard only the faint echo of their names. As he hunted for them, Remy stepped over items that had been thrown from the shelves and maneuvered around upended tables and other furniture.

He peered over boxes, under tables, and in nooks and crannies, but found nothing. His pace grew frantic as he continued, then he realized he was sending himself into a frenzy. Mentally fatigued, he dropped into a chair and thought of poor Leukan sliding down a chair slippery with blood. Images of Tanythe and Leukan, as he had left them, kept appearing. Leukan sprawled on the table, covered in blood that he had vomited, and as good as dead. Tanythe, without her crystal, helpless beside him.

Why hadn't she messaged him through mind talk?

He cupped his hands to his mouth. "Tanythe! Leukan!"

His stomach lurched as he thought he heard a faint reply. Was it Leukan's voice? Then disappointment set in as he recognized the distorted echo of his voice. He was overcome, his insides hollow. Perhaps he should have waited one more day, as Pheodora had suggested.

Remy checked under a table he had missed. Nothing there but dust and debris. He must stop this and resign himself to hoping Leukan had revived and carried Tanythe someplace safe.

But he couldn't convince himself of that unlikely scenario, and kept imagining answers to his recurring question: God in heaven, how did they escape, with Leukan practically catatonic and Tanythe without a body?

He had seen Tanythe's magic. She could have protected them even without her crystal. And Leukan? Perhaps he had actually recovered, gained his true power, and stolen Tanythe away.

Before he fled with the Gov, Remy had noticed her beatific expression, eyes overflowing with devoted love each time she gazed at Leukan, who lay beside her, as still as a corpse. He hadn't moved or blinked since Remy and the Gov had rushed him into the laboratory. They had tried all they knew to cure him, but nothing made a difference. Leukan had a heartbeat and breathed, but remained unresponsive.

Tanythe had never looked at Remy the way she did Leukan. He closed his eyes. The fullness in his heart when he envisioned Tanythe's azure eyes, when he remembered her voice in his mind, flattened into a dry, dull ache.

CHAPTER 41

*R*emy's desperate, failed search through the room with its stacks of trunks and boxes left him physically and emotionally spent. As he straightened the room, rearranging trunks displaced by the quake, he dreaded finding Leukan's mangled body clutching the remains of Tanythe's head, their eyes dulled in a final death.

In the hallway, servants bustled in a haze of plaster dust, hauling debris, sweeping, mopping. Remy motioned to Khalil. "Choose a few of the most reliable workers. Have them ready to clean the laboratory when I come out again. It may be a while, so they can continue out here."

Back in the laboratory, Remy tapped his fingers against his thigh, something nagging at his memory.

He rushed to the back of the room, which looked as bad as the hall. It was still there, worse for wear but intact, and still staring the nastiest stare Remy had ever seen. The third and last head. The man with the beady eyes.

Remy left the laboratory, locked the door behind him, and retrieved a bucket of clean water from Khalil. Back inside, he gathered clean cloths from a cabinet and approached the head, now doubly precious. The only one left. Fighting with misgivings, Remy stared at it for a moment. Like everything else in the laboratory, it was dusted in white. The man's coarse hair looked gray, his dusky skin paler. His eyes radiated malice, but when he noticed Remy in front of him, he affected a more pleasant demeanor. Certain of what he had seen, Remy forced his expression into one as pleasant as possible and studied the head.

"Your companions are missing, and I must hide you for safety's sake. Before that, I need your cooperation when I remove the dust covering you." This was the first time Remy had spoken to him, and the man looked pleased. Perhaps he had been one of those kind souls cursed with a face that put people off.

"I'll take that as a yes," said Remy. Hearing his voice made him feel as alone in the laboratory as the remaining head.

He dipped a cloth in the bucket of water and wrung it out. When he put the cloth to the man's face, the wall nearest them blurred into a great plain, stretching away to a far mountain, an army silhouetted on the crest. The air became heavy with anticipation. An intense, manic energy danced around Remy's body. His fear, his unease, was manifesting this odd occurrence.

Trying not to be distracted, he blotted the man's face carefully, turning the cloth as it dirtied with dust. In the illusion, the army swarmed down the hill towards Remy. The clatter of weapons, chariots, and footsteps of hundreds of soldiers filled the laboratory. Remy dropped the cloth and stepped back.

"Are you threatening me?" Remy blurted. Then regretted it. The other heads had powers. This one had them as well. Best not to antagonize these beings.

The army came closer, near enough to make out the soldiers' faces. "Make it stop." Remy heard the alarm in his voice. The horrific cacophony of the army suddenly muted. The vision came into sharp focus. A man riding a fine stallion halted before Remy and saluted.

By heaven, he had the same face as the beady-eyed man on the table.

Early morning sunlight glinted off his peaked bronze helmet just as the army arrived at a white marble temple. On the steps, a woman with long red hair stood by an ebony-complexioned man. Remy blinked. He leaned forward to better see them.

"Tanythe? Leukan?" Remy called out. Was the army coming to save or harm them? Remy squinted at the vision, but it faded into the laboratory wall.

On the table in front of him, the beady-eyed man's eyes glowed, beckoning images swirling inside. Had those figures on the steps been Tanythe and

Leukan? If Remy could find out where they were, he might be able to save them.

He leaned closer, nose to nose, to peer into the images in the beady-eyed man's eyes. Remy glimpsed Tanythe inside a reflection, but she looked away, her red hair swinging as she turned. Leukan, behind her, met Remy's gaze.

"Tell me where they are," Remy pleaded. "We can help them."

Garbled words appeared inside his mind. The head was attempting to mind talk with him. Remy leaned closer, looking into the man's dark brown eyes, trying once more to catch images of Tanythe and Leukan there.

A rapid movement in the head's eyes. A shadow leapt from the man's pupils. Remy side-stepped and threw his hand out to push it away. In a rush of cold air, something brushed his arm. A dark shape glanced past him. Remy's flesh burst into goosebumps. He batted at where he last glimpsed the dark shape, feeling as if he had blundered into a massive spiderweb.

"Tanythe? Leukan?" Remy cried as he whirled around, desperately looking for them. Had the beady-eyed man brought them back?

Then Remy heard a voice: *"Be still. Welcome me. Together, we can find Tanythe and Leukan."*

Staggering from the visions, the threatening shape attacking him, and the garbled mind talk, Remy tripped over a wooden crate. He plunged to the hard floor and lay there in the debris, jags of pain ripping through his body.

What in Jupiter's name had occurred? Was this another manifestation of his possible madness? He looked up, expecting the shadow to loom over him. Nothing was there.

His yearning for Tanythe and Leukan hadn't and wouldn't fetch them from the ether. Examining the wall for a trace of his vision, he rose to his feet. His palm closed over something lumpy and warm. Remy jerked his hand away and let out a hoarse cry.

The beady-eyed man's head lay beside him, cheek to the floor, staring up at him, his brow furrowed.

Remy scuttled backward. For a moment, he sensed anger flash through the head's eyes, but when the man saw that Remy looked at him, he affected a sad countenance.

That was it. The man was playing him.

Despite being furious, Remy adopted a concerned expression. His fury, like heat from raging fire, radiated from him. He stopped himself from kicking the head across the room.

Thoughts rolled through his brain: 'This is the last head. I cannot destroy it, no matter what its game is.' On the floor next to him lay one of the cloths. Keeping his face turned away, Remy picked it up and dropped it over the head. Dust be damned.

He staggered, his head and legs aching, and rummaged through the cabinets, found a suitable box, and set it on the floor sideways, top open and facing the man. With his foot, he nudged the head inside, closed the box, and locked the cursed thing inside a chest.

The head had tried to do something to him. Remy was sure of it. It lured him close with visions of Tanythe and Leukan. Much like mind talk, but this was different, images instead of words, and exactly what Remy had wanted.

He and walked to the door, intent on leaving. But this was his laboratory. The last head had been locked inside a trunk surrounded by boxes and other trunks, far away from where he would work. The man was only a head. He couldn't touch Remy now.

He mourned all the discoveries he, Tanythe, and Leukan would have made together, all the possibilities. His future had been full of promise, but the earthquake had buried and destroyed parts of Constantinople, killed and injured hundreds or more, grievously wounded Simmery, and quashed Remy's bright prospects.

What would he do now?

"The Elixir!" Remy's voice rang through the laboratory, sending the plaster-dust motes swirling in the shaft of light nearest him.

But first, the laboratory must be cleaned. He rushed into the hall, almost colliding with Khalil, who was mopping.

"I am ready. Have them clean the room fast and carefully. Mind you, they should sprinkle the floor with clean water before they mop up the dust. I want none of it floating in the air like out here."

As the four servants cleaned the laboratory, Remy moved the microscope to a newly cleaned table. He put the incident with the last head out of his mind and concentrated on his task. Remy dampened his cloths and carefully wiped the microscope, cursing that he hadn't thrown a cover over it before he fled.

The servants brought a sense of reality to the room, making the strangeness of what happened with the beady-eyed man fade. In about an hour, Remy would have a pristine laboratory and the silence he relished. He wiped the microscope lens a fourth time, the glass clear and shining. Tomorrow, he would send a request for a room to be built inside the laboratory to secure special equipment like the microscope and Leyden jar, their newest addition. Simmery would send up the request with highest priority.

"Blast." Remy's voice boomed through the laboratory. His outburst made the servants pause. He held up his hand. "Carry on."

The Gov would blame him for Leukan's and Tanythe's disappearance. Not only would Simmery deny his special equipment room, he might very well sack him. In that case, he must be prepared.

He rushed to the cabinet. How many weeks had it been since he checked the Elixir? Too long. So much had happened. Still, he should record the Elixir's status every day. His carelessness could have cost him his last hope.

As Remy turned the cabinet lock, he touched the crystal around his neck for luck. He opened the door slowly.

The vessel stood upright, the sturdy glass clear, not a single hairline crack. Even the small jar, containing the cloth with remnants of Elixir in which the fly had resurrected, was intact. Remy wilted in relief and took a long breath, steadying his hands.

There had been three ounces in the jar. It looked as if the amount was the same, the substance level with the line he had incised in the glass when he had first filled it.

The vessel with the Elixir felt warm, yet the cabinet was as cool as a deep cave. He held the jar as if his life depended on it.

And perhaps, in some small way, it did.

CHAPTER 42

The next day, Remy unlocked his laboratory, hurried inside, closed the door, and relocked it. He breathed in the silence as he took in the sparkling clean surfaces and equipment, the colors vivid sans their white plaster-dust coating. The Gov wouldn't return for at least a week, most likely several, as he recovered from his earthquake injuries. In the meantime, Remy would use the interval he had left to continue his work.

First, he must prepare in case Simmery decided on a brief visit to the laboratory before he was fully healed. The Gov didn't know Tanythe and Leukan were missing, and hiding the beady-eyed man's head could worsen things, for Simmery might think Remy had hidden this head to study by himself.

His whole body protesting, Remy opened the trunk and removed the box imprisoning the last head. With gloved hands, he carefully placed the head in its original spot on the table that had been occupied by the three heads.

After Remy had set him there, the man's crafty eyes followed him as he walked away. Remy cringed, recalling his vision. Like Tanythe and Leukan, the man possessed powers. Only he had proved deceitful and dangerous.

Remy would have to be on his toes. But he had placed the beady-eyed man in the back of the laboratory and was planning to run the Elixir experiment at the front. Not far enough away for Remy by any means, but that was all he could do, given the circumstances.

Putting the last head out of his mind, Remy began. With a surgeon's care, he removed the glass lid on the Elixir jar, inserted a small metal spatula, scooped up a drop of Elixir, and placed it on a slide of thinnest mica.

Through the microscope's lens, the Elixir appeared clear, unlike the water that Khalil drew from the well, which contained rod-shaped and circular organisms. Remy perused his substance log for comparisons and found that the Elixir, viewed through the microscope, resembled honey, but, unlike honey, it was as clear as pure water. He had starred his note about aloe vera, stating that it was most similar organically, as well as being clear with the same mucus-like texture.

He removed the slide. The Elixir drop hadn't spread out on the mica. A fleeting, faint fragrance met his nostrils, and he held the slide closer. A lemony citrus scent filled the air, similar to the Magnolia Grandiflora, which was brought to Constantinople by European gardeners around 1700, seventy years ago. The odor grew stronger and, for no reason that Remy understood, he began salivating.

When he first discovered the Elixir, Remy's hands had been coated with the substance, slick, smooth, and cool, similar to the gel inside an aloe leaf. Remy set the slide on the table. With a clean spatula, he transferred a small amount of the Elixir from the slide onto his fingertip and rubbed it with his thumb. Cool, silky, and wet, the same as his first impression.

Remy smeared what was left of the drop onto his tongue. He tasted nothing. Again, he salivated an alarming amount, so much that it filled his mouth. Afterward, his mouth felt dry, as if he had sucked on a lemon, but with no taste.

While entering these facts into the log, his eyelids drooped. Either the Elixir worked fast to cause drowsiness, or the strain of the earthquake was finally taking its toll. Remy forced his lids open. He must continue, for he may not have this chance again. The laboratory was the Gov's province now, and the Gov claimed the right to anything discovered. But Simmery didn't have to know about the Elixir.

Remy looked over his shoulder at the door he had locked when he first arrived today. He had estimated that Simmery would need time to convalesce properly, but the old rascal could recover speedily and return any day. Any minute. And the Gov had a key.

What seemed a few moments later, Remy raised his head. For a panicked instant, he had no clue where he was. Then he realized he was in the laboratory, sitting in a chair in front of the microscope. It was late afternoon by the look of the light streaming through the upper windows. Blast, he had drifted off. For how long?

He stared at the table, his mind in a fog. Jars with lids, ceramic bowls, his log. He had been working with the Elixir.

And dreamed.

He stood up. Still so drowsy. A vivid dream. Tanythe with a body. So real. She had come to him. They were naked in a sumptuous four-poster bed draped with dark blue velvet, her hair a red slash across the embroidered white-on-white linens. When she leaned over him, her pale breasts brushing his chest, the scarlet curtain of her hair created an intimate chamber where no one could disturb them. They entwined in every position Remy had ever imagined, and some that far exceeded his fantasies. Her touch felt as delicate and ethereal as diaphanous silk, as soft as an angel's wing brushing his skin.

He rubbed his eyes. On his desk, his log lay open, his handwriting small and cramped. The last entry recorded that he had tasted the Elixir. Was that the cause of his dream? Would tasting the Elixir call Tanythe?

The sound of his chair, as he pushed it back and came to his feet, broke the dream's spell. He unlocked the laboratory door, locked it from the outside, and hurried to his office. As he opened the door, stirring up the plaster dust, he remembered he hadn't given Khalil permission to clean this office after the earthquake.

Some items had fallen off the shelves, and his desk lay in disarray on its side, his chair turned over. On top of the liquor cabinet, the remains of a vase lay in shards, interspersed with last week's flowers. The flowers, the same color and type of rose that Phe had given him this morning, lay withered and brown throughout the plaster dust. Remy picked through the broken glass and ended up with a handful of dead petals. He carefully wrapped them in his handkerchief and slid them into his pocket.

Back in the laboratory, he chose a few dead petals that were whole and brushed them clean with a soft paintbrush that he used for other plant specimens. He set a dead rose petal on a square of stiff paper, then plucked a fresh petal from one of Phe's fresh roses and set it two inches away on the same paper. Remy dipped a long-handled, one-sixteenth teaspoon into the Elixir, then held it over the dead rose petal. The gel clung to the spoon until he tapped it, and the Elixir dropped onto the middle of the shriveled brown petal.

The substance sat there glistening, then, as if it were melting, the Elixir expanded to cover the petal.

Impossible.

The small amount of Elixir appeared to increase in volume for the task. Then, as if a wand had wafted over the brittle petal, it became silky, red, and supple, identical to the petal sitting nearby that Remy had plucked from Phe's fresh bouquet.

The transformation proved as rapid as the mangled fly's. He transferred the paper square with the two petals into a small glass case, then sealed the glass lid with wax.

Remy stood transfixed for a moment, staring at the fresh red petals. His brain worked as if it were bound and chained, then broke the bonds and feverishly put together this discovery's potential.

Yes. Yes. Yes.

This experiment could be easily recreated and would convince anyone, even the most critical fault-finder, of the miracle of the Elixir.

Remy glanced at the glass jar holding the substance, sitting on the table, completely vulnerable. If he broke the glass, the Elixir would be lost. Remy became paralyzed by the thought. He had so little of the substance. Could he make or grow more?

The Leyden jar.

Months ago, he had sent the Gov a request to purchase a Leyden jar and had been disappointed when it never arrived with the new shipments. Then, on a grim Monday, Simmery barreled into the laboratory and set a Leyden jar next to the microscope.

"Our lab now has the latest equipment," he had stated nonchalantly, but there was a gleam in his eye.

Electrical experiments with the Leyden jar had been the rage for years, using substances from beer to blood, and had been conducted with varied results. Among these, some had reported volume increase. Remy had never replicated those experiments, but the details had shown that the successful trials used a rather small dosage of electricity.

If Remy ran an electric spark through the Elixir, would it stimulate the precious substance to grow?

CHAPTER 43

*R*emy set the Leyden jar in the middle of an empty wooden table, which bridged two tables on either side, making a U-shape. Alone on the tabletop, the Leyden jar looked odd. He laughed. The unique apparatus could be mistaken for a too-small candy jar with a peculiar top or a miniature butter churn that had lost its handle.

At Trinity College, Remy had observed experiments with the device and found it difficult to believe it could generate electricity. But when he touched the metal ball at the top of the charged Leyden jar, he had yanked his hand away, shaking it and cursing from the sharp sting. Worse than a wasp's. He had never forgotten.

This modern Leyden jar stood eight inches tall with a four-inch diameter. Straight sides. A metal rod ran from within the jar through the wooden lid, ending four inches above it, where it was topped by a metal ball the size of a large grape.

Simmery, bless him, had also ordered a discharge wand—an eighteen-inch glass rod, one and one-half inches in diameter—and a silk cloth, which one would vigorously rub lengthwise over the glass rod. The rod would accumulate static electricity and transfer it to the Leyden jar. Remy arranged these three items on the table.

Then he lined up the other supplies for the experiment in order of usage and set them on the side table. On the middle table, he placed the jar holding the cloth used to blot up the contaminated Elixir, and the smaller jar containing the Elixir which had resurrected the fly.

Remy called his servant Khalil, who lurked beside the laboratory door. "Hurry to the Grand Bazaar. Purchase four large aloe vera leaves, three metal spoons, and two thin brass chains, three hands in length." He placed twenty silver para in Khalil's palm. "Take an araba. I need these immediately."

When he first handled the heads, Remy had peered inside their severed necks. Their blood vessels and muscles were virtually the same as those of humans he had observed in anatomy class at Trinity College. He planned to stimulate growth in the Elixir with the electrical current generated by the Leyden jar. When the current raised the temperature to ninety-six degrees, the temperature of the human body, as discovered by Gabriel Fahrenheit, the German instrument maker, he would stop the current.

To discover when to stop the current, he would first use a substitute for the Elixir since he did not have enough of it for tests. After viewing various substances through the microscope, Remy had discovered that the Elixir's structure most resembled aloe vera. Therefore, he would use aloe vera as a substitute.

In Turkey, aloe vera was known as 'flower of the desert,' and praised for its healing powers. Remy considered his Elixir an even better essence. A gift from the gods.

First, he would discover the amount of electrical current that would heat the aloe vera to ninety-six degrees.

Second. The final experiment. He would apply the same amount of electrical current to the actual Elixir.

Third—the CRUX OF THE EXPERIMENT. Remy hoped that this amount of electrical current would stimulate the Elixir to 'grow'—based on reports from other experiments that had reported VOLUME INCREASE.

Remy lined up the jars that would hold the aloe vera. Then he leaned back in his chair for a moment to rest his mind, but it kept humming along. He pictured the last head, those beady eyes staring malice at him, and sat straight up at a horrid thought: The Elixir had been the residue issued from all three heads, including the evil, beady-eyed head, for they had all been close together on the same table. Yet the Elixir had revived both the dismembered fly and the brittle, brown rose petal. Perhaps the substance only contained the good from each head.

At least it had *shown* only the good, so far.

He would not allow himself to continue with this musing.

Almost ready to start, Remy unlocked the laboratory door so he could call for Khalil to enter, rather than interrupt his preparations. He had to take the chance that the Gov would be absent today.

Checking the clock, he realized Khalil had been gone an hour. Blast. Remy had given him far more para than he needed for bargaining, so he shouldn't have had any trouble completing a purchase. Khalil knew he was waiting anxiously for the aloe vera.

He cracked his knuckles. Percy, a college classmate, swore that when he did this during exams, it gave him greater access to his brain. Percy had always impressed his professors with his performance. It couldn't hurt. Remy needed all his wits about him for this experiment.

Checking the line he had incised on the side of the Elixir jar, Remy found that none of the Elixir had evaporated, but remained level with the line, two and one-half inches—around three ounces. This was all the Elixir that he had.

The only Elixir in the entire world.

CHAPTER 44

*R*emy's heartbeat sped up, slightly vibrating his hand as he gripped the long-handled spoon. He dipped it into the Elixir, three teaspoons per scoop, and emptied it into the smaller jar beside the original. How much could he spare? Too little would abort the experiment; too much would waste the precious substance. He added another scoop. Six teaspoons in total. That would have to suffice.

He wrote *G.E. Shocked* on a paper strip, applied a line of glue, and affixed it to the smaller jar, which would be shocked with an electrical current. He entered this in his log, where he had been careful to keep the nature of the Elixir vague, in case the Gov flipped through the pages, calling it *Substance 'A'* in the *Grand Experiment*, abbreviated *G.E.*

To the best of Remy's knowledge, Simmery did not know about the Elixir. He had discovered the heads by his own devices, but Remy had been far more cunning in hiding the miraculous gel. It looked ordinary enough—clear, gel-like—and sat in a standard laboratory jar.

Thank God it didn't sparkle or glow.

The original Elixir, which would remain untouched, served as the control. Remy labeled its jar *G.E. Control.* No respectable scientist would dare tamper with a declared control. On that jar, he etched a second line beneath the first to show the new level after removing six teaspoons. He set it aside.

He labeled two of the empty jars *Test Shocked*. Once Khalil returned, these would hold aloe vera gel, which would stand in for the Elixir until Remy could perfect the process. With no warning, the laboratory door banged open.

Startled, Remy spun around, knocking several jars from the side table. They shattered on the marble floor, scattering glass in all directions with an echoing clatter.

"Blast," Remy muttered.

Khalil stepped inside, clutching several bags, and closed the door. "Aloe vera not delivered 'til late, Usta," he said as his sandals crunched on the broken glass. Khalil had insisted on calling him 'usta,' the Turkish version of 'master.'

"Next time, open the door slowly," Remy snapped, waving him inside. "Clean this up," he said as Khalil placed the supplies, including large, thick leaves of aloe vera, on the side table.

"What is special about aloe vera? I, myself, grow it," Khalil said, sweeping the glass shards into the dustpan.

"It is a necessary part of the experiment." Remy set the aloe vera leaves in a line on the table.

"I will help with numbers on therm-ter. Been practicing." Khalil moved the dustpan and swept more shards into it.

"Let's test you again." Khalil leaned the broom against a table and slid the dustpan underneath. Then they tried several rounds with the thermometer.

"Good job?" Khalil asked, leaning towards Remy, his eyes large in expectation.

"You will be my official thermometer reader," Remy said, with a smile at Khalil's grin. He needed an assistant, and so far, Khalil had proved trustworthy. But this was one more secret for Khalil to keep, and they were adding up.

Khalil's grin turned serious when he spotted the Leyden jar alone in the center of the middle table. He crept toward it, peering cautiously. "You have a djinni, now?"

"Why on earth would you think that? This is a device for my experiment," said Remy, nonplused. Even if the Leyden jar looked a bit strange, topped by a bright red ball, the metal rod extending into the interior with a chain attached, why would Khalil connect it with a djinni?

Khalil shrugged. "You have heads that do not have a body, yet they live." He looked around.

"You are not supposed to tell anyone about that," said Remy.

"You know about it already, so we can talk. I promise not to scream or run, but may I see djinni?"

"This doesn't contain a djinni," Remy said, removing the Leyden jar's wooden lid. Khalil gaped at the metal rod and dangling chain. He slid the dustpan under the table behind him and stared at the jar as he moved from one foot to the other, eyes never leaving the jar.

"For God's sake, quit fidgeting." Remy poured water into the Leyden jar, stopping two inches from the top, then replaced the lid, ensuring the chain touched the silver conductive lining inside the glass.

"Khalil, cut several lengths of the wire on the supply table. Make them as long as three lengths of your hand," Remy said.

When-Khalil finished, he set the trimmed wires on the supply table. "Small wire. Djinni must be small, too?"

"This jar is empty except for water," said Remy. He saw Khalil smirk. His servant didn't believe him. Why would he, after seeing the heads?

"Fetch one of the metal spoons." Remy laid out several thick aloe vera leaves and filleted one open with the long, sharp knife. "Like this," he showed Khalil, pulling the leaf apart at the cut and scooping the gel into a bowl with a spoon. "Continue until the bowl is filled."

He turned from Khalil and readied his experiment, imagining the reactions of the Society fellows when he told them Khalil's comments about the Leyden jar. Yet he wasn't so different. Remy also had his wishes: that electricity might cause the miraculous gel to grow.

He sobered and got down to business, creating a wire hook and affixing it to the handle of a wooden spoon. Now he needed to determine how much electricity would heat aloe vera to ninety-six degrees, the temperature of the human body.

"Oha! Offering to djinni." Khalil's voice boomed off the walls as he came from the back of the laboratory and studied the hook. His concentration suddenly interrupted, Remy nearly overturned the empty jar. He should be used to that. Khalil had soft sandals and walked like a damn ghost.

"Do not creep up on me," Remy said, frowning. "And there is no djinni."

"No problem. Djinni knows the offering is from you," Khalil kept glancing at the Leyden jar as if he had a nervous tic.

"Khalil, I need quiet for my experiment. You may leave now."

"Please, Usta. I will be quiet as that djinni. I will keep your secrets. I must help with therm-ter." Remy sighed as Khalil began to kneel.

Remy would need assistance. Khalil knew about the heads and hadn't blabbed it all over the city, as far as Remy knew.

"Get up, for heaven's sake." Remy crossed his arms on his chest as Khalil stood up. "All right then. No talking. Do exactly as I say. Now, take this key and lock the door."

CHAPTER 45

*B*efore he began the next phase of his experiment, Remy motioned Kahlil over. "How much aloe vera did you scoop?"

Khalil covered his mouth with his hand, eyes wide under raised brows, making him look as comical as a child's puppet. Confound it, he had told Khalil to be quiet during experiments, but Khalil took that to extremes.

"For heaven's sake, you may speak." Remy didn't have time to play games.

"Half a bowl of the gel. There are leaves left. You want me to scoop more?" Khalil said.

"That should do." Now, to time how long it would take to build a proper charge in the Leyden jar. Remy picked up the glass rod, flipped a one-minute sandglass, and vigorously rubbed the silk cloth along the rod until static crackled in the air. He reset the sandglass, kept rubbing, and felt his scalp tingle. The sandglass ran out. Two minutes of brisk rubbing should be enough.

He glanced up at the sound of movement and heard Khalil gasp at the crackling noise of the electricity while jumping off his stool.

Holding his breath, Remy turned the one-minute sandglass over, starting the sand flowing. Then he set the electrically charged glass rod against the Leyden jar's metal ball, moving it back and forth for two minutes and twenty-five passes. This transferred the electricity into the Leyden jar.

He positioned a jar of aloe vera beside the one holding the newly charged chain, then, with the hook, moved the chain into the aloe vera jar. Shaking the thermometer, he slid it in.

"Khalil, call out at ninety-six."

"I know ninety-six." Khalil stooped to see the numbers. Remy watched the sand run through the three-minute timer.

"On ninety now," Khalil said slowly. "Mercury moving… ninety-four… ninety-five…"

"Ninety-six. Now, Usta, now."

Remy removed the thermometer and picked up the discharge wand, wooden handle with a brass wire in a half circle, brass ball at each end. He had almost positioned one brass ball to touch the ball at the top of the Leyden jar, the other to the foil lining, when a vivid blue arc leapt between them, crackling like miniature lightning.

Khalil let out a cry and jumped back. "Djinni is angry."

"There is no djinni," said Remy as he held the discharge wand in place and the current discharged, the blue lightning fading. He removed the wand.

To double-check, Remy placed his finger on the ball.

Khalil screeched.

Instinctively, Remy pulled his finger away. "Damnation, Khalil." Was his servant trying to sabotage the experiment? Remy gave him a dirty look. With great exaggeration, Remy put the tip of his finger on the ball and left it there. "It is harmless. I have discharged the electricity."

Khalil stared for a moment, clearly absorbing everything. Then he shrugged. "Oh, electricity is *Anglis* name for djinni."

Hmm, perhaps Khalil was correct once more.

With his fingers, Remy lifted the discharged chain from the aloe vera jar and cleaned both the chain and table. He reviewed his notes—charge time, rod passes, temperature—and repeated the process twice more. The results matched.

Confident, he placed the sandglasses in order, set up the jar labeled *G.E. Shocked*, and studied the arrangement.

Steady on. This was it.

The experiment.

CHAPTER 46

*R*emy thought of Tanythe, who knew about the Elixir. Of Leukan and wondered if he had become whole. Of the beady-eyed head in the back of the laboratory, likely watching him even now. Would an electrical current stimulate the Elixir to grow? How long before he would know success.

Or failure?

Patience.

Feeling like a runner at the starting line, he held the glass rod in one hand, took a deep breath, flipped the one-minute sandglass, and rubbed the silk cloth along the rod.

After a minute, he reset the sandglass, continuing until he had two full minutes of charge, just as in his successful trials.

He ran the charged rod back and forth over the Leyden jar's metal ball for another two minutes.

Now to charge the Elixir.

Using the metal hook on the wooden handle to lift the charged chain, he lowered it into the Elixir jar.

A knock at the door.

Startled, he dropped the hook, barely missing the jar. He froze. Khalil had locked the door earlier. "Derrien, are you in there? Forgot my key," came the Gov's voice as he knocked again.

Remy held his finger to his lips and stared at Khalil, who nodded, holding his finger to his lips. Lord in heaven, if the Gov discovered what he was doing this very moment...Remy would not let it happen.

He turned over the three-minute sandglass, then the one-minute. Then set the thermometer beside the sandglasses when someone knocked again, rattling the door handle.

"Derrien? Derrien?" The Gov mumbled something. Maybe he had found his key and would barge inside right now. Please walk away, Remy prayed as a sudden weariness made his body wilt. After the experiment, he would have to hurry and tidy up so it would look as if no one had been here for a while.

The three-minute sandglass had a few grains left. Now.

Remy turned over the one-minute sandglass.

Khalil sat on a stool by the Elixir, eyes focused on the Leyden jar as if a djinni might rise from it.

Remy checked the sandglass. Finished, thank heaven. Hoping the Elixir hadn't received too much electricity, Remy slid the thermometer inside the substance.

Whispering, he said, "Khalil, watch the same as last time, ninety-six. And be sure to whisper the numbers. The Gov should never know we were in here."

Khalil nodded.

Remy glanced at the thermometer. Eighty-eight degrees. He turned over the three-minute sandglass as Khalil glued his eyes to the numbers.

"Eighty-nine," whispered Khalil, squinting at Remy to see if he had heard. Remy nodded as he watched the sand run down. If the Gov had found his key...Remy visualized him hurrying back to his office for a second search. He was a most determined man.

"Ninety," whispered Khalil.

It seemed to take longer than with the aloe. Would he have to recharge the Leyden jar?

"Ninety-three. Now going fast," Khalil whispered as Remy silently tapped his hand against his trousers.

"Ninety-five. It hurrying. Oha, Ninety-six. Ninety-six!" Khalil barely kept his voice to a whisper.

Remy removed the thermometer. Thank God. He shifted his hand toward the chain.

Khalil hissed softly, skittering his hands in all directions, then pointing to the Leyden jar. Remy eyed the door. Had Khalil heard the Gov muttering outside? Or a key rattling in the lock?

As if his brain were a multi-headed beast, thoughts layered simultaneously:

Listening for keys jangling,

Glancing at Khalil,

Waiting for the click of the lock opening,

Worrying if the Gov would burst inside any moment,

Reviewing steps in the experiment,

His bare hand lifting the chain from the Elixir jar,

Had he discharged—

Gesturing toward the Leyden jar, Khalil stood up, waving his arms, hissing as loud as a King Cobra.

A sharp crack snapped through the air. A blinding flash of blue.

Khalil screamed.

Remy's muscles spasmed as if a thousand wasps had plunged their red stingers into every part of his body. A force thrust him into the air. The laboratory flew past to the sound of shattering glass and Khalil's Turkish expletives.

The splintering crunch into the floor stole whatever breath was in him. His mouth opened and closed. He couldn't take in any air.

God in heaven.

His body tingled as if he were a bell that had been rung, the vibrations eddying through him over and over. The laboratory grew dim. Clouds of black specks whorled in front of his eyes like distant flocks of birds wheeling closer and closer, blocking out more and more light. He attempted to raise his hand to shield himself, but his arm wouldn't obey.

"Hayret! Usta, Usta. Oha! Djinni angry. Usta, I xcdzwq snmbvl wrzx..."

Was this the end of him? He envisioned the Elixir that had received the electricity. His hope and his future. Had he broken the jar with his spastic movements? He could see only a few specks of light in the darkness now.

The loud bang of the laboratory door resounded inside his head, blending with the now unbearable burning, growing hotter and hotter inside him. Agitated voices in English and Turkish blared, then faded incrementally, as if they were speeding away from him.

His limbs lay inert, unreachable. How could he save his precious substance? In his mind, he reached out…

My Elixir…my Elixir.

CHAPTER 47

"*D*errien. Derrien, old chap."

"Simmery?" Remy's eyes felt heavy, and barely dragged themselves open as if against a great weight. The Gov's visage blurred in front of him, then Remy's lids slid shut. Had he just called the Gov Simmery to his face? But that was impossible because he couldn't make his lips move properly. What came out had been a shrill moan like the wind through a crack in a door.

"By George, I can barely detect a heartbeat. Derrien, do you hear me?"

Remy tried to open his eyes wide, but his lids refused to obey. Attempting to wiggle his index finger also failed. He should be worried, but it seemed too much of a bother.

"Can you feel that?" The Gov's voice sounded strained.

Remy felt nothing. Then, "Ow!" The word slurred from his lips.

"Thank heaven," Simmery said, his voice shifting away as though speaking to someone else. "I just slammed my fist into your thigh. If you hadn't felt it, it would be calamitous."

Remy blinked. His lids were working again. He caught a glimpse of the Gov, then lost it again. He must have moved somewhere else. Turning his head was a dim thought, which became lost in a fog.

"I've set a damp cloth compress on your forehead. Show when you can feel it. At some point, we'll get you to the guest room."

"No." Remy heard his distorted voice, but the Gov must have understood he didn't want to be in the guest room. If they moved him there again, everyone would hear what had happened, what he'd done. Blast.

Remy couldn't afford the attention. He had done something stupid. Fuzzy images flew by in his mind, then stopped as a barely discernible image grew. He fumbled with identifying it. The sense of urgency became almost manic. It became clearer. The shape of a woman?

No. A glass vessel.

He cried out, but he didn't. His body craved to emit a moan, a call for help, but he might as well have been one of those amorphous creatures he had viewed bumping around in a drop of water under the microscope.

The ELIXIR. Had he toppled the vessels when the Leyden jar shocked him? Had he destroyed the Elixir by trying to grow it?

Simmery's face came into view again. The Gov had probably been watching him all this time. "My God, Derrien. A shock from a Leyden jar killed Count Elstone. You aren't safe yet. Physical symptoms can worsen days after the shock."

Remy closed his eyes. He couldn't feel the compress on his forehead yet. He tried to move his hand to see if it was there. No response. Was he—?

"Derrien? I see you can understand me." Simmery appeared above him. "I'm going to clean up this mess." The Gov left again. Faint sounds came from somewhere. Remy swallowed. His ears popped.

He heard the door open, Khalil's treble voice inquiring about what he was to do. Then Khalil's anguished face appeared in front of him. "Usta. We carry you to the room."

Remy knew his lips moved, that he emitted mangled words, which startled Khalil. He could tell by his servant's gaping eyes and mouth. But Khalil said nothing as he helped the Gov lift him onto a canvas stretcher. As they carried him, he could see Khalil's back, his muslin trousers and long tunic, and the hall's ceiling. They set him gently on a soft bed in one of the posh guest rooms with a view out the window. The tree outside threw a dark shadow on the glass panes. Back here again, injured by his stupidity once more. He pressed his lips together only to have a buzz of pain make him cry out.

It was to Simmery's advantage to make Remy's story flattering because Remy was now his responsibility since the Gov now ran the laboratory. He settled into the cool pillow, the compress wet on his forehead. He had barely moved a muscle, other than being thrust across the room and onto the floor, yet he was unusually exhausted.

* * *

REMY OPENED HIS EYES. The window was dark, reflecting the flame of a candle. A shadow blocked the light. He gasped. The beady-eyed head? Then, Pheodora came into view as she closed the gauzy under-curtains. She turned as she drew the heavy damask ones together.

"Remy. You're awake." She kissed him. Placed her hand on his forehead and leaned close. "Snowy says you had a shock. An electrical shock."

He began to answer, but his eyes, his lips, his tongue had become impossibly heavy. When he next opened his eyes, it was dark, and he was alone. And hungry. He slid slowly up to sitting and collapsed back onto the pillow, his body alternately sore, then numb. A copper bell with a black wooden handle sat on the bedside table next to a pitcher of water and a glass half full of water. He reached for the glass, grasped it, but his weak grip dropped it to the floor with a dull thud.

"Oh, you're awake." Pheodora shut the door and hurried over. She reached under the table and brought up another glass, filled it half full of water.

"Can you sit up?"

He gave her a dazed look. She slid her hand under his head and lifted it enough for him to take a few sips. At dinner, Phe propped him up with pillows, and he managed to eat a little, mostly with her spoon-feeding him after his disaster with the fork. He remembered nothing else until she appeared in front of him, the room aglow with Constantinople's bright daylight.

She asked a few questions. He tried to answer, his voice garbled. Then she left to fetch whatever meal came next. Remy couldn't clear the fuzz from his mind, but when he had a discernible thought, it was something to do with concern over how he would explain to the Gov what he was doing with the Leyden jar and why he hadn't cleared it with him.

The next day, Pheodora left for something that he couldn't for the life of him remember. Remy lay flat in bed, looking at the plasterwork on the ceiling, trying to ascertain how much the shock had affected his mind, praying that it would be temporary.

"Derrien, I see you're awake."

At the sound of Simmery's voice, Remy recoiled. He nearly released the contents of his bladder, but contracted his muscles in time. He must have dozed off. And dreamed. He had been telling the Gov that he was excited to come across the Leyden jar, and before he knew it, had become caught up in an experiment. One that used electricity to stimulate growth in organic compounds suspended in various liquids. The Gov had been listening quietly. Then, with no warning, he had flown into a rage, banishing Remy to his office. "Clerical work only!" the Gov had screamed. "I'll be damned if you'll ever set foot in MY laboratory again."

The echo of his furious voice rang in Remy's ears. By heaven, what a dream.

"Pheodora says you've eaten well and seem to be progressing." Simmery sat near the bed. The silence grew.

Remy was not about to break it. It was all he could do to keep from cringing from the Gov's boiling anger in the dream. Should he pretend to drift off to sleep? But that would put off the inevitable.

"How are you?" Simmery put out his hand, reaching to touch his shoulder, but then withdrew. Remy wondered if he had made some kind of face that put Simmery off. Or had he merely looked frightened?

"Much better. Sore. Numb. Foggy." Remy looked directly at the Gov. At least that's what he thought he'd said, but the Gov seemed flummoxed. Remy must still be jumbling his words. However, the Gov looked exactly like how Remy felt. When he could, should he tell the Gov about the Elixir? The thought made him so weary that his eyes became heavy, and he nearly nodded off.

"The doctor said that after this Friday, you'd be out of the woods. Three days away." Simmery's brow wrinkled. Was he worried? Remy was thrilled that he could feel and move everything. And he was making progress in speaking. Could he be in more serious shape than he had imagined?

Would they cart him off in a wheelchair?

"I h-hope to be better b-before that," Remy said, his words sounding, at least to him, clearer this time. Still, there was that bit of a falter. And his thoughts proved as elusive as wisps of cloud.

Simmery nodded. The man was bursting to ask about Remy's experiment. Surely the Gov had read his log. His log! The remembrance of it had come from nowhere, like the memory of the Elixir.

Remy fought panic as he thought hard. How had he explained his experiments in the log? He had been careful to note the experimental Elixir as *G. E. Shocked*. The second Elixir, the control, he had noted as *G. E. Control*. What had he stated as his goal? To grow the Elixir, rather *G. E.* So all should be well, barring a slip in his notations. If he called it the Elixir, that didn't explain the particularities of the substance. It was just another name, albeit a grand one for an ordinary solution. A solution that Remy would say was composed of substances that he knew might grow if he produced the correct environment.

Should he wait for Simmery to broach the subject? Yet Simmery sat there, watching, just watching. The silence became unbearable. Remy inched onto his elbows, then struggled to sit. The Gov jumped up, assisting Remy in position. Even plumping a spare pillow before slipping it behind his back.

"Thank you." Remy placed his hands on either side of his body, meaning to straighten, when the muscles in his left leg twisted as if someone were wringing it like a wet rag.

"Uh." Remy threw off the covers, swiveled around, and put his feet on the floor. As he attempted to stand, his leg drew up and wouldn't hold his weight.

Simmery grabbed his arms, but Remy ended up on the floor in a heap, the pain in his leg unbearable.

"A c-cramp." Remy almost screamed. "Help." He grabbed his leg, pushing his weight into it, the muscles like iron under his flesh.

The Gov pounded on his leg, lifted Remy, and held him in a standing position. "Put your weight on it. Come on." Simmery tried to direct Remy's body, but his leg hung there, deformed by the constricting muscles.

"Uhh. Can't." Remy crumpled onto the bed, moaning in agony while the Gov massaged his leg.

"Remy?" Pheodora burst in.

"A cramp, bad," said Simmery. He lifted Remy, who moaned again.

"Phe, try to—"

She took Remy's leg and twisted it.

"Remy, push." She held his foot on the floor as Simmery got him into position. Pheodora took his calf and pressed. He thought he might start screaming and never stop. He gritted his teeth and, leaning hard on Simmery, at last set his full weight upon his leg. Finally, he managed to straighten his foot on the floor.

"Don't let go, Gov. Don't set me down." Remy breathed in relief, not daring to let up the pressure on his leg, dreading another cramp.

"Derrien, old chap, I believe the episode is over." Simmery assisted Remy in sitting on the bed. "This happens after electric shocks. Someone will need to be with you at all times until this phase is over. I've been studying the subject."

The Gov looked at Phe. "I can take tonight."

She nodded. "Take the first four hours while I get my things. I will return with my lady's maid and a footman to relieve you. Can you have Khalil stay in case we need someone other than the footman to fetch things?"

After Pheodora left, Remy insisted on standing on his own, but he couldn't do it for long. So, he let Simmery hold him up. Blast. His leg went into spasm again. Simmery held him upright from behind, his arms around Remy's waist, pressing hard against his back, his head above Remy's shoulder.

"Derrien, what the hell were you doing with the Leyden jar?" Simmery asked from behind him, his tone like a musical scale, starting low and fairly pleasant but ending in a snarl.

Remy was helpless.

"No, do not reply. We'll leave it for now." The Gov tightened his arms around Remy's waist. "Just don't die on me." The words fell from his lips, tight and hard, as though they had escaped through gritted teeth.

His arms squeezed Remy tighter then, as rough and as angry as his tone of voice. Yes, Simmery wanted him to heal, but only well enough so Remy could feel Simmery's satisfaction in ruining him.

CHAPTER 48

"*I* love the brightness of these rubies," Pheodora said. She tapped her dangling ruby and gold earrings, watching the way they moved in the mirror, while her lady's maid, Anisya, adjusted the diamond circles on either side of her cloth-of-gold headdress.

"These rubies were a gift from the *kayhya's* lady," Pheodora continued.

Anisya frowned and shook her head. She didn't know of this important official.

"You have heard much about the grand vizier, the first officer in the empire?" said Pheodora, prattling on. As long as she talked, that beady-eyed man inside her wouldn't speak. At least, that's what she had experienced so far in her bizarre captivity.

Anisya nodded while she finished braiding a section of Pheodora's tresses.

"Well, the kayhya is the second officer. He is the most important official as he exercises the authority, while the grand vizier has only the name," said Pheodora.

"Hmm," Anisya mumbled over the hairpins she held between her lips. She finished braiding three smaller sections of Pheodora's hair and pinned the braid in a neat coil next to the headdress.

Using a hand mirror, Pheodora eyed the side of her head in the large dressing table mirror. "Perfect, Anisya. Now to the other side. As I was saying

—after enjoying a meal such as I have never seen, with a vast number of dishes at the kayhya's lady's house, one of her handmaids slipped me a serviette folded to resemble a tulip. When I unfolded the brocade cloth, these marvelous earrings fell into my lap." Pheodora flicked one earring for emphasis. The rubies winked in the morning light from the windows.

"Imagine treating these treasures so casually. Why, any English lady would have presented them on a polished silver tray in a box wrapped in brocaded paper tied in wide satin bows." Anisya leaned close to one earring, peering intently, the movement of her eyes and brows like a market vendor clicking beads on his abacus.

"How much would a jeweler give for these?" Pheodora asked. So far, she hadn't heard a peep from the man inhabiting her.

Anisya, a most practical person, showed no surprise at the question. "One thousand kurus." Anisya smiled. "But I would obtain five hundred more."

"I'd wager you would," Pheodora said, and they both laughed. She took the hand mirror Anisya offered and turned her back to the dressing table mirror, viewing her hairdo and headdress from all directions. "Oh, the braids pinned in circles are charming. Very nice. I'll color my lips while you fetch Sultana from the garden and bring her up."

When Anisya closed the door to her room, Pheodora admired herself in the mirror once more, then put her hand to her chest, feeling for the evil-eye necklace under her blouse. It wasn't there. Odd that she called it that, for it protected her *from* the evil eye, whereas her name for it made it sound as though the pendant *was* the evil eye. She must rename it more accurately. Perhaps she should use the Turkish name, derived from Arabic—*nazar bondugu* —Bead of Sight.

She unlocked her Florentine jewelry box. The pendant wasn't there. Before her bath last night, Anisya had removed it and placed it in the jewelry box, which locked upon closing. Considering recent events, Pheodora needed protection at all times. She shouldn't have let Anisya remove it.

Do you want to find it? Your evil-eye jewel, as you call it?

The beady-eyed man.

Pheodora froze as if a lion were standing behind her, its enormous paws silent on the carpet, the claws extending as it readied to pounce. While she dressed with Anisya attending her, she had tried to forget him, in the same way one attempts to put a nightmare out of one's mind. She would ignore him.

That bauble does not affect me while I am inside you. You *keep me safe.*

An evil-eye pendant appeared in her hand. She gasped. It was the same as her custom-made one, a costly version set in gold on a gold chain, inlaid with the deepest indigo lapis lazuli for the pupil, around that, a ring of sparkling light blue amethyst, then a ring of smooth ivory, and on the outside, a wider ring of lapis lazuli.

It IS yours.

With a minimum of fiddling, Pheodora clasped the chain behind her neck and tucked the pendant into her blouse. It usually clashed with her other jewelry. Besides, she was more comfortable keeping it a secret. She didn't hear any talk inside her head, so it may keep him—

I find it odd that you would expect this market bauble to keep me away.

"Leave me alone. Why are you here? I have no magic." How could she speak to him in this way? What would he do if he were angry? But she had a feeling he needed to use her for something, so she would be safe until he got what he wanted.

I could give you magic.

"Why would I need to do paltry tricks?" Pheodora swallowed hard. Surely, he knew he was making her uneasy. She laughed aloud. She was speaking to a figment of her imagination. And to think she had been questioning Remy's sanity. She found the pendant's chain around her neck and withdrew her necklace from her blouse. From now on, she would give it more prominence. Perhaps that would keep him away.

I can give you more baubles. Or take them away.

The weight of the evil eye pendant on her chest lightened. Fumbling for it, she looked down. Gone. She inhaled, her mouth open in shock, then tried to hide her astonishment from him.

"What have you done with my necklace?" She noticed her voice shrilled at the end of her question. Trying for more control, she continued. "You cannot possibly want this 'market bauble,' as you call it."

Ah, but you *want it. What is it you truly desire? I can give you what you cannot imagine, what you cannot purchase. A wish come true.*

She felt the warm weight of her necklace again and clutched it in her hand as if that would prevent him from stealing it once more. "Leave me alone. That is what I want."

You are angry. Perhaps your husband, a man of natural philosophy, or science as he prefers, would be more attuned to having me as his guest. But surely you can use me while I am with you to gain your desires. You need only command me as you do your lady's maid.

Pheodora remembered attending church, the priests standing on pulpits behind elaborately carved lecterns inside soaring cathedrals and droning on about the devil's clever ways of tempting poor humans. How could she align those sermons with the vision she experienced a few days ago in the laboratory? The head's dark eyes, pools of bubbling lava. One of his hands held a gleaming double battle axe, the other, a hand of the Tarot in which the figures moved on the cards. On half of his head, he wore a warrior's pointed bronze helmet, the other half a conical cap of a shining substance winking with stars. And he had put words inside her mind, 'This power can be yours.'

She couldn't deny the beady-eyed man's magic. As much as she wanted to state that she hadn't been impressed, there was a part of her that was now running through a list of things she wanted. This man knew of Remy—had watched her husband work in the laboratory. He had been there to hear conversations between Snowy and Remy and had seen Remy hurrying around the laboratory, carrying this and that. Perhaps he knew Remy's secrets.

You have only to name what you desire. More jewels, clothing, houses, horses, carriages, lovers. In the vision, you saw my importance, my magic. If you like, I can change another to fit your needs. Tell me what you want from them, and it will transpire.

She wanted to protest that statement. If he was so powerful, why had he been with the other two heads in the debris thrown from the Golden Horn Waterway? And how had it been possible to behead him? Yet, she should take care now. This was no normal spirit, or whatever he might be. After all, his survival lacking a corporeal body was quite extraordinary.

She had suffered consequences before when she argued with men in high places and had proven them wrong. At such times, she had seen how the adage held true: 'Tart words make no friends.'

Over and over, without her even thinking, things she desired popped into her mind. How true that humans can be tempted, even if they think they could never be. Was causing a lost bauble to appear in a lady's hand all that was needed to win her over?

She came out of her thoughts and focused on her room. All was silent now. Her communication with the beady-eyed man, her pondering his offerings, seemed to have taken more of the morning than she realized.

The man hadn't spoken in some time. And where was Anisya with Sultana? Anisya was never late. Had this man delayed them? Had they been harmed?

She hurried outside, feeling relieved at leaving the man upstairs in her room. Foolish. She could never escape him. He was inside her.

Pheodora hurried through the garden, calling their names. She passed the tulips surrounding the main fountain, which made the water look as if it sat in a rainbow. Bending low, she made the little chirp, chirp noise that brought Sultana from hiding. The gardener, tending the herbs and vegetables in the side yard, hummed an atonal tune while a yellow butterfly attempted to land on his red fez. He hadn't seen either the kitten or the maid. Bees zipped from flower to flower, birds trilled in the trees, a natural setting that contrasted with the oddity she had become.

Pheodora turned away, her eyes tightly closed. Back in her room, the man had answered the words she had spoken aloud. She was now fully communicating with what had invaded her.

At a light pressure on her foot, she pulled her skirt up and looked down. "Aha, there you are," she said and hoisted the kitten into her arms.

"Lady," Anisya called. She limped through an opening in the hedge, her skirt torn and dirt smudging her face. "A hawk swooped down for little Sultana. Before he caught her, I threw myself over the little thing, only she zipped out from under me into the bushes. The hawk—his talons scraped my back." She crossed herself, murmuring a prayer in Russian.

Back inside, Pheodora got out her medicine kit and attended to Anisya. Her dress was torn, but the thick cloth had lessened the injury from the hawk's claws. Later, with her maid's wounds properly washed, soaked in honey, and bandaged, and Sultana gulping down a treat in the kitchen, Pheodora retired to her room. But she couldn't banish the thought that somehow the man inside her had delayed Anisya and Sultana, hoping to get what he wanted from her.

On the day she had visited the laboratory and found the disembodied heads, she had become hysterical. Remy had restrained her. He wouldn't let go when the shadow came at her, when it assaulted her. She had pleaded with Remy, and he had ignored her.

If he had let her go, she would have run from the shadow, and this horror wouldn't be inside her. Her maid and little Sulty wouldn't have been in danger. Why didn't Remy trust her enough to listen to what she said?

Is that what she truly wanted? For Remy to trust her? For him to open up to her as he would if she were his best friend? Being his wife and lover wasn't enough.

You saw my magic. I am a magus. That has never changed.

Now that I know your genuine desire, let me go into your husband. If you want him to change to your will, your desire, embrace him, and look into his eyes, then I can work my magic. What could be more natural?

You can have it all. The material objects, the influence over those you know, those who vex you, and those you love. You only have to tell me.

He had heard her thoughts. Could the beady-eyed man do this? Could he change Remy to her desire?

Restless and anxious, she stared out the window, the clouds small white puffs seeming to tangle in the trees. Tangle, like her thoughts. If Remy changed, it would have to come from him. Any other way, and she could never trust his words or actions. Pheodora vowed to ignore the beady-eyed head's temptations of magic and power. He was gaining control, but she must fight it. Remy would come to her in his own time.

Tomorrow, she would go to Nene Rose and appeal to the gypsy for help. Could she keep the beady-eyed man and his temptations at bay until then?

CHAPTER 49

*P*heodora counted on her fingers. Remy had been home from the Society for one, two, three, four days, recovering from his laboratory accident. It was terrible to see him so lethargic, so unlike himself. In that state, he paid little attention to her, never noticing how the beady-eyed man's presence inside her pulled her mind elsewhere. If he were his normal self, would he see that she had changed?

On this, the fifth day of her husband's recovery, Pheodora observed him sitting across from her at the table in the garden, fully dressed for the Society, his cravat neatly in place. This was when she could see him best, with the morning light shining through the foliage, accenting the gray-blue shadows under his eyes. The birds, so quiet after the quake, now sang as if making up time.

Everything that previously weighed upon Remy had been exacerbated by the electric shock and had manifested in his mood, his manner, and his body. The first few days he was home, he rarely spoke of anything that concerned the laboratory. Yesterday, he had made random statements regarding the artifacts and equipment, but never the accident. When he became occupied with reading or another normal activity, Remy would pause and stare into the distance. When she asked if anything was wrong, he would jerk as if she had stuck him with a pin, then look straight ahead, a frightening blankness glazing his eyes.

Snowy had alarmed her when he called the accident *a brush with death*. Just how close had Remy come to losing his life?

Remy, so precise, so impassioned with life, had to be troubled by his state. She attempted to converse with him, but more times than not, he would veer into distraction. He would lurch a bit when he rose from a chair or turned a corner in the house. Snowy had warned them both that bouts of vertigo could occur.

Since late yesterday, Remy seemed to improve. He had gained a steady gait as he walked, sat, and stood, with a hardly noticeable sway to one side. This morning, their breakfast conversation had been, well, normal, thank God. She looked up. Remy leaned toward her, staring into her eyes with alarming intensity.

"I didn't want to tell you, Phe, but this weighs upon me." He broke their gaze and looked down at the table. Inside her mind, she yelled at him, 'No, Remy Edric Derrien, you may not stop now. Please, please talk to me.'

"Before I started my experiment four days ago, I checked on the—uh—heads. Only the man's head was still there." Remy's voice sounded as morose as his expression.

She didn't want to hear or speak about that beady-eyed head.

"I cannot imagine where John might have gone with the woman's head. You know how incapacitated he was." Remy looked up at her from the remains of his breakfast. The flecks of gold usually sparkling in his irises had vanished. His eyes shadowed into a much darker brown.

This was the first time Remy had mentioned the heads since the accident. So the man they called John was part of that group, just as she had surmised. What if—

Pheodora clamped down on the burgeoning thought. It was too awful.

She clutched the serviette in her lap, the embroidery rough on her palm. Her previous thought now sprang fully formed into her brain. What if the red-haired woman inhabited Remy, just as she had been inhabited by the beady-eyed man? Remy had just said the woman was gone. If she were like the man inside her, the woman's head could be anywhere, and she could still inhabit Remy.

Pheodora pondered the odd happenstances after she first saw the heads in the laboratory: the beady-eyed man possessing her, the earthquake, and Remy's accident. Now, days after the quake, the servants had cleaned up the inside of their house. They had discarded the broken furnishings, dishes, vases, chests, and wardrobes and ordered new ones. Pheodora glanced around the garden. The lingering dust had mostly settled, and the gardener had washed off the plants. The tremors had ruined only one vegetable and herb bed when a tree branch crushed the tomatoes, parsley, and cilantro. All else had miraculously survived, thank heaven, for the garden proved a much-needed respite for both Remy and herself.

"Phe, is this troubling you to hear about the—the heads, after your experience in the laboratory?" Remy put his hand on hers. His eyes looked clear, and he seemed to see her.

"Yes, of course. How could I possibly forget the disembodied heads? Their visages are burnt into my brain." Pheodora refused to let her fear of the beady-eyed man show, but all she hid from Remy threatened to overcome her. She blinked furiously. One tear slid down the side of her face, very, very slowly, teasing her with her vulnerability. Was the beady-eyed man doing this?

Remy, however, didn't seem to notice as he drained his teacup. "If memory serves, I think the man's eyes have grown duller." He patted Pheodora's hand. "I must check. He is the only one left. The only one left," he whispered as he gazed over her shoulder, the phrase a ghost of an echo.

Pheodora looked behind her, fearing to see the beady-eyed man somehow materialize as a whole person, his head attached to a body, his dark eyes drilling into her. But she saw only the hedge of roses and tiny sparrows hopping in and out of the branches.

Remy pushed his chair back and tossed his napkin on the table. He stood there, solid, exuding strength. "I should go. The araba is probably here by now."

The man stirred inside Pheodora, growing, moving as if he were a serpent uncoiling to its full size. She stood. Held onto the back of her chair. This was the first time it had seemed possible that the man could emerge from inside her. She closed her eyes for a moment, quelling her tears.

If only Remy hadn't mentioned that beady-eyed head or hadn't noted the man's eyes dulling. There would be no telling what the man would do now.

She was sure he hated that menacing description. What would happen if his head died? A rush of ice-cold filled her body. She put her hand to her chest and let out a moan.

Remy looked at her. His eyes narrowed, but he put his hand on her waist, and they walked through the garden to the house. She wondered if he could tell that there was something different about her. But she forced a smile, and he seemed to let her behavior slip from his attention. He ran his other hand through his curls. When he was worried, his mouth drooped like that of a small boy who had lost his dog. If only she could kiss him, make it better, but she dared not approach him. Not like this, not with a disturbed man inside who seemed to want to leave her and go to Remy.

She walked a little faster, and he picked up the pace when she almost tripped on an uneven flagstone. "Are you that anxious, Phe, for me to leave?"

"No, I want you home early, so if you leave soon, you'll accomplish enough to do that." She stopped by the mimosa tree, pink blooms redolent of raspberries, bees buzzing around crazed by the fragrance. She kissed him on the cheek. That was safe. She wasn't looking into his eyes.

He smiled and started walking again.

"The microscope made it through the quake, but anyone can see that we need a spare, as evidenced by the damage done in Constantinople from this last minor earth tremor," said Remy, in a rather abrupt change of subject. "Earthquakes happen frequently in this part of the world. After all, the last huge earthquake is why we're here."

This was wonderful. Remy was talking about the laboratory. Pheodora struggled to find a suitable comment that would keep the conversation going in a non-threatening way.

"Father has begged me to ask for something he can send us down here in the uncivilized world. It would thrill him to brag that he shipped us a new technical wonder. How he would love to boast that you have two microscopes for your research." Her voice came out sounding surprisingly normal, which begat a normal thought: If her father gifted the Society a new microscope, she could use it as much as she wanted, since they had effectively banned her from the laboratory after her disastrous encounter with the heads.

"I'm not sure the Gov would care to be trumped by your father." Remy shook his head. Was that a smile starting in his eyes?

Again, she felt the beady-eyed man, his words so faint she couldn't make them out. Could this be related to what Remy had observed in the laboratory? With the beady-eyed man inhabiting her, it stood to reason that part of his magic might be divided, neglecting his head enough to cause it to suffer and grow weaker. This may not bode well for her.

As she tried to close her mind to the thing inside her, she found she could function on different levels.

They had made it into the parlor without incident, and she had gotten a more spirited reply from her poor husband. Now, if she could herd him out the door to the Society before the man forced her to kiss him. Who knew if he could transfer from her into Remy if she opened her mouth to her husband's? And what if she suddenly yielded to the temptation to change Remy according to her desire?

The man had talked of giving her magic, giving her what she could not imagine. A general feeling tingled through her now and again that being invaded by the beady-eyed man was not at all about her, but about Remy—that the head was assessing Remy for some task, and she was a means to that end. And that end was her husband. But why would the head want Remy?

"Remy, dear, promise me that on your first day back, you will not work too hard. And don't forget to come home early." She must subtly persuade Remy to leave without him suspecting anything. "Do not make me come and fetch you. You know how Snowy would hate that."

"Dearest Phe, I promise." Remy started for the door. He came back and took her in his arms. "I need you, Phe, you know. I need your rock steadiness, your support." He pulled her closer, his eyes pleading.

Pheodora slipped from his grasp and turned, holding her palm up, keeping him away. She sniffed, and sniffed again.

"A–choo!" Convincing, thank God.

"Bless you," said Remy.

She pulled a handkerchief from the hidden pocket in her *antery*, her favorite white and gold damask Turkish vest, and clamped it to her nose. "I may be catching a cold." She sniffed once more for good measure and plucked a long-stemmed red rose from the vase by the door, offering it to him.

"I love you," she whispered.

Remy held the double-flowered rose blossom close. He closed his eyes and inhaled long and slow.

"Careful of the thorns," she cautioned. Pheodora watched his long black lashes flutter. She envisioned being as close to him as the rose, sharing the delicate fragrance, kissing his bow-shaped lips.

A faint smile curved those lips, and Remy gazed at her as if he knew what she was thinking. "I shall see you this evening."

She closed her eyes, her body yearning to go to him. To tell him everything. To beg for help. But no, Remy must leave. She closed her mind.

He must go away from her for his own good.

CHAPTER 50

*P*heodora stood in the parlor, resisting the beady-eyed man's seductive whisper.

He is your husband. If you want to go to him, you must. We endured an earthquake seven days ago. We could all be crushed today. Go to him. Give your husband an affectionate leave-taking. And you will receive all you ever wanted from him.

She closed her eyes as Remy stepped out the door, his dark hair curling over his white cravat. The man inside her shifted restlessly. Could he do damage without a physical body? His essence alone inhabited her, and, perhaps, as he claimed, part of her soul. A chill traced her spine. Then something soft brushed her ankle.

"Well, hullo there, poppet." She lifted Sultana into her arms, the kitten batting her cheek with a soft paw. Pheodora stroked the calico's fur, white, red, and black, so plush she longed to bury her face in it. Upstairs, she set Sultana on the bed, tapping her pink nose. The kitten meowed, a silky sound.

"Are you ready to go on an adventure, little Sulty?" Pheodora gazed into Sultana's blue eyes, then, from under the bed, lifted a wire carrier with a gold velvet pillow at the bottom. "Now, don't be afraid. This is your cozy traveling spot," she murmured as she placed Sultana inside. The kitten meowed piteously and tried to push her nose through the spaces in the wire, her front claws pulling her body upright.

"As soon as we arrive, I promise I will set you in my lap so Nene Rose can greet you." Pheodora stuck her finger through the wire and stroked Sulty. The kitten purred. Strange, the same thing happened as before. She had thought she was imagining it. When Remy headed for the door, and the beady-eyed man was coaxing her to give him a proper farewell, she lifted Sulty in her arms. Immediately, the head's presence dropped away. Now, when she stroked Sultana, she felt the presence vanish in the same way.

Perhaps she would keep the carrier in her lap. Might that create the same effect?

The araba waited in the front by the portico, and it was the same driver she had hired before. But this driver had never taken her to the gypsy camp.

"*Günaydm*," Pheodora said as he helped her inside. She had been working on her Turkish pronunciation since it was becoming hopelessly entangled with her Greek, French, and German. But the driver's eyes lit with under-standing at her greeting of *good morning*.

He focused on Sultana. "Iyi şanslar?" he said.

"Iyi sanslar," Pheodora repeated as she smiled at Sultana. Just how much luck the kitten brought was one thing she meant to discover.

"Roma camp," Pheodora said to the driver, who waited to close the door until she had settled.

His brow furrowed. He mumbled a Turkish oath that the servants used against the evil eye. "No no, lady, *kötü şans*."

The driver stood outside the araba, hand on the open door. He wasn't the only one who thought the gypsies were bad luck. Was he going to throw her out?

Pheodora reached into her purse and slipped the coachman twenty silver para coins. "This brings more luck," she said as she pointed to Sultana, lounging on the gold pillow in her carrier. The driver looked at the kitten, then the money, pocketed the coins, and walked to the front of the carriage.

Leaning into the padded seat, Pheodora set the carrier in her lap and said a brief prayer for Remy. She added another to protect them all, even the strange heads. After the quake, her first, she was forever alert to any slight tremor in the earth. But she couldn't pray for what was bothering her most, couldn't afford to expose those thoughts to the beady-eyed man.

Out the window, she watched the city pass by like the thoughts that floated idly through her mind. What if the quake compromised the old palace that housed the Society in a manner that no one could tell? A hidden crack straight through to the structure, which held part of the ceiling or a wall that would crumble and crush someone. She stiffened, envisioning Remy looking up in horror at a wall crashing onto him.

The driver must detour. Go straight to the Society so she could check on her husband. She took a breath. This was the beady-eyed man inside working on her, and she would do her best to ignore him. Perhaps the carrier blocked Sultana's effect on her. The kitten was curled up on the pillow, sound asleep, the tip of her little pink tongue sticking out from her mouth. Ah, to sleep so soundly. She wouldn't disturb her.

When she thought of Remy or spoke of him, Pheodora sensed a quickening from the man inside her. That sensation affirmed her suspicion that the beady-eyed man was interested in any path to Remy, including using her. Who knows, perhaps his magic could arrange an injury for Remy so he would be easier to inhabit.

Remy had said they had hired an architect to inspect the building this morning while they attended a meeting in one of the kiosks in the nearby park, where only a few trees had been torn from the earth by the quake. She had forgotten. So, her husband was safe for the moment.

Hmm. A convenient thing to forget if someone wanted to persuade you to change your plans. She was going to see Nene Rose to help Remy. So why did she keep looking over her shoulder, cringe when another carriage passed by, or jump when a street vendor called out, hawking his wares? These were normal street occurrences. She held tight to the carrier and clutched at her evil-eye talisman. She should have purchased a larger one or tried to find a crystal like Remy's.

If only she could make it to Nene Rose's before the feared and unnamed happened.

CHAPTER 51

*W*alking to the Society this morning would be beneficial, Remy told himself. Pheodora had worried that he wasn't healed from the electric shock. She had seen the strange symptoms and observed that, at times, he wandered around in a fog. Surely he had noticed, she had said, eyeing him pointedly.

Of course, he was aware he wasn't quite up to snuff. His memory had been affected. Bits and pieces of thoughts and images floated through a vague haze, which he tried to assemble into something coherent.

It had been five days since his disaster. The Gov had assured him the effects should be gone by now, according to his studies. Hoping to clear his head, Remy swung his arms briskly as he walked. In his right hand, he held the rose Pheodora had given him, slipping the flower into his pocket to avoid damaging it, only to prick his finger. She had warned him about the thorns.

A glimpse of something he couldn't put a name to flickered in his brain, something important. His mind worked on identifying whatever it was, while his overriding thought that simultaneously swinging his arms and working his legs was a promising sign of his return to normal.

He walked through an area wispy with mist, which blurred portions of the buildings and landscape. In places, dust clouds hung in the air from the sudden collapse of buildings or sections of them. Here and there, stacks of the wreckage had been consolidated.

Progress.

Remy stopped and listened. The city had mostly returned to normal: araba bells jingling, the many languages blending into a murmur, hawkers' cries rising above the clomp of horses' hooves, and the clatter of cart and carriage wheels. Different from just after the quake, when periods of silence were broken by loud booms or screams. He heard hundreds had lost their lives, and more bodies would likely be found as rubble continued to be cleared.

Since the quake, the eerie feeling that he was being watched, watched with evil intent, had never left him. Remy put his hand to his old wound, which had begun to throb. Not that again—would he ever be without a reminder of it?

He walked faster and stepped with care over a mound of concrete and brick chunks when a bout of dizziness overtook him. He misstepped. His foot slid on the gravel, and he sloped toward a crevice directly in front of the rubbish. Leaning back, Remy counterbalanced, but his foot continued sliding down the angled crevice wall. He sat hard in the rubbish he had just stepped over, something rigid hitting his rear. Surely, that bruise would curtail his riding Atabey tonight, the first time since his electric shock.

Brushing grime off his trousers and coat, Remy backed away from the crevice. In the surrounding streets, he had encountered more dark, yawning crevices created by the earthquake. His mind wheeled as a remnant of his nightmare rose into his consciousness. He was at the bottom of one of the deepest crevices, which had transformed into the bag containing the heads. Pressing his fingers into his temple, he willed that lingering horror out of his brain.

Remy continued his walk, keeping his steps deliberate, but slowed when his thoughts brought up the image of the beady-eyed man's dulled eyes. With effort, he made the unsettling visual go away and hurried on. His mind, never ceding defeat, insisted upon a reappraisal of his nagging suspicion that Pheodora didn't love him anymore. He reviewed what had happened that morning before he left home and concluded that she simply had a sneeze coming on, perhaps a cold as well. Happened to everyone.

Remy turned onto a street where the effects of the quake seemed minimal.

The air here, strong with the musky odor of freshly turned soil and an indefinable earthy, fecund smell, infused him with an odd energy, a feeling that he could do anything, be anyone. He could change this topsy-turvy world for the better.

Rounding a corner, he faced another area heaped in rubbish, with splintered parts of furniture and broken household items protruding here and there. Shielding his eyes from the glare of the morning sun glinting over the buildings, Remy stared into a second-floor room open to the air, a divan at the rear, pillows still arranged against the backrest, a third of the vivid carpet hanging over the remains of the floor that had fallen away. With a prayer for the people in that home and a thankful one that his own home had survived, he detoured onto another street.

Prayers. He still said them. Even after his laboratory accident, he prayed.

But what god created a firmament that shook, destroyed cities, and unearthed severed heads that still lived? The heads—helpless with no limbs or voice. His nightmare came forward again, of him inside the bag, as helpless as they were, crushed into their flesh in the interminable darkness, and existing in that state for centuries, for millennia.

The earth and its dark soil, its boundless secrets, its depths, and gaping crevices. For reasons that baffled him, he was alternately repulsed and then attracted to these attributes. He was most puzzled by those feelings toward the earth, which made him feel safe and imparted a kind of odd euphoria.

What was the source of these feelings? Remy had never in his life entertained this kind of bond with the earth. He had researched specimens in his scientific studies, paying little heed to the firmament upon which they and he lived their lives. What had changed?

His old wound throbbed now with a vengeance. With a muted grunt, he clutched his arm, envisioning the bullet that burst from his pistol and pierced Leukan, then pierced his arm. Perhaps that gave him a bond with the creature. After all, Leukan was beyond human and most probably had some esoteric connection with the earth. That connection could explain why Tanythe insisted Remy take her crystal and leave her with Leukan in the laboratory during the earthquake. Her crystal was powerful, yet during the crisis of the quake, she gave it up. Was Leukan's connection with the earth such that it had healed him, enabling him to escape unharmed with Tanythe?

He hoped with all his heart that they were healthy and prospering wherever they were.

"Good day, Lord Derrien." The British guard stood at attention as he
opened the Society doors. Remy stared for a moment, aware now that he had
stuck his key in the lock and partially opened the door, the guard taking over
after that.

A little slow in closing the conversation gap, Remy replied in kind and
strolled down the hall. After the electric shock, he experienced similar lags in
his actions and reactions. Thank heaven, they were lessening.

Remy eyed the walls and high ceilings of the old palace. The architect had
approved the state of the building, reassuring the Gov that the quake had done
only superficial damage. Yet a web of cracks, as thin as a spider's silken thread,
spread at the ceiling from the hall's corners, at least as Remy viewed them
from his vantage point. Up close, they would be larger. He hoped they were
not new and were the surface cracks the architect referred to, with no bearing
on the palace's structural integrity. Pheodora had expressed fear about the
quake's effect on the ancient palace.

His thoughts jumped to this morning, Phe standing forlornly by the door,
handing him a rose. Her words, *I love you*, had been like a soft kiss. He reached
cautiously into his pocket and pulled out the rose, careful of the thorns. He
inhaled the fragrance.

"Well, well, Derrien. How are you, old boy? Time has flown, eh? Four or
five days since the shock. Right?" Simmery had emerged from his office. The
bandage covering his head wound from the quake resembled a shrunken
turban.

Remy clutched the rose, winced, and put his finger to his mouth.

"Damned thorns." He grinned at the Gov and replaced the rose in his
pocket. "Lord Simmonds-Snow, thanks to your quick action, I am healed from
the electric shock with no residue that I know of."

"Glad to hear. Step inside my office for a moment."

Remy followed the Gov, resigning himself to a dressing-down for his,
according to the Gov's thinking, careless laboratory accident. Just inside the
threshold, he stopped as a new thought formed in his brain. Blast, had
Simmery looked for Leukan and Tanythe in the laboratory after he found
Remy stunned from the electric shock?

Before he knew it, Simmery was in front of him, staring quizzically into his face. "Derrien, old man, are you quite all right?" He took Remy by the arm and led him to the upholstered chair in front of his desk.

"I-I'm fine." Remy sat down, barely missing the seat of the chair. He had miscalculated the distance. Things like that still occurred, consequences of his accident. Simmery gave him a stern once-over, which signaled that he didn't believe Remy, then bent over a stack of papers on his desk.

"I waited for you so we could go into the laboratory together after the earthquake. Survey the damage. Couldn't handle it myself, not since the trauma of the quake. By God, it has taken its toll on me, Derrien." The Gov looked into Remy's eyes, his own eyes and mouth drawn down, making him look much older.

"I happened to be here in the office that fateful day when Khalil informed me you had just supervised a thorough cleaning of the laboratory. I had stopped in for some paperwork to take with me to the Residency when I heard a racket, then your cry from the laboratory."

Remy caught a strong whiff of the Gov's cologne, Attar Al Paçuli, and cringed inwardly. The cursed fragrance brought memories of when Simmery became furious at Remy's failing to inform him about the heads for the first time.

"You know what happened after that." The Gov sat back. "By George, they are gone. Only one left. And not a word from you."

"After the accident, I thought of it, thought to tell you, but then kept forgetting. I was upset, grieving as if they were old friends." Remy couldn't believe he'd said so much that was true.

"Was the experiment something to bring them back?" asked the Gov.

Remy gaped at him. How could he know?

"Why on earth would you think that? I would need a special compass to find them. I don't have the foggiest idea of where to look." He fingered his crystal.

Simmery took notice.

"Derrien, at the very beginning of the earthquake, you removed the crystal from the woman. She didn't protest. Before the plaster chunk hit me, I saw all of that. The stone has some kind of strange power." The Gov stated that as a fact, when Remy would have wagered he would merely question it.

"I would have considered none of that, that alchemy or what-you-will, but once you see living heads detached from their bodies, the woman a vision of beauty as fresh as a budding rose. John, now a complete person..." Simmery widened his eyes, appearing a bit lost, then continued. "Uh... the heads existing as if they were whole. One rethinks what one believes about the world, about natural philosophy/science."

By God, the Gov felt just as he did. This thought enhanced the growing sensation of his head being stuffed to the brim with cotton wool.

Simmery tugged at his bandage and grimaced.

"Bloody thing. The doctor insists I keep it on for a few more days. Of course, he drops by and changes it out every day." Then he became quiet for too long, his expression serious.

"Derrien, what is the component of the substances labeled *G. E. Shocked* and *G. E. Control?*" The Gov placed his hands on the stack of papers and leveled his gaze directly at him.

Remy fought to keep his expression calm. He should have foreseen this question. Simmery had cleaned up after the accident, so of course, he would have noticed the experiment laid out. Remy had heard that if you must tell a falsehood, it should be close to the truth, but if he mentioned *G. E. Shocked* and *G. E. Control* were a substance he gleaned from the heads, he would never hear the end of it. The Gov would chastise him for keeping the Elixir a secret and suspect him of deceit from then on. He would insist on participating in every experiment.

"Sorry for the delay in answering. Since the shock, my mind is sometimes annoyingly slow." Remy did not want to admit it, but it was the perfect excuse for his delay, especially since the Gov was sympathetic to his *near-death ordeal*. "However, every day I am improving." Remy set one hand in his lap, hiding his twitching fingers.

"What I've discovered about healing from these shocks is exactly as you just described. Thankfully, everyone recovered their full faculties," the Gov said, as he kept his eyes on him. "Have you found an answer to my question yet?"

"Of course." Remy put his hand to his head, which had begun to ache as Simmery interrogated him. "I used the gel of the Aloe Vera plant for the final experiment. The Arabic people call it the flower of the desert. I'm sure you know it has healing properties."

"And what was the objective of your experiment?" Simmery set his finger tenderly on his bandage. Was Remy making the Gov's head throb? Well, tit for tat.

"My objective was to discover how the shock would affect the aloe's healing property. I haven't had time to assess the results." The words Remy said sparked a cascade of ideas and worries inside him regarding the Elixir.

What in Jupiter's name had he done? Had he neutralized the healing power of the Elixir with the electricity? He possessed such a small amount. Was he so foolish as to kill the golden goose? On the other hand, it was possible that the electricity could have enhanced the Elixir's healing power. At this, the rush of energy in Remy's body settled.

Nevertheless, his answer had sounded dull enough that Simmery just might drop the subject. Aloe vera was a common remedy known and used by peasants and royalty in times even earlier than the ancient Egyptians.

Sure enough, the Gov unsuccessfully stifled a yawn.

Remy breathed easier.

"Now, Derrien, give me a full report on those experiments completed before your accident, as well as the ones left incomplete. Not just your notes. A full report. And from now on, give me a preliminary report, however brief, on any experiments you are planning. I need to know. Using our newest equipment can be dangerous, as you are now well aware." Simmery gathered the papers in front of him and stacked them with a thwack, thwack, against the surface of his desk.

Well, that was it. Simmery's voice had been serious, and this was his dressing down. Remy nodded. He had expected more vehemence, even a harsh punishment. Perhaps his accident, *a brush with death* as the Gov had termed it, when Remy heard him informing Phe, had been much more serious than Remy fathomed. By heaven, his electric shock had scared the Gov.

"After all, Derrien..." The Gov paused.

Remy stiffened, ready for the punishment phase.

Simmery looked him in the eye. "We will have an advantage if we collaborate on projects. As you know from experience, two heads are better than one."

Simmery kept his serious manner and tone. He hadn't noticed exactly what he had said.

As if he had received another electric shock, Remy sat straight in his chair, eyes wide open, trying desperately to keep from bursting into laughter.

It didn't help that the Gov sat there, also struggling to keep a straight face, his complexion growing from pink to red as he realized what he had said.

CHAPTER 52

*M*aintaining a straight face, Remy left the Gov's office, the Gov's statement repeating inside his head: *We will have an advantage if we collaborate on projects. As you know from experience, two heads are better than one.*

Remy's mouth twitched. He couldn't hold in the huffs and puffs from smothering a laugh. Once he locked the laboratory door from the inside, he gave in, loud guffaws shaking his body until he slumped limp against the door, tears streaking his cheeks.

His scolding hadn't gone the way he thought. He could say the same for the Gov. Simmery had tried to end on a philosophical note but had delivered a pun in a manner so serious that it made the unintentional wordplay even more hilarious.

He pictured the Gov's grave expression and was reduced to hilarity once more. As his laughter died, he took a steadying breath and looked around, really looked, at the laboratory. For the first time since the accident with electricity, he was inside his laboratory, rather, the Gov's laboratory. He attempted to recall what he had come in for—something specific that had awakened him abruptly this morning, something he must attend to. Layered over that was an item from the meeting he just had with Simmery. Both were important, but he couldn't remember. Damn the accident. He missed his clear-headedness and—

There it was. Inside his head, clear as a bell. He had it.

Then it dissolved as quickly as a sugar confection in the rain. He would get it back. Remy attempted to visualize the fleeting thought, just as it had appeared in his mind a moment ago. A blurry image, an echo of a word. Then they were gone. Twice failed.

These obliterations of his memory had been cruelly teasing him since the electric shock. The particulars of his accident were something else he couldn't recall, but working in the laboratory would most likely help him remember more of what had occurred.

He put his hand in his pocket. The velvety petals of the red rose that Pheodora had given him brushed his fingers. Drawing it out carefully to avoid the thorns, he set the stem in a beaker, filled it with Khalil's water pitcher, and placed it near the microscope. The vivid bloom brought color to the laboratory, reminding him of Phe, whose strangeness this morning had prompted her to give him this flower.

What was going on with her? Perhaps, like the Gov, she feared he had been close to death after his electric shock, and his returning to the Society today made it more real for her. If so, why had she avoided him? That look in her eyes. He'd seen it before. She wanted him as much as he wanted her. The concern that she was coming down with a cold was a poor excuse, but for what purpose?

According to the Gov, Remy could have died from the Leyden jar's electric shock. Remy had heard of people receiving mild shocks but had no idea the small device could deliver a fatal blow.

Now, he would take proper precautions and continue with his laboratory work. He put these morbid wanderings from his mind. The table where he had set up his experiment was empty, the surface shining, the surrounding floor spotless. The Gov had done a thorough job cleaning up the mess, as Remy dimly remembered him calling it. Each day, some small memory surfaced through the fog in his mind; perhaps that meant he was recovering.

He fingered the cloth covering the microscope. Simmery had informed him they employed a seamstress to make this oilcloth protector, which was water-resistant and heavy enough to protect the instrument from small things colliding with it. Remy lifted the cloth. The microscope looked as good as new.

He had feared he might have knocked it over in his spastic movements from the electricity pouring through him.

There was another piece of equipment involved in his experiment. One that was at the forefront of natural philosophy/science experiments. The name hovered on the tip of his tongue, taunting him.

"The Leyden jar," he blurted aloud.

His brain fuzzed. He sat down, overwhelmed.

The word alone set his brain buzzing, his breath coming fast. If thinking of it rattled him so, what of seeing it? Had it been destroyed when he was shocked and propelled across the room? Surely Simmery would have said. Remy began searching, finding the usual beakers, stoppers, and instruments until—

There. It stood in its proper place, red lid secure. His logbook sat beside it, one corner crushed.

Still..something else was missing. Slowly, the word formed.

"The Elixir."

He slammed his fist on the table. "Confound it. How could he have forgotten? How?" Five days since the shock. Five days since he'd charged the Elixir with electricity. Grabbing his logbook, he rushed to the cabinet where he kept the precious substance and unlocked it. Empty.

Had the Gov found the jars? He wouldn't know what was in them. Remy had labeled them obscurely enough. He shut the door, his mind flashing to a snatch of Simmery's voice mentioning containers of a mysterious substance. Surely not. Perhaps he imagined it, fearing the worst.

He could see the jars in his mind—labeled *G.E. Shocked* and *G.E. Control*— left on the table after the experiment. Then the Gov's knock, the jiggling handle. He could recall nothing clear after that.

His stomach clenched, an enormous fist tightening inside, taking him back to that very moment the electricity had fizzed through his body. He had become airborne, a sound echoing in his head. He squeezed his eyes shut, trying to relive when the sound came at him, as if he were in the laboratory that day, suspended in the air.

Shattering glass.

This memory pierced him as surely as if it were a rapier. Had he destroyed the very substance he was desperately trying to save? And destroyed his destiny as well?

The Elixir was all he had left of Tanythe and Leukan. It was the discovery that would bring him respect in natural philosophy/science. And fame, fortune, and most of all, freedom from his father's wishes.

He stood poised, ready to fight, anything to find the Elixir whole, untouched. Then his brain shifted, as it used to, rationing out reasonable steps, cautioning against incorrect action, suggesting practical scenarios.

Whether the jars were shattered or left intact, Simmery would have deduced that they were part of Remy's experiment. Had he disposed of them out of spite for Remy's unprofessional accident? Or, as the Gov had implied, had he been truly upset that Remy had been injured and stowed them away for later? The laboratory rubbish bins were in the back.

On the way, Remy passed by *the* table. One lone head sat there. Remy walked over, his mind placing Tanythe and Leukan's heads beside this one, which sent him into a worrying spiral. Where on earth were they? Had the beings perished during the earthquake?

He stood in front of the beady-eyed man's head. The man's eyes weren't as bright as Remy remembered, but they focused on him and opened wide.

Remy stepped back. His mind flooded with images as if someone had shoved a book in his face and flipped through a series of vivid illustrations: plaster dust coating the laboratory; a dusty, damp cloth; words in Remy's head; a vision of this man with a body, a helmet, a spear; Tanythe and Leukan in front of a white marble edifice. The beady-eyed man had tried to affect him in a terrible way, and Remy had locked him in a trunk.

At the bins, the first was empty. The second yielded only broken beaker glass, wooden shards, rags, wire, a cracked jar with some blackened cloth. Nothing of the Elixir jars.

What would the Gov have done with them? Remy looked through the cabinets near the front of the laboratory again. They weren't there.

He sank onto the floor, head in his hands.

He had failed and possibly impaired his thinking and memory irreparably.

CHAPTER 53

*P*heodora's araba slowed, bells fading as it pulled up before the gypsy camp. A sea of low black tents covered the ground, like an infestation of beetles, each the size of the araba, their rounded carapaces dull in the sun. A fetid smell rose in the breeze. Wrinkling her nose, she gripped Sultana's carrier and stepped onto the ground, wondering if her letter had reached Nene Rose.

"*Hanmefendi,*" called the boy, who had slipped from between two of the tents. The same boy who always met her, clad in the same blue turban and red and black beads, with the same greeting of 'Lady.'

"Nene Rose, Nene Rose," he motioned for her to follow. He must be Nene Rose's grandson, great-grandson, or even great-great-grandson.

"Please wait here. I have silver paras for you when I return," Pheodora said to the driver. He gestured to his cloth belt, where he had stashed a knife in a leather scabbard. At Pheodora's quick inhale, he smiled at her and placed his hand solidly on the hilt. Not a threat, merely a caution to let her know he would watch out for her and little Sulty. She gave him a somber look and nodded, then followed the boy.

As Pheodora walked into the alley of tents, her heart beat faster. She wouldn't care to be here when twilight set in. Even now, to the side in a dark alley, she saw a knife flash. But it turned out to be a harmless metal turnbuckle holding a tent in place. She startled at a tall man lurking near a tent she was passing—

Only a shirt hung out to dry. An eerie cry made her halt, drawing the carrier tight to her chest as a black cat leapt across her path.

She clutched her evil-eye pendant and hurried to catch the boy who waited ahead. Careful to keep her distance from the debris swelling in the alley ditches, Pheodora picked her way along the path, breathing through her mouth. Once again, she fell behind the boy, who moved like a lizard, swerving through bits of trash that didn't make it to the ditch. A rat scurried across his path. Unfazed, he jumped over it. A little further down, the boy stopped in front of a tent that looked like all the others.

"*Hanımefendi*, Nene Rose." In a sweeping gesture, he moved aside the door flap. A cloud of gray smoke flowed out, sweet and spicy, thank the Lord. Holding the carrier at her side, Pheodora stepped into the tent.

Square oil lanterns of clear glass set into brass burned brightly, illuminating the vivid cloths draping the tent walls. Thick Turkish carpets covered the floor. Behind the lamps, a dark shape rose. Pheodora angled toward it and squinted. Gold coins, medallions, and glass beads adorning Nene Rose's bright pink turban reflected the light into Pheodora's eyes.

"Laydee Derrien, please sit," Nene Rose's deep voice boomed in accented English. Pheodora had forgotten the strength of the woman's presence.

Almost in a trance, she set the carrier on the carpet and sat on the intricately carved chair inlaid with mother-of-pearl. She faced a table draped in shining purple silk cloth. Behind the table, Nene Rose took a seat in a gilded, throne-like chair. The gypsy's eyes met hers.

Pheodora stared into the deep black pupils, a gold point of light in each. Fast as a lightning strike, the beady-eyed man moved inside her. An image of him, his head on a body, flashed into her mind: his eyes shut, mouth twisted in a grimace, arms and hands shielding him from Nene Rose.

Pheodora blinked. Had she just seen Nene Rose lean forward, eyes in a squint, then a perplexed expression on her face? Or had she imagined it?

She felt the beady-eyed man squirm under the gypsy's hypnotic gaze. So, the gypsy had glimpsed this man that inhabited her, the same as when one gets a whiff of a lady's perfume.

After unlocking the carrier, she lifted Sultana onto her lap and smiled inwardly as the man's presence faded. The kitten balanced awkwardly on Pheodora's wide Turkish trousers, trying to find a grip on the slippery silk, while sniffing the air as she assessed the new surroundings, her back slightly arched. Then Sultana noticed Nene Rose, stiffened, arched fully, and hissed so hard she tumbled to the ground, landing on her feet.

Nene Rose laughed, deep like the boom of a drum. Sultana's slanted eyes grew into blue circles. "You have a spirited one there," she said.

"She is a dear." Pheodora scooped up the kitten. As if he were going down a drain, the man's presence faded.

Nene Rose tilted her head, eyeing Pheodora suspiciously.

"Show me your left palm," said Nene Rose as she held out her leathery hand, rings of gold and silver sparkling with gems on each finger.

Pheodora leaned forward, her hand resting on the gypsy's. An air of lethargy shrouded her as if she were languishing in a hot Turkish bath after a salt massage. In her lap, Sultana stretched, then reared up and placed her front paws on the table, casting her shadow over the lines in Pheodora's palm as the gypsy studied them.

"Three. One for you. Two for husband. One wants your husband. Your husband wants another one. What are you to do?" Nene Rose's eyes grew large. A force shot out from behind them.

Startled at the soft, but firm, phenomenon hitting her and sinking inside, Pheodora lurched backward in her chair. Sultana's paws slipped from the table edge, claws catching on the silk, but the cloth stayed in place. The kitten wrestled her claws from the silk, leapt off Pheodora's lap, and scampered across the room. Immediately, the beady-eyed man's visage rose inside Pheodora with such a sudden force that she grasped the chair arms in surprise.

Nene Rose stood up abruptly, knocking over the oil lamp next to her. The lamp righted itself, or the gypsy moved too fast for Pheodora to register. The lamp's flame never faltered, burning straight and steady throughout.

"Leave!" Nene Rose's voice boomed like one of the earthquake's tremors.

Staggering to her feet, Pheodora looked behind her. Surely the gypsy had addressed someone who had intruded upon them, but no one was there.

"You. Leave Phe–o–dor–a." Nene Rose pointed her right hand at her, the rings glinting, each one a separate evil eye.

"But–but why?" Pheodora raised her eyes to see Nene Rose, who was suddenly taller. She wondered if she was shrinking, turning into the small girl whose frightened voice had just asked why she had to leave.

Sultana scratched at Pheodora's legs, and she held the kitten next to her chest, the relief at the man's fading presence banishing her fear of the gypsy.

Nene Rose stared hard at them, Sultana struggling in Pheodora's arms. The gypsy sat. Gestured for Pheodora to do the same.

As Pheodora sank into the chair, she became her blessed self once more and stroked Sultana, who snuggled into her lap, purring.

Nene Rose half stood from her throne and bent toward her. She put her index finger to her lips and stared hard into Pheodora's eyes. Waiting.

The gypsy wanted her to be silent. Pheodora nodded and placed her finger to her lips, showing that she understood.

"Your kitten would be more comfortable in the container you brought," Nene Rose said in an amiable voice, different from any Pheodora had ever heard from the gypsy.

Pheodora pulled Sultana from her lap and set her into the carrier, clicking the door shut. As Sultana meowed, angry at being removed from a warm, soft lap, the beady-eyed man's presence reappeared.

Narrowing her eyes, Nene Rose looked her up and down. The gypsy *knew*. Knew that when Sultana wasn't next to her body, the evil man possessed Pheodora.

Nene Rose took Pheodora's left hand, slipped a silver ring with a blue cabochon-cut stone onto her little finger, and spoke in a language Phe had never heard. A slippery sound with a hard consonant here and there. Pheodora's stomach twisted with the strange words, making her dizzy. A sudden pain pounded in her head.

"Now you are just as you were before the spirit invaded you. We can discuss freely."

Pheodora angled her hand to alter the light falling on the stone. "By heaven, Nene Rose, a star."

"Yes, a star sapphire. Six-pointed to show the many ways the star protects you. It quelled the evil spirit inside you *for the time being*. Let us not waste this interval." Nene Rose had a way of emphasizing words that made your blood run cold. *For the time being.* How much time before the man returned and could know and hear and see everything? Pheodora looked around as if she could catch the beady-eyed man creeping up on her.

Nene leaned toward her. "The evil spirit is called Bahl. Knowing its name can help you control it. Know it and you can control him." Nene Rose leaned back. She was finally in the mood to talk.

"Your cat senses evil inside you. Protects you. The spirit wants out. Into someone you love. Yes?" The gypsy's deep voice rose higher as she ended the sentence.

Pheodora nodded, the thought more frightening with Nene Rose acknowledging it aloud.

"Your cat is three colors: white is woman, lunar magic. Red is man, sun magic. Black takes. Removes evil. Very good omen, your cat. Palm again."

Nene Rose let Pheodora's palm rest in her hand and made clucking noises as she studied the lines. Deep wrinkles suddenly etched her face as if someone had inked them onto her skin. The large silver crescent on her red-and-black-beaded earrings, lucky colors, caught the oil lamp's golden light. "Keep cat always with you. So how did you get evil spirit?"

"I—" Pheodora stopped, afraid to say anything about Bahl. Even his name sounded evil. Would Nene Rose believe she was insane?

"A big secret, mmm? Nene Rose keeps them locked up." The gypsy pointed at her forehead and rotated her thumb and forefinger as if she were turning a key.

Pheodora could have sworn she heard the metal tumblers inside a lock click. She sat very still.

In the carrier, Sultana had stopped purring. Nothing from Bahl. This banishment, for *the time being*, was still in effect.

She would have to hurry.

CHAPTER 54

*P*heodora would have to tell the gypsy everything immediately, before Bahl inhabited her again. She took a breath and began. "Five years ago, the great earthquake of 1766 unearthed many treasures from the Bosphorus. The Society of Antiquaries sent my husband to oversee them. In his work, he opened a chest containing three living human heads. This man, the spirit inside me, is one of them."

There. She had said it aloud. Nene Rose nodded, the spangles and coins on her turban tinkling like the wind chimes of tiny fairies. She leaned across the purple silk covering the table, her gaze steady.

"Bahl is banished while you are here." Nene Rose said, nodding toward Pheodora's sapphire ring. "Speak without fear."

"The man came at me as a shadow, and then he was inside my body. He wants my husband. I don't know why and—" Pheodora sobbed. She hated this. Hated being the woman who didn't know what to do.

Something touched her hand. Pheodora screeched, her hands flapping. She had secured Sultana in her carrier and glanced around, trying to find what it was.

"I let the kitten out. She will make it easier for you to tell your story." Nene Rose's voice had changed into a dulcet grandmotherly tone as she crooned sweet things to the kitten. Pheodora sniffed, tears still streaming, and stared as Nene Rose and Sultana communed.

The gypsy reached into her silken sleeve, pulled out a beautifully embroidered handkerchief, and gave it to Pheodora, who blotted tears from her face. Nene Rose took the handkerchief and studied it. "Such sad tears. You will save your husband. Bahl hides what he wants. He truly desires something from the other two found with him. Remember. They are not *like him*." Nene Rose stared into her, her eyes dark as a deep well at midnight. Pheodora would never forget those eyes.

"The spirit, er, Bahl says he can give power and magic, that he can give me whatever I want." Pheodora touched the necklace under her blouse. "When my evil-eye necklace was nowhere to be found, he caused it to appear."

She pulled her pendant out. "That example being a preliminary of the magic or things he could give me, so he promised. Oh, how I wanted to have that magic, that power. I swore I wouldn't succumb to the temptation. But I remember how amazing it was for the pendant to appear in my hand from nowhere. How alluring he was when he said he could direct a person's thoughts to my desire." She looked into Nene Rose's eyes.

"What do I do? How do I rid myself of this Bahl?" Pheodora watched for any change in the gypsy's expression.

Nene Rose rubbed her hands together, her rings glowing in soft pastels. A glimmer of a smile played on her lips. Her wrinkles had vanished, her skin smooth, as if a younger Nene Rose sat before her.

"Spirits easily tempt humans, but you are lucky. Bahl wants to leave. You must see that he does *not go into your husband*. Let him go to another who will harm neither you nor Lord Derrien." Nene Rose placed her hands flat in front of her.

"But who? When? And how?" Pheodora squeezed her eyes shut, yet the tears came again. "Bahl hears my thoughts. He is always with me. Today, I could not kiss my husband goodbye when he left for his laboratory, for I was afraid that Bahl might try to go into him." Phe stroked Sultana, who had settled into her lap.

Nene Rose placed her hand on Pheodora's arm.

Blessed peace exuded from the gypsy, even more than having Sultana in her lap, more so than wearing the star sapphire ring. But when she left here,

Pheodora would only have Sultana and the ring, and she couldn't keep Sultana in her lap or carry her every minute.

"Please, Nene Rose, teach me how to work the ring."

The gypsy raised her arm above her head. "This spell I give you."

Kitus a mu. Bara andatus uneen.

Kial gina. Bara algina.

Kittu tuda m ku. Bara antu tune.

Zianna. Kanpa. Zi Kia. Kanpa.

Inim inim ma. Utug hul a kan.

Lord knows Pheodora had, besides the Queen's English, Greek, French, German, Turkish, and some Russian. This language she'd never heard. An ancient one. She must've looked flummoxed because the gypsy let out a laugh.

"Do not fret. The spell is in here, written." The gypsy placed a finely woven straw box into Pheodora's palm. "Read it aloud the first time you use it. Then you will recall the many words and say them easily as if they were only several simple words."

"This is an English translation:

Where I stand, there stand thou not!

Where I sit, there sit thou not!

Where I walk, there walk thou not!

Where I enter, there enter thou not!

By heaven be thou exorcised! By earth be thou exorcised!"

"Say the spell when you want to prevent Bahl from hearing your private thoughts. Use it when he least expects to hear your thoughts, such as before you sleep. You may use it in other instances, but keep the time brief. If Bahl becomes suspicious, he *will* try to counter the spell. And I cannot guarantee he will fail." The gypsy watched her.

"Do not be fooled. Bahl is powerful. I tell you this not to frighten you but to make you beware. Even with the spell, he still can hear what you say aloud and view what you see." Nene Rose eyed her again, making sure she understood.

"You may obtain five minutes to write or speak freely by pressing the middle of your palm when you say the spell. During that brief time, Bahl cannot access your thoughts, hear what you say, or see what you see. Then you must accomplish your task with haste."

Pheodora looked down at the purple silk draping the table. "So I can never be rid of him?"

"He is eager to go into your husband. Your husband is close to the other two beings. Bahl will use him to obtain what he wants from them. Watch Bahl, listen to him, and feel his mood carefully. When the time comes, make sure he inhabits someone other than your husband."

"How?"

"Your desires will play a part in your guidance." Nene Rose touched Pheodora's ring. The barely discernible star, just a suggestion in the deep blue stone, rose to the surface, shining bright white.

"*Never* remove this ring. If anyone inquires about it, say *it was a gift from your aunt*. If you lose it before Bahl leaves you, send word or come to me right away. Remember, Sultana also protects you."

The lamps blinked and dimmed. The inside of the tent lit as if by a half moon, the atmosphere sultry as before a storm. Incense hung heavy in the air, the fragrance a powerful enchantment each time Pheodora breathed it.

"I will send a black cat for your husband. He must take it with him every-where. It will protect him from the spirit Bahl." Nene Rose stood.

"Wait for the black cat. Keep your little one close." She nodded at Sultana. "You have experienced the kitten's magic."

Pheodora had trouble seeing the gypsy, for she blended with the design of the lapis lazuli blue, ruby red, and emerald green carpet hanging behind her. The incense smoke grew thicker. She fumbled inside her sleeve, pulled out three silver kurus, and laid them on the table. Best to overpay your fortune teller.

"Sultana and I thank you, Nene Rose." Pheodora placed her hand over her heart.

"*Hanmefendi.*" The boy stood in the doorway, a perfect silhouette. He motioned her out. "Do what Nene Rose says." He smiled and nodded, beckoning.

Pheodora followed the boy into the lane by Nene Rose's tent, thankful that he had arrived in such a timely manner, for by herself, she would never find her way out of camp through the maze of alleys. Three gypsy men holding lit torches walked past them toward Nene Rose's tent. A loud whooshing sound brought a burst of heat. She turned, clutching the carrier with Sultana inside.

"Nene Rose!" Pheodora screamed.

The men had set the torches to the gypsy's tent, which was now a mass of orange and blue flames. Yet the outline of the black tent stayed whole, untouched as the flames burned bright and hot. Pheodora stayed rooted to the ground, the smell of incense rather than burning cloth and wood pouring from the flames. Then, all at once, the flames shrank as if a heavy rainstorm had doused them, and the tent stood as it was when the boy first pulled aside the door flap for her.

The boy took her hand. "*Hanmefendi*, we go."

A small line of flames outlined the untouched tent in a yellow halo. No, it was merely the brightness of the sun against the blue, blue sky. Something blurred in front of the tent. Pheodora blinked away her dizziness, but the blurriness stayed in the same place, growing larger. Against the black tent, a figure stood solid. Nene Rose, her hand raised in blessing like the saints in sacristy paintings, her rings shining rainbows in the sun.

"Hurry, *Hanmefendi*." The boy pulled her away. "You bring plenty evil."

CHAPTER 55

On the ride home from the gypsy camp, Pheodora stroked Sultana, who lay curled in her lap, a multi-colored fuzzy ball luxuriating in a warm spot of sunlight. She gazed out the latticed window as the araba trundled through Constantinople, the horse's bells jingling merrily, a contrast to the somber occurrences at Nene Rose's.

Pheodora held her ring to the window. Despite the bright light or angling her hand this way and that, the star remained a faint white shadow in the stone. Had Nene Rose played a trick on her, making the star shine while holding the beady-eyed man at bay with a fleeting spell? Telling false tales about the ring?

She felt no stirrings from Bahl and smiled down at Sultana, who slept blissfully unaware as she blocked the man's presence. Pheodora removed the thin straw box from her sleeve and opened it. The spell was written in a fine hand, black ink on thick cream paper flecked in pale brown like a bird's egg. She began to sound out the words, but stopped before a syllable crossed her lips. Her first recitation called for more preparation. As she replaced the lid, she noticed a piece of paper stuck inside it. Ah, the English translation in the same hand. The box retained the fragrance of the gypsy's tent. Even though Pheodora had experienced peculiar and disturbing incidents there, the smell imparted a settled, peaceful feeling.

Arriving home at last, she paid the driver handsomely, so he wouldn't hesitate to take her back to the gypsy camp. Inside the house, Sultana ran and scratched at the door. Before Pheodora stepped into the garden with her, she asked a servant to bring a meal with sherbet and tea.

Painfully aware of the intruder when Sultana wasn't touching her, she settled at a table in the gazebo and looked at her ring. With no spells in place, it was just a pretty bauble. Focusing inside herself, she directed a strong thought: 'You know much about me, but I know next to nothing about you.'

Ah, but you know more about me from the gypsy who shut me out. What did she tell you?

"I see her often. Some things are not your concern." It felt less peculiar speaking aloud to him now that he had replied. "But what of my first question, that you know much about me, yet I have little information about you," said Pheodora.

I gave you a vision of me when you first saw me in the laboratory.

She hadn't shaken the feeling that she was descending into madness from hearing this voice, then carrying on a conversation. Would she be one of those poor souls who would plunge through the air to their death from the insanity this very thing caused?

I doubt speaking with me will drive you to madness, my dear. You can do that perfectly well on your own, as many before you have.

Pheodora sat up, alert at the faint sound of footsteps, china clinking against china, then the clomping of shoes on the wooden stairs to the gazebo. She had settled in the fanciful structure because it was difficult for anyone to approach silently.

The maid appeared, holding a luncheon tray. Pheodora dismissed her and sipped the cool sherbet, grateful for the refreshing mix of cherries and grapes with cinnamon, cloves, and lemon. She wondered at how she could sit and converse with a spirit inhabiting her, enjoy sherbet, and simultaneously conjecture that she might go mad and hurl herself from some high edifice.

Gazing out at the low branches of the trees that snaked by the gazebo's six open sides and shaded her almost as much as the roof, she gained the same tranquil awareness she had enjoyed at Nene Rose's. The garden always set her right. Could she sustain that as she continued?

"In the vision you sent, I saw the head of the beautiful red-haired lady from the laboratory. She had a body." Pheodora heard her voice, loud over the chirping birds and whirring insects. An image of the beady-eyed man formed in her mind. His brow was furrowed, his eyes half closed as if he were brooding. Mentioning the woman must have bothered him. Perhaps she was his wife or sister.

The woman is a goddess.

In Pheodora's vision, the red-haired woman wore a crown sparked with lightning, so her being a goddess was no surprise. But the man had said *a goddess* in a harsh tone. At least, she had perceived that in her mind.

Pheodora propped her head on her hand. A whiff of the *sarma*—grape leaves stuffed with whatever meat Cook had in the larder, greens, bulgar wheat, and spices with yogurt sauce, made her feel a bit nauseous. A yellow-chested bird fluttered onto a branch outside the pavilion, eyeing the food.

The goddess has vanished, as well as the man. I am the only one left. Perhaps I am looking for them, as is your husband.

"In the vision you sent, you held a battle axe and a hand of the tarot where the figures moved," Pheodora said. *I am Bahl, a magus and a warrior to a great king. Perhaps your history has recorded me.*

Across the garden near the herb bed, one of the gardeners harvested carrots and placed them in a basket, their long, fuzzy stems becoming a cloud of green over the bright orange vegetables. As Pheodora watched him, she pondered Bahl's last statement. When she studied classics with her tutors, they had not mentioned an ancient named Bahl.

"Our poor studies are bereft of many of the past great civilizations. We have found clay tablets written in cuneiform and tomb walls which tell the tales of only a few of the great kings, brave warriors, gods, and goddesses," Pheodora said in a proper tone. "Of Bahl, the elite warrior and magus of kings, I have no knowledge. But there are many tablets and scrolls, the languages unknown and undeciphered."

An odd sensation of numbness tingled around her ankle. She startled, jerked her ankle away, and looked down, preparing to swat whatever it was. Blue eyes peered up at her, and with a meow, Sultana leapt onto her lap.

Pheodora lost all connection with Bahl. Since he had freely given her his name, she could now use it without giving away that Nene Rose had known his name and shared it with her.

"Hello, little Sulty." Pheodora stroked the kitten's head, then ran her hand down its back as the little creature started that odd rumbling specific to cats all over the world. Purring was the perfect word for it.

The kitten was heavier than when Pheodora had found her in the Karacaahmet cemetery, what with her inside meals and pouncing on bugs in the garden. Sultana arched in a stretch, then hopped off her lap and scampered across the garden.

Pheodora sat for a moment as the distraction provided by Sultana dissipated. She tilted her head. When Sultana hopped into her lap, she had become herself once more. Now, after Sultana's departure, she felt Bahl still inhabiting her, ever alert and listening once more.

Careful to look only at the gardener, she pulled the straw box from her sleeve, opened it, and removed the lid. She glanced at the paper at the bottom and looked away when a soft voice came from her mouth, speaking the spell faster than Nene Rose. Her ring became warm on her finger, the star shining bright white in the blue stone. By the time Pheodora realized what had happened, the spell had finished.

She was free of Bahl for a short time now, but she wrestled with this. What could she do knowing that the head still inhabited her, ever alert when the spell released? Whenever the spell broke, he could see and hear everything she said and listen to her innermost thoughts.

She might well go mad before he left.

CHAPTER 56

*R*emy rose from his knees, disbelieving that his experiment had failed so spectacularly. Just then, he caught a glimpse of something shiny out of the corner of his eye. The table beside the microscope had two shelves beneath it. Something he should have remembered.

He crawled over and examined the bottom shelf. Rows of beakers, jars, and bottles lined the space, some full, some empty, a few labeled. He squat-walked in a line, turning jars to check if they had labels. At the end of the first row, he squinted to read a label on one of the last vessels: *G.E. Control*. This was the control Elixir that hadn't received the electric shock. The original Elixir. The substance was exactly at the etched fill line from five days ago.

He said a silent prayer.

The label on the next one read *G.E. Shocked*. This was the Elixir that had electricity run through it. Low on the glass near the bottom, Remy found the incised line showing the level of six teaspoons of Elixir. But the substance was nowhere near the incised line. He couldn't see anything in the bottle. Had the electricity evaporated the Elixir? He ran his gaze up the vessel and found that the Elixir had risen near the top.

The Elixir's volume had increased.

Remy uncrossed his legs, jumped up from his seat on the floor, and fetched a ruler. He held the measure to the glass at the bottom, two-and-one-half inches to the incised line, then another seven-and-a-half inches to the new level. Nearly a three hundred and fifty percent increase. The electric current had excited the Elixir and caused the volume to expand. Now, he could make as much of the Elixir as he wanted, as much as anyone wanted.

He flipped through his logbook. Placing his finger on a few lines, confirmed that before the experiment, he had two jars in the cabinet, one containing the Elixir and a small jar holding a cloth with Elixir contaminated by the dead fly. The original jar with the Elixir survived, along with the new jar originally filled with a small amount of Elixir for the actual experiment.

Yet, when the electrical shock threw him across the room, he distinctly heard glass shattering. Remy cocked his head, then slapped his hand on his thigh, recalling the cloth with the black sticky substance in a broken jar that had been in the rubbish bin—the only jar that had broken.

Then, like a thunderclap, what he had been trying to recall burst into his mind. In their meeting today, the Gov mentioned finding jars labeled *G.E. Shocked* and *G.E. Control*. Fearing he'd been found out, Remy had muttered something about aloe vera, electricity, and healing, ostensibly the truth. The panic he had experienced in the Gov's office sharpened his next thought. Had the electricity killed the Elixir's healing power or enhanced it? Or had it remained the same?

Remy left the laboratory and ran into his office. He stopped inside the doorway.

"What did I come in here for?" he said in a soft voice, as he surveyed the room to jog his memory. A vase of wilted red roses sat on his desk, surrounded by dead petals, brown and shrunken. Roses? No, dead roses. That was it. Using the Elixir, which had received the electric shock, he would replicate the rose petal experiment. On a piece of paper, Remy placed five dead petals, folded the paper into a packet, and placed it carefully in his pocket.

Back in the laboratory, he unfolded the packet of dead petals and set them next to the long-stemmed rose Phe gave him this morning. He pulled off a perfect velvety red petal and set it three inches from a wrinkled dead petal on a white ceramic plate.

Using a long-handled one-sixteenth teaspoon, he retrieved that amount of Elixir from the *G.E. Shocked* jar. Holding a teaspoon over the dried petal, he gave it a sharp tap. One drop fell and spread over the petal, like icing on a cake.

That should be enough. Remy peered closer. The petal looked the same. The transformation wasn't as instantaneous as had occurred with the fly or his first experiment with a dead rose petal.

After ten minutes, nothing had happened. Shocking the Elixir had increased the Elixir's volume but killed the life-giving property.

Failed.

Remy slouched in the chair.

Simmery shook him. "Derrien, wake up. I have news." He waved a letter about. "The Society sacked you." Remy bolted upright. But Simmery wasn't there.

He looked around. He was in the laboratory. The clerestory windows showed afternoon light. He had fallen asleep. Confound it. And dreamed that Simmery sacked him.

Remy stood up. The room spun. He gripped the chair.

Bleary-eyed, he gathered his things to leave, but stopped. He would repeat the experiment. As he tried to overcome the disorientation from his impromptu nap, he fought off excuses. The rose petal experiment today failed. Why not admit it? He should leave, eat, and rest, then return tomorrow, fresh with a day's more healing from his electric shock.

Blast. Remy recalled the deep voice of his scientific studies professor at Trinity College admonishing his students: "Performing an experiment once does not show that repeating it will yield the same results." A maxim that might be either good or bad for Remy's particular experiment.

At this point, Remy couldn't imagine leaving for home and resting. He would only reproduce the experiment step by step in his head until he returned, feeling more frustrated. He placed another dead rose petal on a new ceramic plate. Then he plucked a fresh red petal from Phe's rose and laid it three inches from the brown one.

He dipped the same amount from the *G.E. Shocked* jar and dropped it on the dead rose petal. The Elixir spread as it had in the first experiment.

As he waited, Remy felt as if he were falling from a great height. Had he killed this vessel of Elixir? He stared into the laboratory, seeing Tanythe and Leukan on the table, and the glittering gold, jewels, coins, dishes, and other items found in the same earth that spat them from the sea. Finally, he looked up. The dead petal remained brown and shriveled.

He should go home now. These failures occurred. He shouldn't take it so hard.

Remy started to throw the petals in the rubbish bin, but staying true to his resolve to take care, he retrieved his logbook and entered the date. Pen in hand, poised on the correct page, he turned to view the petals. He looked down at two red, silky petals. Disbelieving, Remy moved closer.

He made sure he was seeing correctly and carefully entered the conclusion of his experiment into his logbook.

The Elixir, *G.E. Shocked* that received the electricity, had tripled more than threefold and could still restore life.

CHAPTER 57

In the parlor, Pheodora ran her hand the length of Sultana's back to her fuzzy tail. With a tiny meow, the kitten raised her white face, an irregular spot of rust red above her eye. Pheodora rubbed the soft black fur between the kitten's rust-red ears, eliciting a muffled roar of purring louder than seemed possible.

"You're my adorable little runt, aren't you?" Pheodora cooed. Sultana meowed and closed her blue eyes, her purrs rumbling louder. Safety from Bahl was the gift Sultana had given her.

"Oh." Pheodora looked up at Remy standing beside her, his morose expression causing her to jerk back in startlement. "Like a ghost, dear Remy. I didn't even hear you come in the door. You're home early."

Her husband mumbled something. Did he say that she loved that mangy cat more than him? Something like that? Remy wore a frown as if it were an item of clothing that was difficult to remove. Cradling Sultana in her arms, Pheodora rose and kissed her husband. He returned the kiss and pulled her close, Sultana leaping from her arms. If Pheodora put Remy off now, with the dour mood he was in, the night would be ruined. So far, Sultana's magic worked, with no sign of Bahl stirring inside her.

Remy kissed Pheodora, removing her jeweled belt. When he lifted the gold-fringed waistcoat over her head, shifting her headdress to the side, he gave a passing caress to her breast. She had almost undone his cravat when she heard one of the servants open the door from the kitchen.

"Upstairs," she whispered to Remy. In a graceful move, he lifted and carried Pheodora to her bedroom, laying her on the bed before she could slip behind the dressing screen to use Nene Rose's spell. His mouth and hands were on her, scattering her thoughts.

Was this truly Remy? His kisses roused fiery sparks inside her wherever he touched. She gasped when he tore her silk smock, the cool brush of his cravat against her skin contrasting with the heat of his hands moving over her body.

The star in the blue stone of her ring shimmered as she wrapped her arms around him. She tried to remember the spell, but what if she got a word wrong? She might call what she wanted to banish.

Her intruder forgotten, she concentrated on her husband as he kissed her deeply. Whatever happened today at the Society hadn't dampened his desire. All day, her guilty thoughts were with Remy after she had avoided his advances this morning. She slid his cravat from his neck and opened his shirt, which he removed over his head. She fumbled with his trouser buttons, his growing desire making it difficult to undo them. With a laugh, she gave up.

He held her gaze as he studied her watching him undo the last buttons. Remy smiled at her reaction when he was free of his trousers. Then he stripped them off, leaned over her, and lay down slowly, pressing his body against hers.

"Phe, I thought I'd lost you," Remy murmured in her ear, sending tingles rippling through her neck and down her spine. "Say it's not true."

"N-not t-true." Phe could barely get the words out as he kissed her ear, his body warm and musky against hers. Kissing her passionately, he worked his way down her body while she ran her fingers through the soft curls of his hair. He planted kisses where she least expected, her body arching into his. Everything and anything faded into the intimate world where only she existed with him.

Remy began advancing upward from between her legs, pausing here and there when he finally rested full length on her, his body radiating a delicious warmth.

She nearly swooned and wound her arms around him, kissing his neck. "Stay with me, Remy," she whispered and wondered if he had heard. This was her useless plea to have Remy help her banish her intruder.

Remy entered her slowly as if they had an eternity to make love. Her breaths became long and relaxed. She wanted him to hurry. She wanted him to slow down.

You must save your husband, or he will be cursed as they cursed me.

Just then, Remy plunged deep inside her.

"Oh," she cried.

How dare you, Bahl. Get out, she spoke inside her mind. In rhythm with Remy, she met him in a place beyond the Society, the living heads, and the Byzantine city. A place where their flesh merged as one.

Your husband will bring you down with him if you do not let me help you.

"Go away," she said aloud to Bahl, then realized what she had done.

"What?" Remy mumbled, his breathing louder than his voice as he moved through his lovemaking.

"I-I." Her mind muddled.

Remy moaned and collapsed on top of her, his body slick with sweat. His eyes sparkled. He kissed her, then rolled to the side, raised onto his elbow, and met her gaze. His curls fell onto his brow and brushed his shoulders, the muscles of his torso defined by his position.

Pheodora reached for him. Her eyes gazing into his.

Silent and as swift as a thought, something left her straight for Remy.

She pushed Remy away, and he landed flat on the bed. Forcing a smile, she planted her body on top of him. Let him complain about that, she thought as she brushed her breasts over his chest and felt him grow ready for another encounter.

Bahl tried again. She had risked this with her husband, letting him get close without Nene Rose's help, but Lord in heaven, Remy had taken her with such passion. After Remy finished, he kissed her, lifted her off him, and lay on his side, facing her. He stared into her eyes and fondled her breasts.

Phe slid closer.

Then she couldn't move, like in the laboratory. She couldn't open her mouth to speak. Lord in heaven, Bahl would go for Remy if she didn't do something.

Still holding her gaze, Remy slanted toward her.

She couldn't push her husband off the bed. She couldn't speak to warn him. *Bahl, stop. You have me. I can give you what you want. Everything you want. Leave my husband out of this.* She could feel Bahl coiling inside her, moving to leap once more through her eyes. Apparently, Remy hadn't felt a thing from what must have been Bahl's prelude earlier. But something greater follows a prelude.

Remy yelped.

He leapt out of bed and spun around and around. His hands scrabbled against his back where Sultana held on, hissing, her claws digging into his flesh.

"Blasted cat. Get her off me, Phe. Ugh, I can't budge the damned thing."

Pheodora lay on the bed in the same position, paralyzed. Then a pain so sharp, as if someone slid a barbed hook through her insides, made her sit up. What had built up inside her flew out. She could sense Bahl loose in the room, trying to find a way to inhabit Remy.

Sultana screeched, an ungodly sound that surely must have come from the depths of hell. Trying to dislodge the kitten, Remy swiped his hands over his back but missed just as Sulty sprang from his back and landed on the carpet, fur standing on end.

Pheodora staggered over and took Sultana in her arms. The kitten stared straight into Pheodora's eyes.

You have foiled me.

Bahl.

Inside little Sulty.

Bahl, I was trying to have relations with my husband, a perfectly normal circumstance for a faithful wife. You have foiled me. *As for my kitten, only a coward would harm an innocent creature,* Pheodora silently replied to the demon from inside her mind.

This is your *choice,* Bahl answered.

Sultana meowed. Her body stiffened. Her blue eyes widened. She went limp.

"Sultana. Sultana!" Pheodora shook her gently, then stopped. The kitten wasn't responding, so she stroked her. A jolt shocked her fingers, and she stared at Sulty expectantly when a force jumped from the kitten's body into her. She couldn't move her fingers. If she tried to wrench them from Sultana, she might hurt the kitten.

Yes, stay still. Bahl's voice sounded discordant in her mind. *I do not hear you welcoming me back.*

"Fix her. You did this. Take it back. Make her well," Phe said aloud to Bahl.

Remy touched her shoulder. "I'm so sorry, Phe. Let me see what I can do." He put his hands on Sultana, his fingers gently probing her.

"It wasn't you, Remy. She saved *you.*"

"Saved me? She attacked me for no reason. Was she jealous?" Remy kept his hand on the kitten as if his warmth might bring her back.

"Cats are far more intelligent than that," Pheodora murmured.

You would destroy a poor animal? She thought in her mind to Bahl, trying to keep the hatred from her expression so Remy wouldn't see. *How would that possibly make me favor you?*

She clutched Sultana closer, tears streaming down her face.

Remy stood in front of her. "Phe, cats jump further than that all the time. Even though Sulty is a tiny thing, the leap shouldn't have hurt her."

"I–I–we must give her a proper burial, Remy," Pheodora spoke her husband's name, listening carefully to each letter, wishing his name were longer so she could better savor it: a multisyllabic name like Bartholomew, Montgomery, or Remington. Perhaps that might rid her of feeling Bahl take up space inside her again. She hadn't had time to appreciate Bahl's absence. It was unfairly brief. Her tears flowed, this time both for Sultana and herself.

Remy put his arm around her, the feel of his body a small haven. She leaned into him.

"Wait, Phe." He moved away from her, eyes bright with excitement, and began opening drawers in her clothes bureau, rifling through them. He pulled out a plain white chemise. "This should do."

He spread the chemise flat on the bed. "Bring Sultana over and lay her on this."

While she placed Sulty in the middle of the chemise, Remy practically jumped into his clothes, rushed to the bed, and wrapped the kitten up like a tiny parcel, leaving a space around her nose and mouth. He lifted the kitten as if she were a baby and rushed to the door.

"Remy, what are you doing? Where are you taking her?"

Don't leave me alone with Bahl. She wanted to speak those words, to plead with her husband. But he couldn't know what had happened to her. She had seen Remy's inspirations pull him away from her before. It might be impossible to keep him here.

"I'm taking Sultana to the laboratory." Cradling little Sulty to his chest, Remy dashed out the door.

CHAPTER 58

*R*emy sped down the stairs with a firm hold on Sultana, bundled inside his shirt so as not to jostle her. Arriving at the stables, he called out.

"Quick, saddle Atabey."

Tarek ran for the tack while Remy led the stallion from his stall, checking the kitten against his chest. Still. Too still. He had hoped his warmth might revive her. To better secure her for the ride, he tucked his shirttail securely into his trousers. As Tarek cinched the girth, Remy double-checked it, then mounted.

Despite his hurry, he was mindful of Atabey's needs and started him at a walk. He scanned the sky. Plenty of daylight left. It was after hours, so only a few fellows would be at the Society, and the Gov had been leaving early since his earthquake ordeal.

A nudge, and Atabey broke into a trot, then a canter. So close now. Three blocks from the Society. Remy left Atabey in a freshly mucked stall and rushed into the back entrance. The Gov's door was closed. No light shone under it. Remy could only hope he had left for the British Residency. Passing Lord Grimond in the hall, they exchanged brief nods. Too late in the day for talk.

In the laboratory, Remy locked the door. Only he and the Governor had keys now that Pheodora had given hers up, or so she let everyone think. He should have the locks changed.

He grabbed a metal tray from a cabinet and rushed to the back of the room, avoiding the lone head on the table.

The beady-eyed man. He should put that demon back in the trunk. On a table far from the beady-eyed man's, Remy knocked the two crates cluttering the surface to the floor, grimacing at the racket. With a prayer, he removed Sultana from inside his shirt and placed her on the tray. He unwrapped the tiny kitten. She looked as if she were sleeping.

His mind free of fog for the moment, Remy's thoughts jumped to the fly he'd once revived with the Elixir. He fetched gloves, ceramic bowls, clean cloths, and utensils. Remy slipped on the gloves. From the *G.E. Shocked* jar, the batch that had grown in volume yet still worked, he scooped an inch of liquid into a bowl. Using the wooden utensil, he spread it over the kitten's fur, pressing gently so it would soak in. When he finished, her fur was wet enough that her skin showed through in places.

He pulled out his pocket watch—6:30 pm. The fly had resurrected immediately. Sultana still glistened with the gel. Tink-tink-tinka-tinka, his second hand advanced. After a quarter hour, he slipped the watch back into his pocket and leaned close to the kitten.

Her fur was dry over three-fourths of her body, so she had absorbed most of the Elixir. Using a clean utensil, he spooned another inch into a clean ceramic bowl and spread it over Sultana, rubbing it into her fur until she was thoroughly soaked again.

Remy settled in a chair, his pocketwatch out. Tink-tink-tinka-tinka. Perhaps this time the Elixir would work. A knock startled him. Simmery? No, why would he knock if he had a key?

Sliding Sultana onto the bottom shelf of the Elixir cabinet, the door ajar for air, he called, "Just a minute, misplaced my key." The truth: he needed a moment to compose himself.

Was he a total failure, a fool, for trying this? Couldn't he face he had killed the kitten whom Phe adored?

Remy prepared to deal with the Gov or give Kahlil a dressing down for bothering him. Either way, he had to get hold of himself. He unlocked the door.

Pheodora nearly fell in. "What on earth are you doing that you had to lock the door? No one is here except me." She looked around the laboratory. "What is that odd smell?" She sniffed around him.

"Why, it's your gloves. What is that goop on them?" She reached out to touch.

"Better not." Remy pulled his hand away. "Something we're trying for our discoveries. Let me dispose of these." Remy hurried away.

Phe must have left the house soon after he had. He chided himself for not suspecting it was her. Must still be foggy from the electric shock.

"Where is Sultana?" Pheodora peered around him.

Remy's face burned with his failure. He had hoped to make Pheodora happy, but could not tell her they should give it another quarter-hour for the kitten to return from the dead. Instead, he would have to think of something else. Was he insane or merely a hopeful natural philosopher/scientist?

He took Pheodora's hands in his. "Dear Phe, I thought Sultana was in a deep faint. I hoped a brisk ride, a change of venue, and special smelling salts would bring her out of it." That took care of the smell Phe had noticed.

Her face lit with sudden relief. "Oh, Remy. It's a miracle. I thought she was surely...g-gone." Pheodora bowed her head, sniffing, trying not to cry. Then, she looked up at him, a bright smile lighting her face. "Let me see her." Pheodora stepped into his arms.

Remy drew a breath. That went well. He chastised himself for being so vague that she had misunderstood. Now she was in for more disappointment.

"Phe, look at me. It did not work. I was wrong. Something very odd happened to Sultana."

Pheodora stared at him, her eyes narrowing in anger.

Remy took her gently by the shoulders so she would look at him. "Phe, I did my best. I thought she would come around."

Pheodora turned her back to him, her shoulders hunched. Was she crying? He hadn't meant to startle her and moved toward her, ready to comfort her, when she suddenly darted to the back of the laboratory. Was she searching for Sultana's body?

He followed the shuffling and metallic clang. She could hurt herself in this place if she weren't careful. Blast, where was she?

She stood before the beady-eyed man's head, calipers raised like an axe, a fresh dent in the table beside it. My God, she would destroy their last specimen.

Remy caught her arms.

"Phe, we don't want to do that."

He pulled her away.

She went limp.

Caught by surprise, Remy braced himself so he wouldn't fall from her unexpected weight. He could see only the back of her head. Had she fainted?

She sprang from his arms. The caliper's jaws smashed into the table with a crash, just missing the man's head, which fell onto its side.

Remy swiveled in front of her and gripped her wrists. "Drop the calipers. I don't want to hurt you."

"He killed her!" Pheodora almost wrenched away from him. But he walked her backward and pinned her against a wall.

"Phe, he has no body. He's been here the whole time. He couldn't possibly have hurt Sultana."

"He tried to slip into you, but when Sultana jumped on your back, she stopped him. Don't you see? He's evil. Evil!" Pheodora kicked Remy. She had tried for his privates but hit his inner thigh.

Remy flinched. What was she on about?

"No. I don't see." Moving so that she couldn't bullseye his privates, Remy let go of one of her wrists. He held tight to the one with the calipers and wrenched them away, watching in satisfaction as they hit the floor.

"Ow! You hurt me." Pheodora glared at him. Then, as if she had just realized where she was, her gaze swept the room.

"Where is the woman?" she asked and stepped back, turning to walk away, presumably to look for Tanythe. Remy did not care to have this conversation. He caught up, took her arm, and stopped her.

"The woman with the red hair. Where is she?" Pheodora's voice shrilled, and she pulled away from him. "Did you hide her?"

Remy thought back to when Phe first discovered the heads. At that time, the beady-eyed man and Tanythe were the only ones in the laboratory. Leukan's head had already been joined to his body.

"She left," he said. That might shut Phe up, and it was the truth. Tanythe had left with Leukan after the earthquake, but Phe didn't know Leukan was associated with Tanythe.

Pheodora faced him. "When? How could she leave? She couldn't possibly move."

"Yes, I know. I have no idea how. The last time I saw her, she was here, then the earthquake began. The Gov was injured. I carried him to the street as parts of the ceiling shook loose."

"You left them here?" Pheodora leaned against a cabinet and glared at him accusingly. "How could you? Have you no decency? I-I would never—"

"The woman told me to take the crystal and leave. To go quickly." Remy blurted. How had he let it slip? He had told no one about Tanythe and Leukan's mind talk.

"Damnation, Phe..."

CHAPTER 59

"*L*ord Remy Edric Derrien, I think you are officially insane." Pheodora pushed away from the cabinet and looked wildly around the laboratory, then hurried down one of the aisles between the tables.

Remy followed. Would she try to attack the beady-eyed man again or attempt to destroy something else?

As he caught up with her. She spun around.

"Keep away from me." She stepped backwards. "I'm taking Derya home before something happens to her like it did to S-Sulty." Tears streaked her cheeks. "When did you become such a walking disaster? I-I don't know what to do with all this." She gestured, indicating the laboratory.

"T-the heads. The robbery. You getting shot. And the electric shock. It almost killed you. What on earth were you thinking, Remy?" She dipped to the floor and scooped up the calipers.

"I'll put an end to this evil." Phe rushed toward the beady-eyed man.

Remy caught her, knocking the calipers from her grip and wrapping an arm around her waist. "Stop, Phe. Destroying him won't change anything. Can't you see that? We can study what made him the way he is. Good can come from that."

"There are things you don't know." She pummeled him with her fists and tried to wrench away, but he tightened his grip.

"Yes, there are many things I don't know," Remy said, dragging her to the door. Outside the laboratory, he locked the door with one hand.

"We'll both ride Atabey home. I'll send Tarik for Derya. We're too upset to be apart now." He lifted Pheodora onto the saddle, mounted behind her, and set Atabey walking. He could feel her smoldering with anger.

"Look, Phe. I know impossibly odd things have happened—"

"You don't know the half of it," she snapped.

He glanced at the half-moon. They would be home before full dark. A relief.

"The woman talked to you?" Pheodora blurted. She had been holding back. "Did she speak aloud, like I am now?" Phe turned and glanced at him, eyes glistening with her tears.

"Could we wait until we're home for this?" She might have forgotten about it by then. But being home would remind her of Sultana. Good lord, Sultana. He didn't have a moment to check on the little thing. If she revived, he had set out dishes with food and water that he had prepared in his optimism. And the kitten could easily nudge the cabinet door open as he had left it cracked at least an inch.

"Absolutely not, we must discuss it now," Pheodora snapped. "This is important, Remy. Did you hear her speak aloud like I am now? Did you hear how her voice sounded?" Phe's voice rose in decibels.

Atabey snorted and shook his head, sensing Phe's rising hysteria. By God, she was upsetting them both. He would bet tears were streaming down her face again.

Pheodora sniffled.

"No, Phe. I have never heard the woman's voice." He was giving her every reason to believe *he* was insane.

She sniffled again. "Well, then how—?"

"Pheodora, please. In my mind. I hear her voice in my mind. And…"

They passed a hotel lit by gas lanterns, shadows flickering over them. Phe leaned to the side in the saddle and turned, her expression so intense it made him tighten the reins. Atabey whinnied and reared.

"Atabey, settle," Remy spoke softly as if they were in the stables. He let up on the reins and wished he could pat the stallion on the neck, but he had to hold on to Phe.

"And what, Remy?" Her voice squeaked as it did when she was most upset. How she could so easily take up a sentence after such an interruption, he'd never understand. But he should answer truthfully. Right now.

"If...if I think a question, the red-haired woman will reply. In my mind, I see and hear her reply. I do not hear her voice as I hear yours." Remy braced himself for a barrage of accusations from his wife.

Before he could see her expression, Phe turned away. She simply sat in the saddle, stiff and straight, the rhythmic clomp of Atabey's hooves on the cobblestones hypnotizing. The night chill settled around them. In rhythm with Atabey's gait, Pheodora swayed closer to him, the warmth of their bodies lending intimacy despite their tiff. Remy's eyelids tried their best to close, reminding him just how weary he was.

"Things like that can happen," Pheodora said, her voice so faint he had to strain to hear.

"Like what?" Remy pictured Tanythe the last time he saw her, the last time he *heard* her voice in his mind. What did it sound like?

"How could you possibly forget what you just told me? What is the matter with you?"

"Phe, I didn't forget. Couldn't possibly forget. And how do you know that things like that can happen?"

"I just know," she said. She was holding something back. After what he had told her, how on earth could she hide anything from him now?

Pheodora stayed quiet except for a few sniffles. Remy put his arm around her, wary and ready to pull it away if she protested. Was she crying again?

"Remy, your crystal. From the woman. Is it magic?"

Remy startled at Pheodora's voice. It carried back to him, so clear and loud it was as though she were speaking into his ear. He did not want to address this subject again. But the crystal pendant around his neck pressed against his chest as if it had come alive. Surely, that was because she had brought it to his awareness. If she had mentioned his knee, he would probably have felt it doing some odd thing now.

Pheodora turned to face him, eyes wide, pupils dilated. "I can practically hear the wheels turning in your head. I know you don't want to discuss this. Can't you see how this is affecting our lives?" She sounded desperate. The laboratory, Tanythe, the beady-eyed man, and Leukan were his to take care of. Well, his and the Gov's. She needn't worry about any of it.

"I've observed," Pheodora continued, her voice weak, "when I bring up a subject, and you don't respond, that is something you've been pondering. One you have no answer for." Pheodora's voice had the annoyingly confident lilt that he hated. Was she trying to bait him? He didn't see how all these things were affecting *her* life. At least, not that much.

"Remy, ignoring me is rude." She sniffed again.

He reminded himself that she had lost a favorite pet and blamed him. A misplaced blame. When Phe said that the beady-eyed man had killed Sultana, everything in her actions showed that she truly believed it. Did she have some kind of connection with him? Was that why she was trying to find out about the mind talk?

"Remy?" Phe sounded worried now.

"Pheodora, I believe that the man is evil. Those beady eyes are malevolent." Hearing the tremor in his voice, Remy knew his fear of that man was real.

"OW!" Phe clutched her head. Was she making fun of him?

"My head." She leaned to the side in the saddle.

He braced his hand tighter at her waist just as she turned and looked at him. Remy jerked back, taking her with him. Lord in heaven, her eyes. Almost all white, but for a fraction of her pupils as they finished rolling up into her head. Remy gripped Atabey with his thighs. Confound it, he had almost fallen off.

"Oh, Remy. He–he's making me—"

"No, not like Sulty. No!" Phe fell hard against Remy's chest. Her head flopped to the side.

Remy caught her, or she would have fallen from the saddle. Holding her straight with one hand, the other on the reins, reminded him of Leukan, limp in front of him, the man's mind and body disconnected. Was this what was happening to Pheodora?

"Phe?" He shook her gently. Her body flopped as if she were a rag doll.

"Home, Atabey." Remy dug his boot heels into the stallion, spurring him into a gallop. He locked his left arm around Pheodora, praying she'd wake.

CHAPTER 60

"*B*ahl." The name slipped from Pheodora's lips, pulling her from a dream she couldn't quite grasp. Had she spoken aloud? Her head on the pillow, she grappled with a deep, unnamed feeling. She sat up, the bedcovers slipping down her chest.

What if Remy had overheard? Bleary-eyed, she checked beside her, but met only an empty pillow, not a bit of warmth left. She squinted at the sunlight beaming through the window. Remy must already be at the Society.

Inside her, the dull ache increased. Chasing fleeting bits of memory, she bowed her head and covered her face with her hands. Last night, she had been riding with Remy. Before that. What? She couldn't recall the slightest detail, couldn't think. She kicked the coverlet off her legs, the cool air stealing some of the bleariness away. Her head throbbed.

"Sultana? Sulty?" Pheodora focused on the shelf where her kitten liked to squeeze into a space between the books, but it was unoccupied. She lifted her gaze to the top of the wardrobe, where Sulty surveyed the room like a queen, then shifted to the window, the kitten's spot for bird-watching.

Anisya must have let her into the garden. Pheodora stood, wobbled, then sat-fell back onto the bed.

You failed.

Bahl. Would she never rid herself of this parasite?

"Failed. What do you mean?" she said aloud, her voice gruff. A memory: calipers in hand, striking the laboratory table, trying to destroy Bahl's head.

Yes, you failed to destroy my head. I saw to that. But before that, you failed to let me leave you.

Pheodora put her feet on the floor, steady now.

"No, my kitten. She—"

"You killed her! She clapped her hand to her mouth at the sudden, sickening memory. *She* kept me from letting you inhabit my husband." The images stabbed: Sultana's still form, Remy carrying her wrapped in a chemise.

She stared at the rug, the tree of life pattern woven in the bright colors of the garden. If only she could jump into that blissful world with its singing birds, its forever-blooming flowers.

I do not deliberately kill small animals. The poor creature simply got in the way of me transferring out of you.

Pheodora pressed her lips together, trying to banish the many angry replies circling in her mind. No need to incite Bahl to do something worse. She lifted the straw box from her jewel casket. At her writing desk, she opened the lid and positioned it in front of her. Pressing the middle of her palm, she read aloud the spell words written on the lid.

"*Kitus a mu. Bara andatus uneen.*

Kial gina. Bara algina.

Kittu tuda m ku. Bara antu tune.

Zianna. Kanpa. Zi Kia. Kanpa.

Inim inim ma. Utug hul a kan."

Her head, clear. Her body, lighter. She closed the lid and returned the box to the jewel casket, then started reciting the spell words with no prompts. The words flowed like her childhood rhyme: in a circle holding her friends' hands, turning and turning until they collapsed, laughing from dizziness. That silly old rhyme played quietly and quickly inside her head:

Ring-a-ring-a-roses,

A pocket full of posies,

A-tishoo! A-tishoo!

We all fall down.

Nene Rose's spell freed her from Bahl. For how long, she didn't know.

She was weary of the demon haranguing her about letting him transfer into Remy, about giving her power if she'd permit him to lead her life. Was Sultana's death her fault? Little Sulty, so brave to attack Remy, making him jump away from her so Bahl wouldn't inhabit him. Tears rolled down her face. She sniffed and blotted them with her sleeve. Had she faced having to choose her kitten over her husband?

Nonsense.

The door opened just a crack. Every muscle in her body jumped. She turned, fearing to see those beady eyes embodied.

"Lady Pheodora, you awake." Anisya sounded surprised. "How you feel?"

Almost limp with relief, Pheodora asked her maid to bring tea and scones, but instead of bowing and rushing off to fulfill her command, Anisya stayed put.

"Gypsy boy here. Won't leave. Must see you." Anisya shrugged. "I send him away?"

Pheodora stared at her maid, who stood by the door waiting for her reply. A gypsy boy. Here. At her home? Was he begging? All that had happened earlier streamed by in her mind, the procession dark and dreary as a funeral march. Nene Rose had said Sultana would protect her. But Sultana was gone. Was the boy sent by Nene Rose?

"Hand me my wrapper and send the boy up to my sitting room in five minutes." Pheodora secured the blue silk tie around her waist. On the way out, she slipped silver coins from her writing desk drawer into her pocket. She had settled on a divan by the window when Anisya knocked.

"Boy, here." Anisya ushered him in. At Pheodora's dismissive wave, she left, closing the door.

"Hanımefendi." The boy who led her to Nene Rose's tent gave a light bow as he held out a basket with a leather-hinged top. "Nene Rose gives it to you."

Pheodora set the basket on her lap. Warmth emanated from it. She lifted the top and peered inside. A kitten, black as midnight, lay curled in a ball, sleeping soundly.

"Nene Rose says your husband keep it by him. Much protect. Black good." The boy put his hands behind his back and shifted his feet, eager to leave. Did he think it might taint him, being inside this *gadje's*, or foreigner's, house?

"What about a kitten for me?" Pheodora teared up at the pitiful pleading in her voice. The boy pressed his lips together and gave her a puzzled look from under his dark brows. When he guided her from the araba to the gypsy's tent and back, he had seen Sultana in the carrier.

"Nene Rose says you *think* you have lost a cat, but you are wrong." He stepped back, his eyes large. Perhaps he thought she might believe he had insulted her.

With effort, Pheodora held back those tears. Nene Rose was wrong. Sultana was definitely—

She could not say the word. "Tell Nene Rose that my kitten died because of the evil man she saw. That…that things are not working as she thought."

"Hanimefendi." The boy looked down at the rug. "Nene Rose never wrong."

He met her eyes. "She says take cat to husband now. Before it is too late." The boy raised his eyebrows, watching to see if she had understood.

"Yes, I will leave as soon as possible. Tell Nene Rose thank you." She set the basket to her side and slipped the silver coins into his palm.

Pheodora opened the door. Anisya came in and placed her hand on the boy's shoulder. "I show boy out."

Speaking Turkish in a low voice, the maid guided the boy down the stairs. The words Pheodora heard as Anisya's voice trailed away would not insult the boy or Nene Rose. Pheodora needed all the luck the gypsies could give her.

She opened the basket's lid. The kitten stretched, yawning, its pearly claws sticking into the cloth lining.

"Hello, little one, your journey is just beginning." She reached inside and tried to pet him, but the kitten batted her hand and backed away. When he tried to climb out of the basket, she scooped him into her arms.

"Boy is gone," said Anisya as she came into the room. She eyed the kitten. "Cat that's black, good omen. From gypsy makes it more special." She looked around.

"Where is Sultana?"

Pheodora burst into tears and waved her maid from the room.

* * *

LEANING CLOSE TO THE MIRROR, Pheodora adjusted her Turkish headdress when a knock at the door ended her solitude.

"Enter," she said, her voice steady after a good cry in blessed aloneness, without that evil demon Bahl. Anisya entered at the same time that Nene Rose's spell exited. The room blurred as if it were behind the veil of tears that Pheodora had just cried. She put her hand to her head.

"Lady, do you have ache of head?" Anisya stared into her face.

You-u-u—

Bahl's voice in Pheodora's head slurred the same as her vision.

A g-gypsy spell-l-l-l.

The demon's voice dissolved into an odd, repeating noise. It sounded like… Could he be laughing? The hairs on her head prickled, and she turned, looking for the malicious being to materialize in the room, his eyes staring evilly into her.

"He's not here," Pheodora said aloud, just so it would sink in. She stumbled to the bed and sat heavily on the rumpled covers.

"Lady, Master left earlier. You want me to fetch him?" Anisya patted her arm.

"N—no." Pheodora lay down on the soft pillow, the covers around her knees. "Bring me some wine."

You forget I am a mage. Your little spell worked for a while, but I am stronger than—

Pheodora pictured the spell in her mind. It spilled from her mouth:

"*Kitus a mu. Bara andatus uneen. Kial gina…*" The words that had come so easily ceased as if they had circled faster and faster down a drain. She tried to pull them back, but all she heard was the frightening sound of Bahl laughing.

I have destroyed your gypsy spell. You best give me freely what I want.

She clutched the covers to her chest, praying he was gone.

If you fail to do so, when I leave, I will seize more than you could ever imagine.

CHAPTER 61

"*W*ait here," Pheodora told the driver as she paid him. Gazing up at the ancient palace, she wondered why the Society had chosen a place surely inhabited by ghosts and ghouls. Hands trembling, she lifted the basket Nene Rose had sent.

.I am expecting your cooperation today. You are aware of what happens when you foil me.

Bahl. He had plagued her since breaking the gypsy's spell. Determined to ignore him, she smiled at the guard, slipped past Snowy's office, and prayed the door stayed shut. After her disastrous visit, where she had discovered the heads, she was persona non grata. And she couldn't recall whether Snowy liked cats. If not, that would be another count against her.

It doesn't matter what anyone likes. It only matters what I prefer. You must put me first or suffer the consequences.

Pheodora shut her eyes as she wrapped her fingers around the evil eye medallion on her necklace.

You know that those ridiculous symbols do not work on the great Bahl, yet your pathetic tendency to hope obscures what intelligence you have.

She knocked on the laboratory door, hoping Snowy wasn't in there with Remy. "It's Pheodora," she called. The lid of the basket bumped up, and she held it down with the weight of her hand just as the door opened. Remy eyed her as if she were poxed.

"Phe? Are you well enough to be here?" Remy sounded concerned.

"I brought you something important." She barged in and set the basket on the nearest table that afforded any space, opened the top, lifted the kitten out, and placed it in Remy's arms.

He gave her the same look he had given her at the door, as if the kitten were also plague-ridden. "What's this?" he said, his frown squinting his eyes into slits.

"A kitten. In Turkey, they believe black cats protect their owner by repelling evil spells better than an evil-eye charm. This one is especially for you. And after all that has happened, there couldn't possibly be any excuse for refusing this little precious." There, she had laid it out succinctly enough.

Amusing. Once more, with the gypsies and the cats.

If Bahl didn't shut up, she would...She gritted her teeth, controlling her temper as the burn of anger kindled inside, stinging her face. She knew her cheeks were red from it.

Something scratched at her ankles.

"Oh!" Pheodora stepped back. She looked down. "Sultana? But it couldn't be." Pheodora scooped up the kitten and held it in front of her. Same markings, same blue eyes. The kitten tilted its head and meowed.

"Remy, you found another kitten for me. It looks just like her." Pheodora hugged the kitten to her cheek. It batted its soft pads against her skin. Their little game.

"This is the exact game Sultana played with me." She kept her eyes on Remy, closely watching his reaction. The slight hunch of his shoulders, the way he looked at her from under his brows, said he had been up to something.

At that moment, the laboratory grew brighter and Remy more distinct, as if a gauze veiling her sight had lifted. Her head felt unconstrained, a great weight falling away. Hah, kittens did work magic. Bahl had gone from inside her.

But Remy was speaking with unusual animation. She focused on him.

"...a great secret, Phe." He sounded excited and turned his head as if he were making sure no one else overheard. "An Elixir I gleaned from the heads. I didn't think it had worked, but it turns out I just needed to use it longer on Sultana. You are the first person I've told."

Pheodora clutched the kitten. She trailed to a chair nearby and lowered herself into it. Her head was clearer than it had ever been. Yet, perhaps she had misconstrued what Remy had said.

"You mean...Sultana was actually *dead*?" She could hear the strain in her voice as if she were talking to that demon Bahl.

Remy knelt beside her, still holding his black kitten. "Dear Pheodora, little Sulty did not have a convulsion. She was truly gone."

"Dead?" The light flared around her, around Remy. She could hear her heartbeat in her ears. Was her husband insane? Did he truly believe he could resurrect the dead?

"You are pledged to secrecy. No one else knows about the Elixir," said Remy, the gold flecks in his eyes glowing.

My God, he was serious. She was the only one he'd told. No one else knew how crazy he was. She must keep him quiet about this.

"Phe, don't look at me like that. It's true." He told her about the fly, dismembered and becoming whole, then buzzing away.

Sultana meowed and licked Pheodora's hand with her rough, pink tongue. She clutched the kitten to her, silently thanking her for chasing Bahl away. Thankful that he didn't hear this.

"Have you fed her?" she asked.

"Who?"

"The kitten in my lap. After you raised her from the dead."

"Don't say it like you don't believe me." Remy had the audacity to look hurt.

"What? Have you listened to yourself? I-I thought the heads were—" What could she say about them except they were an unnatural occurrence. But he knew that.

"I think the kitten is hungry and thirsty." Pheodora rose, then sat down again. She hadn't a clue where to look for food here.

"Probably not. Earlier today, Khalil fetched her a bit of chicken from the market. I have some left if you want. And there's a water dish out for her." He rose to fetch some food for the kitten.

"No, don't bother, just so she had something to eat and drink." She ran her hand across Sultana's back, ruffling her soft fur. "Remy, are you serious about her being dead?"

"You don't believe me?" He had knelt in front of her again.

"Look carefully at the kitten in your lap. Her markings are identical to Sultana's. You said that she played your little game. It is Sultana. And yes, she was dead. And now she's not." Remy tried to stand but wobbled with the black kitten in his grasp. He set him on the floor, got to his feet, and snatched the kitten just before he skittered under the table.

The rumble of the kitten's purring in her lap sparked a thought. Lord in heaven, would all kittens banish Bahl or only Sultana? Nene Rose had said the kitten was special. Pheodora remembered she had said something like that. This could really be Sultana.

"Confound it, Phe. I thought you'd be thrilled that, at last, I'd done something amazing, something very serious." He stroked his kitten. Tiny black tufts of fur took to the air.

"It's been a long several days," Remy said. "I'll ride home with you. Unless you are too repulsed by what I've done." He put his hand to the back of his head, his eyes drooping like his mouth.

"Remy." She stood beside him, adjusting Sultana in her arms. "I need time. I cannot possibly conceive what happened here. *All* the things that have happened here." Pheodora surveyed the laboratory. Would this place be their nemesis?

"I remember you saying that it was very unusual for a kitten to be grievously hurt, let alone killed, by leaping from anything the height of your back. Something else is going on, Remy. And bad things can happen to you, as well as me." Pheodora cuddled Sultana to her chest, the kitten's purr vibrating through her.

She couldn't tell him that Bahl—it seemed Remy didn't know the man's name—had inhabited her, causing the odd things Remy had observed. At least she couldn't tell him outright. She sighed inwardly, thinking: 'I should tell Remy about Bahl. This moment. But I don't know how.'

"Think of all the peculiar things that have happened to you, me, and even Snowy since you discovered the heads. The heads are the cause," she said.

Remy watched her, suspicion clouding his eyes. Was he envisioning her writing letters home about this-this substance he called the Elixir? Telling her Turkish friends, her maids?

She clutched Sulty to her chest and gently touched Remy's arm, closing the gap between them. "Do you know who they are, Remy? Why they were beheaded? What they want?"

Remy shook his head. He still held the black kitten, who straightened its ears and pointed its deep green eyes at Sultana, who wailed.

"I don't know who they are, Phe. There were no clues in the trunk where I found them. The crystal was with them. I felt compelled to take it. Strange. You would say that it called to me, wouldn't you?"

She nodded, the gold tassel on her headdress bobbing out of the corner of her eye.

Remy stroked the black kitten's head, its purring growing louder with each pass of his hand. He squinted the way he did when he was most insecure, and crimped his forehead in a slight frown, his pupils as big and dark as the kitten's in his arms. She knew how he felt. The questions, however much he would deny them, were the same for both of them: Who were the heads? What did they want?

Remy felt the same as she did about Bahl: that Bahl was evil, that the heads could be as well. Could Bahl overcome the kittens' power as he did with Nene Rose's spell?

Sultana meowed. Pheodora clutched her tighter.

The short distance separating her and Remy seemed to widen. Most probably, she knew more about the heads than Remy, especially about one of them. How long had he kept those secrets he just revealed to her? Why hadn't he confided in her? Didn't he trust her?

Pheodora tried to see Remy in a new light. Her husband standing there, holding the black cat from the gypsy fortune teller. Did *she* trust him? Why hadn't she told him about Bahl? Of course, she didn't want to be bundled off to an asylum. But even if Remy, in one of his crazed philosophic conclusions, did stoop to that, she had vast social and political connections. Still…

How could he, discoverer of three severed heads that were still alive, think anyone was crazy? Remy had practically attacked her, defending Bahl's odious head when she tried to destroy it. If Remy knew the truth, he would never consider choosing Bahl over her.

She could hear the back kitten still purring, its green eyes half closed. In the space of a second, they flew open. The kitten jumped to its feet, balancing on Remy's arm, back arched, black fur bristling. It stared at the laboratory door. A rough purr grew into a growl, then became more like something you'd hear out your window on a dark, stormy night, covering any noise that had roused the kitten to its state.

Pheodora cuddled Sultana, thankful that her presence banished Bahl to some place where Remy's kitten couldn't detect the diabolical presence inhabiting her.

The door creaked open. Snowy strolled over the threshold.

Pheodora and Remy looked at the tiny kitten, ready to attack the Gov, and burst out laughing. Incredulous that they could both laugh at this moment.

"Please share the joke. I need more humor in my life." Snowy gave Remy a fatherly pat on the shoulder. "Good Lord, kittens all around. Derrien, I never knew."

"Pheodora thought we needed a competent assistant," said Remy. "Lord Snow, please make the acquaintance of King." Remy held out the kitten, who pushed off Remy's arms and leapt at Sultana. King hung onto Pheodora's arm with one prickly paw, catching on her side sleeve until Sultana swatted him off with a caterwaul. In a sudden burst of strength, Sultana shot from Pheodora's grasp and chased after King.

"Sulty," shrieked Pheodora. She lurched forward to catch the kitten, bumping into Remy and meeting his eyes.

Perfect.

Bahl's voice rose in volume. But only she could hear him. His power flared inside her like sudden flames of a smoldering fire given air.

She must get away from Remy, but her legs wouldn't work the way she commanded. Bahl forced her against her husband.

Desperate, Phe began reciting Nene Rose's spell, "*Ki tus a mu. Ba ra an da tus u ne en.*

Ki al gin...

The surrounding laboratory became muted as if she were in a bell jar, the glass frosting over. The shapes of Remy, Snowy, and items in the laboratory all became faded and flat like pressed flowers fallen from a book's opened pages.

"Pheodora." Remy gripped her shoulders, trying to push her away. "Lord Snow, help. Is she having a seizure? I cannot move her."

She had become immobile, her eyes staring deep into her husband's. She felt Bahl gather his powers like a coiled snake, its body bunched muscle, readying to strike. If Snowy pushed her to the side, she would crash like a felled tree. It would hurt, but Remy would be saved.

From the corner of her eye, she saw Snowy come close, his face next to hers and Remy's. At that moment, something slipped.

Remy vanished.

Snowy's eyes appeared directly in front of hers. Despite her intent to move out of the way, she locked her gaze onto his.

Snowy's pupils dilated in surprise.

Bahl sprang.

"No," she called out as her body hollowed, the word slurring.

Bahl's essence tunneled into Snowy's pupils. The agony. She couldn't release her scream. It radiated inside her, throughout her emptying body.

In the laboratory, the light faded, the day ending in minutes rather than hours. Then darkness, its presence as palpable as a massive mountain pressing upon her.

CHAPTER 62

*L*eukan dipped his hands into the sacred pool, rubbed them together, then shook them dry. He scooped the clear water into his palms, walked over the rough floor of the cave, and poured the water over the smooth white stones marking Tanythe's grave.

With a sharp-edged, flat stone, he dug out a shallow depression near the grave, ensuring it sat lower than the surrounding ground. He glanced toward the altar. Only six oil lamps and as many incense cones from their few devoted worshippers. How different it had been thousands of years ago, when the altar blazed with hundreds of lamps and the swirls and eddies of incense smoke poured from the cave so thick and sweet it perfumed the air of the glorious White Temple on the nearby rise.

Leukan's power had renewed because of his worshippers, but he must take care. Power was simple and fast to use, but their worshippers were new, their numbers sparse. He dared not take his power for granted.

Working as a mortal, Leukan moved back and forth from the sacred pool, carrying water in his palms until it filled the small depression. He placed three flickering lamps and three burning incense cones from the altar around the edge. When the air grew fragrant, Leukan set his satchel on the ground and opened the flap.

"It is time," he said aloud to Tanythe. He saw her eyes widen and eyebrows raise at his deep voice booming through the cavern. From inside the satchel, she looked up at him, a slight smile curving her lips. They had waited long for this day.

Gently, he set her head in the shallow depression beside her grave, the consecrated water feeding her magic. As Leukan raised his right hand toward the grave, the white stones rolled away, and the earth scooped out, spreading gently on all sides. For this, so important, his power held.

Anxious to see Tanythe's reaction, he glanced over. But her head had fallen, her face in the puddle. Reciting a prayer aloud, he righted her head and gently dried her face with his sleeve. She moved her mouth, but nothing came out. They had never spoken since they had been beheaded. When Tanythe had attached his head to his body, their mind talk worked briefly, but that had been the only instance in thousands of years. Oh, to hear her words again, even if it was in his mind.

Finally, his magic cleared the grave. Leukan recoiled in horror, glad that Tanythe couldn't see into the pit. Her body lay there, shriveled and dried like a mummy's. Her lovely pale skin blackened. He turned to her.

She met his gaze, her eyes sad. Questioning. Leukan placed his hand on her cheek.

"Last I saw in this very grave, thy body lay there, living, and as beautiful as it was thousands of years ago when the White Temple was our glory." He had planned to make her whole and have Tanythe in his arms by now.

He turned her head to the altar. "Concentrate on the lamp's flames."

They must leave before the early worshippers arrived. With Tanythe occupied, he knelt over the grave. Her poor body was so desiccated he feared to lift it, feared it might fall apart. Searching the cave, Leukan found a blue ceramic vase filled with a few dried flower stems. As he threw them out, he tested his power. It gathered, clear and strong. Would it be enough?

Submerging the vase in the sacred pool, he filled it and placed it before the altar. The new lamp he offered took the flame fast, then burned bright and steady as he prayed to the pantheon of gods in the Golden Shrine.

Facing Tanythe, he said, "I shall pour sacred water onto thy body,"

She blinked her tears away. Tanythe had read his expressions and knew something had gone shockingly wrong.

He tilted the vase at a slight angle over the grave, letting the water drip delicately on her parched skin. Back and forth he went, filling and emptying the vase, first in drips, then in a steady pour until it was empty. The water beaded and rolled on the wrinkled black flesh as it would on a prune and slid into the grave, leaving a faint sheen on the dark surface of her once-fair skin.

"It is done. We should leave. No one should find us here. Not like this." Ignoring her inquiring gaze, he placed her head in the satchel and secured the latch. They must return to Constantinople. It would take all his power to travel back, but they couldn't stay here. He would find Lord Remy Derrien.

As Leukan hurried to the cave's entrance, he glanced at the sacred pool and paused at his reflection. He held a long shape wrapped in Lord Simmonds-Snow's black cape. Staring into the pool, he waited for the water to shimmer, for Tanythe to throw the cape from her body and stand beside him, her red tresses falling in curls around her lovely, pale nakedness. The beautiful goddess of abundance, the source of life-giving water, of peaceful ponds to raging seas, restored.

But his reflection looked like any other image glimpsed in a body of water, the bundle in his arms merely a long black shape rippling in the sacred pool's shallow current.

Outside the cave, Leukan paused, arms tight around Tanythe's body, the earth at his feet seething with power. He looked up. The heavens, vast and lonely, sparkled with glimmering stars despite the faint blue band on the eastern horizon. A sheep bleated in the distance. The land fell away to vast valleys and mountains. Beyond his sight, the great ocean pounded the earth with waves while cities teemed with life. He was merely a dark speck on this earth.

A lost god with his goddess.

CHAPTER 63

*T*heodora had suffered another episode last night, the second one Remy knew of. He looked up from the microscope. Strange that they both happened here in the laboratory. The first, a few days ago, but this second episode, witnessed by the Gov, had been the most disturbing. Remy had needed Simmery's help to subdue her. She had called out, but her words were indecipherable. Then she fainted.

He tried to shake the memory as he picked up the next slide, which held a piece of thin, gauzy cloth that sparkled silver in the light. Cloth he had found in the trunk, hiding the bag of heads. He had examined this amazing fabric countless times, searching for the source of its unnatural sparkle. As Remy placed it under the lens, a black shape darted across the floor. His hand jerked, crushing the delicate mica slide.

"Blast," he said as he turned, breathing hard, and jumped from his stool. A blur of white crossed in the same direction. Only Sultana chasing King. He sagged in relief and laughed aloud, a nervous cackle. Still, he had every reason to be twitchy. He had brought both kittens with him today, knowing he would soon go home to confer with the physician. Their presence brought a lightness that he sorely needed.

Remy stretched his arms above his head and leaned back on his stool, his exaggerated yawn surprising him. No matter how hard he tried to concentrate on work, his mind replayed last night's events, assembling fragments that refused to fit together. The images dissolved into questions without answers.

Last night, when they arrived at home, he had carried Phe to her bed, where she remained unconscious throughout the night. This morning, he sent a note summoning the British physician from the Residency, then left for the Society. Pheodora's maid, Anisya, would stay by her, keep him informed, and send word as soon as the doctor arrived.

At noon, when one of his footmen appeared with a message, Remy's hands trembled as he stood by the laboratory door and unfolded the note. Just as the footman left, Simmery sauntered in. "Derrien, old man, how is your wife?"

Remy shook his head. The question, in a soft and caring voice, brought up all his fears. "Still unconscious. She hasn't eaten or drunk anything."

Simmery crossed his arms and tapped his sleeve, his gaze far away. "It hasn't been a full day. She'll come round this evening, old man. I'll stop by after I finish here. By then, she'll probably be up and chatting your ear off."

Usually horrified that the Gov would invade his privacy, Remy said not a word. He could use the opinion of a learned man other than the physician. Simmery looked down at the floor. "Sorry, I did not catch your wife when she fell. She took me by surprise. I cannot figure it out. It was the strangest experience." He raised his head.

Remy stepped back at the peculiar expression in the Gov's eyes, something he couldn't put his finger on. It was as if he were looking at a different person. Yet it was the Gov that stood before him, no one else.

Remy waved the note. "The physician is on his way. I must see to Pheodora," he said, hoping his overloud voice would dispel the strangeness emanating from Simmery. "I've only finished with around half of the slides. This waiting makes it impossible to concentrate."

The Gov made a dismissive motion with his hand. "Go, old man." He glanced at the slides sitting in a crooked stack beside the microscope. "Whatever's left will keep for another day."

As Remy sat in the araba on the way home, he suppressed the urge to leap out and strip every last damned bell from the horse's harness. His reaction to the Gov, his inability to concentrate, Phe's situation, all these had him completely unhinged. He closed his eyes, but he was still in the araba, still on his way to face Phe's condition. And the damned bells still jingled merrily as if it were Christmas.

On the seat beside him, the basket vibrated as the araba hit a bump in the road. Remy opened the lid. Sultana and King were asleep, Sultana's white paws around King's neck. Pheodora would probably be missing Sulty by now. He hoped she wouldn't be angry at him for taking them both away for the morning.

The araba let him off at his front portico. Remy tucked the basket under his arm, ran up the stairs, and entered the bedroom, expecting to be met by a bright-eyed, somewhat peeved wife.

"Lady Derrien still sleeps. Nothing else." Anisya stood beside the bed, twisting her apron in her hands.

"When the physician arrives, send him up immediately," Remy said as she left the room. He stroked Pheodora's hair, her face serene in sleep or whatever state she was in, then opened the basket and set the kittens, still sleeping, onto the bed.

Remy squeezed his eyes shut, attempting to understand the last image he had of Phe when they were in the laboratory. Her blue eyes had stared into his. Had they changed colors? He recalled the blue deepening to darkest black. A shiver cut through him, chilling his insides. She had looked possessed. Then that odd stiffness, making her immobile, when he could tell she wanted to flee. Hmm, how could he have known? But he was sure that was what she wanted. Or perhaps she was willing *him* to flee.

That was immediately after the two kittens had jumped from their arms to run about the laboratory. Pheodora had been unduly upset about that. He glanced at the kittens sprawled on the bedcover. Sultana stretched and yawned, her tiny pointed teeth white against her pink tongue, then snuggled next to King. Phe's chest rose and fell almost imperceptibly with her slow but steady breathing, thank God. She was in the same position as when he placed her on the bed last night.

He set his elbows on his knees, head resting heavily in his hands, and watched his wife, who lay still, too still. Pheodora had said the cats would protect them. There was precedent for that. The ancient Egyptians had revered cats. Bastet, an Egyptian Goddess of love, was depicted with a cat's head. Here in Constantinople, one of their Russian footmen had offered that in St. Petersburg, they sent a cat into a house they were about to let to search out and banish evil spirits.

Anisya burst through the open door, and Remy sprang off the bed, expecting the doctor right behind her. He brushed his coat with his hands and straightened it.

"Doctor here. He insists he wait downstairs. Oh." She looked at King. "Black cat here. Very good." Sultana leaped from behind the pillow at King.

"Sultana?" Anisya squeaked as she backed away. Crossing herself, she murmured in Russian, then, after a long pause, said in almost a whisper. "I sit with our lady. Doctor waiting."

Anisya folded her short stature into one of the chairs beside the bed, leaned over, lifted King onto her lap, and started crooning in Russian. Sultana crouched, her tail twitching as she eyed the black kitten purring on the maid's white apron. Remy hurried out, not wanting to deal with Anisya's reaction to the cat returned from the dead, joining King in her lap.

An imposing figure stood silhouetted against the arched windows of the main parlor, looking out into the garden. The British Residency must have misunderstood and sent a Turkish physician, as the man appeared to be dressed in the native costume. Or perhaps, like some British here, he had lately developed an affinity for Turkish dress.

"Dr.—" The physician's name had flown from Remy's mind. "I apologize. In all that has occurred, I seem to have forgotten your name."

The physician turned to face him and stepped away from the window.

"John!" Remy blurted.

John, er Leukan's, gold and maroon turban twisted most spectacularly around his head, his black braids entwined somehow into the head covering. His dark eyes, so dull the last time Remy saw him, sparkled with intelligence. The gold tattoo on his neck glittered, his black skin setting it off like a star in the midnight sky. A blue embroidered silk sash draped over his shoulder and tucked most smartly into a wide embroidered belt embellished with diamonds. By God, the man had recovered. He hadn't been stolen or murdered.

But where was Tanythe?

John, er Leukan, must have followed Remy here; it would have been impossible for him to know where he lived. But being a—whatever he was, perhaps it was easy for him to locate whoever he wanted. And do whatever he wanted?

Suddenly, Remy was breathing hard, his heart beat rapid and shallow in his chest. Seeing Leukan here, in his parlor, obviously healed, sent Remy's mind into somersaults. Remy backed up, his hand going into his pocket, fumbling for the pistol he had forgotten to place there.

Leukan had done nothing threatening, but his sudden, unexpected presence in Remy's home was like a small invasion. How long had this man tailed him? And why? Shadows in the corner by the hearth wavered and became men in unfamiliar, ancient uniforms, eyes blazing under iron helmets, their long spears tipped in gleaming points.

Leukan put his right hand on his heart and gave a slight bow. "John was the name thou and Lord Snow graced me with." A deep baritone carried John's odd accent, and Remy stood stunned at Leukan's phrasing, his Biblical use of *thou*.

The word golden came to Remy's mind, and a wavering ring of that color formed around Leukan's body, then faded like the marauding hordes by the hearth in Remy's now-vanishing vision.

Leukan's dark eyes shadowed, highlighting the golden ring around his irises. A whiff of fresh grass sweetened the room, changing into a peaty fragrance as if Remy were standing in a field freshly turned, the corn silk-colored straw from last year's harvest reflecting the light like the amber beads woven into Leukan's deep black braids.

Likewise, Remy put his right hand on his heart and bowed. "Lord Remy Derrien, your servant, sir. I beg your pardon, Tanythe informed us of your true name, Lord Leukan. To keep my wife from becoming suspicious, we gave you a rather normal English name."

The man smiled. "Ah, I am most relieved that in the condition I was in, I failed to alarm Lady Derrien." The gold ringing Leukan's irises shone for a moment like a ray of sunlight.

"Let me save thee the trouble of a question," Leukan said.

Hearing Leukan speak proved unsettling. Ever since Leukan had robbed him and spoken inside his mind, Remy had imagined a different voice for him. But Leukan's voice was deeper and more resonant than Remy had imagined, giving more gravitas to that refined face. The voice of someone important.

"Please, be seated." Remy gestured to the traditional British maroon-upholstered chairs Pheodora had insisted on, although she had also furnished the room with a Turkish divan stacked in cushions. After Leukan was seated, Remy took the chair across from him, tossing the matching fringed shawl over the back. He stole a moment here and there to study the man in a way that wasn't obvious, and suddenly wondered how Leukan spoke English in a manner that Remy could understand.

"I have my lady fair here." Leukan pulled Remy's leather satchel from under his chair and settled it on his lap. Gingerly, he lifted Tanythe's head from inside and set her on the brass table between them.

"Tanythe," Remy whispered, dizzy at her beauty. She blinked, raised her chin, and the light in her eyes changed as she registered Remy in front of her. He had thought never to see her again. By the Grace of God, she had survived the quake and looked more vibrant than when he had seen her last, admonishing him to leave the laboratory and flee as plaster rained from the ceiling.

He reached for her, then pulled back under Leukan's gaze. Remy had best watch his decorum. He kept his eyes on Tanythe, avoiding Leukan, who must be studying his reaction. Just a minute ago, Remy had heard his own voice, tender, intimate, when he had spoken her name. And he had held out his arms for her, like a lover.

Her voice brushed his mind: *I am joyous that you survived, dear Remy.*

At last, he heard Tanythe, and she had called him *dear*.

"And I the same. I thought. I worried—" Remy, realizing he wasn't alone with Tanythe, became stricken with fear of Leukan's jealousy. He looked over at him. Would the man think him insane, speaking aloud like this?

"I know that thou and my lady speak mind to mind. I could see and hear at the glade when thou found us, when thou worked my lady's magic with her crystal. She was directing thee, and thou was answering her. My lady graced thee with her necklace." Leukan gazed at him with those eyes, as dark and mysterious as a hallowed glade's pool.

Remy's jaw tightened. Was this a challenge? A warning? A test of loyalty? What would Leukan demand of him now?

CHAPTER 64

"*I* have come to thy abode seeking aid," said Leukan, his voice measured, and calm, as though they discussed the weather rather than secrets of eternity. He sat unmoved, regal, not the least perturbed that Remy and Tanythe conversed mind to mind. Yet with such beings, Remy knew appearances deceived. He remained wary.

"Lord Leukan, pardon me." Remy rose quickly, crossed to the parlor door, and turned the key. "No one must intrude. No one must see Tanythe here."

Leukan inclined his head, his lips pressed to a somber line. "We thank thee for keeping us safe all these *mânghas*."

Leukan cannot hear me as you do. The voice darted into Remy's mind. He startled, whipping his head toward Tanythe. Had she granted him favor above her companion?

Because of a curse levied by the very man found with us. The man you refer to as beady-eyed. His name is Bahl. She smiled. By God, she would have laughed had her form allowed it. But as her smile faded, a spark of rage burned in her eyes. She had said that the man Bahl had cursed them. So the beady-eyed man *was* evil. Remy folded his arms over his chest, his glance shifting to Leukan, who betrayed not a flicker of jealousy or doubt as to how Remy was reacting to Tanythe.

Do not fret over Leukan. He is mine, and I his, but we also have those who love us, and we reciprocate. It is our nature. Our worshippers give us life and power, as they have for thousands of years. Tanythe shifted her eyes to Leukan. As if that were a signal, Leukan faced him.

"I need thee. Nay, we need thee, Lord Derrien, to serve as our intermediary, so my lady and I may communicate. That is why I, rather we, have crossed over thy threshold. I hope it has not been an intrusion."

A sharp rap rattled the door. Both men turned, Tanythe's eyes following. "Pardon me," Remy murmured. He stepped outside and closed the door behind him.

"Lord Derrien, this was just delivered, sir." A footman bowed and offered a brass tray. A sealed note lay upon it.

Dear Lord Derrien

I regret being the messenger of this delay. The British physician is away with a patient and cannot be reached. A native physician will attend instead and arrive in about one hour. We sincerely hope this does not cause you any inconvenience.

Yours respectfully,

Sir Reginald Lewis, H.M. Ambassador

BACK IN THE PARLOR, Remy pocketed the key along with the letter. "Forgive the interruption." He hesitated, thinking of Phe upstairs. Should he ask them to heal her? But to call these beings to her side might further undo her. She had nearly broken under the shock of them before. He prayed she would heal in peace.

"Please continue, Lord Leukan." Remy took his seat, more unnerved than he was at his first sight of them, with Tanythe staring up at him and Leukan in his elaborate costume opposite. These beings were in his home, which magnified their utter strangeness. Leukan had kept Remy's satchel in his lap and now held it with both hands as if it were a touchstone. "I have retrieved my Lady's sacred body," he declared.

Remy stared at the man. Surely, he hadn't said what Remy thought he'd heard. "I beg your pardon?"

"I have retrieved my Lady's sacred body," said Leukan, more forceful this time.

The words sent images burning through Remy's mind: Tanythe whole, in his arms, her lips warm against his. The feel of her body held close. Remy flinched, fearful Leukan might read such thoughts.

"We need thy assistance with making my lady whole." Leukan set the satchel on the floor and sat straight as if a burden had been removed from him.

My God. How could he help him put a woman together? How could he make life flow? His mind spun until it clung to a vision of a beaker, its contents clear, a fly buzzing upward toward the light. The Elixir...

Please tell Leukan about the Elixir, urged Tanythe.

As he received Tanythe's mind talk, sounds from the parlor penetrated his concentration on the beings: a closing door, the shuffle of feet, and a butler's polite inquiries.

"Lord Simmonds-Snow to see Lord Derrien." Simmery's voice boomed from the portico.

Remy stood and faced Leukan. He must fulfill Tanythe's request before he leaves the room and politely sends the Gov packing.

He drew a breath. "Lord Leukan, Tanythe bade me inform you of the Elixir." The phrase, *what is done cannot be undone,* ran through his mind.

"I have discovered a substance that heals and renews life. Only she, my wife, and now you know of it. Because I kept the heads a secret from him, Lord Simmonds-Snow has taken over the laboratory. In consequence, I am now subservient to him. He knows nothing of this, and he must not. We must pursue the quest without him." Remy wiped his brow with a handkerchief. His eyes locked with Leukan's. He had laid himself bare before these beings, of whom he knew next to nothing. What had he done? Should he have taken Simmery into his confidence before this? Had he chosen the wrong side? Leukan's gaze sharpened, narrowed, widened again, as though measuring Remy's very soul.

Tell Leukan that I agree, Tanythe pressed.

"Tanythe has spoken that she agrees on this," said Remy. "Please excuse me, I must see to the disturbance in the hall."

He opened the door, meaning to steer the Governor into another parlor. But Simmery had already turned the corner. "Ah, Derrien. No trouble, I trust? We could use the smaller room."

Remy clenched his jaw. The man had already seen Tanythe and Leukan once. What if he thought Remy was harboring them?

"Before I forget, Derrien, the butler asked where my black bag was, then said, 'Go in.' Rather odd. You must speak to him. I could be just anyone—"

Remy took him by the shoulders. "Before we enter, Lord Snow, you must know, this was a surprise to me."

"Nonsense," the Gov said cheerily. "I mentioned coming over here in the laboratory today." He peered over Remy's shoulder. The door was half open, and Remy could have sworn he heard the Gov gasp.

"Good Lord. It is John in the flesh. We feared we'd lost you." The Gov walked past Remy, pushed the door open wide, and sauntered into the parlor until he stood before Tanythe's head on the brass table. "And you have brought the fair lady. How wonderful to see you both healthy and strong after that dreadful earthquake. As you can see, I fared less well." He indicated his forehead bandage.

Remy, wondering how on earth he had left the door slightly ajar, followed Simmery inside. Now and then, the Gov leaned heavily on his cane. He must use it only outside of work to assuage his injury from the quake, for Remy had never seen him carry one at the Society. His voice had an odd twist to it, as though an accent from long ago was attempting to surface.

"Please, Lord Simmonds-Snow," Leukan said, "use my true name—Lord Leukan. It gladdens me to see thee once more." Leukan's stentorian voice rang out in the room.

Simmery raised his eyebrows. The same reaction Remy had experienced after he heard Leukan's odd lilt and his phrasing. Remy reminded himself to be careful. He must not slip and say the name Tanythe or Bahl, for the Gov did not yet know those names.

Remy took the key from his pocket and began closing the door when, out of nowhere, Sultana zipped through the opening. Remy gave the door a final push, but it was thrown open, almost hitting him. Pheodora, bleary-eyed and disheveled, stood there in the same clothes from yesterday. What in God's name was she doing down here?

"Pheodora, you're awake," Remy exclaimed. Where was Anisya? She was supposed to keep watch over his wife. Why, in this condition, it's a wonder Phe hadn't fallen down the stairs.

She stood swaying and stared at Leukan as if she had never before seen him. Then her eyes moved to the Gov. She sucked in her breath. Remy put his hands on her shoulders, steadying her.

"Dear, let me help you to your room," Remy said. He began to steer her out the door. Under his hands, Pheodora's muscles tightened. She dug her feet into the carpet and wouldn't take her eyes off the Gov. Remy had to get her out before she made another scene.

A blur of white, black, and red whipped past them. The Gov's features distorted, then became partially covered by the kitten in full attack mode. Simmery's hands tore at Sultana, and his muffled scream was Remy's nightmare come to life.

"NO!" screeched Pheodora. She wrenched away from Remy's grip and pulled Sultana off the Gov's face, the kitten hissing and pawing, her bloody claws extended. Streaks of blood welled on Simmery's cheeks and forehead from the claw marks.

"You killed her before. Get out!" Pheodora screeched, looking into the Gov's eyes.

Who on earth was she talking to? Simmery hadn't been in their bedroom when the kitten died. Remy studied Pheodora and then the Gov. They seemed to commune, connected with their eyes, both of them not themselves. What was going on here?

Clutching the kitten, Pheodora broke the connection with the Gov and staggered to the doorway, colliding with Anisya, who had just burst through. While everyone stared at Pheodora and Anisya, Remy slid the fringed shawl from the back of his chair and draped it over Tanythe's head, sending her a silent apology.

"My lady." Anisya supported Pheodora. As if in a spell, the maid stood transfixed in the doorway, taking in the blood-spattered Gov. Anisya shook her head as her face paled and she hurried Pheodora from the room. Remy watched them go. He should sack the bloody maid, but Phe needed her now.

"I am deeply sorry, Lord Simmonds-Snow." Remy pressed his handkerchief to the Gov's face. "I cannot imagine what has gotten into Phe. The shock from all this has discombobulated her."

Simmery snatched the handkerchief. "Never was fond of the blasted creatures." He took the handkerchief and held it to the bloodiest side of his face. "They seem to feel the same," he muttered.

Remy glanced at Leukan. The late light turned hazy, casting the room in a vision. Images appeared blurry, submerged, surfacing for a moment, then sinking. Soldiers, helmets gleaming, swords sharp as a scream. Lamps flickering in a cave, a bright red spray—of blood? Remy's stomach convulsed. He could see Simmery and Leukan through the vision's fountaining blood. Leukan clutched the chair arms, his eyes trained on the Gov.

Simmery's face and clothes dripped bright red blood. He gripped a long sword, the razor-sharp blade so threatening that Remy reached for his absent pistol. A cold current swirling with flotsam and jetsam pulled at Remy's feet and legs, dragging him down, down, down into oblivion. His vision darkened. Shapes blurred in the brume.

Remy groped for something, anything, to steady himself.

A strong arm caught him, braced him, steadied him. The chill drained from his body. As if a wall had suddenly collapsed, his vision cleared. Simmery sat in his chair, bloody handkerchief in hand. No sword.

"Lord Derrien," Leukan murmured close, releasing him, "I see thee views the world the same as I."

CHAPTER 65

"Derrien, old man, I stopped by your house this morning to see how Pheodora was, and your butler informed me you were here."

Remy gave a short yelp and dropped his notebook. The Gov had burst into the laboratory, out of breath, as if the Sultan's Janissaries had pursued him.

Simmery tilted his head, lips pursed. Small white plasters cluttered his face, attesting to Sultana's ferocious attack the night before. He peered around the laboratory, obviously expecting Leukan to walk from the back and greet him.

"Sorry, old man, didn't mean to startle you," the Gov said.

"Give some warning next time. I've been on tenterhooks since last night, and this morning, meeting with the doctor about Pheodora hasn't helped." Remy bent to pick up the notebook and dropped his pencil, which rolled under a table.

"Forgive me. How is Pheodora?" Simmery asked.

Murmuring a few unrepeatable words, Remy kneeled, retrieving the pencil. "Same." He looked up at the Gov, irritated at the morning's events. "The doctor said Pheodora had been sleepwalking when she arrived at the parlor with her kitten. Then he had the nerve to diagnose me as overwhelmed and give *me* medicine."

"Well, old chap, that stands to reason, you being overwhelmed. The doctor's opinion on your wife?" Simmery dabbed at a plaster, and it fell off, leaving a spot of blood.

"Prescribed medicine for Pheodora. Thinks she should come round after the shock wears off." Remy stood, pencil and notebook firmly in hand.

"Last night would've put anyone under. When you go home, she'll probably be her same self." Simmery shifted his feet and looked around again. "Since we were, er, interrupted last night, I was expecting an enlightening conversation with John, er, Leukan, this morning."

Remy put his hand to his head, surprised it was still there. Too much brandy from his shock early in the day, amid everything that Dr. Havenard had said, and now the Gov biting at his heels. Remy closed his eyes, wishing he were still in bed, his worries buried in sleep.

Of course, Simmery didn't know. The thought made Remy's eyes fly open. He'd better get on with it. "Last night, after the maid had ushered my wife upstairs, you heard me offer Leukan my house as a refuge. And you heard him accept," Remy said.

Simmery nodded, but his eyes had a hard look, as if he suspected Remy of some devious chicanery.

"I showed Leukan to the guest suite. Saw him remove the woman's head from the satchel and set her on the chest of drawers. But this morning, the maid came to me, upset. Said they were gone, and there was no sign that anyone had stayed overnight.

"Of course, I looked for myself."

"Gone?" The Gov puckered his eyes. "They just left without a word?" He alternately squinted, then frowned as if by a series of quick assessments, he could determine truth or lie.

"Not a word. I sent two footmen to see if they could find anything. But they returned without a clue." Remy glanced over the laboratory. He envisioned Bahl. Tanythe had said that was the beady-eyed man's name, staring God knows what into him from the table in back. What if they had taken him also?

"We had better check on the other head." Remy made his way, fearing what they might or might not find, Simmery following. Confound it, what with all the hubbub last night, he hadn't done the expected polite thing and invited the Gov to breakfast at his home today with Leukan.

"I apologize profoundly, Lord Snow," Remy said with a glance over his

touched something warm and fleshy. A jolt, like the shock of electricity on a wintry day, tingled his fingers. Lord in heaven, he had grasped Bahl's head. Despite the revulsion turning his stomach, Remy kept hold of it.

Simmery locked eyes with him, his crazed expression making him into a stranger. What the hell was going on? This had gone too far. Remy whipped Bahl's head in front of him as if it were a cross against a vampire.

Simmery leapt back, his eyes round in shock.

"Give that to me." Simmery lunged for the head, taking Remy completely by surprise. Clutching Bahl's head against his chest, Remy stumbled backward into a trunk and fell hard on his backside.

His eyes lit with a fervid ardor, the Gov reached down, hands spread, ready to grasp Bahl's head. As his fingers touched it, Remy rolled to the side, the head crushed against his chest. Simmery, still moving toward him, tripped on the trunk and fell forward with a thud, his legs sprawled awkwardly over the trunk's top.

Remy scrambled to his feet and fled the laboratory, speeding down the hall and out the back. It was only when he opened Atabey's stall that he realized he still clutched Bahl's head. Atabey, however, had noticed. The stallion whinnied. Remy started to throw the head away, but instead buttoned it inside his coat.

With his nerves shot and Atabey's near the same, Remy had the devil of a time mounting the steed. He kept looking at the back door, expecting Simmery to burst out any moment, brandishing Lord-knows-what ghastly weapon. When Remy finally settled in the saddle, Atabey swerved to the side, almost pitching him off.

Blast. Even with Bahl's head hidden, Atabey knew it was there and was reacting to it. Lying as low as he could with that damned head inside his coat, Remy whacked the stallion in the sides with his boot heels. Gripping the reins, he held on tight with his legs as Atabey shot down the road beside the Society. The stallion exploded onto the main thoroughfare, narrowly missing an araba.

Angry curses from the occupants faded behind them. Hoping they would make it without further incident, Remy clung to Atabey as they thundered toward home and Pheodora.

Simmery was different somehow, like when a new cook baked scones, the taste was never the same as the old cook's, even with the exact ingredients. The visions Remy had experienced during Leukan's visit: helmeted soldiers, glistening swords, lamps flickering in a cave, and the sickening spray of blood had been a warning that he should be wary of the Gov. And Remy knew why.

Simmery wanted to steal any power Remy had in the Society. The Gov wanted what Remy had. He would steal credit, steal power, even seize the heads for himself.

Atabey clattered past a regiment of the Sultan's Janissaries, uniformed in multicolors of silk, plumed like crested birds. Crouching low on Atabey's neck, the elite guards flashed by: tall, squared-off bork hats, curved swords, vivid cloth belts, long rifles, white stallions aligned perfectly.

By galloping and swerving past the fabled warriors, he'd probably committed a grievous protocol error, one that the Gov was sure to hear about since he lodged at the British Residency. But Remy had his face almost buried in Atabey's streaming mane, and wore no identifiable uniform, only an Englishman's clothes. How could they possibly recognize him?

Always, always, his worries returned to the Gov.

Remy felt a spasm in his stomach. Good lord, he had absconded with Bahl's head and left Simmery in the laboratory with the Elixir.

CHAPTER 66

*P*heodora was the same, not worse, not better. How could she live without food or drink? She was not like the heads, who somehow lingered on, caught in their own strange immortality.

Remy had used the dropper from the doctor to place a few drops of the dissolved medicine on her lips. The drops rolled down her chin. Supporting her head, he slipped the tip between her lips, pulsing the rubber in intervals so she received only a few drops at a time. She swallowed without choking, thank God, but did not stir or open her eyes. He would have to let the medicine work.

His gaze drifted to the chest of drawers, where Bahl's head lay hidden beneath a shawl. The only head left. Leukan had taken Tanythe with him. Before leaving, he had asked Remy's help, and Remy had said yes. What had he done wrong?

Sultana nosed at Remy's shoe, then curled around his ankle. A black paw shot out, swatting her. She darted after King beneath the bed. Their sudden play drew a laugh from him—laughter he sorely needed. Later, he would let them loose in the garden, their scampering a distraction while he brooded over Phe's plight and his own helplessness.

He curved his palm gently against Phe's forehead. Cool, clammy. As far as he knew, in this condition, she had never had a fever, never moved, or even blinked. He hung his head, drummed his fingers on his calf, and jumped as something furry batted them. Sultana crouched on the carpet, blue eyes on Remy's fingers, tail twitching. Before he could blink, she was on his leg, claws sinking into his flesh. He laughed and shook his leg, but she clung on until he gently swatted her off.

As soon as Remy heard from Tanythe, he would ask her to help Pheodora. Tanythe could heal. He had experienced this healing firsthand when he found Tanythe in a glade by a stream. Remy stroked his wife's hair, so soft, light yellow like a just-opened blossom.

Oh, Phe.

Only last week, they had breakfast in the garden, watching the kittens chasing butterflies into the flowers. Pheodora, leaning back in her chair, cradling a cup of tea, had commented on how she loved the garden, the kittens, and him. Remy teased her about listing him as third in the things she loved.

Just this morning, he discovered that Leukan and Tanythe had absconded sometime in the night. Then, talking with the doctor hadn't offered him much hope regarding Phe. At the Society, he had encountered Simmery, suddenly a different person.

Remy pinched himself on the thigh. Pain shot through his leg. He was not dreaming.

Disappointed, Remy considered the room and the noticeable quiet. Phe still breathed that drugged, slow breath of deepest sleep. But something had changed. Remy eyed the shawl covering Bahl's head. He imagined those beady eyes glaring through the weave, straining toward Phe, toward him. Tanythe had called the man evil. Now Remy felt that malevolence, a chill leaking through the cloth.

He lifted the head at arm's length, the shawl an ineffective barrier, though it mercifully hid the eyes.

In his study, he opened one of the many doors in a huge, unwieldy piece of furniture that had come with the house. Pheodora wanted to have the servants cart it away, but the garish colors, the inlay of rare woods and stones, and the peculiar carvings of creatures and plants, so unusual for a country with a portion of the population that shunned images, caught Remy's fancy. He had insisted on keeping it.

Standing on a stool, he reached up high for the dark blue door's handle. At the back of the empty compartment was a door, the same light green as the inside, making it difficult to detect. When he first explored the cabinet, Remy had discovered the hidden door only because the light that day emphasized its outline on the compartment's back wall.

The secret compartment's size surprised him. It would serve. Bracing himself, he stepped down from the stool. As he lifted Bahl's head, the shawl's edge caught under Remy's leather sole and slipped off, revealing the head.

The man's skin had paled, beady eyes dull, when before they were sharp, black, and full of malevolence. Bahl's head felt warmer than when he had held it against his chest as he tried to escape from Simmery. Could the man have a fever?

Bahl squinted.

Remy would not have those beady eyes glaring malevolence into him, so he pressed Bahl's face against his chest. Grunting from bruises gained in the earlier struggle with the Gov, he lifted the shawl from the floor and draped it over Bahl's head. He hadn't realized his injuries would be so blasted sore from that little dust-up. Call it what it was. By God, Simmery had attacked him.

Gathering the shawl like a sack under and around the head, Remy climbed up on the stool again. Carefully balancing, he lifted the head high into the secret compartment and tucked the edges of the shawl around it. There was room to spare, as if the space had been custom-made for a human head. Remy closed the secret door, restacked books in front of it, and shut the main compartment door. He would be glad never to see Bahl again.

The kittens darted around his feet as he hurried back upstairs. Anisya rose when he entered. Phe lay unchanged. He sat, took her hand. Something more must be done. He would summon the doctor again.

Come.

Mind talk, for the first time since Tanythe and Leukan disappeared.

Tanythe? Remy thought her name inside his mind.

It is I, Leukan.

Again, Remy thought his answer, *I understood only Tanythe could mind talk with me.*

I spoke with thee when I came for our heads. Hast thou forgotten? Leukan's words were clear in his mind.

N-no. I could never forget that. Remy's thoughts shaped words—and an answer returned. Still astonishing.

I can speak with all but Tanythe. We need thee. Come.

Where are you? Perhaps now Leukan would reveal where they had been hiding.

I will lead Atabey, thy stallion. Come. Bring the Elixir. Let no one follow.

Remy stared at Pheodora. He hadn't realized that he had jumped to his feet. Leukan's mind talk was unexpected. Remy gave Anisya instructions on how to give Phe the drops, then rushed downstairs and wrote a note summoning the doctor, telling him to speak with Phe's lady's maid, that he was called away and would be back later this evening.

Blast. He had not asked Tanythe for help with Pheodora. Should he bargain that he would aid them if they healed her? How could one deal with these beings?

He must ask in his voice, aloud, when he was face-to-face with the beings. But first, he had to return to the laboratory and fetch the Elixir.

And avoid the Gov.

CHAPTER 67

*A*s Remy hastened toward the stables behind his house, he faltered mid-step. Was he utterly bereft of reason, leaving Pheodora ill with a mysterious malady, only to run in obedience to a voice within his mind? He pressed his fist hard to his temple and leaned into it, as if to steady his wavering resolve.

What of Phe? What if something happened to her when he was absent? But he shouldn't be long. The Elixir would act swiftly upon Tanythe. She was, after all, one of the sources. His stride quickened. Atabey had led him true before, when Tanythe first called, guiding him to that isolated glade far from the city. God knows where Leukan had gone this time.

Atabey nickered in greeting while Tarek cinched the saddle. "It has not been long since our return from the Society, my fine fellow," Remy murmured, tousling the stallion's silken forelock. Beams of afternoon sunlight streamed through the slatted roof that covered part of the stable's outdoor area. It had been a long day already.

Tarek handed him the reins. Heading to the Society once again, Remy tried different phrasings of his request for healing Pheodora. He had the least formal relationship with Tanythe, so it would be best to address her since she had healed him at one time. Besides, he had never shot her.

Remy settled Atabey into a stall at the Society's rear stables. On the lookout for Simmery, he unlocked the back door and crept through, hoping he wouldn't meet anyone.

In the laboratory, the natural light from the window was adequate, and he took care not to leave any traces of his presence since that morning. He cleared a space on a back table behind a stack of boxes, where the Gov would have to search him out if he came into the laboratory, then rushed to the cabinet where he had stashed the Elixir.

How much Elixir should he take to Tanythe? It was imperative to leave some for his fortune, his reputation, and Pheodora. But the Elixir would enable Leukan to connect Tanythe's head with her body. Perhaps that was the sole reason he had discovered it. His thoughts betrayed him. He envisioned Tanythe whole, holding her in his arms, her sigh warm against his neck.

His decision made, Remy removed the jarl labeled *G.E. Shocked*, containing the Elixir increased by the electricity. It was full to the brim, holding seven and a half inches. Remy poured almost all of that into the jar for Tanythe. Next, he removed the bottle marked G.E. Control, containing two and a half inches of the original Elixir.

In his notebook, he recorded the total Elixir left: three inches. He would have to use the Leyden jar once again to make more. Tingles shivered through him, a haunting memory of the electricity coursing through his body.

A key rattled in the lock. Remy froze. Only Simmery possessed another key.

Trying not to break anything in his haste, Remy steadied his hand and placed the jar with the remaining Elixir into the cabinet. His hand shook as he locked the cabinet door. Then he set the bottle containing the Elixir for Tanythe on a clean cloth and wrapped it for cushioning.

The laboratory door creaked as it opened. Remy held his breath, trying to control his panic, but laughed silently to himself. Finally, a positive result from procrastination—he hadn't yet had the hinges oiled.

As quietly as possible, Remy slipped the Elixir inside his new leather case. Before he latched the flap, he stuffed a cloth next to the bottle and another around it so it would stay upright.

Simmery's footsteps sounded as if he were deliberately setting each foot down as loudly as possible. Did he know Remy was in the laboratory?

The Gov murmured under his breath. He had recently begun doing that as if he were having a conversation with himself. Remy found it unnerving. If Simmery discovered him back here, he would be more suspicious about what Remy was doing than if Remy showed himself.

Why had the Gov returned to the laboratory? He knew Remy had run off with the beady-eyed man's head. But there were many other discoveries than the heads, which had been given short shrift, what with all the unusual events. Someone at the top must be leaning on Simmery. If so, the Gov would probably stay until the end of the day.

Remy picked up a spare notebook from the top of the cabinet. He removed the pencil that marked his place. With the pages spread in front of him, his pencil poised, he strode toward the front.

"Which table are you starting on, Lord Simmonds-Snow?" Remy asked as he glanced at his notebook.

"Huh?" The Gov whipped around as if Remy had caught him stealing. Remy eyed him and, with effort, kept a smirk from his face. Simmery was on the defensive. So Remy had made the right move.

"On which table are you starting?" Remy repeated innocently, pretending to check his notebook.

"Uh, I have not yet decided." The Gov stared, the same look as this morning that had set Remy to flee, as if the Gov would ask something of him that he knew Remy didn't want to give. Remy tried not to flinch at the hair on the back of his neck prickling.

"Well, I must meet Pheodora's physician," Remy said in what he hoped was his everyday voice while he forced himself to walk at a normal pace toward the back of the laboratory, where he picked up his satchel.

"I should be in tomorrow, Lord Simmonds-Snow," he called, pretending it was just another day. He could barely hear Simmery's reply, but it sounded normal. After he locked the door from the outside, Remy sped down the hall as if Simmery were a demon chasing him, waving a bloodied knife.

Monitoring the back door, Remy practically jumped into the saddle and set off at a brisk trot. As they continued down the street, Remy checked behind, then all around, and with a loud exhale similar to Atabey's snort, sat up normally in the saddle. No one had followed that he could tell. Remy patted his new satchel. Now, where to?

But Atabey never hesitated. The stallion trotted down the street, across a bridge, onto a barge, then disembarked in Uskudar, the Asian section of the city.

The sun sat low on the horizon, the long rays making the azure sky hazy. Pasted near the opposite horizon, the full moon looked out of place amongst the wispy clouds, a ghost of itself in the sunlight. After what seemed an interminable amount of time, Atabey entered Karacaahmet Cemetery, a Muslim graveyard centuries old that he and Phe had been meaning to tour. The tall tombstones, a world different from the short, stocky ones in Britain's graveyards, stood like crowds amongst the towering cypress trees' shadows and the shrubs' deep green foliage.

As Atabey made his way through the twists and turns to heaven knows where, Remy would occasionally whirl around, sure that someone followed, only to notice a tall tombstone leaning at a steep angle over the main path. Or, he would glimpse a black-shrouded figure gliding up one of the steep steps, disappearing into the hundreds of gleaming white tombstones, one of the many women here to pay their respects.

Atabey picked his way up a series of wide steps, climbed a steep hill, then walked a bit faster up a curved stone path. The stallion hesitated, shook his head, and then turned into a section of tombs set in a thick grove of cedars.

"This cannot be correct," Remy said aloud as they passed domed sepulchers like miniature mosques with tall, silent bell towers.

Let Atabey lead. Thy steed has done well.

The voice rang sudden in his mind. Remy nearly cried out. He gripped his legs tightly around Atabey and clutched the reins. Hellfire. Why couldn't Leukan have conversed with him in increments over the time they were traveling? Remy could have used the reassurance.

As if Atabey had heard Leukan's mind talk, he pricked his ears and eased into a brisk trot. They stopped at a wrought-iron gate topped with ornate brass spires, the tips sharper than Remy thought necessary for an ornamental fence. The tall fence meandered around an elegant sepulcher tucked in a glade of lofty cypress trees, their black trunks like shadows of something best unseen. With its golden pinnacles, white marble towers, and arched insets, this sepulcher was not one of the largest tombs Remy had passed, but it looked to be one of the wealthiest.

The setting sun lit the marble a fiery orange, the gold pinnacles so bright they appeared molten, as if they would melt and streak down the brilliant white towers.

Atabey stopped at the gate, waiting patiently as Remy fumed. Damn this Leukan. A sepulcher, a place of the dead. Would Leukan and Tanythe be waiting for him amongst shrouded bodies? He'd better dismount and try to open the gate. Scowling, Remy had pulled one foot from the stirrup when the gate clicked and began to open, surprising him so he almost lost his balance.

Blast. He set his foot firmly in the stirrup as the gate opened fully. Just then, the sun slanted onto the sepulcher at a different angle. Black areas marred the marble surface as if it were infected with a leprous fungus. Remy stared hard.

Cats. Sitting in the arches, on the ledges, in impossible places where it seemed they had access only via flight. They dawdled there, blinking their slanted amber eyes as if they were the devil's own, warning Remy away.

Atabey breezed through the fully opened gate as if he were headed to his stables for a fine supper of oats. Eyeing the cats, Remy held his coat close against the sudden penetrating cold inside the grounds. This strange chill, his flesh suddenly hard and devoid of warmth—was this merely his fear made manifest? Remy gritted his teeth at the cats' piercing hisses and yowls resounding like human shrieks echoing off the tombstones. They entered the sepulcher through the open gilded doors.

Wide-open doors.

To the best of his knowledge, Remy recalled that sepulchers were sealed. But this sepulcher had been waiting for them. A trap? Remy's muscles tightened, readying him to spring to defense. He tugged the reins and directed Atabey to turn around.

But the stallion squealed in anger. He jerked his head forward, almost pulling the reins from Remy, and trotted inside the edifice. As they entered a magnificent hall, Remy looked up, astounded at the hallway's soaring ceiling, which was higher than indicated from the outside. He caught the fragrance of a patchouli-like incense.

This place resembled a palace more than a tomb. At a blur to his left, Remy whirled around, almost toppling off of Atabey.

CHAPTER 68

*I*nside the sepulcher, Atabey raised his head, ears forward as if someone were approaching. Remy, stunned by the hall's immensity, dimly noted Atabey's subtle signal, heeding the more obvious: the stallion's breath visible in the cold air, his hooves ringing on the marble floor, and the slap of his tail swishing in discomfort.

Suddenly, Leukan stood before them. With a terrified squeal, Atabey shied away. Remy pulled the reins in the opposite direction, gaining control. As Atabey danced in fear, Remy eyed Leukan. Good Lord, the man was kitted out like a sultan: a ruby-red cylindrical hat edged in jewels, black braids looped over his ears, a deep purple jacket with an endless-knot design of gold brocade, and a green silk shirt bound at the waist by a jeweled crimson sash. Like in a painting of a djinni, he wore trousers in lapis blue, ballooning above curved-toed jeweled slippers.

"I regret startling this magnificent beast." Leukan held the back of his hand to Atabey, the gems in his rings glimmering as if they would come alive any second. Atabey whiffed, then stuck his nose close and let Leukan stroke his neck. "A fine stallion," he said.

"I trust Atabey brought thee with no complications." Leukan turned and gestured down the hall. A man emerged from the dim passage.

Remy nearly screamed. Strangely, Atabey remained calm. Who on earth would Leukan know in Constantinople? And how would he have enticed them into a tomb?

"This is Majidi. He will care for Atabey." Leukan nodded at the man.

Majidi bowed, his long dark hair rippling like a battle banner, blown by a wind that Remy could neither feel nor hear. The man blurred as if he might fade before Remy's eyes.

Atabey wouldn't care for this at all. Remy would not have his horse upset by this creature. He dismounted and took the reins, guiding his stallion close beside him, but Atabey nudged his back, pushing him forward. He nickered to the man as if he were Tarek. Remy stood there with his mouth open while Majidi lifted the reins from his hands. Atabey walked placidly away with him.

"Majidi is a creature of the horse from the Persian deserts," Leukan said as Remy watched his horse being led down the long hall, the man's hair blowing behind his back over his indigo robe. Oil lamps glowed in the marble hall's niches, their light dimming as Atabey ambled out of sight. A cramp gripped Remy's gut. Would he ever see his horse again?

"H-how did Majidi come to be here?" Remy asked, attempting to lessen his panic, his voice cracking.

"I summoned him. He will care well for Atabey." Leukan indicated an arched doorway. A door that Remy had not noticed before was now open wide. He squinted at the bright light streaming from inside, then looked behind him, wary of another being similar to Majidi appearing. The gilded doors at the front entrance had closed without a sound.

Remy put his hand to his throat as if that might help him swallow. He and Atabey were shut inside a tomb at night in a strange, faraway cemetery with two beings who seemingly couldn't die and a mysterious man summoned from the deserts of Persia. At this moment, Remy was speaking to one of the beings, formerly headless, who had risen from the grave to steal his head. Remy had come here voluntarily to help place the woman's head on her body. This was pure insanity, and he was willingly participating.

He could be sealed inside this sepulcher for eternity, wishing for Atabey at his side so they could flee into the fresh air. Remy checked the front doors. Still shut tight.

And what of Pheodora, mysteriously unconscious, the doctor perplexed.

Remy must go to her. Now. "This is a mistake. I'll not stay. Bring my horse." Remy moved toward the front doors.

"Be not afraid." Without appearing to move, Leukan stood beside him. He took Remy by the arm before Remy could react. "Come."

Leukan had never touched him before. Remy jerked away but didn't dislodge Leukan's hold, which was strong yet unthreatening, like a soothing pressure on sore muscles. A great calm overcame him, clouding his feelings and dulling his senses.

"But my horse, and I must return to my wife." Remy heard his pitiful voice, weak with fear. The gold tattoo on Leukan's neck glittered, and Remy envisioned the tattoo broken where the blade had severed his neck. A strange fragrance clung to the man, pleasing, yet foreign, unsettling.

"Lord Derrien." The use of his name by Leukan made Remy's predicament in this place real. But, as in a nightmare where you cannot wake, he could not find the strength to dislodge Leukan's hold, could not find the will to insist on leaving, could not form his lips into the whistle that would bring Atabey thundering to him.

"Lord Derrien, please do not think of this as a tomb, which has disagreeable connotations for most. We chose the cemetery for its privacy. This building could have been set in any part of the city." Leukan gripped Remy's arm tighter and led him toward a doorway blazing with light.

They entered a chamber. Huge lamps hung low from the impossibly high ceiling, their source of illumination hidden. Jewel-toned carpets softened the marble floors. Rubies, emeralds, and diamonds winked from the gold wainscoting covering the lower walls. Leukan removed his hand from Remy's arm and gestured to an area with several tables set on a lustrous carpet.

Remy, dear.

"Tanythe." Remy heard the reverence in his voice as he put his hand on his satchel, his courage reinforced by knowing the Elixir was inside. How could he ever greet Tanythe properly when he didn't know her title? Had he disrespected her?

Her head sat regally on a gilded table with curved ivory legs. Behind her, a large, polished wooden table held a long, bulky object wrapped in black. There was something familiar there. Remy studied it. The Gov had at first accused him of accidentally taking his superfine cape from the hooks in the laboratory, but Remy had done no such thing. Now, he was proved correct. The black cloth covering the object was Simmery's cape.

"I have Tanythe's body," Leukan said softly, taking hold of Remy's arm. Once more, Remy experienced the same sensation, as if he had imbibed too much wine, his head dizzy, his thoughts foggy.

"I must warn thee. Prepare for a shock." Leukan removed his hand and walked over to the table. "If it pleases thee." He motioned for Remy to stand next to him.

Remy did not move. He had already been shocked. Coming here was proving quite enough. His eyes darted to the closed door across the room. When had it shut? Was it locked? He had not heard a click, and there was no bar secured across it. He turned away from the thing on the table covered in Simmery's cape, sprinted to the door, and took hold of the gilded handle. It came off in his hand.

He moved his hand up and down, weighing the handle, horror rising. He looked back. Shadows—from where?—flickered over Tanythe and Leukan. For an instant, he thought he saw skulls, rictus grins, and hollow eye sockets. Panic surging inside, he pounded on the door with the handle. Solid. The gold boomed like a gong. He stopped. My God, what was he doing?

"I must get some air," he shouted over the reverberations. If he did not leave now, he might start shrieking.

Leukan stood before him, his hand suddenly on Remy's brow. The booming ceased. Silence fell, broken only by the flickering shadows and the gleam of gold and jewel-light. Remy's breath slowed, heavy, like the first drift of sleep.

"Lord Derrien, I beg thy pardon. I am afraid I have made thee feel most unwelcome. Please come and join us." Leukan gently guided Remy to a seating area near Tanythe that he had not noticed. He sat in an overstuffed chair. A hearth fire burned in a marble fireplace, giving off just the right amount of warmth. Where had that come from? Leukan poured golden liquor into a crystal snifter.

"Please, refresh thyself." Leukan sat near him, a drink in hand.

Remy dear. Leukan wants to show you my body. That is all. Tanythe. Her mind talk soothed him.

" I-Is that—" He glanced at the table.

Yes. My body, wrapped in Lord Simmonds-Snow's cape. Do not fear. In the quake, Leukan seized it to shield me.

Leukan gazed at Remy, his ebony eyes full of expectation, the thin gold rims shining. Afraid the man might do something alarming, Remy set down his drink. Then he remembered that Leukan and Tanythe could not mind talk with one another."

Tanythe tells me her body lies there, beneath the cape. She bids me not be afraid."

"Lord Derrien, please accept my profound apologies for rushing things. I thank thee for sharing her words. As thou can imagine, I am most eager to have Tanythe here in ways that she is not now." Leukan sipped what Remy discovered was superb brandy.

"Thou shouldst know—" Leukan leaned close to Remy, the gold ring around his black irises as bright as a sunbeam "—that when I last saw Tanythe's body, it was as alive and as beautiful as her head is now." Leukan motioned toward Tanythe, who watched them both, her expression pleasant.

Remy's muscles knotted. He thought he might have to jump from his chair and hop around to relieve the cramp in his leg, but with a protracted stretch, it lessened. What was Leukan telling him? Remy had experienced enough of strangeness and horrors.

"Shall we proceed? It may take all three of us to find a solution." Leukan extended his hand in a slight gesture for Remy to rise, and they walked to the table together. Leukan held his hand over the object, and the black cloak rose, floating free.

Remy craned forward. He didn't see a body. Instead, there was a blocky, blackened mass, fissured like charcoal, long and grotesque.

"Tanythe's body," whispered Leukan.

shoulder at Simmery as they walked. "If all had gone the way I visualized, we would now be enjoying breakfast with Leukan and, er, discussing his history."

Simmery grunted. "I was looking forward to that."

Remy and the Gov stood in front of the table. Bahl was there, just as Remy had left him, thank God. Well, it was good in one way, not in the other. After all, Bahl wasn't Remy's favorite head.

"He looks worse for wear. Do you agree?" Remy asked the Gov.

"Y-yes." Simmery's voice broke.

Remy stared at him. Simmery rubbed one of the plasters on his forehead. He had never shown any sentimentality regarding the heads. Yet his voice, that frown. He looked up at Remy and visibly regained his composure.

"Where do you suppose Leukan has gone?" Simmery asked, his voice weak, then stronger.

"I cannot imagine. If you recall, he appeared with no warning at my home. Before you arrived, I attempted to discover where he had been since the earthquake. That would have given me some clue as to where they might be now. Leukan answered my questions most courteously but gave no factual information. Then, after a long pause, Leukan mentioned something about searching for Tan—the woman's body." Remy cringed inwardly. How could he have let that slip out? Did he want to sabotage himself?

"Good Lord. Has he found it?" Simmery didn't give any outward sign that he noticed the word slip or the slight tremble of emotion Remy couldn't keep from his voice. Still, Remy couldn't keep the images from forming in his mind: To see Tanythe as a whole woman, to hear her voice, to—

Simmery stared at him.

For a moment, Remy thought the Gov had heard what went through his mind about Tanythe, but that was impossible. Simmery had about as much intuition as a stone.

Then, with such an abrupt move as to seem frightening, the Gov stood face to face with him. So close Remy felt his breath, Simmery's eyes alight as if he might whip out a dagger and use it to some grisly effect.

Remy staggered back, colliding with a table.

"Leukan will return. The man needs our help," Remy strangled out the words. He scrabbled his hands across the table behind him, feeling for something he could use to clobber some sense back into the Gov. His hands

CHAPTER 69

*H*ow many times would he fail? He was Bahl, the Great Shaman. He had transferred his essence into Remy's wife, the stubborn Pheodora. With a woman's wiles, she had sensed his plan to seize her husband and avoided intimacy. Each time she thwarted him, his fury deepened. If he did not break her soon, she would drive him to madness.

Late this morning, he had his chance. Pheodora took the accursed kittens to the laboratory. The small demon kitten she called Sultana, whose presence in Pheodora's arms foiled him, had leapt away from her, allowing Bahl's presence to influence her again. Running to catch the kitten, she collided with her husband. Husband and wife stood face to face, staring at one another.

Perfect.

At that moment, Bahl coiled to strike. He froze her body in place, the position ideal for his leap.

Bahl sprang.

But the Governor blundered into them, stumbling against Remy and shoving him aside. Bahl barely made it inside Remy.

He exulted. Finally, closer to his goal. Now, he could easily access Tanythe, as Remy took every chance to be close to the goddess. Soon, Bahl would command boons from the gods. Soon, he would be one of them. Through

Remy's eyes, Bahl found Pheodora, still spell-stuck from his power, and was surprised at the hostility Remy had for his wife. Strange. He looked for the governor but saw only Remy, who held Pheodora by the arm.

Bahl's exultation began crumbling. How could he see Remy if he were inside him? Where was the governor? His triumph curdled. *By the Conjurer's Blade, it cannot be. Hhe was inside that buffoon, Lord Arthur Simmonds-Snow.*

Bahl flexed the Governor's fingers, testing the body he now wore. Something had blocked him from Remy. A force not his own. He recalled what he had glimpsed through Pheodora's eyes: Remy bending close to her, a glint swinging from his unbuttoned vest. A crystal on a silver chain.

Bahl knew it. He had once held that stone himself, stolen from Tanythe's severed body, crimson hair matted with blood as her blue eyes stared into nothing. The crystal had nearly burned through him with power. Centuries later, it hung from Remy's neck, blazing protection. No wonder he had failed. The goddess herself shielded Lord Remy Derrien.

Bahl gritted his teeth. Rather, Arthur's teeth. The answer was clear. If he could not have Remy, he would shape this new vessel into his weapon. He suggested Arthur acquire a weapon other than his pistol. The Governor obediently slipped one of the Society's surgical blades into a case and hid it in his pocket. Better. A silent weapon, suited for closed rooms.

Next, he guided Arthur's hands to draw out a small trunk from beneath a table. The size was right. Empty, with room to spare. Perfect for Bahl's new strategy. Arthur carried it to the Society's carriage without question.

Another time in the laboratory, Bahl had seen Remy mooning about Tanythe like any supplicant before a goddess, hovering, eyes vacant, lips moving in silent conversation. He could tell that Tanythe spoke in his mind. The goddess confided in him. Bahl's plan had been flawless: inhabit Remy, stand near the goddess, charm or threaten her into granting immortality. Yet the stone and Pheodora's clever resistance had ruined all.

In Arthur's body, he had tried once more, lunging toward Remy in the laboratory, but Remy thrust Bahl's severed head at the Governor. The shock recoiled through both men, and he failed again. The Englishman proved as resourceful as his wife. More caution was needed.

He retreated within Arthur. The Governor proved pliant. When Bahl whispered to visit Remy and check on Pheodora, Arthur accepted as if it were routine duty. Convenient. Arthur remembered nothing of the laboratory debacle. That suited Bahl. This time, there would be no blundering force, no necklace in the way.

This time, he would move with subtlety, strike unseen, and catch Lord Derrien by surprise.

CHAPTER 70

*A*t Remy's home, the butler recognized Arthur. "Good afternoon, Lord Simmonds-Snow. Lord Derrien is in the stables, attending to his horse. I shall inform him you are here."

Bahl dictated Arthur's reply, and to his satisfaction, the Governor repeated the words precisely: "Wonderful. I will meet him there. In Lord Derrien's note, he directed me to collect an item from his study. He mentioned I would know it when I saw it." Bahl had Arthur add a genial chuckle. "If you would direct me there, I will be on my way."

The butler eyed the trunk Arthur held. "Would you like me to carry that for you, sir?"

"Thank you, but I have a reasonable grip," the Gov replied as Bahl had directed. He followed the footman, who opened the study door and gestured for Arthur to enter.

"No need to wait. I know the way out." Arthur said, again, just as Bahl ordered. He was truly an easy one to manipulate.

Now, to find his head. Bahl had Arthur search the obvious places in the study, desk drawers that were large enough, and a corner cabinet, while Bahl sent his magic through the home to trace Remy's most recent steps. The thin threads where Remy had most recently been crisscrossed the house like a

342

snail's slimy tracks. On this floor, there was a bright trail straight from the front door to the study. Bahl had guessed correctly.

In the study, the tracks converged in front of a massive armoire with painted sigils and carved images of birds, flowers, and strange humanoid creatures. Remy had left a footstool by the middle of the armoire, probably from his last visit. At Bahl's command, Arthur mounted it clumsily. Bahl cursed inwardly at the Governor's lack of grace, but he steadied himself and opened one door after another until he found his head, unharmed. Yet its eyes were dull, and its complexion had paled.

He had lived for centuries tethered to the gods, his severed head thrown into the same stained bag as Tanythe and Leukan, sustained by their divine essence. How easy it was to take such power for granted. Now, staring through Arthur's eyes at his diminished form, he understood: without the gods, his immortality would fail.

He must find them soon. Or perish.

Per Bahl's instructions, Arthur secured Bahl's head in the trunk and lugged it to the carriage, where the coachman met him and lowered the footstep.

"Situate us at the end of the drive nearest the street behind the rose hedges. We must be hidden, yet able to see a horse leave the stables." Arthur pointed to the far end of the circular drive. Bahl supposed the stables were in that direction, and was pleased with how his instructions integrated with what Arthur knew.

"Lord Derrien will be riding a chestnut stallion. Follow him. Mind, keep back enough so he won't suspect we are following. When he arrives at his destination, stay close but hidden." The coachman nodded his understanding, then closed the carriage door.

While they waited, Bahl cast a spell on Arthur, using much of the man's energy. As a bonus, he discovered he had more control when Arthur became tired. Meanwhile, through the carriage window, Bahl studied the passing crowds: a man of the Tiklitat nomads, tall, thin, his light brown beard scraggly, his cap adorned with coins and beads. Walking in a loping gait, a young Winter Dweller with a pallid complexion and dark brows overtook a short, squat, red-haired man in bright robes. Shrouded in indigo robes and veil, a woman glided by, followed by a dark-skinned girl holding a baby, and three children waddling behind like ducklings. After them were three jaunty men carrying—

There, that one. Bahl directed Arthur to step from the carriage toward the young man whose image he had put in Arthur's brain.

"May I have a word?" Arthur called politely as Bahl sent a burst of magic to the young man in worse-for-wear pantaloons and a dingy striped tunic. As he turned his toward Arthur, he brushed a hank of dark hair out of his face and walked over. His strong shoulders, stocky build, and muscular arms and legs reminded Bahl of his own body, long lost.

"I need a footman. You will receive wages in addition to room and board," Arthur said. "What is your name?"

The young man grinned. "Juba, Bey Efendi." He eyed the carriage with interest, pupils dilating. Perfect. The lad addressed Arthur with respect and was impressed by the fine carriage.

Juba nodded. "I will take your offer, sir."

Bahl had Arthur reach into his pocket and give Juba ten para in silver coins. "Of course, there will be more later," Arthur said, according to Bahl's instruction.

"Çok teşekkürler, Bey Efendi," said the young man.

Bahl scrutinized him with care. The young man had said, 'Many thanks.' Bahl suggested that Arthur smile while Juba looked at the coins. The young man pocketed them quickly as if they might float out of reach, then opened the carriage door for Arthur. He closed it gently, then climbed onto the footboard at the rear.

Moments later, Remy rode by on a chestnut stallion, a fine specimen of horse. Bahl kept him in sight as Remy constrained his horse to a walk. When he was several carriage lengths ahead, Arthur banged on the carriage ceiling, signaling the coachman to pull out.

Dulling Arthur's senses, Bahl instructed him to open the trunk. Inside, his head's lackluster eyes and complexion were worrisome, and he directed Arthur to place his hands on either side of the head, while Bahl suffused it with magic. Immediately, Bahl's eyes shone brighter, and his complexion became less pale. Latching the trunk, he rested it in his lap and devised a new plan that excluded Remy, who had proved as bothersome as his wife.

The carriage rolled through stately boulevards, past edifices that reminded

Bahl of King Gydrl's great palace. Though none matched its splendor. The city bustled with foreigners from many lands, still it felt smaller, poorer than his memories of Reklitabi Geite.

To Bahl's surprise, Remy guided his horse onto a ferry, and they waited while the coachman arranged for the carriage to board as well. Debarking, they discreetly followed. At last, the carriage took a sharp turn, and Arthur leaned with the curve as Bahl spied Remy guiding his horse into the Kara-caahmet cemetery, of all places.

A land of the dead. How fitting.

As Bahl pondered why Remy would travel to a cemetery, he edged his way into Arthur's brain but held back, gaining control bit by bit, careful not to cause confusion. He needed Arthur under his power, but still sharp enough to execute instructions and quick moves.

As the carriage stopped to see which direction Remy would take, Bahl looked out the window. They were in a grove of stately cypress trees, the imposing tombstones pale ghosts lurking through the foliage. Under those trees, it was near dark, whereas the sky above still glowed blue in the bright sun as if the day were divided into two separate worlds. The sun's rays pierced the carriage window directly into Arthur's eyes. He glared as he moved to the shadowed side of the seat, watching the tombstones that seemed to advance in slow, menacing steps toward him.

Remy rode through the gates into the open doors of an ornate sepulcher, its ancient design strangely pristine.

Juba, the new footman, jumped from the back of the carriage and opened the door. After Arthur emerged, Juba tarried beside the carriage, obviously spooked by the cemetery's long shadows gradually overtaking them in early twilight. Bahl had Arthur assure him they were in the correct place, then order him to carry the metal trunk inside.

"Wait here. We may be long, but do not leave." Arthur spoke softly to the driver.

"Follow me, Juba," Arthur said, looking the young man over. Bahl congratulated himself on his fine choice. He had always desired to be as handsome as this young man.

They slipped inside the gilded doors. Far down the hall, they glimpsed Remy's stallion heading down a dark passage as Remy disappeared in the opposite direction around a curve. The horse's hooves on the marble floors drowned any noise their footsteps made, and Bahl found Arthur could be surprisingly light on his feet. The sound of male voices echoed through the building.

Remy and Leukan.

So this was where they had been hiding.

CHAPTER 71

*R*emy stepped back, his fist clenched. He turned away, the image of the blackened chunk of unrecognizable horror on the table stuck in his brain. Was this some kind of perverse joke? His stomach convulsed. He doubled over and ran, but never found a receptacle. The vomit spattered across the marble floor, fouling the tomb with its stench.

A pressure on his back startled him into retching again. Leukan removed his hand.

"Lord Derrien, please. Neither Tanythe nor I wanted to shock thee with this revelation." Leukan flicked his fingers, and the vomit vanished along with its odor. Remy straightened, amazed that his body had returned to normal.

"Th–that is Tanythe's body?" Remy's voice wavered as he dared to stare at the chunk of black substance. The horror on the table mocked every memory he held of her. Leukan only nodded, unfazed.

"Yes. But when I last saw Tanythe in her grave, she lay as lovely as thee see her here," he gestured to Tanythe's head on the gilded table.

Dear Remy, you possess the Elixir and know what it can do. Leukan is powerful, but depleted. Rising from his grave, piecing himself together, and retrieving my body has left him little to spare. We are new to your world and not yet fully restored to our fullness. Tanythe smiled at him, radiant despite her state.

Dear Lord in heaven. That smile. Remy had once scoffed at the impossibly romantic legend that a war started over Helen of Troy. Yet in that moment, with Tanythe's luminous eyes upon him, he understood how a face *could* launch a thousand ships.

She was counting on him to help Leukan. What if the Elixir failed? Remy had seen its miracles with the fly, the rose petals, even Sultana. But this? Could it restore a body reduced to charcoal? He steeled himself. Glanced at the table, at the fissured chunk of black.

His breath came fast and shallow, the walls closing in. Despite Leukan's smooth talk that this palatial building could be anywhere in Constantinople, the hard facts of where Remy had ended up bore down on him. He was in a tomb with strange beings, virtually a captive, prepared to use an Elixir, which he gleaned from them, to resurrect a woman's body that had been transformed into a block of charcoal.

Confound it. Was he insane? He glanced at the enormous room's door, closed. Would he ever see the light of day again?

Turning away from Leukan beside him and Tanythe's beautiful head on the gilded table, he covered his eyes, hot tears burning from grief and fear. He would never hold his Tanythe. Never feel her beautiful body next to his. Never hear her lovely voice say his name aloud.

He was on his knees when he felt a hand on his arm. A gentle touch.

"Lord Derrien?" Leukan's voice was soft with an inflection Remy had never heard from him. Concern, perhaps?

Remy looked up. Leukan was staring at Tanythe's body, his brow furrowed.

Remy, dear. There is hope. Please tell Leukan. Can you imagine how he must have felt when he first saw my poor body?

Remy tried to stand, but his strength wavered. He accepted Leukan's assistance but couldn't meet his eyes. "I beg your pardon, Lord Leukan. Tanythe's message just now. There is hope for you both."

Remy slipped the satchel's strap from his shoulder and set it on a table next to the wall behind Tanythe's body. Three large burning oil lamps, ensconced in an arched niche above, illuminated the area. As gently as if it were the holy grail, Remy set the bottle on the table and unwrapped the cloth from around it.

"The Elixir," he said. And he told Leukan about the fly and the rose petals. Then he explained how the Elixir had brought Sultana back from the dead after Pheodora had accused Bahl of killing her kitten.

Leukan looked at Tanythe when he heard the name Bahl, and she met his eyes.

"When thou first discovered the Elixir, was Bahl contributing any?" Leukan eyed Remy with those dark eyes, the thin gold line around his irises glittering as if he thought Remy had ulterior motives.

"The Elixir appeared on the table unconnected to anyone," said Remy.

"How shall thou use the Elixir?" Leukan shifted his gaze to the thickened, blackened body. Remy couldn't read his expression.

"The same way as on Sultana, unless you know a better way." After all, they knew more about healing.

"First, let Tanythe bless the Elixir." Leukan looked over at her.

And Leukan must bless it after that.

Remy repeated Tanythe's words. He set the Elixir in front of Tanythe. She focused on the glass bottle. He couldn't tell what she was doing to bless it, but her eyes never strayed from the Elixr. He waited in silence for what seemed an hour.

Give the Elixir to Leukan.

Dutifully, Remy relayed Tanythe's message. He wouldn't want Leukan to think he had interrupted Tanythe's blessing when he removed the Elixir and gave it to him.

Leukan angled the bottle, studying the substance before he set it on the table next to Remy's satchel. He held his hands over the Elixir, his lips moving silently.

Remy startled at the sudden movement by his side, He must have gone into a kind of trance from Leukan's silent spell. He had not been aware of Leukan finishing his blessing of the Elixir, or of him moving. But Leukan stood beside him, holding out the bottle.

"What dost thou need for this procedure?" Leukan asked.

Remy named his tools. And then, with no interval that he remembered, found himself in front of a small table next to the one holding Tanythe's body, his requested supplies neatly laid in orderly rows. He looked behind him, then all around, as if that would bring an explanation.

Working a miracle with a foggy mind would be impossible, but then, when had he possessed a rational mind since encountering the heads? A laugh escaped his lips, and Leukan stared hard at him.

"I apologize. I…Ah."

Leukan nodded sagely. "I know of the peculiar ways humans express anxieties. Art thou prepared to begin? If thee need something more, please make it known."

"I have what I need to begin." Remy inhaled to steady himself and picked up one of the wooden utensils, testing it as he studied the wreck that was Tanythe's body. In the blackened bulk, there was a vague shape of legs, arms, and a misshapen chunk where her head would be. What evil had done this to her? He stopped himself. Emotions could only hurt what he would accomplish.

"How did this occur?" He asked Leukan. It took some effort to keep his voice level and steady.

Leukan shook his head, his countenance grim. "I know not. When I rose, I opened her grave. She was whole then, as beautiful as now. Only later did this affliction come."

Leukan cast a somber gaze at Remy. He stroked his rings absently. Gold too bright, set with stones of otherworldly hue. "Thou saw me soon afterward."

"When you came to the laboratory and stole, er, took your head, and Tanythe's and Bahl's. That was directly after you awoke from your grave?" asked Remy. He would never forget that mysterious robber. Remy put his hand to his old wound, then took it away when he realized what he was doing.

"Much later. After I awoke, I needed time to regain some power, enabling me to find my head, and then travel a far distance to secure it." Leukan's gaze drifted, voice heavy with memory. "I became aware when I first sat up in my grave, the dirt cascading from me. I saw I was in our cave, our first sacred temple."

Temple? A cave temple? Wondered Remy. But this was not the time to interrupt and ask who Leukan was.

"Tanythe's grave lay next to mine. After I had regained strength, the first thing I did was remove the earth from her grave. Her body was alive and as lovely as thou see her beautiful head here." Leukan gestured to Tanythe, who smiled a radiant smile. "I resolved to find our heads and make us both whole."

Bahl's beady eyes, glinting with avarice, flashed unbidden in Remy's mind. Why this image now? With effort, he forced the disturbing image away as Leukan's dark eyes seemed to peer inside him.

"Can you see into my mind?" asked Remy.

"I saw thy vision of that despicable, evil head." Leukan glared, rage simmering in his eyes. Remy stepped back, his hands out. What could this being do to him if he were angry? No one would ever find him in this tomb. And Pheodora? Oh, why had he left her in the state she was in?

But he was here in his role of natural philosopher/scientist. To help Tanythe. Perfectly reasonable. Perfectly professional. Perfectly insane.

"I cannot see into thy mind. But the image came alive. It was more than an image. That is why I know." Leukan's voice had calmed. "We must rid thee of his malevolent influence after we complete our task."

Leukan stood over Tanythe's body. "Let us begin."

Remy reached his hand out, then pulled it back. "I must check this black substance. I request your permission to touch her body." Remy had hesitated to ask. This was not like other experiments.

Leukan nodded. "Do what thou must."

Remy put forth his hand. He hadn't asked for gloves, as they would hinder much of the information he would glean with bare fingers. He pulled his hand in. Could he go through with this? He could not touch Tanythe's body.

"I gave thee permission. Thou would not be here if we did not trust thee." Leukan's voice rose. Was he angry? They had brought Remy for a task. He must be the professional that he was.

Tanythe's body felt hard, like a piece of coal. The substance was not as brittle as it looked; otherwise, how could Leukan have wrapped it in the cloak and transported it here? He pressed on an extended ledge near where her foot might be, but nothing chipped off, thank God.

"Water beaded off of it," Leukan said.

Remy held up the wooden utensil. "I need several more wooden ones, the same shape as this, but treated so the wood won't absorb." He glanced down at the table. What he had asked for now sat next to the Elixir. Remy unstoppered the bottle of Elixir and removed a small amount of the substance with the utensil. As he spread it on Tanythe's body, the Elixir glided on like warm butter, and that small amount covered much more than he had expected.

"I need two porcelain plates, black, so I can see the Elixir on them."

They appeared.

One utensil was for scooping Elixir onto the plate, the other for spreading it, and there were spares. Remy became lost in scooping and spreading. As he worked, he envisioned the black substance becoming soft and supple and as pale as Tanythe's beautiful complexion. He stepped back. The entire surface glistened with Elixir. There had been enough. He dared lift the bottle. Only a quarter of an inch remained.

"What magic are you working here, Derrien?" The familiar voice came from the direction of the entrance.

Remy whipped his head around.

The Gov stood in the doorway, flanked by a tall, sturdy Turkish lad.

CHAPTER 72

*R*emy gaped toward the doorway. What in hellfire was the Gov doing here? His grip slackened, and the Elixir bottle slipped. He lunged—

Instead of crashing to the floor, the bottle hovered at his waist. Snatching it midair, he sagged in relief and set it carefully on the supply table.

He stared at Simmery framed in the sepulcher's doorway and tried to wrap his head around this uncanny intrusion. Had the Gov noticed his fumbling with the Elixir? Or was he absorbed in surveying the palatial sepulcher, wondering why Remy was in a cemetery with Tanythe and Leukan? Remy sidled in front of the table that held the black log-like substance that was Tanythe's body, while Leukan, his Eastern finery glittering, strode forward and faced the Gov, blocking Remy's view.

"Lord Simmonds-Snow, I would have thought a man of thy stature possessed more courtesy than to intrude upon a private gathering." Leukan's stentorian voice resounded through the sepulcher.

Remy edged out from behind Leukan so he could see the Gov, who scowled.

"I call this a professional breach of conduct. As Derrien's superior, I have every right to be here." Simmery barged further into the room, his lackey following with a small metal trunk from the laboratory. Was the Gov aiming to steal Tanythe's head?

"Juba, give the man in English clothing the trunk," the Gov commanded as he removed something from his pocket.

Lugging the trunk, Juba walked over to Remy. What was Simmery, the ultimate snob, doing with this street peasant? The boy, smelling of sweat and dust, held the trunk out to Remy. It proved awkward and heavy, and Remy had to hold it with both hands. With this move, the Gov had effectively disarmed him. Remy turned to set it under the supply table, but Simmery started speaking.

"Stand in front of me, Juba." His voice had an odd tone that presaged some event, like a magician giving a command to his assistant before his grand finale magic trick.

Remy, not wanting to miss what the Gov had in mind, gripped the trunk, bracing it against his thighs, and positioned himself where he could see better. Juba stood obediently in front of Simmery, displaying unusual calm, even when he noticed Tanythe's head on the gilded table. It was obvious the Gov had a plan. If he or Leukan could figure it out, then they could deflect him, but so far, Remy hadn't a clue.

Watching for any signal he might send, Remy kept an eye on Leukan, who crept toward the Gov and Juba. The Gov didn't seem to notice. Juba stayed still but glanced uneasily at Leukan, blinked, and pushed a lock of his hair off his face. His eyes darted from Remy to—

A spray of bright red burst into Remy's eyes.

Remy's scream, shrill as a banshee's, blared in his ears as he staggered backward, colliding with the table holding Tanythe's body. It tilted back, partially lifting him off the ground. Blinded, Remy flailed his arms, trying not to fall, and lost hold of the trunk. It crashed to the marble floor with a metallic clang. He had barely regained his balance when a loud thud behind him extended the racket. Had Tanythe's body fallen off the table?

Remy couldn't see. He swiped at his burning eyes. Couldn't fathom what was going on. The sickly tang of copper seeped into his nose and mouth. He spat, blinking furiously. Would the Gov attack him when he was helpless? Where was Leukan? Why hadn't Tanythe spoken to him?

He saw light, then dim shapes. He wasn't totally blind. As he wiped his eyes, he could make out Juba lying on the floor, blood spurting from his neck. Juba's severed head lay a few paces from his body. A sick pulse throbbed through the chamber, seeping into Remy's bones. The room fuzzed as if it were going to vanish. Remy grasped for anything solid and gripped what seemed like a tabletop.

When the room blurred back into view, the Gov stood by the gilded table, holding Tanythe's head by the hair, a laboratory knife's sharp point at her eye.

Leukan sprang at him, but collided with an invisible barrier, collapsing near the Gov, who was out of reach. As was Tanythe.

"You dare not come nearer." The Gov glowered at Leukan, a sight that, from its familiarity, made Remy's mind flash through images, trying to place that look. Simmery had no powers. How could he repel Leukan like that?

Remy hurled himself forward, but his shoulder struck the same invisible wall. Just as the knife sliced into Tanythe's cheek. Crimson streaks flowed down her pale skin.

I am deadly serious. Another attempt, and I shall take out her eye." The Gov's eyes shone in that unnatural way, familiar, but Remy still couldn't place it. Simmery must be afraid his deflection field might fail at any time. Otherwise, he wouldn't threaten them.

"And no tricks of the mind," he warned, his gaze flicking between Leukan and Tanythe. "If you attempt speech within Derrien's head, I shall know. I won't mind carving up this piece of flesh I hold in my hands."

Remy kept his face impassive, though dread coiled in him. The Gov had given no sign that he knew about mind talk. And he must not be bluffing about casting spells, Remy thought, or Tanythe would have spoken to him, given him a way to defeat the Gov.

Something was deeply amiss.

"Derrien, seat Juba in the chair," the Gov said.

What? Remy glanced down at the body. The boy's body still leaked a little blood, though less than any human should. He checked Leukan for some guidance, but he was completely focused on the Gov.

"Derrien, if you wait any longer, she will have only one eye."

Remy stooped and placed his hands under Juba's arms. In lifting him, Remy slipped in the blood on the floor. Making sure of his footing, Remy dragged Juba through the blood to the chair and heaved him into place.

What of Tanythe's body? He couldn't look, wouldn't give the Gov a clue that the black chunk, wherever it was, meant anything.

"Derrien, keep Juba upright." The Gov brandished the knife next to Tanythe's eye. Positioning himself behind the chair, Remy braced the limp corpse from behind, bile rising in his throat. A moment ago, those dark eyes had been alive, fixed on his. Now he was a husk. Juba's body was still warm. Remy felt his legs wobble.

"Leukan, bring the trunk."

In a barely perceptible movement, Leukan straightened his hand, aiming three fingers at the Gov, who flinched. With a furious scowl, the Gov slipped his knife into Tanythe's eye. The orb popped free, rolling across the bloodied floor, grotesquely white against the red, her blue iris coming round again and again. Would it never stop?

Remy's grip on Juba weakened. The boy's body, leaning precariously to the left, collapsed partway off the chair. The foul taste of bile rose into Remy's gullet. Frantic, he tried to choke it down, but retched onto poor Juba. The Gov's gaze pierced Remy, and he moved the knife to Tanythe's other eye.

Remy jumped to attention, grasped the body through the blood and vomit, and pulled it back onto the chair. He kept his mind blank as he studied Simmery for any clues as to what the man, now a stranger to him, might do next.

Leukan, his mouth a grim line, lifted the trunk just as the Simmery had commanded.

"Set it in front of Juba," said the Gov. He angled the knife's blade nearer Tanythe's only eye. "Kneel and open the lid."

Leukan had trouble opening the partially crushed lid, damaged when Remy had dropped it. He banged on it with his fist, then set the trunk on its side, lifted it, and hit it hard against the floor.

The lid broke open.

Bahl's head rolled out.

Remy, breathing hard, clutched Juba, barely able to keep the lad's limp body upright. He had hidden Bahl's head securely in his house. He stared at Simmery. "H-how did you find it?"

The Governor's grin was wolfish. "I am cleverer than you can imagine," he said, his voice gleeful.

"Leukan, pick up the head." Simmery pointed the tip of the knife at Tanythe's eye. "Gently."

In the dead silence, Leukan's breathing filled the room, his face a mask with no emotion as he lifted Bahl's head from the floor. Not wanting to irritate the Gov, Remy tightened his grip on Juba's body, keeping it as upright as possible while glancing in revulsed fascination at the muscle, bone, and veins in the lad's severed neck.

The Gov regarded Leukan intently as his knife glinted next to Tanythe's eye. "Place the head in the proper position on Juba's neck," the Gov said.

His face as gruesome as a gargoyle, Leukan eyed Simmery and the knife. He placed the head properly on Juba's neck and held it there. At a sickening sucking noise, he jerked his hands away and watched as Bahl's head settled. The jagged flesh of Bahl's neck joined with Juba's until Remy, holding tight to Juba's body, could find neither scant scar nor redness.

Bahl's head slowly swiveled on Juba's body and looked up at Leukan. Juba's body twitched. His hand reached out, fingers groping spider-like, and latched onto Leukan's arm. Disgusted, Leukan recoiled, and Juba's fingers lost their grip.

Remy let go of Juba and stumbled back. He was tempted to glance through the open door to see if Atabey was, by chance, waiting there, saddled and ready to spring him from this place. Yet he dared not remove his eyes from Juba, returning to life.

Whose magic was this?

The Gov had none that Remy knew about, and Leukan had no reason to reconstitute Bahl. All this magic and savagery must be Bahl's. Yet how in God's name had the Governor become his instrument?

CHAPTER 73

*J*uba's body, with Bahl's head perfectly attached, staggered from
the chair. As he walked, if one could call it that, his legs splayed
like a newborn colt's, barely keeping him upright, while his torso
lurched side to side, threatening to send him sprawling onto the sepulcher's
floor.

Remy silently repeated, *Fall on your face, fall on your face, you bloody monster.*
But Juba remained upright, beating all odds. The Gov, his lips moving as if he
were praying, still held Tanythe by the hair, knife at her only eye, his focus on
Juba.

Even with his deep inhales, Remy couldn't suck in enough air. Sweat
streamed down his forehead. He peered through the doorway into the hall.
Perhaps Leukan had summoned Majidi to assist them, but he saw no movement and heard neither human nor horse's footfalls. Leukan stayed bent over
the chair that had held Juba's body, his hands bloody on the chair's back, his
regal silks, jewels, and brocades stained dark with blood. Could the Gov, by
forcing Leukan to place Bahl's head on poor Juba's body, have broken this
extraordinary being?

Remy's body grew as cold as the sepulcher. His muscles wound so tight he
thought he might be shrinking. Was it possible that Simmery, or whoever he
was now, had defeated both Tanythe and Leukan? Could it be that Remy, a

natural philosopher and man of science with no magic, was the only one left in the tomb to deal with the madman and the monster alone?

How could he have left Phe unconscious, then traveled here to become a pawn in this strange spectacle, and most likely face his end? No one knew where he was. He and Atabey would never be found. What would happen to Pheodora?

From across the room, Juba turned his newly attached head slowly with purpose, Bahl's dark, beady eyes more alive than Remy had ever seen them. Malicious eyes sighting him. Juba inhaled, air wheezing through his lungs as menacing as a low growl. His broad chest puffed up, and his body tried to straighten, but he remained bent forward like an elderly man in need of a cane. Juba took halting steps on stiff legs. Then, in a lurching stride, he started toward Remy.

Remy's neck prickled. He should do something intelligent and strategic. Yet he stood mesmerized as if Juba were a King Cobra, swaying his scaly body, the hood's dark markings turning into huge, smudged black eyes. Ten paces before Juba could stride right up to him and do heaven knows what ghastly thing, Juba turned.

Like a golem just created, Juba lurched toward his master. His clumsy feet banged against the gilded table, crashing it to the floor. Tanythe's head had sat on that table before all hell broke loose. But now, the Gov held Tanythe hostage.

Juba, oblivious, almost careened into Simmery, his movements as jerky as a string puppet. But he clumsily adjusted his course and, by some miracle, stood in front of the Gov and placed his hands on the Gov's shoulders. They stood forehead to forehead, staring at one another.

Remy caught Leukan's attention and tilted his head and eyes in the Gov's direction. Now was their chance. But Leukan, still dazed and barely standing, shook his head.

So it was up to Remy. He would free Tanythe.

Remy started toward Juba and the Gov. Just then, they broke apart. Remy halted. But it was too late. The Gov had seen and scowled. He held Tanythe's head high, her one eye wide in terror, then slapped the knife to her face, resting it next to her eye. The edge sliced into her cheek. More blood.

Simmery said something indecipherable to Juba, who placed his hands on either side of Tanythe's head and pulled it towards him with a lover's touch. The Gov still gripped Tanythe by the hair while Juba opened his mouth, his incisors unusually long.

He sank his teeth into Tanythe's neck.

"No!" Remy cried out, abruptly silencing himself when he realized he had given his feelings away to the Gov and Bahl. As Tanythe squeezed her eyes closed in a grimace that transformed her beautiful face, Juba repositioned her head, his mouth still on her neck, his throat moving up and down.

By heaven, Juba was drinking Tanythe's blood.

Remy's mind turned one way, then another, but he could not comprehend this repugnant act. His body burned with his inaction, a raging fire of hatred and outrage sucking the life from him like Juba's debauched deed on Tanythe. He silently railed against this creature, but anything he attempted would harm Tanythe. If this ever ended and they survived, she would judge him a coward. *He* judged himself a coward.

With a grunt, Juba straightened. He let go of Tanythe's head. It swung back and forth in the Gov's hand. Her lids closed. Was she dead? While Juba wiped the dripping blood from his mouth on his sleeve, Remy squeezed both hands into tight fists, his face still burning. Tanythe's blood was inside that monster and gave him? Immortality? Immense power? The list could be endless.

Juba lurched away, his eyes brighter, his gait stronger and more human-like. Remy glanced at Leukan. He was looking at the floor. Had he seen what Bahl had done? Just then, Leukan shot a look at Simmery that should've disarmed him. Yet the Gov stood, defiant, the flat blade of the knife pressed hard against Tanythe's cheek. Leukan's eyes shifted to Juba, who stumbled but recovered and walked toward the door.

Simmery's hand trembled. The knife moved a short distance from Tanythe's face. It slipped in the Gov's grip, the tip facing downward. "Don't you dare," Simmery said, his hand shaking worse the more he glared at Leukan. Simmery's eyes had changed markedly, making him resemble the old Simmery. The knife drooped.

Leukan charged him.

"Pursue Juba," he yelled at Remy.

The Gov brandished the knife at Leukan and backed away, his other hand holding Tanythe's head. Leukan knocked the knife from his hand and reached for Tanythe's head. Remy couldn't just stand there, silently rooting for Leukan. He turned and ran after Juba, who was nearing the open door leading to the hallway. The monster swayed to the left and banged into the doorframe, but swerved upright when he heard Remy's footsteps pounding behind him. In a surprising burst of speed, Juba sprinted across the hall. Just as he tried to lift the bar from across the front door, Remy tackled him, jerking him back to the inside of the sepulcher.

"You won't escape, you bastard," Remy said.

But Juba twisted around, his leg clipping Remy's foot. They both fell hard on the marble floor, Juba on top. The monster's flesh was burning hot, amplifying the stink of blood and vomit covering him. Juba pinned Remy to the floor and grunted something as his mouth opened, his incisors coated in blood—

Tanythe's blood. Still warm, it dripped onto Remy's face as the monster made for his throat.

With all his strength, Remy pushed at the monster's chest, meaning to heave Juba off him, but it was as if an enormous stone lay on his body, slowly crushing him. Bahl's beady eyes scrutinized Remy, squinting in that supercilious way of a foe who has bested you. He opened his mouth. The incisors looked longer than before, his breath as foul as a sewer.

Using every bit of strength he could muster, Remy threw punches at the creature. This couldn't happen. This was a nightmare—

Bahl's teeth broke through the skin on Remy's neck. Remy screamed with the horror of it. God in heaven, did he scream.

Then Bahl bit deeper. Remy nearly fainted with the pain and abhorrence as the warmth of his blood flowed over his neck onto the floor, pooling under him. A bitter, coppery smell. He was helpless against this force, an oppression beyond any he had encountered. A wickedness that made his body react in ways that repulsed him.

Remy felt the demon's blood mixing with his, flames flaring deep inside. His body burned with rivers of this force threading throughout, the flow creating a searing chorus.

The demon calling for his soul. Remy's bitter surrender, the sickening sound of Bahl sucking his blood, haunted him as he slid into a dark tunnel, gliding faster and faster with no control, with no idea of where he would end up.

Vague noises in the tunnel. Pitch black everywhere. All had become still. He couldn't move but was lighter somehow, and his breath came easier. There were noises and movement nearby.

"Derrien. Derrien." The voice was familiar, but far, far away. Someone shook him.

"Get off me!" Remy punched and kicked. He wouldn't let Juba or Bahl or whoever he was do it again, not again. The monster.

A hand slapped him on the cheek, hard. Remy opened his eyes.

"Leukan? Confound it, that hurt—"

"Be still, thou art bleeding."

Remy put his hand to his neck. Leukan caught it midair, stopping him. "Leave it until I decide what to do." Leukan bent closer, intent on Remy's neck.

"No." Remy hefted his body to the side as he tried to push himself up. Blast, he couldn't even turn over. Juba had done something to him when he took his blood. With the blood went his strength. What else did he take? Remy couldn't get rid of the sight and feel of Bahl, as close as a lover, his greedy eyes looking straight into his own, his breath hot on Remy's face and reeking of Tanythe's blood. Remy shook with loathing.

Leukan seized him by the shoulders. Remy shrieked. He was certain he had lost the contents of his bladder.

"Derrien." Eyes like gleaming black onyx, a gold ring around each iris, met Remy's.

"It is I, Leukan. I will not harm thee." He pulled Remy to a seated position. Remy veered to the side. Let out a sob. He couldn't even ball his hand into a tight fist.

"Derrien, I must attend to the wound on thy neck." Leukan held him as he swayed, then laid him gently on the floor. "Keep thy head turned like this. Do not move."

Remy closed his eyes, shutting out the sepulcher. If he could only shut out what had happened. After Bahl attacked him, Remy couldn't stand Leukan so close. It wasn't so long ago that Remy had found Bahl in the stained linen bag with Leukan and Tanythe. What if they all wanted the same thing from him that Bahl had taken? A slight tremor snaked through his hands as he tried to summon the strength to escape Leukan and leave this place. The tremors increased exponentially. He struggled to stop them, but all he could see was Bahl's ravenous eyes, his body on top of him, something vital being stolen.

"J-Juba, where is he?" Remy asked Leukan.

"I have taken care of him," Leukan said. "Lie still."

At the sound of Leukan's deep, soothing voice and the words he spoke, the tremors in Remy's body ceased, and he felt safe for the moment. Yet images intruded in his mind: Tanythe, blood dripping from where her eye had been; the Gov wielding a bloody knife; and Bahl, his head on Juba's youthful body. Bahl's beady eyes were more potent than Remy had ever seen them, potent with purest evil. It was clear Bahl was in full command of Juba's body. Poor lad, he had looked so proud to be serving the Gov.

But what about the Gov? How did Bahl persuade him to do his bidding and give him magic? And now that Bahl was controlling Juba's body, was he still in control of the Gov's?

Inside, Remy felt a tingle of cool, then warmth. Whatever Leukan was doing, it was working. Curious, Remy turned his head.

Leukan sat facing him, eyes closed, his palm turned toward Remy's neck, his other hand placed above his heart. Concentrating on Leukan's palm, Remy sensed something transferring into his body. He trusted Leukan, whatever being he was, to help him. The sensation made him sleepy, and Remy realized he had shut his eyes, but he didn't remember consciously doing that. He commanded his body to open his eyes. At first, he thought his eyelids were stuck closed. That was not it. It was as though an aged servant were raising window blinds, his feeble muscles working in another continuum.

As Remy laboriously opened his eyelids bit by bit, he glimpsed the malicious glint of Bahl's dark pupils behind Leukan. He recoiled in panic, but Leukan had said clearly that he had taken care of Bahl. This must be an afterimage, one that he would have to work at removing from his brain. When his eyes fully opened, he saw Leukan in the same position, his hand over him, healing. Then Remy raised his head.

Bahl hovered behind Leukan.

A tingling stirred in Remy's blood as if the liquid in his veins called to the demon. He ignored the odd sensation and readied himself to jump up and attack Bahl. But he stayed on the floor, held there by Bahl's intense stare, and, cursing to himself, watched the demon set his sights on Leukan. He shut his eyes, but the image of Bahl's eyes had burned into his brain. His body vibrated, and his blood sang, urging him to go to the monster.

Remy fought it, thinking of Leukan and Tanythe and poor Pheodora. The blood singing faded. In the quiet, Remy found strength. He opened his eyes. Bahl was still waiting in ambush behind Leukan.

"Leukan, behind you," Remy shouted.

Leukan's eyes flew open just as Bahl jerked him backward.

"No." Remy leapt up, shook uncontrollably for a moment, and fell flat on his face. Leukan's voice traveled along the floor in what sounded like a chant.

Struggling to his hands and knees, Remy saw Leukan heft Bahl off his back. Leukan staggered into the room where Tanythe was, then paused, hands on his knees, catching his breath. With great effort, he straightened and met the monster, who came at him, hands out like claws.

A flash of silver streaked through the air.

Bahl leaned forward, clutching his stomach, his hands around the knife protruding between his fingers. The same knife that the Gov used for his grisly torture. Blood colored Bahl's hands and seeped into his tunic.

Puzzled, both Leukan and Bahl stared at the knife jutting from Bahl's stomach.

The monster jerked the knife from his stomach just as Leukan swung to hit him. In a blur of motion, Bahl danced backward, waving the blade in a confusing series of swirls.

Remy must've blinked, for out of nowhere, the knife wavered in Leukan's chest. In a rage, Leukan went for Bahl, then halted, swaying as if he might fall.

Tanythe appeared by his side. Tanythe. Whole. Her head attached to her beautiful naked body as if she had always been whole.

Remy rose to his feet. He saw only her, his brain overflowing with questions. Leukan's wide eyes, open mouth, and arched eyebrows must've been a mirror image of Remy's. They both gawked at Tanythe, who gave them a brief smile, then moved quickly to Leukan. She placed her hands around the knife, pulled it out, and tossed it to Remy.

That was the last thing he expected. He just stared at it, flying towards him. Then his instincts kicked in. Remy thrust out his hands to catch it, nearly pitching headfirst onto the floor again as the knife clattered at his feet.

Leukan glanced at Remy, his expression as serene as the Buddha.

"Catch Bahl," he said in a clear, firm voice.

CHAPTER 74

The healing from Leukan coalesced inside Remy's body. He bent to the floor and grabbed the knife Tanythe had thrown to him.

The knife that Tanythe threw into Bahl's stomach.

The knife Bahl had ripped out and driven into Leukan's chest.

The knife Tanythe had pulled from Leukan, and tossed it to Remy.

But Remy had missed catching the knife, and it clattered to his feet. Now he seized it. A burst of energy jolted through him, sending him careening after Bahl, as uncoordinated as Juba when he came back to life, his blood tingling, drawing him to the monster. If Bahl took his blood again, Remy wouldn't survive, but if he played this right, the demon wouldn't get the chance.

Bahl had almost lifted the metal bar from across the sepulcher's front door. Remy charged and drove the knife toward Bahl's back, using all his strength so it would go deep.

The monster turned with inhuman speed. The blade had only grazed his side, drawing blood. Face twisted in fury, Bahl struck Remy's chest with a blow so powerful it hurled him into the wall.

Remy opened his mouth for air, but couldn't breathe, couldn't move. *Bloody hell*, the monster had rendered him as helpless as a fly with no wings. Bahl pummeled him again and again, fists slamming into him as though he were a punching bag. Remy crumpled to the floor, landing hard on something uneven. The knife. One mercy. Bahl couldn't stab him unless Remy moved.

The fire in his blood began again, surging hot through his veins, singing in a strange, haunted language and timbre, overcoming him like quick-acting poison. Using that vile strength, he lifted the knife, slipped it through the back of his belt, and struggled to his feet.

The desire to go to Bahl, to do his bidding, was irresistible.

Bahl held out his arms in an open embrace, evoking an incredible longing in Remy. The voices grew painfully loud, the harmony hypnotizing. Their rhythm sang now to the beat of Remy's heart, to the beat of Juba's heart, Bahl's heart.

In the interim of those beats, Remy called desperately, silently to Tanythe. But he heard nothing over his raging blood. The choir blended into a rousing demon chorus. The voices swelled, the messages intense, hypnotic. Remy longed to throw himself into Bahl's arms like a lover. Step by step, he moved closer.

Bahl's eyes glowed like a beacon.

Remy walked quietly into the demon's embrace. The chorus harmonized into a softer tonality as if beginning a new stanza. What in heaven's name had he done? Bahl's arms closed around him, enveloping Remy in the smell of blood and vomit, but to Remy, it was the sweetest fragrance.

Inside the lilting voices, Remy caught something that drew him away from Bahl, something familiar. In that moment, he saw clearly where he was, and the stench again became unbearable. Slowly, he slipped his hand to the knife at his belt. In one swift motion, he drove it into Bahl's kidney, pushing it to the hilt.

Bahl roared, crushing Remy tight in his arms, either in desire for Remy's blood, or the knife had done its work. Remy's blood sang louder.

He knew at any moment, the monster would go for his neck.

A voice pulled him away from Bahl's magnetism. Was it inside the singing? He rammed his knee into the monster's groin. Bahl's arms flung wide.

Remy leapt back, then smashed his fist into the demon's face.

No reaction. Remy hit him again. Bahl staggered, still on his feet. Remy struck the monster's chest and seized him by the arms. He yanked the bloodied knife from his belt and raised it to stab him again. But Bahl twisted loose and bolted into the hall.

Remy, clutching the knife, raced after him, slipping in the blood trail Bahl left. The metal bar across the front doors lay in pieces on the floor. The doors wide open.

He tackled Bahl on the portico, but the monster heaved him off and flung him into the bushes. Still grasping the knife, Remy struggled to untangle his limbs from the bush where he had landed. *Damn, these thorns.* In increments, he extricated himself without regard for tearing his flesh and bounded onto the porch, knife in hand, ready to end this fight for good.

The porch was empty.

The greenish light of a full moon reflected eerily off the golden doors. Remy stood there, sniffing the cedar-scented air for the smell of blood and vomit. At a sudden clatter, he startled in a palsied jerk and almost cried out. The sound of carriage wheels on stone.

Of course, the Gov must have arrived in the Society's carriage, bringing Juba and Bahl's head. Bahl, now transformed by the most offensive magic into a new man, had stolen the carriage. Served the Gov right.

Remy listened until the noise merged with the wind rustling the trees.

He looked up. The moon, shining like a new silver coin, was swiftly covered by gray clouds. The portico plunged into darkness.

Inside the sepulcher, Remy saw no one. He walked further in, aware of the splendor ruined by bloodstains. Had they abandoned him? He hurried to a figure on the floor. The Gov lay beside drying pools of blood. He could be dead for all Remy cared.

Facing away from him sat a sumptuously upholstered, high-backed divan Remy had never noticed before. A heavy weariness descended on him, compressing all his worries and fears into the need to flop down upon the divan. Remy hurried to the front and almost threw himself on top of Leukan, who lay there, eyes closed.

He leaned over him. Leukan's chest wasn't moving. Remy reached out to check the jugular vein in his neck. Was he—

"Resting. In a special way." Tanythe's voice filled his mind. Pulse racing, Remy couldn't move for a moment. Then he turned.

She stood in front of him.

Tanythe. Whole. Her lovely body gleamed like Botticelli's Venus, scarlet hair falling down her back, skin pale as the inside of the seashell that bore the goddess from the sea.

Questions fluttered like a flock of unruly birds through Remy's head. There were too, too many. He reached for her beautiful face to wipe the blood dripping from her hollow eye socket, from the deep gash on her cheek, but dared not touch her. Neither would he have dared touch Botticelli's painting.

A low moan behind him. Remy jerked toward the sound, dreading to see Bahl ready to pounce. Behind the divan, the Gov attempted to stand but made it only to his knees, eyes wide without the crazed look that had so alarmed Remy previously.

The Gov murmured something about Leukan and Tanythe. Remy leaned toward him just as Simmery's pupils rolled up into his head, his eyes stark white, and he smashed into the floor like a freshly axed tree. The back of his head hit with a sickening thud, bounced once with a weaker thud following.

He lay there as still as a corpse, his clothes smeared with Juba's blood.

Tanythe peered at Remy and angled her head toward the Gov. Taking it as an order, Remy sank to his knees beside him. The musky smell of the Gov's Attar Al Paculi mixing with the scent of blood soured his stomach, and Remy turned to the side. He took a breath free of the odor, then checked the Gov.

Remy looked up at Tanythe. "His breathing is slow, as is his pulse. There is bleeding from a large bruised area on the back of his head. He might have a concussion, a commotion of the brain. But we must wait and see."

Blood trailed down Tanythe's cheek from her vacant eye socket. Macabre tears to match this evening's horror. Naked, she stood like a queen, more beautiful than he had ever imagined, her skin glowing like a priceless pearl. She held out her hand. Remy rose, scarcely breathing. He would embrace her. Kiss her. Protect her.

Something slammed into Remy's leg, off-balancing him. He fell halfway to the floor, caught himself, but keeled headfirst onto the Gov, whose eyelids fluttered, his body convulsing. As Remy tried to untangle himself, a fresh drop of bright red blood appeared on his hand. He looked up.

Tanythe leaned forward, her eye cavity bleeding.

The fury came roaring through him so quickly that Remy scarcely noticed

369

he was breathing hard before he looked down and saw his hands around Simmery's neck, squeezing the life from him.

"Bloody hell, you destroyed her eye and scarred her lovely face. You blasted swine." Remy spat out vile words as his body poured more and more strength into his grip on Simmery's flaccid neck. He would avenge Tanythe, make her see how much he loved her, what he would do for her.

Simmery's mouth opened with no sound. His legs jerked.

"Die." Remy spat the word. "Die."

CHAPTER 75

Soft hands with calm strength pried Remy's fingers away.

"Stay your wrath, dear Remy," said Tanythe.

Remy looked up at the goddess, his mouth agape. He had never heard Tanythe speak aloud. Her voice mesmerized him, the words delicate chimes swaying in a heavenly zephyr. Yet they failed to declare love for him. Instead, they simply chided him as one would a child.

Tanythe sat beside him on the floor. The force of her presence so close left him reeling. Her bare flesh exuded warmth and a wondrous fragrance so tempting that Remy forced his hands behind his back, fingers interlocking into a tight fist to keep him from taking her into his arms and ravishing her lovely, bare body.

Her remaining eye gazed into his.

"Bahl possessed Lord Simmonds-Snow. Let us hope the man survives this." She placed her hand on the Gov's forehead. Simmery lay still, his neck ringed in bright red from Remy's attempted choking.

"Will he recover?"

"Yes, dear Remy, I think he shall become normal now." She removed her hand. She was shivering.

"But h-he...your eye. And that vile Bahl." Remy couldn't say the words describing what Bahl had done to her. He reached out to caress Tanythe's face, the teeth marks and bite on her lovely white neck, but his hands wouldn't obey. He glanced down. His hands, now numb, rested on his knees. With his Elixir, he had hoped to be a hero to her and the world.

Remy was still kneeling on the floor next to Simmery when he raised his head to see Leukan take Tanythe in his arms. He placed his hand over her eye and draped the Gov's black cape around her pale body. The long cape dragged through the blood drying around them and encircled her, covering her nakedness.

From under his brows, Remy glowered at them. Cooing to one another like lovers, they had forgotten he was even there. He should have hidden the accursed cape after Leukan whisked it from the black ruin of Tanythe's body.

Leukan removed his hand to reveal her eye restored to its loveliness, her cheek as smooth as porcelain. Tanythe gazed at Leukan, her eyes shining in delight. They were lost in one another, the most beautiful beings Remy had ever seen.

"Leukan." The way Tanythe spoke his name. The tenderness. She had always mind-talked Remy's name with fondness as if he were her pet. Perhaps he would be nothing more than that, save for in his dreams.

Then, as if a bubble that had held the pair safe in all their magical glory had burst, Leukan stepped back, breaking their embrace. Remy snapped out of his jealousy. He became aware of the palatial room, the blood on the floor, and that he was inside a sepulcher in a cemetery where a murder had occurred. Where diabolical magic had sent a monster into the world.

Remy assessed Leukan, this being who enraptured Tanythe. His brocade jacket, bloodstained from the knife wound and ripped at the shoulder and hem, hung loose after his scuffle with the Gov and Bahl. Remy squinted at a curious area on Leukan's shirt where a splotch of bright red blood had appeared. The area grew a bit, stagnated, then, after several minutes, grew once more. The splotch was spreading. Spreading in a rhythm. He didn't know if these beings had the same anatomy as humans, but it looked as if a random number of heartbeats sent more bright red blood onto the darker stains of Leukan's green shirt.

Remy felt Tanythe *see* Leukan's chest, felt her anxiety before he turned and looked up at her. She placed her hand over the wound, and a thin line of blood trailed over one of her fingers.

"Bahl's spell on the knife," said Leukan. "I cannot stop it."

Tanythe's eyes had a faraway look. For a long moment, she was silent, her hand resting on her lover's chest. Remy thought he could hear Leukan's heart pulse each time the blood stain grew.

"When I threw the knife into Bahl's stomach, *my* spell penetrated him as well," said Tanythe. "Pray he is unaware of it, for that is the intent. The spell will destroy him from the inside out. But this. . ." She held her hand above Leukan's wound. "When Bahl stabbed you, this new spell, a curse from Bahl on the governor's knife, entered with the blade."

Shaking his head, Leukan moved her hand from his wound. "Thee must take care with this curse. Bahl used almost all the sustenance he was draining from Lord Simmonds-Snow, hence his stilted movements in Juba's body. But after he drank thy blood, Tanythe, Bahl revived. Even with the power I had left, I could not stop him." Leukan sounded breathless. "And now, I am weakened."

Leukan's chest rose and fell. Remy could hear him breathing hard, like a thief fleeing the scene of a crime. More blood trickled onto Leukan's shirt. He placed his hand on Tanythe's, which again rested on his wound. "I feel thy power pouring into me as if I were an empty vessel. Oh, Tanythe, if we both deplete ourselves, we may never return."

She pressed her forehead to his, keeping her hand on his chest.

Their connection opened onto Remy, deep and soul-reaching through the ages. A river tapped, flowing pure in secret places under the earth. Their desire for one another, a passion inextinguishable, from the basest physical to the angelic ethereal.

As one, they gazed down at Remy, still sitting beside the Gov, who hadn't moved. Remy knew he had overheard what he probably shouldn't. Had felt what was forbidden, but they well knew he was there. They simply did not mind, as if he were a servant or a pet.

Again, they became absorbed in one another, mind-talking now. He could tell by their expressions, by the twinge of energy that rippled through him, the same odd energy he had felt when Tanythe's voice sounded in his brain. Like one color juxtaposed to a different one, he had experienced a specific feel for Tanythe's mind talk, another for Leukan's.

Tanythe turned to him. Was that pity in her eyes?

"Dearest Remy, Bahl took my blood, which is supposed to bestow immortality. The caveat, which would not occur to that demon, is that the blood must be given willingly. As it is, my blood will sustain him and make him powerful, but it will turn on him soon." She closed her eyes.

Within seconds, the stifling oppressiveness of what had occurred transformed into a freshness. All around him, Remy saw a spring meadow's long grasses rippling in a balmy breeze. He breathed in the wondrous green fragrance, more precious to him than any costly perfume.

Tanythe opened her eyes. The long grasses faded slowly, as if blown away one by one, like a dream upon awakening. The odor of incense mixed with blood permeated the sepulcher.

Leukan removed Tanythe's hand from his chest. Their eyes met. The mind talk between them, still only impressions, made Remy squirm in the discomfort of being excluded. After a time, Tanythe looked down at him again.

"When Bahl stole my blood, I was—" She looked at Leukan, and he reached for her other hand. "I was violated in the worst way possible. I thought all was lost." Then she smiled, her face glowing. "Your Elixir worked a miracle, dear Remy. Without it, I would not have survived."

The hum of mind talk filled him. A scene appeared before his eyes: a pool of water, its angled ripples reflecting golden sun rays breaking through the ceiling of...a cave? A place strange, yet in the back of his mind, Remy knew he had been in that place. The sunlight on the water's surface grew impossibly bright. Tanythe floated in the pool. The water tinged blue on her naked body, her scarlet tresses flowing around her like a diaphanous gown. An oil lamp reflected in a jasper altar, gold coins scattered on the surface, bright in the flickering light. Beside the coins sat a silver chalice set with glowing pearls and sapphires.

All familiar, yet Remy had beheld none of those mysterious scenes in this lifetime. He placed his hands in front of him, positioned as if he held the chalice, envisioning placing it on the altar, an offering to Tanythe. Then he shook his head, put his hands to his side, certain that Tanythe's and Leukan's mind talk hummed in his brain, fading the cave's flickering flames, the chalice's glistening jewels, to where he could almost understand what they were *saying*. And in that moment, he distinctly *heard* Tanythe's *voice*.

She and Leukan were in the same position in the sepulcher, standing near him, and the Gov. Tanythe was looking into Leukan's eyes. Yet, in a way Remy couldn't explain, she also gazed into his own eyes, her lovely lips murmuring a name that he had never heard but so familiar it caused an ache in his heart.

Abdosir.

CHAPTER 76

*R*emy checked on the Gov. He hadn't moved since Tanythe placed her hand on his forehead, but the bruising from Remy's attempt at choking him had faded to almost nothing, and his breathing had become normal. He was healing from Tanythe's intervention.

Remy stood up, stiff from the sepulcher's floor, pins and needles pricking his legs. He shook his left leg to wake it and lost his balance, righting himself awkwardly. The room quit spinning. A few feet away, Tanythe and Leukan stared at him. How long had he been lost in the vision Tanythe sent?

"Abdosir." The name fell from his lips. The name Tanythe had called him. He turned away from their unnaturally bright eyes as the vision of him with Tanythe returned, more vivid than when she first sent it. He had held her naked body next to his, his lips caressing hers. They had merged, the feeling like winging to the heavens.

"You were a prince. You were my lover long, long ago, and now you are here." Tanythe stood next to him, here in the sepulcher, so close he could embrace her and find that heaven once more.

Remy became aware of Leukan eyeing him with those dark eyes, the gold around his irises glinting. But Leukan knew all of this: Abdosir with Tanythe. She took Remy's hand, her black cloak opening, revealing the flash of soft breast, a rose-pink nipple, and led him to the table where the black log had been.

Scattered over the floor were pieces of the hard, rough substance that had been her body. It looked as if a rotten tree trunk had broken apart.

"That was not what you both thought it was," Tanythe said. "The sacred cave formed a protective carapace over me, disguising my body. A protection against the forces Bahl was, and is, increasing."

Leukan's eyes showed the same surprise that quivered through Remy.

She let go of Remy's hand and picked up a piece of the carapace. It lay in her palm, looking for all the world like a lump of coal.

"A temporary cocoon, like a butterfly's." She dropped the piece to the floor. It bounced once, making a ringing noise, then landed, parts of it crumbling. Tanythe, her hands dusted in black, brushed them lightly, vanishing the dust.

"Remy dear, you fell against the table, tipping it. My carapace tumbled to the ground and broke open. By then, the Elixir had soaked through and brought me to consciousness. I could see, even though my head was still separate. Like a lodestone to metal, the Elixir linked me to my body in time to intercept Bahl."

The Elixir bottle that was on the table appeared in her hand, the pitiful little of the substance left barely perceptible at the bottom. Remy shuddered. If he had veered to the left, the supply table would have tipped, sending the Elixir to the floor, shattering the glass. The carapace would have stayed on the table, protecting but imprisoning Tanythe.

Remy's mind careened down the thread of events: Bahl, having taken Tanythe's blood, would have gained the strength to overcome Leukan. Tanythe wouldn't have joined with her body, therefore wouldn't have intercepted Bahl.

Remy doubted that he or Leukan, afraid of harming her, would have attempted to break the carapace. He grimaced as he imagined Bahl killing him in a way as gruesome as he had killed Juba. A god-like Bahl, working out eons of jealousy, would have done even worse to Leukan. Remy could only hope that Majidi, fleeing to the desert with Atabey, would have been spared, the only two other than Bahl, to depart this ghastly night in the sepulcher.

What would have become of Tanythe? Bahl would have taken her head and tried to extract the essence of her immortality until she had no life. But he would have ignored Tanythe's body, unidentifiable inside the coal-like carapace, and abandoned it in the sepulcher for centuries to come.

A soft touch brought him from his disturbing thoughts. He turned to Tanythe.

"What happened may not have been perfect, but it was for the best. Bahl is strong for the time being, but his evil will meet its comeuppance with my blood's revenge." Tanythe set the Elixir bottle in his palm and folded his fingers around it.

Remy wrapped the bottle in the cloth that he had left beside it on the table, secured the Elixir in his satchel, and looped the strap over his shoulder.

Putting her hand to her cheek, Tanythe tilted her head as she studied Remy. "The Elixir made me whole." Her eyes were blue, as blue as an infinite sky. Remy saw Tanythe in a diaphanous robe, offering herself to him. He almost moaned as the vision faded.

"Your...ah..." She said something in a clipped yet musical language, which seemed to have the cadence of a mixture of Italian and Russian, then glanced at Leukan, her brows raised in question.

"Natural philosophy. They call it natural philosophy or science now, what we named sorcery in our time," Leukan said.

"Yes, Remy dear, working your natural philosophy, your science. You do it well." Tanythe met Remy's eyes. He drifted closer to her. She found the silver chain around his neck, her hand against his skin, and fondled the crystal as she lifted it from inside his shirt. Locked in her gaze, the images from his vision danced once more before him. He was Abdosir, holding her naked body to his, kissing her perfect lips, possessing every part of her, savoring the way her eyes fluttered closed with his kisses, her lashes dark on her pale cheeks. She called his name as he pleasured her—whatever name, Remy or Abdosir, blurred with the saying.

At one time, her lips changed, became broader, her kisses heavier with a brush of roughness like whiskers. Surprised in a dreamy, slow way, Remy gazed into dark eyes ringed with gold, blackest-black braided tresses interwoven with amber beads. Leukan cradled his cheek in his strong hand, bent and whispered into his ear, his breath warm as a zephyr.

Remy wrapped his arms around Leukan and pulled him close, part of his mind wondering that he held this being, that he had caught the thief who stole his own head, whom he had shot. Kisses from another direction, and Tanythe's red tresses draped across his chest. Her body the inside of a fragrant flower, the pollen golden flecks on his flesh. He burrowed inside the smooth petals, returning again and again like a crazed honeybee. Remy lost all thought to a world indescribable beyond his comprehension.

It seemed forever. It seemed like no time when Remy opened his eyes.

Above him, Tanythe stood beside Leukan, his arm around her, the black cape barely touching the floor, silky, rippling around her bare feet. But Remy had been standing beside Tanythe, embracing her. She had reached for his necklace. His, but doubtless hers. Had she taken it?

He touched his chest and found the crystal against his skin. She had been with him, in his dream, in his vision. Leukan had been there as well. Remy touched his lips. Leukan had kissed them and more, much more.

Tanythe and Leukan smiled down at him. Smiling with him, the same expression on their faces that he felt was on his—the look of one physically sated, love-struck. The cape, velvety against his face, moved in an odd, dream-like motion which brought remnants of Tanythe's kisses. He tried to grasp his crystal, her crystal, but it slipped away in a sprinkle of light. The black of the cape, a night bereft of stars, the moon a memory, darkness all around him, soothing as velvet.

Something called to him far in the distance. Momentarily disquieted, Remy glanced in the direction of the sound, but again turned toward the wondrous beings. They were not in sight. He reached out, further and further, but couldn't find Tanythe or Leukan.

A distant resonance, pulling him away. No. He shut it out. It repeated. Persistent.

A nicker echoed down the hall.

Atabey? No. It was too soon. He could not leave them. Not now. The sound of horse's hooves rang on a hard floor, drawing him back. He couldn't hold on.

Atabey. Definitely Atabey.

Remy raised his head, his hands pushing him up from the cold floor. Was he clothed? He glanced down, sure that he had felt their bodies, their kisses on his bare skin. Yes. He remembered. These clothes, his clothes. The sound of hooves, louder now. A welcoming snort and nicker.

Majidi, his body blurring, led Atabey through the open golden door. The stallion whinnied a greeting and nudged Remy, who struggled up to greet him.

"Atabey." Remy heard his own voice. It sounded far, far away. He rubbed his stallion's neck, soft and silky, reminding him of something in his dream, his vision, but it was gone before he could seize it. The familiar feel of his horse beside him. Good? Odd that Atabey didn't react to the blood. Yes, Remy recalled that there was blood on his clothes, blood on the floor. He glanced away from his horse. He was in—

A tomb?

The blood. Gone. The lamps flickered, their shadows like maddened creatures scurrying for an exit. Like a tidal wave, scenes flooded back, all that had happened. He squeezed his eyes shut for a second and opened them. He was back, fully aware. Damn it all.

And Tanythe? Leukan? Remy stepped in one direction, then another, whirling to check every corner of the sepulcher.

"They have gone back." Majidi's voice slurred, louder, then softer, as if it were distorted by the wind like Majidi's long, long hair.

Remy received the reins from Majidi. When they both held them at once, Remy could have sworn his own feet left the ground for a second, as if he might float away. Then Majidi vanished. Atabey turned and whiffed. A sad farewell.

The temperature dropped. It was cold now. Like a tomb. Remy almost laughed. It had seemed a palace when the magical beings were here. But now—

"Derrien, where is this place?"

Simmery's voice made Remy jerk to the side. The Gov lay on the floor, his head raised. Remy gaped at him. By heaven, he would have mounted Atabey and galloped away, abandoning Simmery in this cold crypt. He had forgotten that the Gov lay on the floor, unconscious. An eerie chill ran through him.

Simmery sat up and brushed off his clothes. There was no trace of blood on them.

"I say, old man, we were having a drink, and then we're here? Decidedly odd." Simmery sounded inebriated.

Remy led Atabey over to the Gov. He wasn't about to let go of the stallion, his only means of escape. Remy looked behind him. Most of the oil lamps had been blown out as if a celestial wind he couldn't feel had swept through the tomb.

And the walls seemed closer than before.

He helped the Gov to his feet.

"Are you up for a ride?" asked Remy. He held the Gov's arm, steadying him.

"Ready as I'll ever be." For a moment, Remy had the brief impression that the Gov's reply was the opening to a drinking ditty, that the Gov might suddenly burst into a rowdy, off-key version.

"Afraid you'll have to ride in front of me." Remy helped the Gov onto Atabey and set his hands on the saddle's pommel. He looped his satchel strap over his head, tugging it crosswise on his chest, then mounted quickly so Simmery wouldn't fall.

The tomb grew colder by the minute. Indistinct voices came at him from all directions. The walls, yes, they were closer, the room smaller than minutes before. They must leave this place now.

Simmery looked around. "We'd best be going," he said, his voice high, a squeak at the end. Nerves, most likely. Atabey quirked his ears back and forth, shifting restlessly, but Remy stroked his neck and, with a few whispered words, trotted Atabey out of the room into the entry hall. The gilded door behind them slammed shut with an explosive bang like a firework.

Atabey neighed, rearing on his hind legs.

"Lean forward, Gov!" Remy yelled.

He grasped the reins with one hand. Threw his arms around Simmery, pushing him until his face was on Atabey's neck and pressing himself to the Gov's back. Remy desperately hung on. The stallion burst out the front doors, leaping over the steps, and shot through the open gate into the night as if a trumpet's blast had signaled the start of a race. Over the clatter of Atabey's hooves, Remy heard the distant scrape of metal, a long, unnatural scream in the silent graveyard. The sepulcher's gate closing.

When Remy had calmed Atabey and made sure the Gov had no discernible ill effects, he kept his stallion at a brisk trot, the full moon adequately lighting the paths. He would rather have Atabey gallop out of this place, but if the stallion hurt himself, he and the Gov would be in an impossible situation, stuck here with a lame horse and God knows what demons. He kept a hand tight on the reins, his other arm around the Gov, wary of Bahl's presence, afraid that he might rush at them from behind one of the tall gravestones or leap from atop a sepulcher.

A breeze tossed the shadows, giant ghouls rushing in all directions in the eerie light of the full moon as they left the graveyard behind.

Remy dared not look back.

CHAPTER 77

"*N*o need to crush my chest, Derrien." Simmery sounded annoyed at Remy's arm around him, keeping him upright in the saddle.

"Sir, hold firmly to the pommel. You had a shock back there. I'm not confident you've yet recovered." Remy tried to gauge the Gov's state of mind since Bahl had possessed him. Then dispossessed him according to Tanythe, who claimed the Gov hadn't been aware of his actions.

After they exited the cemetery, Atabey slowed, and Remy took his first full breath since they had broken out of the sepulcher, a ponderous weight lifting from him. Still, the remnants of fear hovered about like cobwebs that no amount of brushing and slapping could banish. The trees and shrubs lining the streets loomed like watchful silhouettes.

As they passed beneath an extinguished street lamp, the eerie light of the moon made hedges into globular monsters, and the street dogs rustling through the dark foliage into ghosts. Simmery remained quiet. Remy didn't want to rouse him by asking questions. Who knew what the Gov might do if he was set off again? Remy had felt no weapons as he patted him down when he lifted the Gov into the saddle.

"Blast!" Remy exclaimed. The cool night air carried the scent of salt as he gazed at the distant city lights far across the seemingly endless Bosphorus, its waves looking treacherous under the silvery moonlight.

"What?" Simmery squeaked. Remy could feel him tensing in the saddle.

"I need to arrange for a conveyance. Let me help you get seated on that bench under the street lamp. You'll be safe there while I talk to the men loading that barge." At least Remy hoped the Gov would be safe. Who knew what had followed them from the cemetery?

The workers hauled a large box similar to a horse's stall from a storage shed and assured him they had room for two more passengers and a horse. After they secured the box in place on the barge, Remy calmed Atabey and led him up the gangplank, situating him in the stall. Luckily, the stall was open at the top and afforded a view over the front gate, much like Atabey's stall in the stables at home.

Remy gently woke the Gov and assisted him to a cushioned bench on the barge. "We'll be home before you know it," he said, hoping the Gov could stay calm for the ride.

Sure enough, Simmery slept nearly the whole crossing. On shore, Remy made sure he was awake, then assisted him into the saddle, and they were off. Now, if he could just take him home without incident.

At last, they arrived at the British Ambassador's Residence, which blazed with oil lamps tinting the darkness golden yellow. Carriages lined up at the portico, disgorging ladies and gentlemen in evening dress. A reception or party. Just his luck.

Remy guided Atabey to the back and found the servant's entrance. Several footmen were gathered around the steps, talking. One smoked a pipe.

"Where are we?" The Gov sounded a little more like himself.

"The British Ambassador's Residence, where you live. Servant's entrance, sir," Remy said with authority. He didn't want Simmery pulling rank now. "There's a reception commencing, and you are not properly turned out."

The Gov grunted assent.

Surely, the Gov would have recognized this place. After all, he was living here. Had Bahl's possession made him simple-minded? If only Remy could obtain a clear look at Simmery's face to see the expression in his eyes, but the Gov sat in front of him, and even if he turned around, it was too dark to get a good look. Then the thought occurred that Simmery would never have seen the servant's entrance. Of course, it was unfamiliar.

So, his question was not delusional. A good sign. Perhaps the Gov was coming into his old self.

Remy motioned for a footman, gave him the reins, and dismounted. He helped Simmery from the saddle, thankful that once he was on the pavement, the Gov got a proper footing even though he swayed like a tree in a gale. Remy held him by the arm, fingers on his other hand flexing as if each digit longed to clasp itself around the Gov's neck and finish what Tanythe had stopped him from doing. Images from earlier danced in front of him.

Despite these distractions, Remy managed to speak in a proper voice to the footman.

"I'm afraid Lord Simmonds-Snow is in his cups tonight. Help him to his rooms and make sure he gets settled. Mind, he has a gimpy leg from an injury, so best keep hold of him." Remy handed the Gov to the footman, who took Simmery's arm just in time to avoid a calamity. He awaited an angry rejoinder, but the Gov looked a bit glassy-eyed and seemed to concentrate solely on keeping upright.

"Your name?" Remy asked the footman.

"Harbunkle, sir." The footman wrapped his arm around Simmery's waist, and off they went. Remy swung into the saddle. He turned Atabey toward home just as a bone-numbing fatigue washed over him, and he swayed in the saddle worse than Simmery. Managing a shallow breath, he gasped for more. He could breathe, but it wasn't enough. Would anything be enough to fortify him against all that had transpired this night?

The moonlight rendered the streets and buildings unfamiliar, as if it were another world. He had just escaped a world of splendor metamorphosing into one of horror. Remy looked behind him. Figures walked the street: a strolling couple, two men laughing, a group of young men, and a trio of dogs nosing through a pile of rubbish. Nothing out of the ordinary. Not like in the cemetery.

Who *were* Tanythe and Leukan? Why couldn't he bring himself to ask them? He had not been afraid to pose the question, but whenever he was around them, everything else, *anything else,* took on more importance. He fumbled for the crystal under his shirt, gasping when he couldn't locate it, then clutching it with all his might when he found it at the end of the chain. In front of him, above the cobblestones, an image of Tanythe wavered in the moon-light, then dissolved into Pheodora in her Turkish costume, her many jewels glinting.

Pheodora. The image of poor Phe in bed, unresponsive, flooded his mind. Remy hurried Atabey towards home. Only a few more streets. Phe. Was she better? Was she up, waiting for him?

He clenched his fist. Why, oh why, hadn't he asked Tanythe to heal his wife? Would his affinity for Tanythe kill Phe? He loved his wife. He did not doubt that. Still, he was drawn to Tanythe, whom he could never have.

It was clear she was Leukan's, but she had said Leukan knew about her affair with Abdosir, and Leukan seemed unperturbed about the whole thing. Hard as it was to believe, he had felt the connection through this man Abdosir, who had lived centuries ago, a man who had loved Tanythe as he did. Now, it felt right and good. He sat straight in the saddle, and, as Atabey flicked his mane, Remy emptied his head, preparing for mind talk.

I have hardly any Elixir left for Pheodora. Please, Tanythe, heal her like you healed me at the stream. Remy sent his mind talk. Would it reach Tanythe wher-ever she was? Atabey's hooves clomped rhythmically on the cobbles, and Remy clutched the reins in both hands, inside himself, unseeing, listening for Tanythe's answer.

He jerked in the saddle at a sudden touch on his leg. Remy swatted at it.

"Sorry, master. You were dozing." Tarek stood there, looking a bit abashed.

Atabey tossed his head, and Remy let go of the reins as he dismounted. His legs were as unsteady as Simmery's, but his head cleared the moment he set foot on the ground. The hay's sweet green smell and the freshly turned earth odor of the horses in their stalls had him wide awake. Odd how the attach-ment to the earth worked on him. More and more, he had become aware of that. He must delve into it and discover what it meant.

"Very well, Tarek. Give Atabey extra everything tonight." Remy rubbed his hand down the stallion's nose, then left the stable on his way to the house. A few lights shone through the windows. It must not be as late as it seemed to him.

At last, upstairs. The ever-present moon shone through Pheodora's window. Remy lifted the oil lamp on the bedside table, illuminating Phe, who lay in bed in the same position as she had when he last saw her this afternoon. She looked gaunt now, worse than when he had left. How could she be given water or food when she wouldn't respond?

Oh, Phe. He had failed her. Off in a dreadful tomb, doing what? Helping Tanythe and Leukan. And they had left him. Without any thanks.

He had envisioned Phe healed because of Tanythe's imagined answer to his plea. But it looked as though nothing had changed for Pheodora since this morning. Remy lifted the satchel's strap from his shoulder and set it on the bed. He unlatched the flap, lifted out the bottle wrapped in the cloth, and held it against his chest. Closing his eyes, Remy sent the same message in his mind.

I have hardly any Elixir left for Pheodora. Please, Tanythe, heal her.

How long he sat there with his eyes closed, he couldn't say. Perhaps he had dozed again. He still clutched the bottle to his chest and set it in his lap as he unwound the cloth, hoping against hope. When he held it up, the same amount of Elixir was at the bottom as when he last checked at the tomb.

Precious little. The last of his Elixir, save for the two and a half inches in the bottle at the laboratory. He opened the wardrobe door and set the bottle with the small amount of Elixir in the back, behind a hatbox. On his way out, he snatched the candle from the holder on the table by the back door. Remy saddled Atabey himself and was at the laboratory in no time. With the stallion settled in the first stall at the back of the Society, Remy fumbled his key in the dark and almost dropped it.

No one was at the Society. The hall was a straight path to the laboratory, lit by the moon through the roundel with just enough light to find his way. Inside the laboratory, he set the candle he'd brought in one of the empty holders. They never had enough candles. Remy was always on Kahlil about it. He struck a match from the box. No candles, but lots of matches. A faint stink of sulfur accompanied the bright yellow flame, then dissipated as the candle took fire.

Heart thumping, Remy opened the cabinet and held the candle to the inside. No overflow shone in glossy mounds around the bottle. He sighed in disappointment and moved the candle closer to the Elixir bottle. The meager light could not pierce the dark inside the cabinet enough to check if the amount in the bottle had multiplied.

Once more, he sent mind talk to Tanythe. The same message.

Then he lifted the bottle, set it on a table, and leveled his eyes with it. He brought the flame next to the Elixir, illuminating about two and a half inches of liquid.

"Bloody hell." The same amount as when he left.

He needed a miracle.

CHAPTER 78

*A*s he locked the Society's back door, Remy patted the satchel held securely across his body. It held the last of the Elixir. Again, he sent the same plea to Tanythe in his mind and wondered how many castles in the clouds he thought he could build.

A cool night breeze carried the odor of wood fires, making him feel colder still. Moonlight shone on the Society's stables and lit Atabey's eyes like a bright star, but the yellow hay remained a dull gray. The stallion nickered a greeting and banged his hoof against the stall. He was as ready as Remy to be home and done with this harrowing night.

"Tanythe. Leukan. Lord Simmonds-Snow," Remy said with a pause between them, and unwittingly conjured a scene in the sepulcher: Tanythe and Leukan looming over him, and the Gov, blood drying around them. Remy could barely comprehend all that had occurred just a few hours ago. He glanced at the stables, the back of the Society building, the narrow road leading to the street, a common scene so normal that he forced himself to see it just so he could penetrate the blur remaining from the cemetery.

The ride home from the Society, a route he and Atabey had taken countless times without a thought, had been like slogging through soft sand. When they finally arrived, Tarek was slow to rouse from his blanket in the stables. Yawning, he shook hay stalks from his hair. As he took Atabey's reins, Remy eyed the hay behind Tarek and fought the urge to throw himself down into the soft mound, escaping into blissful sleep with no dark dreams lurking at the edges.

But he must stay alert. He trudged up the stairs. Mind talk. Was it all a ruse? Had any of this truly happened, or was he trapped in some sequential nightmare that took up each day, relegating his actual existence to only a dream?

"Pheodora," he called softly as he opened the bedroom door, hoping against hope she would sit up and scold him for his absence. He lit the oil lamp by the threshold. She slept, unmoving, the same as before. The kittens, bigger every day, raised their sleepy heads, blinked, then cuddled closer to Phe.

Remy hurried to the wardrobe, fetched the small amount of Elixir he had brought from the sepulcher, and placed it on the bedside table. He set the Elixir from the laboratory next to it. Two and a half inches from the laboratory and one-quarter inch leftover from helping Tanythe. Two and three-quarters inches. The total amount of Elixir he had in all the world.

His career, his hopes, his wife's life measured in inches.

He thought of his family. His father, the Most Honorable Marquess of Wearsely, the most senior rank in the peerage, beneath duke, the exalted position that had been drummed into him since birth. His status as a younger son meant he would receive no inheritance unless his father granted him an allowance or his elder brother, upon inheriting the title, chose to provide for him. Unless Remy found a suitable living, his father planned to purchase a church position for him, effectively exiling him to a small backwater English village for the rest of his days.

The Elixir could change all that. The Elixir would make his name.

Pheodora, the kittens, their home here. What would their life be if he failed as a fellow in the Society? What would his life be if he failed Pheodora?

Remy lifted the bottle containing the most Elixir just as an object landed hard in his lap, jarring him. "Confound it, Sultana." He dropped the bottle, dove for it, but knocked it onto the bed, and barely caught it. Sultana swatted his hand, claws sticking into his palm. He brushed her aside. Holding the bottle, he thought for a moment. If he were to proceed with his plan, this room would need to be much warmer.

With care, Remy stowed the bottles safely in the cabinet under the bedside table. He set a log in the hearth, tucked kindling around it, and struck a match.

The kindling caught quickly, setting alight the dry log, tiny yellow flames marching along its surface. His mind quieted by the dancing flames, he stuck more kindling under the log and stood in front of the hearth. The kittens joined him, purring louder than the log's cracks and pops, as Remy became entranced by the red and blue flames joining the yellow ones, the warmth making them all drowsy.

He roused himself from his stupor.

Pheodora slept on.

Remy pulled down the covers and discovered that Anisya had changed Phe into proper night clothes. Visualizing removing the many layers of her Turkish costume, he silently thanked the maid. Pheodora did not stir as he slipped her gown over her head and settled the covers loosely over her naked body.

Clearing the bedside table, he left only a candle in its glass shade, then placed the vial with the least Elixir, his tools, and a china plate. As the heat from the fire filled the room, Remy shucked off his jacket, unwound his cravat, and pulled his shirt over his head. He would be working hard to save Pheodora, and worried as he was, he would have preferred a room on the cool side but did not want Phe to catch a chill.

Remy emptied all the Elixir from the one bottle onto the plate while he mind-talked the same prayer to Tanythe. With a smooth wooden tool, he applied the clear substance over Phe's face and head, marveling at how each small amount seemed to melt into a greater quantity, the same as how one drop covered the rose petal in his first experiments.

The room was even warmer now. He brought out the last bottle and emptied every bit of the two and a half inches of Elixir onto the plate. Then he slipped the covers below Phe's shoulders and applied more Elixir to her chest and down her body. He hadn't put the Elixir on the back of the rose petal or the back of Tanythe, and followed that protocol. Phe's body glistened.

He looked up. The fire was almost out. He must have entered a kind of trance while applying the Elixir. Another log and more kindling revived it. He checked on Pheodora. Still the same. Her skin shone with the Elixir, yet she felt dry. He pulled the covers over her.

"Please give her back to me," he murmured. It was a prayer, but addressed to whatever entity might hear.

CHAPTER 79

*R*emy clutched the bottle of Elixir, but Bahl, in Juba's strong, youthful body, wrenched it from his grasp. Springing for it, Remy knocked it from Bahl's hand. The bottle arced upwards as if it would take flight. Cursing, he leapt after it, but his hands closed on empty air.

Like an eagle, the bottle soared higher until it became a speck against the sky, then vanished. Remy kept his eyes to the heavens, scanning the area where he last viewed the bottle. Why had he felt a tangible relief when the last of his Elixir had vanished?

Indeed, the sensation was more like a burden removed than a flimsy relief. His eyes clung to the patch of cloudless blue sky where his Elixir had disappeared. Tanythe's eyes came to mind, that same shade of blue. He squinted. Something seemed to form in the same area where the Elixir vanished. It was growing. By Jove, it was hurtling toward him.

Hands outstretched, Remy scuttled back and forth, following the bottle's descent, when he tripped and sprawled on the hard marble floor, his breath nearly knocked from him. Wheezing, he lurched upright, hands open, just as the bottle smashed into the floor.

Glass shards sprayed everywhere, pricking his legs and arms. He turned his head away, cheeks stinging. That was the very last of the Elixir. He struggled to his hands and knees, arms lifted to the heavens as if another bottle might land in his embrace.

"Nooo!" His scream tore the air. The scene shifted.

He lay on wooden planks beside a bed. Raising his head, he searched the floor for the bottle's shards, for the remains of the Elixir, but the floor was not marble. Two tiny fur bundles warmed his chest. The rest of him felt as cold as a tombstone.

The hearth fire had died, leaving only the sour odor of charred wood. King stood on shaky legs, stretched his front legs longer than Remy thought possible, and stuck his rump in the air, his tail straight up, stiff as a tiny bristle brush.

The nightmare lingered, in color and so fresh, Bahl's beady eyes pouring malice into him as if he could fill Remy like an empty bottle. Remy willed the images from his mind, but they slunk into the shadows, waiting to pounce when he least expected.

Pheodora.

Remy sat up. She lay motionless under the covers. He checked her wrist. Her pulse the same steady beat. Perhaps fainter than last night. *Please, bring her back.*

The two Elixir bottles sat on the bedside table next to the lamp and various tools. Remy. Lifted one bottle. Empty.

Then the other. Empty as well.

He sank to the floor.

He had nothing. Nothing.

CHAPTER 80

*H*alf an hour later, the doctor still hadn't arrived. No sign of an araba or English carriage coming down the street. Remy turned from the parlor window, picked up the tray with Pheodora's favorite tea in case the Elixir had worked its miracles, and headed upstairs.

A shrill scream pierced the stairwell.

The tray dropping from his hold, clattered, forgotten on the stairs. Remy took the steps two at a time. He shouldn't have left her with the maid, even for that small amount of time. Had Pheodora awakened, disoriented?

He burst into her room. Anisya turned from the bed, tears streaking her face. "I-I think she—" The maid broke into sobs.

Remy pushed her aside.

Pheodora looked the same, pale, her gauntness exaggerated. He placed two fingers on her neck, feeling for her heartbeat. Pressed his cheek to hers and placed his finger under her nose. No breath, no pulse. He shook her. Her complexion tinged a slight blue around the edges, the same as her lips.

"I came as soon as I got your message, Lord Derrien." The doctor hurried to the bedside and set his bag on the floor. He held Pheodora's wrist, fingers placed strategically, put his finger under her nose, and lay his head upon her chest.

His shoulders sagged. He faced Remy.

"I am so sorry, Lord Derrien. It happened fast." The doctor guided Remy to the grouping of chairs in the corner and sat him down. "Did your wife ever come out of it?"

Remy shook his head. How would he know? He had been in a tomb, lusting after a creature who had taken advantage of him.

"Shall I contact anyone? I can arrange to...have her made ready for the funeral." The doctor placed his hand on Remy's shoulder.

"Leave us be for now. Thank you." Remy put his head in his hands. The doctor's footsteps became echoes of other footsteps: Leukan's when he greeted Remy in the sepulcher, Majidi's when he appeared to stable Atabey, and the Gov's when he sauntered into the sepulcher with Juba.

Anisya's voice as she bid the doctor farewell broke him from tunneling further into his living nightmare. The front door closed. That was it. The doctor had confirmed what they hadn't believed.

It was over.

The room brightened as the morning advanced. Light glared on Pheodora's still body, mimicking sleep, mocking him with the illusion she might stir at any moment. How dare she leave him alone now? What on earth had happened to her? A perfectly healthy woman of nineteen years.

"Lord Derrien." Anisya peeked through the barely opened door.

"Leave," Remy said, harsh and hoarse.

He took Phe's hand. Still warm. In the light from the window, her skin glowed. He expected her to open her eyes. Murmur, '*Oh, you're watching me sleep again,*' her eyelids fluttering as she drifted back to her dreams.

"Forgive me, Pheodora." He dropped to his knees, clutching her hand. He would leave for home, for England, next week. There was nothing for him here now. He put his head down, tears soaking the covers.

Remy paced. He would arrive home defeated, scorned by her father, blamed for her death. No glories for his blasted natural philosophy/science. The Elixir was gone, finished, and any evidence of immortality had picked up and left. He started shaking at the thought of entering the laboratory once more. The green, green English countryside called to him, cattle and sheep grazing, white church steeples. A life of exile in some parish. Perhaps that would be all he had left.

He looked around the room where he and Pheodora had been happy, mostly, and sat beside Phe, taking her hand in his. That's all he could think to do. Sit and stare at her beautiful face—

A small shake of the bed. Remy whirled toward the motion. The kittens. They settled around Phe as if nothing were wrong. Remy cocked his head. Could he have been too hasty? But the doctor... He scowled. The doctor had been no help. Like natural philosophers and scientists, doctors were not gods.

Phe's hand was still slightly warm. He let go and snatched a pillow. With his teeth, he ripped open a seam and fished out a fluffy feather. Tossing the pillow aside, he held it under her nose.

The feather's delicate down lay as unruffled as if it were blown glass. He let it float down onto the bed. A kitten pounced on it. A white kitten. Where the hell had it come from? King and Sultana roused from their slumber and drowsily watched the intruder.

The white kitten stretched its paws and swiped at the feather, which floated upward on an air current. Lifting its head, the kitten stared, fluffy white tail switching back and forth, eyes wide as it tracked its prey. One eye darkest brown, almost black with a gold glint, the other azure blue. Remy could not move a muscle, but his mind raced as if it were being pursued.

He reached into the bedside cabinet and removed one of the Elixir bottles. Holding it to the light from the window, he angled it. A smidgeon of the Elixir pooled at the bottom. He pulled out the cork, held the bottle over Pheodora, and positioned it above her lips. He turned the bottle upside down. The substance, less viscous than when he had applied it to Phe's body, plodded down the inside of the glass. The Elixir gradually curved into the bottle's shoulder, turned sluggishly at the neck, then merged at the rounded glass collar as if it had all eternity at its beck and call.

Remy let himself blink, squeezing the dryness from his eyes as the substance curved into the bottle's lip, creeping down. A bulbous drop formed at the lip's edge.

Remy repositioned it just above the crevice between Pheodora's lips.

The drop grew longer. And longer. Remy held his breath, grasping the bottle just so.

At long last, the drop fell.

Please let this nourish Phe.

The drop slid between her lips. Remy still held the bottle in the same position, hoping against hope for another drop.

From the corner of his eye, a fuzz of white. He broadened his vision for the first time since he tipped the bottle upside down. The white kitten had crept onto Pheodora's head, paws resting on her smooth brow, its dark eye and blue eye staring at Remy.

There was no mind talk that he was aware of, but on either side of him, a separate presence presented itself. Remy knew not to look. It would break the spell that had been introduced into the room.

The white kitten arched its back, fur raised to twice its sturdy size, soft paws balanced delicately on Pheodora's forehead. Remy breathed in the euphoric atmosphere, basking in the presence of those who had shown him that natural philosophy and science extended far beyond the scope of his scholarly textbooks.

CHAPTER 81

"Gods?" Remy set his teacup on the wrought-iron table, the clink of the china saucer against the metal ringing like a miniature cymbal. A bird took flight from the pink blooms on the Persian silk tree, the sound of its wings like someone clapping in the far distance.

"Yes, gods. I am absolutely certain." Pheodora's voice had grown weaker as they conversed across the small table, and he could hardly hear her over the chirping birds and rustling leaves. She had insisted on having a late breakfast in the garden, *in the sun*, she had stressed. From her mouth to God's ear, the always-bright Constantinople sunshine, as comforting as a hearth fire, beamed into the clearing where the servants had arranged the furniture. But the breeze blew cooler than he thought was ideal for her.

Remy tucked the Angora shawl, soft as a cloud, around Phe's shoulders. "Are you sure you are not chilled?"

She shook her head in a slow movement, conserving her strength, and nestled into the throne-like wicker chair he had the servants cart out, especially for her. Pale gray circles shadowed the space under her eyes, which had grown a bit brighter from the infusion of sunshine.

Gods? Truly? Remy held his questions. Pheodora seemed to diminish with every sentence, as if her words were leeching away her substance. She sighed and leaned back, the shawl bunching around her shoulders.

398

At some point, Pheodora had gently slipped into sleep. The sun haloed her fair hair. He rose, aching to hold her, his glowing angel, but instead sank back into his seat. She needed her rest. He settled and watched her from across the table as she dozed, thankful that her lips and skin no longer bore the ghastly blue tinge he had tried to banish from his memory.

It had been two days since Pheodora returned to life. Since he had used the absolute last drop of his Elixir. Since the white kitten had taken up residence. Since he had mind talked with Tanythe.

She had praised him for saving Pheodora, when Remy knew very well that it was Tanythe, Leukan, and the white kitten who had saved Phe, rather saved her *through* the white kitten. During the mind talk, he had finally asked who she and Leukan were.

You know who we are, dear Remy. Why would you ever ask me outright? That would be like asking your mother who she is. In the life you are living now, you have a particular turn of mind. The most obnoxious idea that you must have what is plainly shown to you explained as if you were a child.

At Tanythe's last comment, Remy had sunk into himself like a snail, his slick, jellied form reversing into its hard shell.

Dear Remy, that is what your world calls science or natural philosophy. Yes, some wonderful benefits will eventually come of it. But some things must be held above that propensity.

He had peered out of his shell, once more brave. When he asked Tanythe if she and Leukan had sent the white kitten with each eye the exact color of their eyes, one azure and the other dark with a golden rim, she had smiled.

Oh, he could tell, even through mind talk, that there was a smile on her face, that she was playing with him, exactly like the white kitten that Phe had named Osiris —

The Egyptian God who rose from the dead.

Tanythe did not answer in words.

A sensation overcame him. The world receded. He existed in a brighter, more vivid place where his reach extended farther than he could see. His mind unfolded as if it had burst from a tight bud into a magnificent, multi-petaled flower.

Remy could still summon that experience. A sacred, secret gift from Tanythe.

Across from him, Pheodora roused from her nap, the bright sunlight limning her in gold. She tilted her head, her hair falling over her shoulder in a river of pale yellow.

"Remy, before I had to rest, you seemed surprised to hear that Tanythe and Leukan are gods." Her voice sounded stronger. She straightened, removed the saucer covering her teacup, and took a delicate sip.

Remy leaned forward, almost spilling his tea. Fumbling with his cup, he set it upright. "I had no idea they were god and goddess. How did you find out?"

"Bahl told me."

"Bahl," Remy said the name with too much anger, but refrained from blurting his questions. How did she know about that evil being? How did she know him by name? In Phe's delicate condition, he must let her tell him what she could. There was always later. At least, he hoped so. Only a few days ago, there was not.

He kept picturing Pheodora from that awful morning, her lips blue, her body unresponsive to his desperate attempts to revive her. As she relayed her story, Phe leaned toward him, her shawl slipping from her shoulders, and Remy heard the extraordinary background of those three found in the bag.

He waited for her to pause, catching her breath. "Phe, shouldn't you rest? I fear for your health if you continue relating this now." Remy reached across the table for her hand. Still warm.

She smiled. A smile that spread warmth into him. "Remy, my love. This is my way of expunging these things from my soul."

So, he sat, rapt, consumed with her tale while fighting with the worry that she would overdo, that reliving this extraordinary experience would harm her, despite her protests.

Pheodora told him of Bahl possessing her, just as he had Snowy. Disturbed but listening intently, Remy paced beside the sword lilies, the magenta blooms bright in the sun, while she filled in the details that explained the mysterious events they had both endured, suffering on different sides. As he listened intently, he compared her experiences to his, when Bahl was one of the three heads in the laboratory, when Bahl possessed the Gov, when Bahl's head had fused onto poor Juba's body.

Remy glanced over his shoulder. The shadows under the huge rose hedges were so dark it was hard to see into them. He stiffened. The fear that Bahl lurked there, his eyes like a gun's double barrel aiming for him, grabbed Remy as if he were still the demon's victim in the sepulcher.

He scowled at the bushes, then focused on Pheodora, who mentioned the red-haired woman's head that she had seen beside Bahl's in the laboratory. Apparently, Bahl was the only one whose name she knew.

At last, Phe leaned back, silent. She fixed him with her eyes. The sun, having continued on its elliptic, had left Pheodora shivering in the shade. Remy tucked her shawl close around her. He sat beside her. Took her in his arms. "Pheodora, my love, I have learned at least one thing."

She leaned into him and looked up. "Mmm, what?"

"I fear we have experienced quite enough to fill a lifetime and more, leaving us with innumerable questions about life and death. But there is one thing of which I am certain."

She studied him, her eyes intent, waiting for him to enlighten her with sagacious pearls of wisdom.

"I am canceling our tour of Karacaahmet Cemetery," he said.

Phe leaned away from him, eyes wide. Then she laughed hard and loud, like she did when they had first come to Constantinople. She lay her head on his chest, grinning but exhausted.

"Your little joke was worth it." She gave him a weak smile. "I am ready to go inside," she said softly, her voice like the tiny mewl of a runt kitten. Remy lifted Phe and almost tossed her over his shoulder, for she weighed so little. But her cheeks and lips were as pink as the garden's lovely roses. She wrapped her arms around his neck as he carried her through the garden.

"Remy dear." She sounded like Tanythe.

He stopped, his feet firm on the flagstones.

"You sacrificed your precious Elixir for me." Pheodora leaned her head against his chest.

Had she mind talked with Tanythe? Pheodora had been dead when he forced the last drop of Elixir from the bottle onto her lips. He had never said a word about what he had done.

No one knew except Sultana, King, and Osiris.

CHAPTER 82

*A*s Remy hurried to his laboratory, Simmery stepped from his office into the middle of the Society's hall. "Derrien, how is your wife?"

At the sound of Simmery's voice, Remy looked up, his thoughts scattering, and barely avoided slamming into his superior.

"Pheodora is coming along," Remy said. The curt tone of his voice didn't seem to faze Simmery. This was the first time Remy had been to the Society since the cemetery incident, since Pheodora had returned from the dead. The first time to see the Gov since he had deposited him at the British Residency. Yet his kindness towards the weakened Gov in the immediate aftermath that night had now blossomed into full-blown revulsion.

Remy turned away from the Gov as a gallery of vivid images from the sepulcher appeared in his mind. Remy forced his mind away from the horror of that night. Tanythe had said Bahl possessed the Gov, just as he had possessed Pheodora. Remy swallowed hard and faced Simmery. If he didn't do it now, he would never be able to.

"Lord Simmonds-Snow, how are you?" Remy chose his words carefully, not wanting to lead the witness, so to speak.

"Wonderful. Fully recovered from that nasty bout of bilious fever."

Remy stared at his superior, disbelieving, then, with effort, recovered a more normal, conversational expression. "So glad to hear it." He kept any sarcasm from his voice. Lord in heaven, that's what the Gov wanted everyone to think had been wrong with him. Or did Simmery truly believe he had simply been ill? However, Pheodora remembered many details of Bahl possessing her. By the same logic, Simmery should have remembered as well.

"Must check on the laboratory." Remy hurried down the hall. Behind him, he heard the Gov's footsteps fast gaining on him.

"Derrien, continue with opening the trunks on the two back tables." Simmery walked alongside him now. "What with meetings and paperwork this week, I will be hard-pressed to read your reports." His voice was lighter. Almost happy.

At the laboratory, Remy stuck the key into the lock, Simmery leaning close as if he would confide something. The musky-sweet scent of the Gov's Attar Al Paculi engulfed him, dragging back the sepulcher scene. The tart tang of blood mixing with that cloying cologne. Remy was gripped with the powerful urge to flee.

"However, I must touch on your recent ongoing tasks and completions." Simmery continued rattling off a list of what he would do and what he wanted from Remy.

Exaggerating his movements, Remy turned the key to the laboratory and opened the door. Perhaps seeing that he was about to begin his work would convince Simmery to return to his own office. Or would the Gov keep on and mention the heads or Bahl's possession of him? Would he demand that Remy explain why he had kept the Elixir a secret?

"I am puzzled as to why we have not made more progress. However, it has gone relatively smoothly, except, of course, the robbery." Simmery clapped him on the back, and Remy, incredulous, looked him full in the face.

"But that's water under the bridge now," Simmery said, following him inside. "The place is in tip-top shape."

The Gov walked to the microscope. "The Society jumped right in with obtaining a new one, eh?" He turned and smiled at Remy, clearly expecting praise for his part in the procurement.

"Thanks to your effort, Lord Simmons-Snow. Otherwise, that space would be vacant, and we would still be begging them." Remy grinned back at the Gov, who nodded sagely.

"By the way, give my regards to Pheodora. And tell her not to be so scarce around here," Simmery said.

Remy stared at the Gov's back as he turned to leave, a spring in his step. Simmery had banished Pheodora from setting foot in the Society, much less in the laboratory.

Just inside the door, the Gov turned and looked at Remy, whose muscles tightened, his jaw stiff in apprehension. Here it comes, the classic Simmery sword-in-the-gut, now that he has you unsuspecting.

"By the by, Derrien..." He pressed his fist to his chin, his mouth in a twist as if he were calculating a tough math problem. He looked up. Remy saw the whites of his eyes.

No. He wasn't looking up.

Blast, he was convulsing.

Remy caught the Gov as he collapsed, lowered him to the floor, quickly removed his own jacket, and placed it under Simmery's head. His pulse was slow, but he was breathing. Remy glanced at the door, unlocked, thank God. If needed, he could call for help. He looked down into the Gov's open eyes.

The Gov blinked rapidly, his mouth twitched, then his body spasmed.

Convulsing again.

Remy loosened the Gov's cravat, unbuttoned his shirt, and opened his jacket to give him as much room to breathe as possible, watching him carefully in case the seizure worsened. The spasms receded until the Gov lay still, his eyes closed, and Remy started to call for help to move him into a guest room, but Simmery's eyelids flickered. With a sudden inhale, he opened his eyes wide and clutched Remy's hand.

"Derrien." His voice creaked. He struggled to sit up, and Remy assisted him.

"I-I hurt Tanythe. And someone else." Simmery moaned. His grip tightened, almost painful, but Remy bore it as he considered what it must be like seeing out of those eyes, thinking with a brain that the demonic Bahl had possessed.

Remy studied the Gov, who lacked that malicious stare, Bahl's stare, that had so recently terrified him when Simmery had been possessed. His eyes were a bit panicked, but held just the amount of gumption with a hint of mischief that was the old Gov.

Remy welcomed the person who stared out of those eyes.

Lord Simmonds-Snow was back. "Tanythe told me that Bahl had possessed you. That I must forgive you for what you did to her, to the other one." Remy refrained from mentioning poor Juba's name, fearing how it might affect Simmery if he humanized the poor boy.

The Gov, eyebrows knitted together, lips pursed, let go of Remy's hand.

Wary, Remy said, "Remember Pheodora's odd behavior in this laboratory? Bahl possessed her also, then tried for me. While you helped me settle Phe from her frenzy, Bahl miscalculated and jumped into you—"

The Gov gasped.

"—instead of me," Remy said.

Simmery pulled back, eyeing Remy as if he were demented.

Remy shook him gently. "You are shed of him. Why would Tanythe tell me to forgive you if it were not true that you are now Lord Simmonds-Snow, an honorable and righteous man?"

He let go of the Gov. "You are free now."

Simmery slumped a little. "And...Bahl?" he asked with caution and raised his head, looking around as if the demon were inside the laboratory once more.

If he told the truth, could Simmery handle it?

The Gov grasped Remy's hand. "Derrien, you *know what happened*. You must tell me. You don't think I can take it?" He met Remy's gaze. "You said Pheodora was possessed. You said she is now doing well. If she could take it, so can I."

"Pheodora, uh, had it easier than you," said Remy.

The Gov leaned close. "Tell me."

Remy exhaled and stared at the laboratory floor. The things that had taken place in here and in the cemetery. He rubbed his temple. He should call for help if Simmery convulsed again. Twice now, and the Gov hadn't hurt himself. A doctor should examine him.

"Derrien. What happened to Bahl? You must tell me, or I will go insane waiting for him to come for me again."

A good sign that Simmery mentioned he could go insane. Ironic as it was, it showed a semblance of sanity. Remy would try a mild version of the truth. "Bahl made Leukan place Bahl's head on the other person's body—"

"Body? How did the person lose his head?" Simmery looked stricken. "The

405

young man. I-I slit his throat. I remember the knife, the voice telling me to…"
Anger filled his eyes. "I was the one doing these things Bahl did. *You* saw it.
They saw it. Why did no one stop me?"

"Yes, all of that. Suffice it to say that Bahl had his plan thought out, and you
obeyed because he had control of you. No one could stop you, or Bahl would
make you hurt Tanythe more." Could Simmery take this like he said he could?

The Gov looked away. "And how did Bahl escape?"

Remy told it briefly. And Simmery took it.

He leveled his eyes at Remy. "So now Bahl has a body and is out in the
world?"

"Tanythe threw a knife at him." Here, the Gov winced. Remy rushed past
that reference, wishing he had slurred his words more. "She put magic into
that blade. Tanythe seemed confident that it would take care of Bahl."

The Gov stared intently over Remy's shoulder.

The change in the room became palpable. The air weighed upon Remy as if
there were suddenly someone else in the laboratory. Was the presence
creeping closer behind him? Tanythe or Leukan? Or, a shiver shook Remy.
Bahl come to pay vengeance?

His mind frantically searching for the nearest thing he could use as a
weapon, Remy turned. There was nothing there that he could see.

"So Tanythe and Leukan are gone?" asked the Gov.

Remy faced him and nodded.

"As is Bahl?"

Remy nodded once more, his words stolen by all that had happened.

"So, we are back where we started?"

"Yes and no," said Remy, his voice a croak. It was an honest answer, as it
referred to everything, including the Elixir.

The Gov chuckled softly. "Yes, dear boy, I see." He patted Remy's shoulder
and held out a hand. "Give me a boost up, will you?"

With Remy's help, the Gov stood, a bit shaky, his eyes full of his old, impossible self.

"Back to work, eh?" He clapped Remy on the back and tried to press the
door handle. "Derrien, would you do the honors?"

Remy opened the door and watched Simmery stride back to his office. He
closed the door, locked it, and leaned heavily against the cold wood. Should he

have insisted that Simmery travel to the embassy in the Society's carriage? See a doctor and rest in his rooms for several days?

Until Tanythe's magic from the knife blade took effect, Bahl could enter their lives and wreak havoc at any moment. The demon could reclaim Pheodora and the Gov as he renewed his hold on them from the deep recesses of his blood.

CHAPTER 83

Suddenly suffused with weakness, Remy hobbled to the nearest chair and lowered himself into the seat. He hadn't realized what a strain it had been, reliving the horror of the cemetery with the very man who had helped create it. But the Gov wasn't truly Bahl.

He methodically unwound his cravat, the silk a nuisance against his skin, and let it fall into his lap. Leaning forward, elbows on the table in front of him, he propped his head in his hands. Terrifying images flitted through his mind, but he forced himself to release them. He had lived through those things and survived. At last, a merciful quiet blackness stilled his thoughts.

Vigilant, he raised his head.

The laboratory exuded calm. The brass fittings of the new microscope gleamed, his papers stacked neatly beside it next to a closed box of slides. King slept in his basket, a ball of black fur, his water and food bowls still full. Remy leaned back in his chair. This was the very table where he had placed the heads. He rose too quickly, the chair clattering to the floor with a final bang. No one came pounding at the door. Remy set the chair upright and pushed it back under the table. The heads were gone. Done with. And Bahl, though he had escaped, would be neutralized by Tanythe's spell.

Months ago, when Remy first arrived, his position had been the chance to become a renowned natural philosopher/scientist and return home to

England famous. Instead, it had become a nightmare, where unnatural forces had nearly killed him. By the narrowest squeak, he had survived.

Now, he was content that things were no worse. Pheodora was at home, healing. He whispered a quick prayer. Simmery was merely his superior, not his adversary. At a sudden prickle on his neck, Remy absently brushed off the insect, or whatever it was. The area on his skin felt warm and wet. What on earth? He pulled his hand away.

Blood?

Lord in heaven. The very place where Bahl had bitten him and drunk his blood. A strange heat fizzed through his neck and coursed through his body, his blood burning, just as when Bahl mesmerized him. He pressed his cravat on the wound, desperate to stanch the bleeding.

How could he have forgotten? He had never been fully healed from the demon's bite. Leukan had been in the process of healing him, but Bahl attacked before he could finish. When Remy finally found strength enough to aid Leukan, his tainted blood had drawn him instead to Bahl, like maggots to putrid flesh.

Later, when Bahl wrapped him in his arms, Remy became helpless, but he had fought free, cast off the demon's grip, and forced him to flee the sepulcher.

Rushing inside, he had found Leukan bleeding from Bahl's stab wound, Tanythe frantic to help him, and the Gov convulsing. No one, not even Remy, had recalled that Bahl had drunk Remy's blood, that the healing had never been completed.

Majidi claimed Tanythe and Leukan had gone back. Wherever "back" was. Desperate, Remy grasped the crystal at his chest and tried mind-talking with them. No response.

Remy had held the cravat to the bite long enough to stop the blood flow. He removed it and pressed a clean area of the cloth to the bite. Only a small streak of blood.

Relieved, he set the cravat on the table where the heads had once lain. Perhaps his blood, near the place where theirs had rested, might connect him. Needing their help more than ever, he closed his eyes and called them, waiting in silence.

When he opened them again, he saw a small puddle on the table. Clear liquid, something dripping into it. Tears. Confound it, he was crying. He hardly cared. No one cared. He had sacrificed everything for Tanythe and Leukan. What in God's name would happen to him now that Bahl's blood had suffused into his? Would he feel what Pheodora and the Gov had endured? Possession? Madness? Would he only realize he was possessed too late, when he stood, knife in hand, over the mangled body of someone he loved?

"Usta. What?"

Khalil stood beside him.

Remy startled, blotting his eyes with his cravat.

"Oha!" Khalil pointed at Remy's neck. "Usta, you have bite of *Obisch*." He backed away, palms out, his eyes wide. Fumbling, he finally pulled his evil-eye necklace from inside his shirt and let the symbol hang on his chest.

Remy touched his neck, then looked at his bloodied fingers. Why wouldn't the blasted wound close?

Khalil, still at a distance, gaped at Remy's neck.

"Obisch?" Remy asked, wiping his hand on the cravat.

"Someone who dies, then comes back not dead," Khalil whispered. "Fly at night. Take blood from peoples." He edged closer, peering at the mark. "Where did you get this?"

Remy laughed.

Khalil stumbled back, nearly falling. What would his servant do if he told him the truth? That it had happened in a sepulcher, in a battle with a demon returned from the grave? Instead, Remy stretched his arms high, feigning ease.

"Do not worry about it, Khalil. I believe the bite is from a rat in my bedroom. The servants are catching it today. I'll be safe enough."

Khalil gave him the same skeptical look he had worn when Remy swore there was no djinni in the Leyden jar. And yet…Happenstance had proved that untrue to some extent. To this day, Kahlil asks him how he feels, then asks about the djinni who attacked him.

"Fetch lunch. I need to continue cataloging." Remy said in a voice that Khalil should read as 'end of discussion.'

With a long exhale, Remy pulled his satchel from its hook by the door and drew out the two empty Elixir bottles. Peering into the cabinet, he ran his finger along the shelves. No residue. Nothing.

He set the bottles inside, lingering on them. Tanythe and Leukan, however improbable, existed. Bahl, as well. All the extraordinary things he had experienced were now a part of him. He touched his neck. He had learned more than he had ever dreamed, about science, about himself, about the mysteries of gods and demons.

And he was a better man for it.

Mostly.

"For old time's sake," he murmured, locking the bottles away. He'd best return to cataloging.

Among the larger crates and bundles at the back, he found a newly made crate. Prying it open, he stared at a well-preserved stone urn. When he rested the heavy jar on his hip, it came to his shoulders, the circumference filling his arms. As he cushioned it on a piece of gray carpet, he still could not place the writing, a broad line brushed in red paint diagonally across the surface, hung with swirling strokes that looped back on themselves and ended in delicate flourishes. Except for a few hairline surface cracks, the jar was in wonderful condition, with an intact, sealed lid.

He ran his fingers over the pitted exterior and lurched backward. A vast panorama opened in his mind: the thief in his black robe, holding each of the three heads in turn.

Remy stepped away from the urn. The red script seemed to pulse. The lid had remained intact for centuries, keeping whatever lay inside. Or guarding whatever was in there.

Was the writing a warning?

A curse?

A magic spell?

He thought of Pandora, the first woman, fashioned as punishment by a wrathful Prometheus, and the sealed urn, erroneously referred to as a box, entrusted to her by Zeus. Her curiosity loosed all the world's evils.

He held his hand over the cover. Took a breath. Touched it. Still supple after ages.

A vision slammed into himA spray of blood, Bahl's jarring chords grinding through his skull.

His hand wouldn't move as he tried to pull it away. He panicked. Would he have to rip the seal open to be free? What horrors would he unleash?

Something heavy dropped on his shoulder. Green eyes stared into his.

"Confound it, King. You made my blood run cold." Remy fought for breath.

Ears flattened, tail waving like a fuzzy black serpent, the kitten slinked down his arm, claws digging into his entrapped hand, and hissed at the urn.

In a split second, Remy's hand sprang loose from the seal. King jumped onto the floor by the urn. With a yowl, he sprang high as if bitten and scampered off in a flash of back fur. At the same time, Remy jerked his hand away from the urn's seal, clutching it against his chest.

The seal remained closed.

Scrutinizing the urn, Remy scowled and edged toward the door, spinning around twice to be sure it hadn't crept after him. He would not, could not, open it.

Clutching his blood-stained cravat, he stood by the door. A muffledW sound broke the silence. Instantly alarmed, he turned sharply, scanning for the source. *My God, was it the stone urn? Had the seal broken on its own?*

Near the door, a basket's leather-hinged lid thumped up and down. Relief swept through him. Remy laughed, opening it, only to have King hiss, back arched, fur spiked, bristling as if struck by lightning.

"You want to leave as much as I do, don't you?"

The cat's green eyes glinted.

Casting one last glance back into the laboratory, Remy closed the basket and slipped it over his arm. He pressed a clean fold of the cravat to his neck, grimacing at the renewed seep of blood.

Then stepped into the hall and locked the door behind him.

* * *

A SHADOWY THREAT looms over Constantinople, and no one suspects the danger that's about to be unleashed. **Experience the sweeping battle between good and evil in:**

The Demon, the Scientist, and the Blood Enigma—you won't believe the outcome! Released in 2026.

* * *

DOWNLOAD FOR **FREE**, the Prequel to *The Goddess, the Scientist, and the Elixir*:

The Scientist's Bride and the Spirit Curse. **Lost in a shadowy city where magic deceives, Pheodora hides a terrible secret.**

Scan to get The Scientist's Bride and the Spirit Curse

* * *

I WOULD REALLY APPRECIATE it if you could help me out with an honest review of the book you just read:

The Goddess, the Scientist, and the Elixir.

CONSTANTINOPLE •
CITY OF MANY NAMES

Constantinople, a city at the heart of empires, has worn many names across centuries. From its humble beginnings as a Thracian settlement to its prominence as the jewel of the Byzantine and Ottoman worlds, each name tells a story of conquest, faith, and transformation.

Timeline of Constantinople

Originally: A Thracian settlement whose earlier name is largely unknown. While some sources suggest the name *Lygos*, this lacks strong historical documentation.

667 BCE: The Greeks from Megara founded *Byzantium,* naming it after their leader, Byzas.

196 CE: Roman Emperor Septimius Severus razed the city and rebuilt it, renaming it *Augusta Antonina* in honor of his son. However, this name was rarely used, and the city continued to be called Byzantium.

330 CE: Constantine the Great rededicated the city, officially naming it *Nova Roma* (New Rome). Despite this, it became widely known as *Constantinopolis* ("City of Constantine"), a name formalized shortly after. Coins bearing "Byzantium" circulated for a time before the change was fully implemented.

By the 1st Millennium CE: Greek speakers commonly referred to trips into Constantinople as *eis tēn polin* ("into the City"), a phrase that eventually evolved into the name *Istanbul* centuries later.

1453: The Ottoman Turks conquered Constantinople. Though the Ottomans used names like *Konstantiniyye*, the city remained widely known as Constantinople in non-Turkish languages.

1923: The Grand National Assembly of Turkey established the Republic of Turkey.

1926: The Turkish Post Office officially adopted the name *Istanbul* for international use.

NATURAL PHILOSPHER
OR SCIENTIST?

The world of *The Goddess, the Scientist, and the Elixir* rests on real currents of thought from early modern England.

Historians such as Deborah Harkness, in *The Jewel House*, show that by the late sixteenth and early seventeenth centuries, "natural philosophy" was often the preserve of gentlemen who valued speculation more than messy experiment. Yet alongside them, merchants, craftsmen, and a few bold scholars were already calling their work *science*—hands-on, practical, and rooted in observation.

By 1771, when Remy Derrien steps into his laboratory in Constantinople, that tradition is alive and well. His experiments, measurements, and discoveries are part of a lineage that began long before the nineteenth century gave "science" its modern sheen. Remy is a man standing where curiosity, craft, and scholarship intersect.